Perilous Cove

Perilous Safety Series - Book 1

RICH BULLOCK

Perilous Cove

Published in the United States by RichWords Press and Createspace, an Amazon.com company. First Edition.
Manufactured in the United States of America

Bible quotes from:
THE HOLY BIBLE, NEW INTERNATIONAL VERSION®, NIV® Copyright © 1973, 1978, 1984, 2011 by Biblica, Inc.™ Used by permission. All rights reserved worldwide.
Book cover design by Robert Henslin

vCS112312
ISBN: 061567108X
ISBN-13: 978-0-615-67108-6

FOR SHERYL

Who lets me hide behind a laptop screen year after year as I wrestle with the craft of writing, and listens kindly as I talk about word counts, plots, locations, and about people who don't exist but who have become some of my best friends.

ACKNOWLEDGMENTS

My thanks to: Tom Stephen and Jim DeFrates, two friends who encouraged me to finish this book in the first place. Lee Starkey, who graciously volunteered as my first reader of the newly completed book, and returned great feedback and encouragement. Several other test readers who all made the story better—they are amazingly important to any writer. John Bogacki, Site Manager and Light Keeper for Piedras Blancas light station on the rugged California coast, whose behind-the-scenes tour and lighthouse lore fired my imagination, especially when he led us up the ladder to the top of the tower on a stormy day. Ben Sandler, who furnished information about the St. Louis area. Tim Smith, fellow author and another encourager. Authors Gayle Roper and James Scott Bell, who gave selfless direction and feedback in mentoring groups at the Mount Hermon Christian Writers Conferences. My critique group: Rebecca Luella Miller, Eric Wright, and Rachel Marks. Rob Henslin at www.rhdcreative.com for an awesome cover. And finally Carol, who inspired the story, lived the real-life version (which was much different than in these pages), and came through victorious.

Perilous Cove

Part One

- 1 -

He'd killed before. Once. Not that he was particularly opposed to it.

Tarz Broderick kicked the shoe of the man sprawled against the wall. The schmuck's head came up and his eyes slowly focused. Duct tape secured his wrists and ankles. Three outside wraps with three more in-between. Inescapable.

"Nick Moreno, I presume," Tarz said, watching the man's eyes dart wildly as consciousness returned. Blood ran from his temple, staining the once white dress shirt.

Tarz turned to survey the small desk area and sighed. It could have been simple, easy in and out. The office should have been deserted. But that's why they called it work, as dear ole daddy liked to say—often right before a whipping.

Tarz yanked the handles of the filing cabinet, a four-drawer, putty-colored unit of superior quality. Locked. He didn't have time to mess with finding a key, so he hoisted his pry bar, wedged it into the drawer crack, and drove it home with his palm.

He could have come back later if he'd known someone would be in the office, but he'd rounded the corner into the L-shaped office and there Nick had been, working under the light from a single desk lamp. Oh, well.

Plus, Tarz didn't have time to waste. He'd promised to drop by his sister's apartment tonight. Dumb girl had gotten pregnant by a married man. She wasn't saying who—knew her big brother too well to give up the slimeball's name.

Tarz shrugged and worked the bar back and forth against groaning metal. Family was family. The money for tonight's job would buy a nice baby gift for sis, plus keep him living high for a couple of months at least.

And next week's job… Tarz smiled at the thought of the much larger *remuneration*—word-of-the-week from his Improve Your Vocabulary calendar. Arson paid pretty well, but combining it with a hit—well that elevated Tarz to a new level in his career. In a way, tonight with Nick Moreno was a practice run for next week. Tarz' fingertips itched in anticipation and he patted his right pants pocket to double-check the packet of matches.

The filing drawer popped open, squealing on bearings long overdue for grease.

"There's no excuse for neglecting the simple maintenance of fine equipment, Nick. Shot of WD-40 does wonders." Tarz fought the temptation to look around for some lubricant. In a few minutes it wouldn't matter.

He thumbed through the drawer's packed folders, searching for the information he was paid to find. There it was: 16 Corporate Center Drive, St. Louis, MO. A fire in a business park. He removed the thick manila folder and opened it on the desk.

Though a poor fighter, Nick was an organized man, a virtue Tarz appreciated. The folder's Table of Contents listed a CONCLUSION section and a reference to POTENTIAL SUSPECTS. The fire hadn't been one of Tarz' jobs, but he could admire another's work. He flipped through the text, lingering on several photos of a burned commercial building. His fingers stroked the glossy pictures of blackened walls, skeletal desks, and collapsed beams.

Beautiful.

The phone rang, and Tarz jolted into the file cabinet drawer, gouging his back.

The ringing sounded obscenely shrill in the ghostly silence of the office.

Probably the little woman. Tarz glanced at the framed photo on the desk, a smiling foursome in bright colors. Nick sat in a straight-back chair while his pretty blonde wife stood behind him, her hand on his shoulder. A blonde teenage girl knelt with an arm on Nick's leg, and a boy with striking resemblance to Nick stood tall beside the mother. Tarz' teeth ground together. The perfect family. Nothing like his own.

The phone fell silent. Tarz slammed the offending file drawer shut.

The folder's suspects page held a single address and name: 423 Old Country Road, Steerman, MO. He read the suspect's name, a smile pulling the corners of his mouth.

"Well, well." He had to admire the old bat. No wonder she was willing to pay for Moreno's arson report on the burned commercial property. According to the notes, the report hadn't been filed yet. Perfect. He'd definitely find a copy shop before turning the report over to her.

Tarz closed the folder and waved it at the bound man.

"Always good to have insurance, Nick." The man struggled against the tape around his wrists and ankles. His right eye had nearly swollen shut now, and blood ran from the wound and dripped off his jaw. Probably a slight fracture around the eye socket if Tarz knew his injuries...and he did.

For a moment he simply looked at Nick, weighing his next move. He could use the crow bar to put Nick out of his misery right now, or he could let him live and enjoy the last of his life, even if it was only a minute or two longer.

Decision made, Tarz turned away. It wouldn't be half the fun if he couldn't imagine Nick watching. Waiting.

Tarz opened the first of two large soda bottles and drizzled its contents across the open drawers of folders and across the mahogany desk. With the second bottle, he created a trail down the hall carpet to the back door of the office where he tossed the bottles into a wire trash basket. Plastic melted immediately in a fire, obliterating fingerprints. Couldn't be too careful.

"Ac-cel-erant." He let the four syllables roll off his tongue, the last two speeding together, mimicking the meaning of the word. It sounded, well, professional.

Pungent fumes filled the air, and he touched his right thigh where his dad had once splashed gas. The hard scar tissue still itched.

Tarz opened the matchbook cover, exposing the row of red-tipped sticks. Straightforward, yet so effective. Beautiful in their design simplicity. They'd been called Lucifers when first invented.

When ten years old, he'd accidentally discovered their awesome potential in some dry brush behind an old barn. The vision of the towering flames, the shrieking of the three horses inside the structure, still brought a shiver—and a smile.

As he gripped one match to tear it off, a scratching noise came from a doorway to his right. He snatched up his pry bar and crept to the wall near the opening to the tiny break area. His eyes watered in the fume-laden air as he peeked around the doorframe. A cardboard box, circled by red ribbon and a large bow, sat on the linoleum floor and contained the source of his near heart attack.

Smiling, he laid down his weapon and picked up the warm bundle.

"Hey there."

The puppy licked his hand and face in exuberant enthusiasm, free at last of its cardboard prison.

Tarz opened the outside door and checked the alley before stepping out. Juggling the folders and squirming puppy took some doing. He propped open the self-closing door with his knee while he tore one match free. He held the matches outside in the fresh air, struck and lit the one, then touched the flame to the rest of the open book. They ignited with a small whoosh and flared intensely, briefly revealing the dark brick alley walls and shadowed dumpsters. He held the book up, admiring the surging fire, and rotated it until the match stems all caught. Then in one smooth motion, he flipped the matchbook onto the fuel-soaked carpet and kicked the door closed.

The steel security door muffled a much larger, satisfying whoosh. On the other side of the building came the tinkling of shattered windows.

Shushing the puppy, Tarz pressed his ear against the cold surface and listened to the escalating crackling. His heart sped up with the sound of the inferno, and he wished just once he could be inside with the beautiful yellow and orange.

Tarz sighed and straightened. In the dim light of the strip mall alley, he could barely make out the stenciled lettering on the sign on the rough wall: *Nick Moreno, Independent Insurance Investigations, St. Louis, Missouri.*

On the wall below the sign, a cut chain dangled from the office's sprinkler system emergency shutoff valve. Water wouldn't spoil this job.

He gazed longingly at the door while scratching the wriggling dog's chin.

The only bad thing about using duct tape was you couldn't hear them scream.

The mahogany coffin sat on steel beams that spanned the thinly disguised pit. Natalie Clayton took a sip of bottled water and winced as the liquid singed her raw throat. Her stomach churned in revolt at even the tepid water, reminding her she'd been up all night hugging the toilet.

She let the bottle drop to the plastic grass, unable to tolerate more pain from any source. Wasn't her husband dying enough? She shifted on the hard chair trying to ease aching muscles. But the pain spread from within.

"Jack Clayton was a good man, a loving husband, and a devoted son." Chaplain Harris used his handkerchief on his forehead, then stuffed the soaked rag into the front pocket of his shapeless black polyester suit. Jack's mother had chosen the chaplain. Natalie couldn't see her mother-in-law from where she sat. Just as well.

Natalie shifted her eyes from the coffin and concentrated instead on a five-inch earthworm that had just crawled out of the fresh grave and gone still, as if resting from its arduous climb up the wall of the six-foot hole.

"It's always hard when a loved one is taken from us so suddenly. We ask why, but there is no answer." His jowls wobbled as he sadly shook his head. "We seek peace, but often it flees from us just when we need it most. The great, universal spirit has his—or her—own plans and ways. We can't understand." More jowl shaking.

The worm moved again, and Natalie let its silent maneuverings drown out the babble of the sweaty man. *Lumbricus terrestris*, if she recalled correctly from her college biology—the worm, not the man. The nightcrawler had several redeeming qualities in nature. Of the chaplain, she couldn't be sure.

Natalie ran a hand over her face and, though her head felt like it was stuffed with cotton candy, tried to concentrate as the chaplain droned on. This was her husband's funeral; he deserved this homage. Her stomach knotted again, sending a wave of heat and pain. She only knew she wanted this day to be over so she could grieve in private.

Natalie looked downslope toward the cemetery pond and its spraying fountain. Shimmery waves rose from stone grave markers in the Missouri heat, like translucent spirits ascending to heaven—if such a destination even existed.

A loving husband, Chaplain Harris had said. Maybe at first. She twisted the simple gold band on her finger. August twenty-fifth, only three weeks away, they would have been married eleven years. Now they'd never make that milestone.

Never-to-be celebrations stretched endlessly in her future. Jack might be at peace, but he'd left the pain behind for her.

Natalie rubbed the spot between her eyes where the headache pulsed. The frenzy of activity the last few days—Jack's heart attack while mowing the lawn, the cardiac care unit, all-night vigils, meetings with doctors, the phone call from a frazzled nurse, and then, finally, the funeral director—everything led up to this singular point in time: the end of a man's life. How could a person be so alive one minute and then permanently gone from the world the next?

Is this it? Is this what I have to look forward to? Natalie sighed, rocked against the pain, and clutched the one tangible thing remaining—a folded American flag in honor of Jack's military service before she'd met him.

Donna Montgomery, Natalie's one good friend, gave her hand a squeeze. She leaned toward the woman who several guests had assumed was Natalie's older sister because of their strong resemblance. But even with Donna, Natalie kept her deepest feelings private. The years with Jack had stifled something in her.

Natalie took a cleansing breath and returned the squeeze of Donna's hand. "Thank you for being here."

"I wouldn't be anywhere else."

Donna was the one who sat with her at this same cemetery two years ago for the funeral of her parents after their car accident. It was Donna, not Jack, who slid an arm around Natalie then, as she did now. Jack had nearly killed this friendship, too. Natalie vowed that would change.

The chaplain mercifully concluded his remarks, thanked everyone for coming, and stepped to one side, arms bowed around his protruding belly, hands crossed at the wrist. Natalie glanced at the grave edge. The worm had disappeared. Maybe she could, too.

Mr. Jeffries, the funeral home director, slid into the empty seat beside her, an ill-conceived comb-over failing to hide his shining bald head. A cloying cloud of aftershave traveled with him and her stomach roiled.

Not a leaf moved on any tree, and the air pressed down like a sweaty palm, flattening even the real grass, yet Mr. Jeffries patted her hand with a soft touch, dry as old bones. "Mrs. Clayton, everyone at Mountainside Chapel is here to help in any way possible."

Natalie mumbled polite thanks but inwardly scoffed at his sincerity. What did he propose to do, come to her house and finish cutting the grass? Fix leaky faucets? Provide a high-paying job to take the place of her husband's income? She shook her head. Empty promises. She'd had enough of those in her life. He remained in the chair to her right, Donna on her left.

Surrounded, yet alone.

She started to get up, to move, but several guests stopped at her chair to offer condolences.

Such a shock. So young—only forty-seven. Too soon. So very sorry. Time heals all wounds.

They wished her wellness, luck, and happiness, phrases that had once seemed appropriate to Natalie. Now they held no meaning at all.

Mr. Jeffries resumed his patting and she glanced down in surprise. She hadn't noticed he'd stopped. Perhaps it comforted him more than her.

A sense of finality crushed Natalie. What now? She knew what wives did, but thirty-nine-year-old widows? She retrieved her hand from Mr. Jeffries and rubbed it over her face in an attempt to wipe away her new reality. Instead she nearly gagged from his cologne now imparted to her hand and face. Maybe she could wash it off with some of the bottled—

"I'll take that."

The familiar female voice ripped the solitude more than the gunshots from the honor guards' twenty-one-gun salute.

Hilde Clayton stood directly in front of Natalie. With a move as quick as a rattlesnake, Hilde tore the flag from Natalie's grasp, then leaned close to Natalie's ear. "He was *my* son. Do you hear me? *My* son." Her whisper rose in volume.

Jeffries rose, palms out. "Please, Mrs. Clayton."

Natalie peered at the narrow-faced woman, silhouetted by the high sun, the triangular flag now clasped to her impeccable, severe black suit. Natalie tried to feel sympathy. Hilde Clayton had just lost Jack, her only son, and her whole world had revolved around him. She had to be in great pain. But Natalie felt nothing for her mother-in-law but dislike.

The familiar bitterness oozed like a poison from Hilde's thin lips. "You meant nothing to him."

Natalie's cheeks grew hot as the few remaining guests close enough to hear turned and stared, some curious, some open mouthed. Jeffries stepped in between them, while Donna tightened her arm around Natalie's shoulders.

God, please make her go away.

A tall man with chiseled features and carefully styled gray hair took Hilde's arm and urgently whispered in her ear while surveying the crowd. Hilde shook him off, pushed around Jeffries and leveled her boney finger inches from Natalie's face. "You were no wife."

Natalie had had enough. Her sight blurred with her own rage before the woman's rant. She shook off Donna's arm and shifted her weight to stand.

"That's enough." Jeffries blocked Hilde and forced her back a step. His position pinned Natalie to her chair.

The cold, burning eyes released Natalie and snapped to Jeffries, acknowledging the man for the first time. Jeffries retreated, almost into Natalie's lap. Then Hilde glanced over his shoulder at the staring guests. She tugged the hem of her suit coat, flashed an apologetic half-smile, cocked her head in her familiar trademark way, and waved her hand in a practiced manner, communicating the proper mix of self-deprecation and sorrow.

She was so good.

The tall man made another attempt to pull her away from the scene, but she subtly peeled his fingers from her arm, pushed around Jeffries and again leaned close to Natalie. Hilde's hissing murmur held more dread for Natalie than yelling. "You'll get nothing of his. Do you hear me, Natalie?"

Jeffries took Hilde's arm. "Let me escort you to your car, Mrs. Clayton."

Hilde turned a killing glare on him. "Take your hands off me."

Jeffries did.

Hilde leaned down to Natalie, voice low again. "Trash. You're nothing but trash."

Donna gasped, but the words were familiar to Natalie.

With that dismissal, Jack's mother lifted her chin and smiled appropriate grief for the crowd. Jack's honor flag still clutched in her arms, Hildegard Clayton dabbed her eyes with a lace handkerchief as the tall man led her to the news cameras waiting discretely by the black limo parked on the paved path.

Fifteen minutes later, Natalie opened the front door to her house and entered. The cool air washed over her, wonderful relief after the oppressive heat of the cemetery. Donna followed her in. This was only Donna's second time in the house, and Natalie watched her friend survey the living room, assessing decorating and furnishings. Natalie stroked the fuzzy back of the brown corduroy sofa. Jack had chosen it, as he had most of the furniture.

She hated brown.

"Are you hungry?" Donna deposited her giant purse on the floor with a clunk. "Can I fix you something?"

"My stomach isn't doing too well."

"Well, it's not your fault. Funerals are awful times, barbaric if you ask me. I don't know why we don't do away with them entirely."

"That's not what I meant." Natalie gave a weak smile at her friend's crusty way of coping with death. "I was up all night with the flu." She wobbled toward the stairs where she caught the newel post as a brace. She swayed in place. "I hope you don't catch it."

"Never mind about that," Donna steadied her with a hand. "What do you need?"

"Bed."

"Good idea. Come on." Donna helped her up the stairs and into the master bedroom. *Her* room now. No longer *their* room.

"It was so hot under the tent today, I think that made it worse."

Natalie's skin burned with fever as she eased onto the king-sized bed, aware of how huge it seemed without Jack's knees and elbows bumping her.

"It was *way* hot. I thought my pantyhose were going to melt." Donna hurried into the master bath and returned with a cool washcloth that she draped on Natalie's forehead. "You should try to eat something, too. You're all bones as is. I'll go make some toast."

Donna turned on the light as she went out. Heavy gold drapes kept the bedroom in a perpetual gloom. Before their marriage, Natalie had dreamed of a light and airy bedroom, with pale yellow walls, white sheers, a vaulted ceiling, and a paddle fan spinning lazily on warm evenings. But Jack insisted it was too frilly for him and chose taupe walls, brown carpet—and the gold drapes that matched the ones at his mother's house. Natalie wanted to rip them down right now and send them out with the garbage.

Remorse overwhelmed her. How could she be so selfish? Jack was gone and she was thinking about redecorating? Jack's car keys lay on his dresser. He'd never use them again.

A heart attack, a blockage of a tiny blood passage, and suddenly *never-agains* redefined her world, her future. Never again would they eat together, watch television, never go...well, they hadn't gone out in months. Not together anyway. Still, there was a comfort to Jack's presence; the simple awareness of another person held back the loneliness just a little. No longer.

Donna returned with the promised toast, a glass of iced tea, and a digital thermometer she'd found in the bathroom. When it beeped, Natalie checked the readout—one hundred two—and fell back against the pillows. No wonder she felt dizzy. She dutifully swallowed two aspirin Donna brought, wishing there was a pill to fix her other pain.

Donna settled herself in the bedside chair. "You never told me much about Jack. How did you meet?"

Natalie nibbled the lightly browned toast and studied her friend's face, but found no hint of judgment. It was true she hadn't talked about Jack much in the four years she'd known Donna. Four years. Had it been that long since she started working at Emerald Escrow and Title?

She and Donna worked on the same floor and, during her first week when everything had been so confusing, they literally bumped into each other in the restroom. Donna dropped her lipstick and they both bent to retrieve it. When they stood and got a good look at each other, it was like staring in the mirror: same hair color and cut, same height—even the same charcoal outfit. They both grinned, then laughed. An instant friendship had developed. But while Donna chatted non-stop about her husband, Chet, Natalie mostly listened and kept her home life private.

"We met in college." Natalie sipped the icy drink. Though sweetened, it tasted bitter. She set the glass aside and tried more of the toast. "Jack graduated eight years ahead of me, spent time in the army, then came to work in the finance office at the school. I met him in my senior year." She added a sugar packet to the tea.

"So, he asked you out?" Donna sipped her own tea and evidently thought it didn't need doctoring.

Natalie shook her head, immediately regretting the movement. "Not at first. We had some mutual friends, and we bumped into each a few times over the years." She smiled at the memory, so long ago. "Then the friends began getting married and we attended the weddings. Eventually, they all moved away and it got down to the two of us. I was twenty-eight when we married." She didn't mention the pregnancy that compelled the union.

"I take it Jack's mother wasn't in favor of your marriage?"

Natalie's glass clattered as she set it on the nightstand. "She refused to come to the wedding."

Donna tucked stray hairs behind her ear and lifted her glass. "Wow. Mother-in-law from you-know-where, huh?"

Natalie smiled at Donna's automatic softening of the language. Donna was a churchgoer, but didn't come across as overly religious. Natalie liked that, and she'd accepted Donna's invitation to attend one Sunday. She might have gone back except for Jack's insistence that religion was for the weak.

Donna shook her head. "That was a difficult encounter today."

"I think it set a new record." Hilde had barely let Natalie into her house over the years—never without Jack. The woman wielded words like a cat o' nine tails, and Natalie knew well their flesh-ripping sting. Natalie suddenly realized she'd never have to talk to her mother-in-law again if she didn't want to. Jack's death gave her distance from Hilde, but at a terrible price.

"Well I definitely won't vote for her," Donna proclaimed.

Hilde Clayton had worked her way up through the city council to the mayor's spot, then to county supervisor, then had been elected to the state legislature. Now she had her sights set on the governor's spot in next year's election, and her campaign was well underway with television and print ads. Natalie had to hand it to her; the woman knew how to work the press and crowds. The public loved her energy, can-do attitude, and not-so-subtle stabs at her opponents. Few knew the real Hilde.

Donna sipped her drink. "Were you and Jack happy?"

"Of course," Natalie blurted. "He was a good man." Her friend shot a questioning look, and Natalie concentrated on another sip of tea, wincing at the acidic taste. Maybe it was the memories that were bitter.

A few minutes later, Donna left for home to check on Chet, but not before insisting she return and spend the night in Natalie's downstairs guest room. Too weak to argue, Natalie lay back with eyes closed and envisioned a vaulted white beadboard ceiling with cooling paddle fan. Sounds of the house crept into the bedroom: the hum of the refrigerator, the loud ticking of the mantle clock in the living room. The clock was a post-wedding gift from Hilde, addressed only to Jack. Natalie vowed to stop the pendulum and get a decent night's sleep.

At eight o'clock, Donna returned, armed with an overnight bag, 7-Up, and saltines. Natalie obediently nibbled a few crackers while Donna planted herself in the chair by the bed and recounted humorous stories from her church activities. Natalie didn't feel up to responding, but she marveled at Donna's love for the people in her church.

An hour later, Natalie could barely keep her eyes open. She slouched down against the pillows. "I'm afraid I'm not very good company."

"That's okay, hon." Donna squeezed Natalie's shoulder, adjusted the pillows, and rose to leave. "You get some rest. Tomorrow will be a new day. A better day. I'm gonna pray for you."

Natalie closed her eyes and let fatigue drag her body deep into the mattress. She heard Donna's soft footfalls on the carpeted stairs as she headed downstairs to the guest room.

Tomorrow. A better day.

How could it be any worse?

- 3 -

Natalie woke with a start and sat up in the pitch-black room, straining to hear what woke her. She ignored the lingering headache and breathed rapidly. A glance in the direction of the digital clock revealed only darkness. Was the power out?

She felt for her slippers with her toes, then shuffled to the closed door. She pulled it open, and stepped into the hall. The nightlight wasn't working either. Natalie hated to be alone in the house, but Donna was here, and the thought gave her some comfort.

A muffled noise downstairs stopped the breath in her throat, and her mind raced to identify the source. Was it Donna? It sounded like it originated in the garage, which sat directly below the master bedroom. What would Donna be doing in the garage? The hair on the back of Natalie's neck stood up, and the desire for a flashlight pressed hard as she crept down the stairs.

Halfway down, she froze as the garage door under the stairs banged opened. Dim orange light brightened the hall below, revealing the shadowy figure of a man running past the bottom of the stairs before the door slammed shut. He carried a tiny flashlight and turned right, into the kitchen. He hadn't seen her pressed against the wall, but surely he'd heard her heart thudding.

She heard the distinctive squeal of the backyard sliding door opening, then it closed with a bang. Silence followed. Maybe he was gone, but she didn't dare move.

A crash in the garage sent her rushing back into the bedroom.

Someone was still down there. She fumbled for the cordless phone by the bed, pushing buttons until she found 911. She put it to her ear. Dead. She recalled Jack telling her only the kitchen phone would work in the event of a power outage. The kitchen wasn't an option—the man might still be there.

Donna! Was she all right?

Natalie stumbled from the room and down the stairs. Her slippers called a soft clap-clap, and the need to reach Donna now overpowered fear of the intruder. At the bottom, she crept past the garage door to the guest bedroom. Donna's door stood ajar. She pushed it wide and stepped into pitch black.

"Donna," Natalie whispered. No answer. She willed her eyes to take in more light as she moved to the bed and felt for her friend. "Donna." Blindly patting the covers, Natalie found a form at the far side of the queen sized bed and shook it. "Donna. Wake up. There's someone in the house. We need to get out."

She imagined the prowler sneaking up behind her and spun to check. No one was there, but an orange glow emanated from under the hallway's garage door. Someone was still out there.

She climbed on the bed and pulled on Donna's arm. "Donna." Still no response. Leaning over, Natalie clutched both shoulders and shook. "Please, wake up!"

Another crash and a loud thud came from the garage. Natalie spun and the acrid smell of smoke hit her nose at the same time her mind recognized the glow.

Fire!

With renewed effort, Natalie shook her friend, no longer trying to be quiet. "Come on. There's a fire. We have to get out." Her hand slipped off Donna's shoulder and came away wet and sticky, the iron odor of blood unmistakable.

"Donna!"

An explosion blew the garage door open and spewed red flame across the hallway and into the room. Her arm came up automatically to protect her face and heat seared her back as she shielded Donna.

As the fire retreated momentarily, she lurched across the room and slammed the bedroom door, blocking the worst of the inferno. Smoke filled her lungs and she doubled over in a fit of coughing which ripped her already raw throat.

The thin bedroom door glowed at the edges and she retreated until the backs of her knees hit the bed. In the dim light, smoke poured under and around the door, spread across the ceiling, and climbed down the walls. They would die in minutes if Natalie didn't get them out of the house. She ran around the bed and cast aside the heavy drapes, baring the window to the backyard. For an instant, the menacing darkness immobilized her. What if the intruder was still out there, watching her? Waiting for her? She shook her head. It didn't matter. They had to get out.

The window lock stuck and her hand slipped off the catch, ripping a fingernail to the quick. She yanked the latch again and the window ground open. Fresh air flooded into the room and she gulped it hungrily. But it poured between security bars Jack insisted upon. Where was the release? She'd never used it.

Natalie fumbled on the left side of the window, then the right, gasping in relief as her fingers closed around the pin. She pulled it out, but the security bars didn't release. Shaking the bars did no good and time was running out.

Another bang in the garage catapulted her into action. Natalie gripped the cold steel and shook hard; they rattled but didn't budge. The pin was out; they must be stuck. She picked up the heavy table lamp from the bedside and smashed repeatedly at the bars. They held fast and the shattered pieces of the lamp showered her feet.

In the darkness, the fire reached a new level of life as it added sound to its repertoire of destruction. Paint sizzled like frying bacon on the door, it popped and crackled in the hall and finally grew to a roar. She could feel heat radiating form the door.

Natalie turned her attention back to the bars. She needed something heavier. A swipe of her arm cleared the oak nightstand where the lamp had stood. She wrestled the awkward piece of furniture chest high, then hurled it against the bars. It bounced back into the room, landing on her right foot and sending a current of blinding pain shooting up her leg and into her skull. Smoky air erupted from her lungs and she collapsed onto Donna's limp form, gasping for breath.

Red light brightened the room as the door bowed inward at the top. Paint melted and transformed into fiery rivulets. The light switch sagged and rained droplets into the dark. Flames marched up the wall and crawled across the ceiling toward her, dragging death in their wake.

Ignoring her foot, Natalie pushed off the bed and heaved the nightstand above her head. This time she threw her whole weight behind it and rammed it against the steel. Once. Twice. On the third thrust, bolts gave way and the security grate crashed to the ground, followed by the nightstand.

Crackling flames covered the ceiling, and Natalie's ears blistered as she pulled Donna up and got her shoulder under her friend's arm. Tears blinded her and she wheezed and coughed in the swirling soot. Gathering all her strength, she draped Donna's limp form over the windowsill. With a final heave, she shoved her friend into the night.

The bedroom door collapsed, and red fire burst into the room, consuming the fresh oxygen and igniting Natalie's hair. She dropped to the floor and batted the flames with her hands. An old throw rug, a gift from her Aunt Wena, padded the hardwood. The cleaner air at the floor gave her strength, and with a final breath, she wrapped the old rug around her head, stood and leaped through the window as flames licked her legs.

Fire burst from the opening, searching for her as she sprawled on the steel bars, nightstand, and Donna. Natalie sucked large lungfuls of cool air and then forced herself to move. Donna's dead weight fought her as she untangled her friend's arm from the bars and dragged her off the debris. Once on the cool grass, she dug her heels into the soft soil and pulled Donna to the middle of the back lawn. Crickets calmly continued their chorus, and frogs in the drainage ravine behind the back fence croaked with summer enthusiasm, a strange counterpoint to the increasing roar of destruction before her.

Natalie turned and watched in fascination for a few seconds as the fire spread along the eaves in both directions. Smoke poured from the eyebrow vents on the roof. The kitchen windows were orange squares, lighting the yard with throbbing light. Then two explosions rocked the house, showering her with glass shards and burning embers, and silencing the neighborhood wildlife. Natalie opened her eyes to flames pouring from her home's windows and roof. Above the angry crackle of the orange tongues, shouts erupted from the neighboring houses. The heat from the inferno now formed an updraft, emptying the lawn of smoke and pushing it skyward into the night. Cool air washed across Natalie and Donna.

Sticky wetness ran into Natalie's right eye, but she ignored it. In the roiling red light, Natalie turned her attention to her friend. Cradling Donna's head in her lap, she brushed grass and soot from the woman's peaceful face. She turned so she could see better in the flickering light, sought the source of the blood—and found it.

In the distance, sirens screamed the promise of help. But Natalie's own screams drowned out all other sounds as she stared at the kitchen knife buried in her friend's blood-covered chest.

- 4 -

Detective Addison Conner arrived before dawn, summoned from a restless sleep by the Chief's high priority text. Strobes and spotlights lit the night, creating an unworldly effect, which never failed to get his blood pumping. A dozen emergency vehicles pointed their noses toward one house.

Fifty or more spectators dressed in pajamas and bathrobes pressed against the police tape ringing the property, blocking his view. But above the level of the vehicles, a dark plume of smoke blotted the stars, alternately highlighted by red and blue pulses.

A quick check of his daughter in the passenger seat revealed her curled up against the door. Though Mandy had just celebrated her fourteenth birthday, Addison still couldn't bring himself to leave her at home alone in the middle of the night. He knew he was overprotective, a fact Mandy flung at him regularly, but after Elizabeth's death, she was his world. In four short years Mandy would head for college, leaving him alone for the first time in many years.

"You'll be okay, sweetheart?"

"Of *course* I'm okay, Dad. I can't believe you dragged me out here in the middle of the night." Mandy gave him her perfected eye-roll and pulled the blanket tight about her shoulders.

Addison sighed, then closed the car door, keyed the remote lock, and ducked under the yellow tape. He surveyed the scene, automatically scanning each face for his partner, Arnie Trujillo. He spotted him talking with the fire chief under the glare of an emergency floodlight and hustled over to join them.

Arnie greeted him. "Morning partner. I just got here."

"Hey, Arnie." Then he nodded at the chief. "Bob. What's the situation?" Addison's tennis shoes squished in the wet front lawn where they stood, surrounded by debris. Broken glass sparkled, a smoldering sofa and two mattresses lay in a heap, and piles of what appeared to be blackened clothing or drapes gave off noxious smoke that robbed the air from his lungs. Firemen, covered with soot, their eyes reddened, noses streaming black phlegm, moved in and out of the house, rolling up hoses and replacing equipment on the rumbling trucks. An acrid stench of burned, wet carpet and wood mixed with the melted tar from the roofing and hung thickly over the neighborhood in the heavy pre-dawn air.

Fire chief Bob Torey coughed, shrugged out of his Steerman Fire Department coat, and wiped a dirty hand across his dirtier face. "Well, the call came in at 2:27 AM—six neighbors called within two minutes of each other. They all heard explosions—probably the car gas tanks. But the fire had been going for a while, and the house was almost fully engulfed when the first units arrived at 2:36 AM. Garage seems to be the point of origin. Then it spread to the downstairs hall, then into the upper rooms. Very heavy structural damage to those areas. Parts of the kitchen and the south end escaped the worst of the flames, but have severe smoke, water, and heat damage."

Addison stared at two men in yellow coats poking around in the gutted garage. Bright work lights shone in the space, visible through the demolished rollup door, half of which lay in the driveway in a twisted heap.

"Is that the arson team in there?"

The chief glanced over his shoulder where Addison pointed, then nodded. "Yeah."

"Pretty fast on the scene for them." Arnie pulled out his notebook and began writing.

Torey nodded. "Normally we'd wait for daylight. But the fact that one of the victims has a knife in her chest is a good indication of a suspicious fire, don't you think?"

They all turned at the sound of a gurney bumping through the side gate. The M.E.s weren't in a hurry as they rolled toward the yawning coroner's van, black body bag securely strapped to the cart.

Addison traded glances with Arnie. "I didn't get that on the message.

Did you?"

Arnie shook his head. "Just said to show up pronto." He turned back to the chief. "How many involved, Bob."

"One more, but she's alive; out back with an EMT team. The dead victim is a woman, too. The rest of the house is clear." Torey turned away as someone called his name, then said over his shoulder, "If you want to talk to her, you'd better hurry. She needs to get to the hospital, but refused to leave while her friend's body was still here."

Arnie and Addison retraced the emergency techs' route, and emerged from the dark side-yard into another surreal scene at the back of the house. Extension cords trailed from the fire engines to portable work lights sitting on a low wall on one side of the back yard. The colors were slightly wrong, turning the grass gray and tinting people's faces bluish. The reek of fire was so strong here, Addison swore it clung to the grass and gummed onto his shoes.

Two EMTs were helping a woman onto a second gurney and adjusted it to a reclining position. As the techs moved, the low lights cast huge shadows on the fence and walls of neighboring houses, giving the impression of giants at work in the yard.

An IV bag hung from the gurney mast, the line snaking into the woman's soot-covered arm where white tape stood out in marked contrast on her blackened skin. A tech tucked a dark blanket around her legs and pulled it up under her arms. People thought the brown color looked warm, but a tech had told Addison they were simply more practical. Brown didn't show blood.

Arnie stopped short and whispered to his partner. "She looks pretty bad."

Addison nodded, then approached the group and studied the woman. She gave no sign she noticed him. Her eyes were open and her hands busy, alternately twisting and smoothing the edge of the blanket. Dark blonde hair hung in burned tangles. Whole sections nearly gone where angry red patches stood out on her scalp. Soot smeared her forehead and nose. Dried blood marked at least a dozen small cuts on the right side of her face. The left side was hidden by a gauze bandage, soaked with bottled saline. Dried blood coated both hands like she'd dipped them in a can of paint. But what struck him most was the haunted look in her blue eyes, sharply revealed in the harsh light.

Addison moved to the other side while one of the EMTs collected equipment and stacked it on the foot of the gurney.

"Ma'am, I'm Detective Conner from the Steerman Police Department. Could you tell us your name?" She didn't respond, staring somewhere over his shoulder, perhaps at the plume of smoke rising from her ruined home.

One of the EMTs reported she'd been non-responsive since they arrived, other than insisting she stay with her friend.

"Ma'am? Is this your home? Do you live here?" Instead of speaking, her eyes closed and she began shaking.

"Blood pressure's dropping some more, Barry," the female EMT said to her partner. "Sorry, detectives, we've got to transport right now."

Arnie and Addison backed out of the way and watched while the techs tightened the straps and then wheeled the cart to the ambulance. He and Arnie followed. Thirty seconds later the rotating strobes came on and the siren whooped twice. The vehicle wove through the tangle of emergency vehicles, dodged two news vans, and sped into the dark.

Interviewing neighbors filled the next hour and a half. Although several had heard popping noises right before the big explosions, no one saw anyone suspicious. The house belonged to Jack and Natalie Clayton, but Jack had died and his funeral had been the day before. The woman might be Natalie Clayton, but none of the neighbors were sure as the arriving fire and EMT staff had quickly surrounded both the women. Strangely, no one said they were friends with either of the Claytons.

At first light, Arnie suggested Addison take Mandy home, then meet him at the station. They would head for the hospital together.

"Mandy. Come on, let's go." Addison rinsed his coffee cup and set it in the dishwasher. He wanted to get to the hospital soon to talk with the fire survivor. Although the visible burns hadn't appeared terribly serious, painful wounds often triggered shock, dangerous if not treated promptly. And he had no doubt she would feel pain when she stabilized.

Her escape had to have been close. A few more seconds…

His fireman friends had told him many times how fast fire moved. He'd once seen a Christmas tree safety video made by a fire department for showing at the holidays. The firemen used an old house and put a dried-out tree in the living room, then touched it with a candle. It went up so fast even the professionals were caught unprepared and scrambled to get out of the room before it became a deathtrap.

"Can't I just stay here, Dad?" Mandy whined from the hall bathroom. "I'm not a baby anymore, you know."

A smile turned up the corners of Addison's mouth. Yeah, but you're *my* baby. "Nope. Gotta go. Ellen is expecting you."

"Ellen's probably not even awake yet."

He grunted in agreement. Got that right. Both girls were the same age, and in his experience no fourteen-year-old woke before eleven o'clock on summer vacation. But with school starting in two weeks—well, they'd better get used to it. Addison straightened his tie in the entry mirror, the one he and Elizabeth discovered at a St. Louis flea market on their first anniversary, right after they moved from California to care for her dying mother.

Keys in hand, he opened the front door to the promise of another scorching Missouri day, simmering air already laden with humidity. Sighing, he thought for the hundredth time it would be good to be near the coast again. He started the car and cranked the air conditioning to maximum. Mandy came out and put on such a great show trudging to the car he couldn't help but grin.

"This summer hasn't been the most exciting for you, has it?" Addison ran his hand through her beautiful hair as she settled into the seat. She reminded him so much of Elizabeth. Mandy and Elizabeth had been inseparable. They shopped, went to plays, constructed school projects, decorated the house, and took care of Grandpa, Elizabeth's father, until he'd passed away four years ago. In a way, Addison was glad the old man died before he saw his daughter succumb to the same cancer that took her mother, his wife.

"It's been okay. I wish we could do more together, though." Mandy slumped against the passenger door. "It seems like you're always working."

The truth, so plainly spoken, left little room for response. Addison drove in silence to Ellen's house where he pulled into the driveway and set the brake. "Come here." He circled Mandy with his arms and drew her to him. "I'm sorry, hon. You're right. This job is too much at times." He breathed in the scent of her hair, herbal shampoo mixed with lingering smoke from the fire scene. It wasn't fair to Mandy to drag her into his dark world.

They held each other for a few minutes in the quiet morning. Over

Mandy's shoulder, he spotted Ellen's mother leaning against her open front door, watching. Reluctantly, he released his daughter. He elicited a promise to start her required reading of Tale of Two Cities, and acquiesced to her counter demand of KFC for dinner.

He backed the car into the street and drove toward the station with the depressing awareness his life consisted of too much work, fast food, and saying goodbye to his daughter. Something had to change.

- 5 -

Natalie came awake in the sunny hospital room and tried to hold on to the tranquil, if not luxurious, surroundings. She wanted nothing more than to forget the last few hours, including her time in the Emergency Room, but the memories were as seared into her mind as the blistered red welts on her skin. Both seemed more painful than she could endure. Not even the sleep-inducing pain medication could chase away the awful reality of Donna's death.

The jarring ambulance ride had made Natalie sick to her stomach again, but the Emergency Room was worse as the nurses and doctors stripped away her clothing and dignity during the examination. They poked, prodded, and x-rayed before allowing the pain medication, which blissfully swept her away…for a while.

Turning to stare at the cheery yellow curtains, Natalie's eyes overflowed as she recalled her friend's limp body, cradled in her arms.

Why, God?

Her tears ran unchecked onto the pillow.

Arnie Trujillo pulled the unmarked car into a parking place and Addison got out in the shadow of Nickerson Memorial Hospital. The modest two-story structure wouldn't rate a second glance in a larger city, but Steerman, Missouri was fortunate to have a good hospital. The Nickersons, fourth generation cattle ranchers, turned the accidental death of their son into a permanent benefit to the town through their generous gift. Other bedroom communities relied on the over-burdened St. Louis medical system.

He grabbed his coat to cover his shoulder holster. Sweat immediately trickled down his temple into his collar. Over ninety degrees and not yet nine o'clock.

"Whew." Arnie shrugged into his own coat. "Gonna be a hot one today, amigo. Hope the AC is working inside." They hurried into the building's interior.

While waiting for Addison at the police station, Arnie had called the hospital for information on the woman. They stopped at the reception desk to request the doctor be paged, then headed upstairs to meet the woman they now knew was Natalie Clayton.

Dr. Billings met them at the nurses' station and flipped open a chart. "Mrs. Clayton was in mild shock when she arrived at the E.R. at 4:31 AM. No major injuries. Fractured second metatarsal in her left foot. Several mild to moderate contusions, and a dozen or so lacerations, mostly minor." Dr. Billings pulled a pen from his white lab coat, tapped it down the page. "We pulled several small pieces of glass fragments from the cuts." He looked up. "I guess there was an explosion of some kind?"

"Yes." Addison leaned against the counter, already weary. "The gas tanks of the cars exploded, blowing out the windows of the house. The two women were only about twenty feet away."

Billings bit the end of the pen and raised his brows. "Two women?"

"The other one didn't make it."

"Oh." Billing's mouth shaped the word. He looked down, resumed his tapping while scanning the notes. "Mrs. Clayton registered a fever of one hundred two point three and suffered some smoke damage to her lungs." He looked up. "We did get out of her that she'd thrown up the day before, so she probably has the flu or some kind of mild virus, confirmed by the initial blood work. With the smoke inhalation, it put an additional strain on her lungs. We're watching for signs of bronchitis. She's on oxygen, antibiotics, and pain meds."

Arnie spoke the question before Addison could. "What about her burns? She looked pretty bad when we saw her."

"Well, they're certainly painful, but they're mostly superficial—first degree in layman's terms—with a few small second degree spots on the back of her neck, scalp and hands. Six to ten days and she'll be okay, although the deeper burns will take longer to build new skin. We'll probably release her in a couple of days, depending on how her fever and cough are doing."

"She sure looked a lot worse." Addison shook his head. "At least her hair did."

Billings nodded. "Yes, her hair took the brunt of it, all right. But its thickness protected her scalp for the most part." He shrugged. "Hair grows back."

They thanked the doctor and watched him walk away. Addison thought of his lovely Elizabeth when the chemo destroyed her hair, causing it to fall out in huge clumps. When he found her in their bathroom, tear tracks streaking her face, he'd tried to put a positive spin on it and quickly found out how important hair was to a woman's self-esteem. As he and Arnie turned toward Natalie Clayton's room, Addison thought the doctor wouldn't be so cavalier if it were his own wife.

He let Arnie knock on the half-open door and lead the way around the empty first bed to the one by the window. The woman didn't respond when Arnie spoke her name, nor did she turn her head from the window. Addison studied the left side of her face, marked by several small cuts and red blotches. He winced at the burned hair. Some strands lay twenty or more inches across the pillow. But parts were gone down to the scalp where a greasy salve covered the burned skin. Soot and bits of debris smeared the pillow surface. How would you even begin to treat these burns? Did you cut the hair off? He didn't know. He stepped around the end of the bed into her line of sight.

"Mrs. Clayton? I wonder if we could speak to you for a few minutes. If you're up to it, I mean." Addison cleared his throat and watched her eyes shift from the window to his face.

She wrinkled her brow and spoke in a scratchy voice. "Who are you?"

"I'm Detective Conner and this is my partner Detective Trujillo. We're from the Steerman Police Department." Addison pulled the side chair from the corner and sat down. "Do you feel up to some questions?"

Her nod gave permission to proceed.

As gently as he could, he tackled the big one first. "The woman with you this morning...could you tell us her name?" Tears immediately spilled from her eyes and her body shook with silent sobs, followed by coughing. Addison reached for the box of tissues and pulled out several for her. He helped her pull the nasal oxygen cannula away so she could blow her nose. A light dusting of freckles ran down her nose and across each cheek. Where the fire hadn't touched her, the complexion of a super model shone through. Addison sat down to give her a minute.

"Donna," spoke the chaffing voice. "Her name is Donna Montgomery." Arnie's pen scratched down the information in his notebook. It matched the registration information from the car in the Clayton driveway. "Her husband's name is Chet." This brought more tears, but she recovered faster.

He shifted in his chair. "Can you tell us what happened, Mrs. Clayton?" They took notes as she described the events, beginning with waking to a noise.

Typical of some victims, Addison observed Natalie Clayton distance herself from the experience, recalling the details with a calm worthy of someone reading a newspaper article. Her strength impressed him, especially when she described pulling Donna from the house and finding the knife in her chest. He liked to think he'd be as brave in the same circumstances. It always amazed him how people found the strength to do what they had to in crisis situations. As she finished her narration, he caught Arnie's eye, seeing the same respect on his face.

The bed rattled as Arnie leaned against the side rail. "Is there anyone you can think of who would want to harm you or Mrs. Montgomery?"

"No. I have no idea who would do this."

"Could it be someone who wouldn't want your mother-in-law to succeed in her run for governor?" Arnie asked.

Addison noticed a slight wince on Natalie Clayton's face at the mention of Hilde Clayton, and she didn't respond to Arnie's question for nearly a minute.

"I don't…I mean, how could that have anything to do with this?"

After more questions regarding her husband's cause of death, bank accounts, life insurance, and business partners, they obtained her permission to search the house for any helpful information. She also gave approval to access bank records and life insurance information. Then they went through the fire sequence one more time. At the end of thirty minutes, she cleared her throat and Arnie reached for the water on the stand. After a sip, her eyelids fluttered closed, then open. She turned to Addison. "What happens now?" He wondered that the fire had spared her incredibly long lashes.

He stood and tucked his notebook in his inside jacket pocket. "We'll talk to the fire inspection team next, and our forensic team is at the house now. The doctor said you'll be here for a couple more days. We'll check back with you before you're discharged."

"Is my house gone?"

Addison stared at his shoes. "Pretty much. Cars, too. I'm sorry." He felt deep sorrow for Natalie Clayton. To lose so much in one week.

As they left the curtained enclosure, Addison turned. She lay with eyes closed, perhaps asleep. But not a sleep of rest. Not with the events of the previous few days.

He turned and ignored his partner's raised eyebrows. "Let's go."

- 6 -

After an emotional meeting with Chet Montgomery, Arnie and Addison drove the shocked man to the morgue for the official identification. Addison hated this part of his job. The soul-wrenching grief of the survivors never failed to resurrect his own pain all over again. Sometimes those left behind grew angry, even violent, and took it out on the messenger. But he felt it his duty to treat both victims and families with respect and graciousness. He remembered what it was like to be numb and out of control.

From the morgue, Arnie caught a separate ride to meet the arson and forensics teams at the fire site, while Addison took Chet home and waited while he phoned his two daughters and pastor. Addison called Jack Clayton's business partners, then joined Arnie at the Clayton home.

Yellow crime scene tape stretched across the driveway, around a parkway tree, and up the left side of the wrecked structure. Sweltering heat poured in as Addison opened the car door, carrying with it the pungent odor of burned wood, plastic and fabric. Leaving his coat on the seat, he shielded his eyes against the noon sun. Roiling, dark thunderheads rose in the west. Weather forecasters predicted afternoon showers and a break in the heat, but then again, they'd been promising for two days. Maybe this time they'd be right. Even a light rain might wash some of the stench of fire and death from this quiet neighborhood.

Fire scenes might look spectacular—even eerily beguiling—at night, but the light of day brought gritty reality and anything but beauty. The two-story Clayton house no longer matched its neighbors in the tract except in basic layout. Two-car garage on the right, master and second bedroom upstairs above and behind the garage, living room in the center front, with a den/office/bedroom on the left. The kitchen and lower bedroom occupied the right rear. Danger of collapse had compelled the fire crews to brace the garage area with timbers to protect the inspection team.

Soot stained the house black above every window and door. The remains of the burned contents sat in a soggy mound where the front lawn had once been green and cared for.

Arnie called to him from the interior of the garage where he knelt between two gray hunks of steel.

"Porsche?" Addison inclined his head toward the once sleek sports car on the left.

"Carrera." Arnie stood and attempted to brush soot off his pants with dirty hands. "Ah, man. Corrine is going to shoot me for ruining these pants." His wiping attempts merely spread the mess.

"Better keep your gun locked up, partner." Addison grinned at his friend. Corrine loved her husband fiercely, but never missed a chance to bust his chops in fun. Arnie peeled off the latex gloves and tossed them on a pile of trash. Addison handed him some paper towels from a roll sitting on the driveway with other equipment. Arnie brushed his pants.

Addison gestured toward the two arson team members tweezing bits of material into an evidence bag. "Find anything yet?"

"Yep. Definitely set. The gas tanks of both cars are punctured, something sharp like an ice pick or punch, so the fuel leaked out onto the floor. Found a book of matches with the cover folded back. Looks like the perp lit it and tossed it into the pool of gas."

"Effective."

"Definitely. The burning gas under the cars heated the tanks until they boiled and ruptured. Then…boom!" Arnie shook his head, sadly observing the blackened car. "Shame to do that to a Porsche."

"Expensive car for someone who didn't make much money." The other car appeared to be an older sedan.

"I thought Clayton was in some kind of investments?" Arnie asked as they stepped out of the garage and under the shade of a tree. He picked two bottled waters out of a cooler of ice and handed one to Addison.

"He was. But, his pay was mostly commission based and, according to his two partners, Jack didn't carry his weight. In fact, the partnership agreement was worded to allow two partners to remove the third if specific proportional sales volumes weren't achieved. Kind of a safety valve."

Arnie took a long drink. "Let me guess—Jack got voted off the island?"

"Not yet. But probably imminent. They'd been having talks with him for six months, sort of do or die. They're faxing me a copy of the agreement and their earnings statements for the last twelve months."

"So Jack had money problems."

"Not sure yet. Maybe the Claytons had other income, inheritance or something, or maybe Hilde Clayton helped them out. From what I hear, her husband left her pretty well off."

Arnie turned to the house. "You thinking this is someone's way of collecting on a debt Jack owed?"

"Could be." Addison walked to the gaping hole where the front door once stood and stepped inside. The stench of smoke and water—not unlike wet charcoal—assailed his nose, and bore no similarity to a cozy fire on a chilly winter night. He pulled a handkerchief from his pocket and held it over his face.

Black mounds marked the location of a sofa, chairs and dining room table. One painting remained on the living room wall, toasted to a crisp, while another lay in ashes on the floor. A charred clock sat on the fireplace mantle, never to chime again.

The right side of the house behind the garage stood in ruins, but the left side of the living room, farther from the source of the flames, was better preserved and revealed a small hallway.

"There's an office back there." Arnie pointed to the area. "The door was closed, so other than smoke damage, it's in pretty good shape." He led the way into the hallway, past a bathroom to a back room.

When he and Elizabeth moved to Steerman, they had looked at houses in this tract. The developers sold this model as a four bedroom, or three bedroom plus optional den/office. A desk stood in the center of the rear wall below the window where a bed might go, a closet to the left on the other outside wall. A four-drawer steel file cabinet filled the right corner. A dusting of soot covered the papers on the desk and the carpet squished beneath their shoes. Any valuables needed protection quickly to avoid mildew in the hot weather. Addison made a mental note to contact Natalie Clayton about it. He could arrange for a recovery service to preserve the contents of the room.

A pull on the bi-fold closet door revealed golf clubs, several coats, two banker's boxes on the floor, a sleeping bag and numerous small boxes on the shelf. Addison started on the lower boxes, bottoms already soggy. They couldn't be lifted without falling apart, so he removed the lid in place. Arnie pulled down the upper ones and sat them on the desk.

Addison's first box held Jack's high school yearbooks, sports trophies, and college textbooks. He'd just lifted the top off the second box when Arnie exclaimed, "Now this is interesting."

"What?" Addison stood and walked to the desk. Arnie held up a blond woman's wig and pointed into the box. The light coming in through the smeared window reflected off a small gray cash box.

Arnie shoved the wig toward him. "Hold this. I'll get the forensic guys. They're trying to get prints off the kitchen slider."

- 7 -

A nurse woke Natalie around one in the morning to check her vitals, disconnect the oxygen per the doctor's order, and give her Tylenol for pain. After dozing most of the day and evening, she found herself wide-awake and again buried in grief for Donna's death. Who could do such a thing? And why? It made no sense. Curled into a ball, she let the tears flow. First Jack, now Donna. Of all her injuries, the pain in her heart hurt the worst.

Poor Chet. Natalie had met the towering man many times when he came by Emerald Escrow and Title to pick up his wife. At six foot five inches, he'd been a massive giant once, but a heart attack and subsequent health problems had left him shrunken and stooped. Yet he always greeted her with a warm grasp of his large hands and a broad smile. His trademark colorful wide suspenders made him easy to spot. He loved Donna so much. Now he faced the future without her. And Natalie faced the future without Jack.

The five o'clock news had shown endless video loops of her burned home, a picture of Donna with the headline *Murder Victim* under the snapshot, and Natalie's own driver's license photo. According to the on-the-scene reporter—an anorexic blonde with too-bright red lipstick and a chrome-yellow blazer—the police had no suspects yet, but were working every lead. Two of Natalie's neighbors testified of a family-oriented neighborhood. The Claytons were a quiet couple who kept to themselves. Nothing like this had happened before.

Then they shifted to footage of the state capitol in Jefferson City and pictures of Hilde giving a speech when she'd won her seat in the House of Representatives. The story had closed with another reporter in front of the hospital here, quoting doctors as saying Natalie Clayton, daughter-in-law of State Representative Hildegard Clayton, was recovering from injuries.

Natalie had turned off the television, unable to stomach any more. Being the victim instead of a bystander changed everything, and Natalie didn't think she'd watch news reports in the future with the same detachment—if she watched them at all. She feared everyone's pain would be a reminder of her own.

Finally, she pulled herself up from the sorrow, wiped her tears, and shifted in the bed, taking care not to bump her broken left foot, which throbbed whenever the pain medication wore off. Her new roommate on the other side of the curtain shifted, too, the stiff hospital sheets crackling with the movement. The woman had undergone some kind of eye surgery, and bandages wrapped her head. Whenever she rolled on her back, she snored.

The dim nightlight above Natalie's bed illuminated the acoustic ceiling. She counted the larger holes in the tiles—anything to take her mind off the last few days. Although she disliked a dark room, it was a little too bright for her. The squeak of a nurse's rubber-soled shoe out in the hallway drew her attention to the muted life-sounds of the hospital: the clank and dripping of the janitor's mop pail, the clatter of cart wheels delivering meds, voices from the nursing station several doors down.

According to Dr. Billings, she would be discharged day after tomorrow. Suddenly, she realized she had no house. Where would she go? She ran her fingers through her hair, instantly regretting the pain-inducing touch. In the dim light, her hands glistened with antibiotic ointment. She pulled a tissue from the box and carefully wiped around the burned areas on her fingers.

The bedside stand lacked paper or pen, so Natalie began a mental "take stock" list, a method learned from her father. It felt strangely disloyal to Jack and Donna, but Natalie couldn't help applying her organizational skills. She imagined the ceiling tiles as left and right columns. On the left she "wrote" what was gone: her friend, husband, home, and cars. The "remaining" side list contained a mother-in-law who hated her, and a low-end job at Emerald Escrow and Title. She didn't know the checking account balance since Jack paid all the bills and gave her some cash each week. She hadn't had her own checkbook in years. She would need to get to the bank right away and see where things stood. Her parents' home and land had sold eighteen months ago and Jack had invested the proceeds in growth funds through his company, so she listed that as an asset. She'd have to call his partners and find out how the investments were doing. And, of course, there was Jack's life insurance policy.

Unable to think of anything else, her mind settled on Jack. When they'd married, she'd been anxious to escape her controlling parents. They weren't bad parents, but their tight reign chaffed on her, their only child. They made most of the decisions about school, activities, friends, jobs and boyfriends. Even after college, every time she talked about wanting to move out and find her own place, it seemed they had a countering argument. In the end, it had been easier to remain at home while she worked.

But eventually the stifling closeness choked her and sent her running to the first man to take more than a passing interest in her. That wasn't all bad, was it? She and Jack had loved each other. Still she wished mom and dad were here now to hold her and tell her what to do.

Independence was overrated.

Her parents had done one thing right. They'd moved to Steerman and bought twenty acres at the edge of town, right before community development exploded. Their house sat on a rear corner with the remainder of the property fronting the blooming commercial district. The surrounding properties were quickly built out, and their vacant land fetched almost five hundred thousand dollars when sold. Jack had promised her that, with the right investments, it could double every seven years. He'd given her a spreadsheet last month, showing substantial growth.

She had no idea what it would cost to rebuild her home, but the insurance should cover most of the expense. At least she wouldn't be destitute.

However, the question remained: Where would she go when discharged?

After an hour of tossing and turning—as much as she could with her foot and IV line—Natalie needed to go to the bathroom. The woman in the other bed snored lightly and Natalie didn't want to wake her with any commotion. She felt surprisingly better, so instead of calling a nurse, she carefully climbed from the bed and lowered herself into the waiting wheelchair. Her left foot throbbed now that it was lower than her body, and she almost climbed back into the bed. But that wouldn't solve still needing to use the toilet. With the IV bag hooked to the chair's post, she wheeled into the bathroom and pulled the door closed before turning on the light.

Getting from the chair to the toilet was an easy task, as long as she minded her foot. When she finished and balanced on one foot, she caught a glimpse of herself in the mirror and nearly sat back down in horror. Dozens of cuts marked her face, but it was her hair that froze her in place. Huge hunks were gone, and what remained contained bits of black soot and a greasy salve. She looked awful. Picking up the brush from the provided toiletry kit, she worked gently at the knots and tried to get the worst of the debris out. What she needed was a shampoo, but it would have to wait until tomorrow or later.

Tangles forced her to go slowly, beginning at the ends and working up. She'd finished half when a noise from the room startled her. Muffled moans and the rattle of a bedside rail were followed by a scream, crash, and cries. Natalie hopped one-footed to the door and pushed it open. In the muted glow of the over-bed night light, a man wrestled a pillow over her roommate's face. The woman pounded his arms and kicked at him.

"Hey! What are you doing?" Natalie took two steps toward him, but her IV line pulled her to a painful stop.

The intruder spun to face her, his face covered with a black ski mask with white-trimmed cutouts for eyes and mouth. For a moment, Natalie had the weird sensation she was in a bank robbery. Voices sounded from the hall. The man looked back and forth between the two women, dropped the pillow and ran toward Natalie, shoving her into the bathroom and slamming the door.

She kept her footing and pushed the door open again. The man was gone, but her roommate was screaming for security and flailing for the call button. Now shouts for security erupted down the hall. Natalie hopped and dragged her wheelchair to the bed.

"It's okay. He's gone." Natalie tried in vain to comfort the screaming woman, but one flailing arm caught her across the nose. She lost her balance and toppled to the floor, taking her IV bag with her. It burst and liquid soaked the back of her nightgown. Something warm and coppery flowed across her mouth and dripped from her chin. The unmistakable smell of blood assaulted her for the second time in as many days.

Light flooded the room and a stern-faced nurse shouted at her. "What are you doing?" Behind the nurse, people rushed into the room.

Natalie lay on her wet back. "I was just going to the bathroom. I saw a man attacking her." She put her hand over her face as the tears fell.

A tug on her wrist drew her attention. She found the nurse kneeling and reading her identification band. "Natalie Clayton," the nurse said.

"Yes." Natalie wiped her tears, and her hand came away smeared red. She tried to still her heart rate. "This is my room."

The nurse's facial features softened and she apologized for shouting. "Here." She got behind Natalie, helped her into the wheel chair. With a drill sergeant's efficiency, the nurse issued orders to the rest of the group to summon the police, get a dry nightgown for Natalie, and find a new room for both women.

A uniformed man with 'Hospital Security' on his shirt stood in the doorway, talking into a radio. Aids rushed out to check on other patients. Natalie's roommate continued to scream about someone trying to kill her.

Natalie turned to the nurse. "Where did the man go? What's going on?"

The nurse pursed her lips and glanced at the uniformed man, then said, "We're moving you to another room."

- 8 -

Addison paced the living room, glancing again out the front window to see if the street held any interesting activity. Of course it didn't, not at two o'clock in the morning. He'd gone to bed at nine thirty, exhausted from the early morning. Now he paid the price.

The Clayton/Montgomery case bothered him. Motive was key in any murder, and though Donna Montgomery was the murder victim, it made sense she might have been in the wrong place at the wrong time. From Natalie Clayton's statement, it seemed probable the killer thought only one person was in the house. Otherwise he wouldn't have made so much noise after setting the fire. He'd probably already stabbed Donna Montgomery.

Addison walked to the kitchen and pulled an orange soda from the refrigerator. The popping of the top brought a memory and smile. During his teenage years, he and his brother, Ben, used to get up a couple of nights a week, drink sodas, snitch cookies from the jar, check out the dark fields and stars from their back porch windows, and talk. Subjects ranged from what they planned for the weekend to dreams of the future. Once in awhile they'd spot a raccoon or coyote in the blue light of the moon. On warm summer nights they'd walk barefoot through the cool grass down to the boat dock and dangle their feet in the lake. His mom never did figure out how they went through so many sodas in a week.

He let the orange fizz swirl across his tongue and asked himself for the twentieth time if Natalie Clayton had been the target. It didn't make sense to go after Donna Montgomery at a strange house, and then leave the home's owner alive upstairs as he set the fire. He and Arnie had ruled out burglary, because a burglar wouldn't torch the house. A burglar might do that to cover an accidental killing, but this didn't appear accidental, not with the electricity switched off at the circuit breaker panel and the smoke detectors ripped from the ceilings. No, this was definitely a murder with arson cover-up.

He set the half-full can back in the refrigerator and headed to his bedroom where he changed into his running clothes. Days were so hot it was dangerous to exercise, though he saw crazy people doing it everyday. A few laps around the neighborhood in the relatively cooler night air sounded good right now.

Addison stepped onto the front entry, quietly closed the door. Moisture-laden air bathed the quiet street, and the floral scent of his neighbor's roses and jasmine lent a tropical feel to the night. He used the handrail for a brace and stretched. When his muscles loosened up, he began a slow run down the sidewalk, letting his mind wander. Some of his best thinking came while running or in the shower. More than once, Elizabeth had threatened to cut off the hot water if he didn't get out.

They didn't get many murders in Steerman, though the population had exploded over the past few years. As his old chief used to say, "Crime moves to the suburbs on the heels of the people." Burglary statistics were up for the third straight summer, fueled by hot-weather boredom and the quest for easy drug money.

Addison longed for the small town of his youth. Storm Lake held many great childhood memories. As his feet pounded the dark concrete, he smiled, and admitted he probably remembered more good memories than there had ever been.

School dismissal in June opened the door to adventurous summers, filled with fishing, boating, water skiing, swimming, family barbeques, and camping trips. Grandpa Conner led the annual trek to the beach for the California grunion run, a middle-of-the-night expedition, which, more often than not, ended in disappointment. Trying to pick the right night—two to six days after a new or full moon—Grandpa poured over almanacs, fishing lore books, and tide tables. A miss resulted in long car rides each way, during which he and Ben slept in the back of Grandpa's station wagon.

But when the old man guessed correctly, the water and beach came alive with the silver-sided five-inch fish, burrowing in the wet sand, laying their eggs, and escaping in the next wave. For a half hour, Addison and Ben would scurry across the dark beach, grabbing the slippery fish, stepping on seaweed and dodging waves. A successful "hunt" earned a sleep-in, followed by a brunch of deep-fried grunion, coated with Grandma's corn meal batter. He and Ben liked the hunt better than the taste of the fish, but they always made a big deal about how good fresh grunion were, if nothing more than to please their grandfather. As they grew older, they discovered grunion weren't too bad if drenched in enough ketchup.

Addison rounded the corner of their block and picked up his pace. He wanted Mandy to have that sense of family, but now with Elizabeth's father gone, there was no family left in Missouri. Sure, their church filled some of the gap, and they had good friends whose support during Elizabeth's illness got them through the most difficult time of their lives. However, several months after her death, church ladies began dropping hints about getting remarried. Nothing blatant, just a comment now and then about Mandy needing a mother. Now at the two year mark, their matchmaking was far from subtle. More than once when dining at the home of friends, a single woman "just happened" to stop by "for a few minutes." Addison knew they had his—and Mandy's—best interests at heart. But it bugged him big time. He'd taken to turning down invitations, which isolated Mandy and him, even further.

Addison slowed his pace from the sudden sprint to a more sustainable run, angry with himself that he let this thinking get to him. It wasn't easy to disconnect from a marriage of 16 years. A great marriage. In some ways, he wanted to just keep running, away somewhere, but he knew that solved nothing.

For Mandy's sake, he needed to make changes. Perhaps he *should* begin dating, though the whole idea scared him to death. At forty-four years old, he ought to have self-confidence, but it all went out the window at the thought of asking a woman on a date. No help at all, Arnie threatened to set him up with a cousin who had a "good personality."

The familiar outline of his house emerged from the darkness and he slowed to a walk, hands on his hips, gulping large quantities of air. He had no idea how long he'd been running, but his muscles felt hot, taxed, cleansed. Wiping the sweat from his forehead with the edge of his tee shirt, Addison turned up the brick path to the door. Another day would begin in a couple of hours, bringing another sunrise and a chance to start fresh. As he reached for the doorknob, the cell phone in his shorts pocket beeped.

Addison arrived at the hospital after 5:30 in the morning, reluctantly leaving Mandy by herself. They'd wanted him there earlier, but he'd delayed until the summer sun was lightening the eastern sky. He wasn't leaving her at night, rather at dawn. Being a single parent constantly challenged his ability to be two places at once.

A security guard checked his police ID at the main entrance. They weren't taking any chances. Addison suspected it wouldn't do any good now. No criminal would hang around with police swarming the scene. The elevator bulged with a patient bed and staff, so he turned to the stairs, taking them two at a time to the second floor. Another guard stopped him as he opened the hallway door, and then directed him to the nurses' station to meet the hospital administrator.

Ten minutes later, Addison walked down the hall to a room with yet another guard at the door. The patient name holder on the wall was empty. He knocked softly, then pushed the door open and walked in.

Natalie Clayton sat upright in her bed, twisting a tissue into tiny ropes. Bits of it littered the pastel blue blanket. Her face showed a mixture of concern and relief when she recognized him.

"Detective Conner."

"Good morning, Mrs. Clayton." Addison stopped at the end of the bed.

"Perhaps you'll tell me what's going on. No one else will." She wadded up the tissue and hurled it toward the trashcan under the window, missing by a foot. A sigh escaped her lips. "Sorry. Just tell me what's happening…please?"

Her anger surprised him and he detected the slightest pout on her full lips. He concentrated on the view of the parking lot for a moment. Addison moved to retrieve the errant trashcan shot, then turned back to her. "Mrs. Clayton, someone tried to smother your roommate."

She nodded, covered her mouth and said quietly, "I know. I was there. Is she okay?"

"Yes. She is pretty shaken up, but she's been moved to another room and we have a policeman guarding her." He pulled a visitor's chair to her bedside and sat down. "I need to ask what you saw. Do you feel up to it?"

She nodded again, so Addison asked her tell him everything.

"I had to go to the bathroom. My roommate was asleep and I didn't want to wake her, so I got into the wheel chair myself. Probably not a smart thing to do, but I'd been sleeping all day and was a little bored, too, you know?"

He nodded and jotted some notes and let her go on. He didn't want to interrupt with questions until she finished. She told of combing her hair, then hearing noises and a muffled scream. She shouted at the man, who then pushed her into the bathroom and ran out. Then she went to the woman's side.

"The nurse said she found you on the floor by the other woman's bed, is that right?"

"Yes. I tried to help her, but with her bandaged eyes, she didn't know who I was and hit me across the nose. I lost my balance and fell. That's when the nurse came in—and then everyone else."

Addison noted the discoloration spreading from the bridge of her nose. It looked like she'd at least have mild black eyes, as if the woman needed any more injuries.

"Did you recognize the man?"

"No. He had on a ski mask."

Addison asked about height, weight, clothing, odor or cologne, hair color, accent.

"He never said anything, just looked at both of us and then ran out. I can't remember exactly, but I think he may have been wearing green hospital scrubs, or at least something loose-fitting like that. Everything happened so fast." She blew her nose again, this time setting the used tissue on the bedside stand. "Did anyone else see him?"

"No. No one saw him."

He paused to give her time to assimilate the information. Addison chose his words so as not to scare her. "We think he may be after you and got the other woman by mistake. It's possible this is the same man who killed Donna Montgomery and set fire to your house."

"Me? Why would he be after me?" She slumped lower on her bed, eyes wide.

"I was hoping you could tell me. This can't be a coincidence."

Natalie Clayton shook her head slowly. "It doesn't make any sense. I'm not important to anybody."

Addison stood and rubbed the rough stubble on his chin. He'd have to shave in the locker room at the station. He moved to the side of the bed to gain her full attention. "Dr. Billings said you can be released today, and I think it's a good idea to get you out of here. We need to move you to a safe place, where the media can't find you. And because of your broken foot you'll need someone to help. Do you have somewhere you can go? A relative or friend?"

She stared at the edge of the sheet, rubbing it between her fingers like she had when he'd first seen her in her backyard. "No. I don't have any family left."

"Your mother-in-law's?"

Natalie closed her eyes and pinched the bridge of her nose, wincing at its tenderness. "Definitely not there."

"Surely there must be someone you can stay with. A friend from work? A neighbor? Someone from your church?" He couldn't believe anyone could be so isolated from people.

She'd stilled, to the point he checked to make sure she was still breathing. Her body seemed to shrink into the crisp bed linens and he strained to hear her answer.

"There's no one."

- 9 -

"I said I'd get her." Tarz's fingers hurt from gripping the minuscule cell phone. When would electronics companies learn that real men wanted a phone they could hang onto?

No, that wasn't fair. He shouldn't blame the equipment—it performed its function perfectly. He switched the phone to the other hand and flexed his fingers. His hand hurt from banging open the fire exit door at the hospital when he dodged security.

"You said the same thing after you killed the wrong woman."

The old bat's irritating voice crawled up his neck and twisted the muscles in a tight knot. He resisted the urge to fling the phone across the room. "How was I to know she had a double?" he growled.

"And the woman in the hospital, was she a double, too?"

He was beginning to regret the day he heard Natalie Clayton's name. How could so many things go wrong on one simple job? First Jack died. But did anyone think to tell him? No. He'd been surprised to find the Porsche in the garage, but hey, who was he to argue when someone wanted a hit and torch job, with a substantial advance payment? All the joy of watching the fire from down the street disappeared when he later found he'd missed the target.

The hospital—that had been close. He'd barely made it out of the building and down the block to his truck before the cops flew by, lights flashing. He'd almost had a heart attack, just like ole Jack. He jerked the phone from his face and choked out a laugh while the old woman prattled on about what she'd do to him if he failed again.

Jack got what he had coming. He'd never been any fun. No sense of humor whatsoever. No *heart*. Tarz laughed again, cupping his other hand over the phone mic as he doubled over, wheezing and in tears.

Gradually the needling buzz cut through his fun and the grin dropped away quickly as it had come. He interrupted the steady stream coming from the phone.

"I *said* I'd *get* her, and I will." She began to speak again, but he cut her off. "I'll get Sis to get me her location. It might take a few days, but I'll find her. And when I do, I'll be the last thing she sees."

- 10 -

The noon sun beat down mercilessly as they pulled into the driveway of an unassuming house. Natalie sat helplessly as Detective Conner ran around and opened her door.

"Detective, are you really sure about this? It just doesn't seem right." Natalie twisted in the car seat to face him, but he was already at the trunk, retrieving the wheelchair.

"I already called her. This won't be a problem." He positioned the chair near her and set the brakes.

Exiting the car with her broken foot and bandaged hands proved much harder than getting in. Natalie inched herself out of the deep bucket seat.

He reached for her, then dropped his arms, evidently as unsure as she about how to help.

Eventually she wiggled to the edge of the seat, leaned forward, and stood up on her good foot. Conner moved behind her and placed his large hands on her waist to help her pivot into the chair. A rush of heat radiated over her skin and left her dizzy with the scent of his aftershave. No man had touched her with such intimacy since she and Jack were married. Even Jack hadn't touched her physically in the months before his death—she didn't know why and he refused to talk about it—yet somehow this contact seemed a betrayal of her vows. Finally settled in the chair, she chided herself. The detective only assisted her into the wheelchair. How could she have such thoughts with Jack's funeral only two days before? Maybe it was the pain meds.

As they wheeled up the walkway, Natalie took in the neighborhood of modest ranch-style homes. Her own home was much newer and larger, or rather it had been. But here the mowed lawns and colorful summer flowerbeds showed a pride and individuality missing in her manicured tract with its Homeowners Association-hired gardening service. Picket or split-rail fences surrounded some of the yards, and rose bushes and wisteria climbed trellises against garages in wild glory.

Two doors down, an older man pruned a hedge in the shade of a huge sycamore tree. Even from here, the sweet smell of its leaves suffused the air, reminding her of summer outings at the river north of town. When the man noticed Natalie, he stopped clipping, slowly straightened, and stared as they approached the front door.

What must he be thinking? Embarrassment colored her cheeks brighter than the first-degree burns, and she concentrated on the bricks passing beneath her feet.

She shook her head. This was a bad idea. Even if Addison Conner was a policeman, she didn't know the man. He seemed nice enough, but what if his house was a mess inside? Or maybe he lounged around in his underwear while watching TV all day and smoking smelly cigars. And what if his teen daughter had no interest in helping her over the next few days? She'd definitely not thought this through. She should insist he take her back to the hospital. They could keep a guard in the hall, couldn't they?

Natalie opened her mouth to insist on going back when cool shade enveloped her as they passed under the porch overhang. Before Addison could reach for the doorknob, the front door opened to reveal a stunning, raven-haired beauty, whose purple top and white shorts contrasted with incredibly long, tanned legs. Seeing the girl's wide, muscular shoulders, Natalie's first thought was, where was the teenage girl? Her second thought was Xena Warrior Princess. The girl's large eyes widened momentarily, no doubt at Natalie's appearance, but they softened so quickly Natalie wondered if she'd imagined it. Natalie hoped she camouflaged her own amazement as well as the girl.

"Hi. I'm Mandy," the girl said in a husky alto and extended a slim hand. "You must be Natalie. Please, come in." The girl's wide smile swept aside the uneasiness Natalie felt.

Mandy stepped back to let them into the cool interior of the house. Even with the short travel distance from the car to the house, the hot air had felt like fire again on her skin.

The three stood—and sat—awkwardly for a moment.

"Okay," Addison said with a smile and rubbed his palms together. "Well, I guess we'd better lay out the house rules," He maneuvered her chair through a wide doorway into a bright kitchen.

Her dream kitchen.

This room had the butter colored cabinets Natalie always wanted. White pinstriping trimmed each door, and frosted glass on several cabinets hinted at glassware and dishes within. White appliances and tan, travertine tile floor added to the cheery setting. So different than the corresponding room in her house.

Lemon scented the air. There were no ashtrays with fat cigars. In fact, the only sign of decay was a pathetic Creeping Charley plant in a hanging basket by the window, yellow and brown leaves indicating needed care.

Mail spilled across one end of the breakfast bar next to a wall-mounted phone. Pens and pencils protruded at all angles from a decorated round can, a grade school project of Mandy's, perhaps.

Natalie gave her attention to the detective, anxious to see what rules he had in mind. Staying here wasn't her best idea ever, but what choice did she have?

"First, since you're now officially our house guest, you need to stop calling me 'Detective' and start calling me Addison."

Natalie shifted from the wheelchair to a whitewashed, spindle back oak chair in the breakfast nook bump-out which overlooked the back yard. "What other rules are there?"

"Yeah, Dad." The corners of Mandy's lips turned up as she crossed her arms and leaned against the counter. "What other rules?"

Addison scratched his head. "Uh, no loud music after ten o'clock. No dishes left in the sink. And don't feed the dog from the table."

Mandy pushed off the counter and stood inches from his face. She poked her finger in his chest and said, "First of all, we don't have a dog. And second," another poke, "*you're* the one who leaves his dishes in the sink."

"I'm reforming," he said, moving away from the girl to straighten the already straight napkin holder on the bar. "And you're the one with the loud music."

"I'm reforming, too." Mandy flashed Natalie a smug look.

"No fair. Reforming was my idea first."

As they continued the back and forth, Natalie stared in awe at the two. She'd never seen people banter like this and not have it grow into a fight. Maybe on TV it happened, but never in her family. Addison and Mandy obviously loved each other and were completely at ease. Natalie's parents could never... Well, they were dead now, and she didn't want to remember the bad things.

Addison had told her Mandy was fourteen years old, but even in Natalie's limited observation of the girl she seemed way more mature. Maybe that was due to Mandy losing her mother. Though Natalie had been thirty-seven when she'd buried her parents, she recalled vividly the feeling that her early life was over. For the first time in her life, she'd felt all alone, which seemed strange at the time since she and Jack had been married nine years by then.

In this house, she had expected a flighty teenybopper, replete with permanently attached iPod, pink everything, and requisite bubblegum. She stared at Mandy's Navajo-style earrings with purple and white stones set in silver that coordinated beautifully with her outfit. Mandy was obviously an exception to the rule.

Mandy's voice broke into her thoughts. "Natalie, while my dad the cop is busy thinking up more rules, can I get you anything? Would you like some ice tea?" She held up a pitcher.

The tears came unexpectedly as she remembered Donna saying nearly the same words the night before she died. Natalie wanted nothing more than to curl up in a ball in her own safe place; however, that place no longer existed. A warm hand rested on her shoulder and she looked up through blurry eyes at Mandy's pretty face.

Sunday morning brought Natalie new energy. The flu symptoms had vanished during the night and, after a glance in the bathroom mirror, she resolved to tackle her hair. Addison and Mandy had left for church and Natalie had the run of the house.

Using her ragged fingernails, she peeled the protective bandages from her fingers and examined the burns. The small blisters hadn't popped and looked better. The doctor said she could bathe if the blisters remained intact. Natalie practiced lowering herself into the dry tub and then getting out. She didn't want to be stranded. Once satisfied, she filled the tub with lukewarm water and lowered herself into it, draping her taped left foot over the edge.

Though cool, the water still stung her hands and neck where the worst burns were, but she needed to cleanse away the dirt. This morning she'd again found bits of soot on her pillow. Perhaps the water could wash away the guilt she felt for Donna's death, and the regret for not being a better wife to Jack. Sliding down, she let the water cover her face and rinse the grime from her ruined hair.

An hour later, Natalie heard the garage door rise while she sat at the kitchen table reading the newspaper. The update story about the hospital attack reported the police had no leads, but she already knew this from Addison. Natalie's photo was printed again as well as repeated speculation of a connection of the attack to Donna's murder. A quote from Hilde stated Natalie was "in our prayers." She shoved the paper aside as the door to the house opened.

Mandy's cheery "We're home!" made Natalie feel like she belonged in this house. It wasn't permanent, but for now she relished the hominess of this small family.

"Hey, you washed your hair." Mandy made a beeline to the refrigerator and began pulling out items.

"Yes. I couldn't believe how gross it was. Still is, I guess." She shook out the towel she'd wrapped around her head and let the wet hair fall free. No way did she want hot air from a dryer on her sensitive skin.

Addison came in from the garage, dressed in chinos and a striped short sleeve shirt. He said hi and that he was going to change.

Natalie watched the girl sauté two chicken breasts in a skillet of hot oil and minced garlic. She added a splash of white wine and Italian seasoning and covered the pan. Mandy moved with the sureness of an accomplished cook. The room soon filled with the mouth-watering odors of a fine Italian eatery.

Addison, dressed in gym shorts and a tee shirt, poked his head into the kitchen and announced he was going for a run. She'd barely worked her way up to his ball cap, emblazoned with FBI in large white letters followed by "Not!" in canted red letters, when he made for the front door.

She'd hardly seen him in the last few days, having left her in Mandy's care. The detective had a demanding job. Natalie turned back to his daughter. "Is there anything I can do to help?"

Mandy held up tomatoes and carrots. "Are your hands up to chopping?"

Natalie nodded and hopped over to the counter. She didn't like the confinement of the wheelchair. Addison had said there were some crutches in the garage he'd dust off for her this afternoon.

Mandy handed her a paring knife. "Here you go. I'll wash some lettuce for salad."

As they worked in companionable silence, Natalie stole glances at Mandy's short haircut. No more than three or four inches long, she had a lightly gelled spiky style on top, while the sides framed her face but revealed pierced ears. Sort of a soft punk style.

"What?"

Embarrassed for being caught staring, Natalie concentrated on a carrot.

"Is there something wrong with my hair?" Mandy fingered her pointed sideburns.

"No, nothing's wrong." Natalie smiled, remembering her own self-consciousness at fourteen. "Actually, I was admiring your haircut. It's beautiful."

"Oh." A huge grin spread across her face. "Thanks." Mandy patted the last of the lettuce leaves between paper towels before continuing.

"I got it from my mom. The hair color, I mean. Dad's got the towhead blond thing going you know," Mandy waved a lettuce leaf, "but my mom had black hair."

"Have you always had short haircuts?" They worked in silence for a few minutes.

"No." The sadness in her voice kept Natalie from replying. Mandy pulled a large bowl out of a cabinet and began ripping lettuce into small pieces, using more force than warranted.

Natalie dumped the cutting board of chopped finished tomatoes and carrots into the bowl. Nearby, a shallow Delft bowl adorned with Dutch windmills contained assorted teas.

"Would it be okay if I heated some water for tea?" Mandy nodded and Natalie turned the burner on under the teakettle and returned to the table to wait for it to heat. Her left foot had begun to throb and she eased into the chair with a sigh.

Mandy set the chicken aside to cool, opened a soda from the refrigerator, and leaned against the bar. "My mom died a couple of years ago. But I guess you knew that."

Natalie remained quiet and watched emotions play across the girl's attractive face.

"We were really close, you know? She was a great mom." A shuddering sigh escaped and, for a moment, Natalie thought she might cry. "She was always planning things for us to do, like going to the lake to rent paddle boats and feed the ducks, or to movies, or just stopping for an ice-cream cone."

The teakettle whistled its interruption. Mandy filled a mug for Natalie and brought it and the tea bags to the table. She sat opposite, running a finger around the rim of her soda can.

"After she started chemo, her hair came out in clumps. She always wore her hair long with straight-cut bangs, kind of like those pictures of Cleopatra in the movies, you know? Exotic. That's what everyone called her. She looked so different than other people around here."

Natalie nodded and dipped her tea bag in the hot water. She'd seen a photo of Elizabeth Conner on the living room mantle. Slightly slanting eyes and high cheekbones did indeed set the woman apart from the norm. Mandy's eyes were more like Addison's in shape, but retained the nearly black color of her mother's. It never failed to fascinate Natalie how a child could be such a blend of two parents, both in looks and personality. She wondered what her own baby would have looked like. Blonde hair like hers or brown like Jack's? She'd never know.

"It was like each hank of hair took a little more out of her and there wasn't anything I could do." Even after two years, the sorrow weighed down Mandy's shoulders and glistened her eyes. "I had the same color hair, same cut. Dad always said we looked like twins."

Realization dawned on Natalie and she sat back. Twins who no longer looked alike. Mandy's full hair would be a constant reminder to Elizabeth Conner of her own lost youth and health, and a reminder to Mandy that they were no longer twins. The words popped out of her mouth before she could stop them. "You cut your hair."

"I went to the shop on the way home from school one day and told them to buzz it as short as possible. They wouldn't do it at first until I explained about my mom and told them I'd do the first pass with the clippers. I still had to argue with them, but they were off the hook then and just had to help me make it look as good as possible." The corners of Mandy's mouth turned up slightly. "Dad was home on his day off and he almost killed me when I walked in the door."

"What did your mom say?"

"Nothing. Her hair wasn't completely gone yet, but as soon as she saw me, she picked up her purse, left the house, and came home a half hour later with the same buzz cut."

"Twins again."

"Yep. For a while, at least, until even her short hair disappeared." Mandy walked to the counter and began chopping the cooled chicken for the salad, her back to Natalie.

Again amazed by this family, this woman/child, the love and dedication they showed, Natalie stared into the back yard. Sun-drenched orange marigolds glowed in beds along the lawn. A lemon tree stood in the opposite corner, heavy with large yellow fruit. So much color and light both inside and outside of this house and family, yet bad things happened to them, too. Why would God let something like cancer enter the world? Wasn't he powerful enough to do anything to prevent it? If not, what kind of God was he?

A hummingbird zoomed toward the window and stopped inches away, intent on feeding from bright zinnias growing tall above the window sill. She could see every hue in its iridescent feathers. The bird seemed to keep an eye on her through the glass as it darted from one flower to another, dipping its long beak deep into the center to drink up sweet nectar. Then, just as suddenly as it had come, it disappeared across the yard and over the fence. If God was truly the creator of the world, he'd created a world of vibrant color, variety, and beauty.

It was this family, though, that so intrigued her. The love between them was palatable, even with the mother not here. Mandy finished the salad preparation and began filling glasses with ice and water.

Natalie's own childhood memories held none of the warmth Mandy spoke about. She had thought her upbringing to be normal, but now she wondered. Vacations had been rare. Trips to the park or the ice-cream shop simply hadn't happened. Jack had been much the same, seeing no need for the frivolous in life.

Anger swelled at all the missed childhood experiences, things she hadn't even known were missing at the time. Oh, probably she did know, deep down, like in the quiet times as a girl when she read under the covers at night with a flashlight. It was in that dim cave she'd discovered travel, adventure, romantic holidays, and fantasies of life beyond her hometown.

Once, after seeing a circus on TV, she'd dreamed about being a lion tamer, wearing a cobalt blue sequined leotard with a white sequined cowboy hat and matching boots. She wielded a white leather whip. And though it never touched the giant cats, it convinced them to obey her every command. For weeks she drew pictures of the lions, tigers, and leopards, meticulously capturing every stripe and spot. She sketched their cages, the circus ring and equipment, all under a giant, striped tent with red, white, and blue pennants flying high atop the main pole. She used her middle name and became Samantha, Queen of Cats, and toured the world, performing before cheering thousands. Samantha, Queen of Cats wasn't afraid of the powerful beasts in the ring, or beasts outside the ring either.

Natalie had even read up on colleges offering degrees in care and training of wild animals. But she had learned life didn't often follow dreams, nor allow for them. She'd grown up.

She sighed and glanced at the sun rays blazing a path across the kitchen floor, dust mites swirling happily in the twisting currents. Maybe she could take a trip to the lake someday with Mandy. They could rent a paddleboat.

Addison returned from his run, showered, and joined them in the kitchen. Before they ate, he had them join hands and offered a simple prayer of thanksgiving. This, too, was a new experience for Natalie. Other than funerals and weddings, prayer certainly wasn't part of her life. She'd always imagined prayer something performed by ministers or "sent up" during crisis by someone on a sinking ship, like Titanic. Never had she held hands with others while praying, and never had anyone prayed for her by name as Addison did now. She couldn't seem to get a full breath.

After his amen, she concentrated on her salad, unsure how to respond.

That evening they played Scrabble, which she hadn't done in years. Addison pouted like a little boy when both women topped his points, with Mandy winning on a triple word score. At times, Natalie felt like an intruder, watching the easy banter between father and daughter. Yet the two made every effort to include and encourage Natalie.

When Addison made popcorn and brought it and a two-liter Pepsi to the table, Natalie tried to remember the last time Jack had served her anything. She couldn't. He'd been a private man, not needing shows of affection. After a while, she convinced herself she didn't need it either.

In bed later, with the soft sounds of music drifting from Mandy's room—volume in strict accordance with the house rules, she noted, her lips curling involuntarily in a small smile—Natalie replayed the events of the day, realizing for the first time how flat her life had been. It wasn't Jack's fault any more than hers. Fact was, she'd settled, something her Aunt Rowena always warned her against. "Never settle; go get what you want."

But life was no longer the same as it had been. Jack was gone, she didn't have to deal with his mother anymore, and she had no home, no car, and no money. The flatness had vanished—for better or worse—literally overnight. Everything was new territory. What would come next?

"Hey, partner, look what I found." Arnie hurried into the detectives' area and laid a stapled sheaf of papers on Addison's desk.

Addison shoved aside another case file. "Life insurance policy?" He thumbed through the document, which gave off a strong odor of smoke. "On Natalie Clayton."

"Emmy at the crime lab called me. They found it in the locked cash box. Nothing else of significance." Arnie leaned over his shoulder.

"Who's the beneficiary?" He scanned pages for the information.

Arnie pointed to a line of text. "The husband." He plopped down at his opposing desk, switched on a small fan and put his face in front of it, drying his damp hair. "It's for two million dollars. And, the policy is only six months old."

Addison looked in surprise and leaned back. "Two million? That's a lot of insurance for the low income earner of the house. So you're thinking...?" He trailed off, waiting for Arnie's take.

"Always in murder you look first at the spouse and for money."

"But it wasn't the spouse who was murdered, it was Donna Montgomery. Plus, Jack Clayton was already dead."

"I know." Arnie leaned forward. "But I interviewed Montgomery's coworkers at Emerald Escrow and Title, and several commented on how much she and Natalie Clayton looked alike. Practically twins."

"You think the killer got the wrong woman." He made it a statement, not a question.

"It explains another try at the hospital. Got the wrong woman the first time."

Addison stood and looked out the window, thinking of Natalie using the hospital bathroom while her roommate was attacked. He'd come to the same conclusion as Arnie. "Okay, let's think this through. The husband was dead. If you've got him hiring someone to kill his wife, why would the killer go ahead with the murder? And why try the second time at the hospital?"

Arnie thought for a minute. "Maybe the perp lives out of town and didn't know about the husband's death."

"I can buy the not knowing for the first attempt, especially if the killer wasn't from around here. But I'm having trouble with the hospital attack. By then, the murder and fire was all over the news. Jack Clayton's death was reported over and over as background for the bad luck of the grieving widow and as son of State Representative Hilde Clayton. How could even a killer be so out of the loop not to see something about that?"

Arnie conceded it unlikely.

Addison poured some coffee from the pot on the credenza, and sat back down. It smelled like burned rubber, but he took a sip anyway. "Unless the attacks aren't related." Arnie shot him a skeptical look and Addison held up his hands, palms out. "Okay, I know. It's a lot of coincidence. I'm just trying to ask the questions the chief will ask."

The office aid, Sharon Tanner, brought in another stack of papers and deposited them on Addison's desk.

Arnie used the interruption to grab a cup of coffee for himself. "Yeah. But it does seem like Natalie Clayton is the target." He sipped the coffee and grimaced. "Say, how's it going with her staying at your house? She and Mandy getting along?"

"Yeah, it's going pretty well." Addison stopped as he noticed Sharon still stood by his desk. She was an early forties blonde who'd worked for the department a couple of years. He knew from Gladys, the dispatcher, that Sharon was pregnant, though not showing enough he'd have noticed without Gladys' legendary inside scoop. Sharon wasn't married, but obviously had a serious boyfriend. Her drawn expression and time off the last few days evidenced the continual morning sickness that plagued her. She normally worked on reports for the uniformed officers, but filled in for Gladys on breaks and lunch hours.

"Did you need something from me, Sharon? A signature or something?"

"Oh. I, uh...no. Sorry." She gave a little smile, then a frown, then turned and left the room.

Addison raised his eyebrows at his partner. "Wonder what that was all about?"

Arnie shrugged. "Beats me. She's been a little weird since she got pregnant. Must be hitting her kind of hard. Evidently the boyfriend is married."

"Ouch." Addison hadn't heard that part of the news. He thumbed through the new papers.

Arnie set his coffee cup on the desk in disgust. "Man, this stuff is so rank it should be illegal. I know cops are supposed to be oblivious to bad coffee, but a man has to draw the line somewhere."

"Maybe we should buy some French roast?" Addison said, and then laughed at Arnie's response about the chief paying for it.

"So, what about the Clayton woman staying with you?"

Addison leaned back. "So far, so good. Mandy's been a great help to her, plus it's given Mandy something to focus on during the summer break. Natalie's quiet, reserved really. Still hurting physically and emotionally, of course. We haven't talked much about the situation, but I get the feeling her husband was a little controlling. It's like she doesn't know how to interact with honest people and take them at face value, you know?"

Arnie nodded. "When I was a kid, I had this little dog that had been beaten before we got him. If we moved too fast or shouted, even laughed, he would cringe and whine. Had him eight or ten years—never did get over it. Do you suppose hubby Jack hit her?"

That was something Addison hadn't considered. It wasn't a conversation he wanted to broach with Natalie, but they had to figure out the motivation for the crimes. Every day that slipped by put them farther away from Donna Montgomery's killer.

Armed with paper and pen, Natalie spent Monday morning trying to piece her life back together. She made a thorough list, then checked off each item as she finished it, jotted notes, and added still more items as she thought of them. She called the auto insurance company and talked to an adjuster. He promised a call back after he obtained a copy of the preliminary police report. Unfortunately, her policy didn't include provision of a rental car. He suggested she check the home and fire insurance and see if it would cover a vehicle rental.

Next she called her bank and inquired about replacement checks. The woman verified Natalie's personal information and promised immediate temporary checks, but Natalie halted when the woman asked the address for the checks. What should she put down? Her house was destroyed and she wouldn't be living there for months at least. Not until she found out how the homeowner's insurance worked and whether she could afford to rebuild. Finally, she gave the address anyway since there were no other options, and said she'd try to get to the bank tomorrow to pick up the checks.

She cancelled the newspaper delivery and arranged for mail to be held at the post office. For a replacement driver's license, the Missouri Department of Revenue required her birth certificate or passport as well as a utility bill to prove she had a residence.

After a call to the water company to arrange for a duplicate of the last bill, she fell back on the sofa and rubbed her face, wincing as she scraped one of the tender red welts that were now beginning to itch like a sunburn. Most of the burns had proved minor and were healing quicker than she'd imagined.

Her birth certificate and passport—a long expired one from her college semester abroad in London—were in their safe deposit box at the bank. Perhaps Addison could take her. She could get some cash at the same time and use taxis for other trips until she could replace her car.

There were so many things to decide, and what energy she had begun the day with quickly deserted her. She tossed the unfinished list on the coffee table and curled into a ball on the soft green couch, pulling up her feet. Tears welled as she thought again of Jack. He'd handled all the money, paid the bills, took care of insurance policies. Took care of her. She hadn't even called the homeowners insurance company yet. In fact, she wasn't sure what company Jack had used since he was continually shopping for a better deal. How could she find out the information? Should she just call insurance companies until one of them said they were the right one?

Sudden anger at Jack sprang up and she pounded the cushion in frustration, filling the air with dust. She stopped in embarrassment. It wasn't Jack's fault. Maybe he could have done better involving her in their finances, but picking up the pieces after his death wouldn't have been so impossible except for the fire destroying everything.

She signed and closed her eyes to blot out the memories. But the memories didn't retreat. Instead she dreamed.

Natalie was back in her house, in her bedroom. Something had awakened her. A sound. Her feet fumbled for the slippers in the dark. The power was out. She took the familiar steps to the door and opened it to the hall. A thump in the garage below startled her, but she'd known it was coming. She moved down the stairs, fearing what waited. Halfway down, the door to the garage opened, spilling orange light into the hall below. Natalie froze on the steps, knowing a man would run past. There —he was moving in the hall. But he didn't continue into the kitchen as before. This time he stopped at the foot of the stairs and, as if sensing someone above him, turned slowly.

Heart in her throat, Natalie tried to run back up the stairs, but her feet were held fast by the gold carpet. It knew she'd hated the color and it took its revenge. Her pulse hammered and she hauled at her feet. Even in the darkness, she could see the despicable carpet loops twining over her blue slippers, knotting together, and snaking up her ankles. Panic squeezed the air from her lungs. In seconds the man would see her.

Fire burst through the garage door, lighting the hall and revealing Donna coming from the guest bedroom. As Natalie struggled to pull her feet from her slippers, she fell back onto the stairs. Immediately, long gold carpet threads encircled her arms, securing her like Gulliver. She shouted warning to Donna, about the intruder, about the fire. But though her mouth opened, no sound came forth.

Through the swirling orange smoke, Donna calmly walked toward the bottom of the stairs, toward the man still hidden in shadow. Natalie fought the fibrous restraints, ripping some loose only to have them replaced by new ones.

Sweat drenched her tee shirt and soot rained down on her, acrid smoke filling her lungs as she screamed in silence.

Shallow breaths. She had to take shallow breaths. Carpet strands wound around her neck, threatening to cut off her air entirely.

Below, Donna reached the man. Did she know him? Then Donna turned to Natalie. Her eyes were glazed over, face expressionless in death. One of Natalie's bone-handled kitchen knives protruded from Donna's blood-soaked nightgown. The dead woman raised a hand in farewell and turned away, disappearing into the dark living room.

The strands across Natalie's neck tightened more, choking her. Fire raced up the walls to the two-story ceiling, lighting the room and smothering her with its furious heat. She would die here, strapped to these stairs by her own carpeting, punished for hating the color Jack picked.

The man now faced her, identity hidden behind a black ski mask with white trim around the eyes and mouth. The mouth laughed at her and the man bent double in mirth.

Something familiar. The eyes, or the crows feet showing at the edge of the cutouts—but she couldn't think. Her vision dimmed as she thrashed in a desperate attempt to get a breath of cool, sweet air, but she could see the man reaching for her, stretching his hands toward her throat. She screamed again and again as fire leapt between the stair balusters and ignited her clothing.

- 12 -

"Natalie?" Addison stood in the doorway from the garage, brown grocery bags in each arm. The woman before him thrashed about on the couch, grunting, swatting her legs, and fighting the lavender chenille throw wrapped around her throat and head.

Dropping the sacks on the floor, he knelt before her and blocked her flailing hands while he tried to unwrap the material from her throat. Natalie thrust upright, sending him crashing into the coffee table. Her piercing scream nearly shattered his eardrums. Though she looked right at him, her eyes darted right and left, unseeing—or at least not seeing anything in this room.

Addison made another grab for her hands. "Natalie!" His shout registered and he watched awareness return to her wide eyes, terror turning to horror, to embarrassment, and ultimately to tears. She collapsed against him, sucking deep breaths.

"It's okay, Natalie. It's okay." He wrapped his arms around her soaked back and pulled her close.

Sobs wracked her body and strong fingers dug into his back. Nothing he said stopped the wails that escaped her throat, so he moved up beside her and rocked her like a child, carefully stroking her damp hair.

Addison left the door to Natalie's room ajar so he could hear if she called. Shaken by her emotional meltdown, he sank to his knees in the living room and retrieved two oranges from under the end table. He scooped the other spilled food items into the grocery bags, and carried everything to the kitchen. Then he dropped into a chair. His shirt was soaked from her tears, but he didn't move to change it.

Not since Elizabeth's cancer and death had he experienced or witnessed such strong emotion, and he knew not to dismiss it. His grandmother once told him people are too quick to erase the evidence of grief and sorrow, that we all need time to process the pain and heal. Pretending life must go on only buries the hurt.

Like Natalie, both Addison's parents were gone, but at least he had a brother and wasn't entirely alone in the world. Not that he saw Ben much, the last time being Elizabeth's funeral. Had it been two years? Truthfully, he hadn't wanted to face the sympathy from his brother. He heard enough of it on their phone calls. Over the months, he didn't think he could take a prolonged visit, though Ben had invited them multiple times and threatened to come kidnap him for a day. Somehow, two years had slipped by. Way too long.

With a sigh, Addison pushed up from the chair and put away the groceries, discarding five broken eggs. A glance at the clock told him Mandy would be home soon from a friend's house around the block. He put a pot of water on the stove to boil and started some ground beef sizzling in a pan, adding some diced onions from a bag in the refrigerator.

He had no appetite, but it was his turn to cook. Tonight's fare would be his "almost-famous" Sloppy Joes on mashed potato pancakes. Arnie had several creative names for the dish and refused to try it, but it was one of Mandy's favorites.

Working the potato peeler, Addison reflected on the day's work. He needed to ask Natalie about the two million dollar life insurance policy. Most women didn't carry that much insurance. Most men didn't either. That was an awful lot of coverage for a middle-class woman with no kids and a regular job.

He sighed, knowing he had to ask about possible abuse by Jack. After her nightmare this afternoon, it wasn't something he wanted to do, but it might tie into motive if Arnie was right about an attempt on Natalie's life for the insurance payout.

"Dad, what are you doing?" Mandy stood in the kitchen doorway, holding her iPod and staring at the potato in his hand. He frowned at the tuber, several sizes smaller than it had been, then sheepishly dropped it in the simmering water.

"Oops." He grinned at his daughter. She deposited her music player on the table and peered into the sink full of potato slices mixed with very few skins.

"At the rate you're going, there won't be enough to mash." Mandy picked up a spatula and broke up the sizzling hamburger. She pulled the splatter screen out of the cupboard and pointed it at him. "You forgot— again." She positioned it over the meat. Grease splatters coated the stovetop. "You get to clean the stove this time."

"Rats." Although Addison enjoyed doing some of the cooking, it wasn't his first love…not like Elizabeth who could turn anything into a gourmet meal, complete with candles, napkin rings, and after-dinner mints. He watched his daughter add seasoning to the ground beef with practiced ease, measuring nothing. She was so like her mother. It took him two tries before he could swallow.

"How come your shirt's all wet?" Mandy asked, breaking him out of his memories. "And where's Natalie?" She poured tomato paste and water into the meat and replaced the screen.

"I, ah, she's…"

"Right here." Natalie stood in the doorway, eyes still swollen and red. She balanced on her left foot. "Hi, Mandy. How was your time at your friend's?"

"Good." Mandy said cautiously, shooting a sideways glance at Addison, then back to Natalie. While Natalie took a seat at the table Addison caught Mandy's eye and gave a slight shake of his head.

- 13 -

Natalie was ready to go on Tuesday when Addison came home during his lunch hour. She'd tied one of Mandy's scarves around her head and, although she looked somewhat like a Gypsy, it hid her disastrous hair. The burns on her face had reached the peeling stage, so she'd applied liberal amounts of moisturizer. The sky blue tee shirt and jeans belonged to Mandy, too. With a belt pulled tight they fit at her waist, but she'd had to roll up the legs several inches to account for their difference in height.

They stopped at the post office first and picked up a large sack of mail, most of it junk. Addison set it in the back seat. Next was her bank. Addison helped her out of the car. She balanced on the door as he handed her the crutches, old ones he'd had in the garage. Inside, she met with a woman named Lydia in the accounts department to pick up the temporary checks. Before handing Natalie the checks, Lydia asked if she would be making a deposit to her account.

"Deposit? What do you mean?" Natalie planned to withdraw money to purchase clothing and all the other necessary items.

The woman, Lydia, looked uncomfortable. "Well, we usually don't even give out checks for accounts with such a low balance, but what with the fire and all...we made an exception in your case."

"I don't understand. I know there is plenty of money in our...in my account." Natalie's paycheck went in by automatic deposit every week, and Jack used that account to pay the bills. He'd told her so.

Lydia cleared her throat. "Mrs. Clayton, your balance is seventeen dollars and sixty-two cents."

"Seventeen dollars? That can't be. My weekly paycheck is over three hundred dollars." Jack had told her the bank had made errors before, and now, just when she needed money the most, they'd made another one. She shook her head. "You must have the wrong account."

The woman swiveled the computer screen so Natalie could see for herself. Her name and address appeared at the top of the screen.

"I can pull up the account activity if you'd like to review recent transactions."

"Please."

Lydia clicked the appropriate menu choice and Natalie searched the screen. The most recent transaction stared back in amber on black background, a withdrawal for twelve thousand dollars in cash. She searched for the date and gasped. The morning of Jack's death.

Natalie rubbed her eyes. How was that possible? She remembered he'd come to the bank that morning before he'd had his heart attack. But what did Jack need all that cash for? And where was it? She'd looked in his wallet after his death to get his insurance card. There had only been fifty or sixty dollars in it. Maybe he'd moved it to their savings account to get a better interest rate. She asked Lydia to check the balance of their savings account.

Lydia rotated the screen back typed in a few numbers. A frown crossed her features.

Afraid to ask, Natalie held her breath.

"Your savings account was closed twelve days ago. All the funds were withdrawn at that time."

Natalie cleared her throat. "How...how much?"

"Eighteen thousand ten dollars and twelve cents."

"That's not possible." Natalie fought for breath. Tiny stars danced at the edge of her vision. She concentrated on her white knuckles where she gripped the Formica desk. Jack always told her they had plenty of money in their savings. Where had it gone?

"I'm sorry." Lydia looked like a caring person. But Natalie didn't want caring...she wanted their...her money. How would she get her life back in order without money? She caught Lydia's surreptitious glance directed over Natalie's shoulder, and turned to see several customers waiting for new accounts. Not wanting to make a scene, she mumbled her thanks for the checks and staggered to where Addison stood by the door.

"Problem?" Addison bent to look into Natalie's downcast eyes. He couldn't hear her whisper and she had to repeat it.

"The money's gone."

"Gone?"

"Withdrawn. On the day Jack died." She told him about the amount and raised her eyes to Addison's. "I don't know what's happening."

Addison asked if she had a savings account or accounts at another bank. She told him about the closed savings account. "Jack always kept track of all the finances."

"Did you see a copy of the withdrawal slips?" At her frown he took her elbow and headed toward the bank manager's office. A show of his police badge gained an immediate audience with the man, and Addison tersely explained the situation.

"We need to have copies of the savings account closure form and the checking withdrawal. And copies of the signature cards, too," Addison added as the man picked up the phone.

After a few minutes a young woman knocked on the open door and handed the manager some papers. He spread them on the desk.

"This is the checking withdrawal, signed by Jack Clayton."

Addison compared the signature to the one on the signature card given at the time the account was opened. It appeared to match, but Addison was no expert. He'd have it checked later at the crime lab in St. Louis. Next he pulled the savings closure withdrawal forward. At the bottom it read Natalie S. Clayton.

She shook her head. "I never signed that."

Taking the signature card, he held it next to the form. If it wasn't a match, it was a good forgery. At his raised eyebrows, Natalie shook her head again. "It's not mine."

Addison turned to the bank manager. "Do you have surveillance videos going back this far?"

"Yes, but they're rotated offsite every Friday. We'll need to retrieve them from the archives at our security company."

Addison thanked the manager and gave him his card with contact information.

As they headed for the door, Natalie remembered the safe deposit box and her passport. She signed the access form at a teller window, then went through another round of red tape because she didn't have her box key. Natalie agreed to the ten-dollar charge for a lost key, deducted from her depleted checking account, and then went into the vault while Addison waited. She returned with a plastic bag bouncing against her right crutch and headed for the exit before without saying a word.

Natalie sat with the bag on her lap, pondering the contents and wondering how so many things could change in so few days.

"Did you get your passport?" Addison closed his door and buckled his seatbelt.

"Yes, I did." Natalie looked at the man beside her. How different he seemed from Jack. She'd always trusted Jack. Well mostly—except her inheritance of her aunt's house in California. She'd kept that a secret, using her office address for all the legal paperwork. Now she was forced to trust this complete stranger, live in his house, eat his food. Even wear his daughter's clothes. In only a few days her life had turned upside down. How could she trust anyone again? Yet she had no choice.

"Addison, there's something I need to tell you." She looked straight ahead.

"Okay. I'm listening." He started the car to get the AC going, but made no move to drive.

"There were other things in the safe deposit box besides my passport." She inhaled deeply to gather momentum. "I found a stack of cash. I counted it."

"And?" Addison turned to face her.

"A little over $9,000." She heard him breathe, but he didn't respond. "But that wasn't all. This was in the bottom of the box." She held the bag out to him, opening the top so he could see in.

- 14 -

Addison wanted to go to the police station immediately, but Natalie pleaded with him to make two stops, first at the Steerman Water Company for a copy of the latest bill, and then at the Department of Revenue so she could get a new driver's license. For once the DOR lines weren't out the door and, when her turn came, she presented the water utility bill as well as her passport and birth certificate from the safe deposit box.

The efficient woman behind the counter typed in her info and printed a temporary license, assuring her she the permanent one would arrive in three weeks. Addison refused to let her use any of the cash from the bank until it was processed for fingerprints, so she borrowed the replacement license fee from him.

As she exited the building, she gasped and stopped short.

Addison spun around, eyes alert for any sign of danger. "What's wrong?" His hand rested on his gun.

"No, it's okay," she said to reassure him. "It's…I just realized. Before the funeral, I wrote out a check to the mortuary for Jack's service. They must not have deposited it yet. It's going to bounce."

With efficiency she found increasingly comforting, Addison escorted her to the car, started it to get the air conditioning going, then called the mortuary and explained the situation. The deposit had been delayed for a few days due to illness of the secretary, but the director said the check was dropped in the deposit box last night.

Natalie pinched the bridge of her nose, trying in vain to stem the oncoming headache. Now she'd have to pay an insufficient funds charge as soon as they posted the check against her account.

"I'm sorry to get so personal, Natalie, but I imagine the funeral was pretty expensive."

"Almost $4,000."

Addison nodded. He didn't want to leave her alone in the car, so he called the station and asked Sharon—still covering for Gladys—to look up the number for Natalie's bank, then called the bank manager and explained the situation. The man agreed to flag Natalie's account to hold the mortuary check until the lab released the cash.

Natalie leaned back in her seat and closed her eyes. "Thank you for doing that. The simplest things seem to be so overwhelming. Like yesterday when I..." Her voice trailed off, as she remembered the nightmare.

"It's okay. Just getting through your husband's funeral is huge."

"I was lucky that Jack's mother had already purchased a plot for the family."

"For all of you?"

"Uhhh..." Her face colored in embarrassment.

Addison raised his eyebrows in question.

She concentrated on her too-big flip-flops—also from Mandy—and shook her head. "Not for me. Just for Jack."

"Had they bought the plots a long time ago?"

She shook her head again, not wanting to explain that Hilde purchased three plots five years ago when Jack's father died.

His touch on her hand brought her eyes to his. "Natalie, don't you find that a little strange?"

Her vision blurred with tears. What answer could she give?

Instead of taking her home, Addison drove straight to the station. He had Natalie give her fingerprints for comparison on the money, then sit in the waiting area while he went to find Arnie.

"Hey, Arnie. How's your day going?" Arnie sat among stacks of folders and paper, typing furiously on his keyboard.

"Been better." He didn't look up, shoulders hunched in concentration.

Addison sank into his chair, for once thankful for the comforting squeak. "Ditto."

Arnie finished typing, then swiveled from the computer screen and rolled his neck. "What's up?"

"I took Natalie Clayton to her bank today. Had a few surprises." He gave Arnie a concise listing of the events, including the cash.

"Interesting."

"Plus, this little item was in the safe deposit box." Addison sat a plastic evidence bag on his desk so Arnie could see it. His partner rose partway from his chair to look over the piles of reports.

Arnie nodded. "Thirty-eight snub nose. I'm liking the husband on this more and more."

"Arnie, nobody got shot. And it's the *deceased* husband you're suspecting."

"No matter." He lowered himself back into the desk chair. "We need to follow the money."

"I know." Addison rose with a sigh. "Natalie is in the waiting room. I need to get her home so she can do more calling on Jack's life insurance, the home insurance, and some other things. Can you run this gun and cash by the crime lab guys? If possible, we need to release the cash soon." Addison explained about the funeral expenses.

"Will do, amigo."

They filled out the necessary evidence log. As Addison rose to go, his desk phone rang. It was the bank manager trying to reach Natalie. The only contact information they had was the detective. Addison asked him to hold, then called Natalie from the waiting area. He stood nearby as she said hello.

"Yes, this is Natalie." <pause> "No." <pause> "Well, yes, my husband always paid it." <pause> "I don't understand. What are you saying?" She turned to look at Addison. He couldn't tell what was happening, but saw the helplessness in her eyes. Suddenly she groped for his chair and fell into it, crutches clattering on the tile floor. "Yes, I see." <pause> "Yes, I understand." <pause> "I...I don't know. I'll have to call you tomorrow."

Addison answered Arnie's questioning glance with a shrug.

"Yes, I'll call soon. Thank you." Natalie slowly replaced the receiver, as if doing it silently would also silence the bad news.

"Natalie?" Addison turned the desk chair, forcing her to focus on him. "What did he say?"

When she spoke, her voice sounded flat, dull. "He said he forgot to ask when I was going to pay the back mortgage payments. He said we are four months behind on the payments, and his loan office is talking about foreclosure." She paused and broke their connection, choosing to focus on the items on his desk. "I have thirty days to bring it current or they will take the house."

She began to laugh, quiet at first, then escalating into sobbing tears. Addison knelt down and took her shaking hands. She let him pull her close, he kneeling on the floor and she bending forward in his chair.

Arnie wrote on a pad of paper and held it so only Addison could see.

Money problems. Staged burglary gone bad. Wife's life insurance.

All Addison could do was nod.

Natalie excused herself to go to the ladies' room. She splashed her face with cold water, angry with herself for another crying jag. When had she become so weak? The blotched countenance in the mirror answered for her. It happened over eleven years ago when she and Jack planned the wedding. Or rather when Jack planned it. He made the decisions about the hotel, caterer, photographer, flowers. Even the honeymoon. The only good thing about the situation was his mother had refused to help.

She'd had her heart set on New England to see the fall colors, but Jack insisted on a primitive resort in Costa Rica. New England would be too cold and she would enjoy the warm water and beaches.

"I know what's best."

She shook her head and tore a paper towel from the dispenser. He'd actually said that. Why had she caved so easily?

For what must have been the millionth time, she thought of her miscarriage. How might their lives have been different if she'd had quality medical care? Her hand covered her stomach, remembering the botched D&C and emergency operation that followed. It wasn't Jack's fault, but regret and anger still gnawed her insides, just as the surgeon's knife had so many years ago.

- 15 -

After returning to Addison's house, Natalie sat at the kitchen bar and called the life insurance agent to ask about Jack's policy. After waiting on hold for several minutes, Mr. Murray came back on the line.

"Yes, I have the file before me. What can I do for you?"

"I'd like to find out…" Natalie paused and rubbed her temple. "I'm sorry, this is difficult to do without sounding…"

"Inappropriate?"

"Uh…yes. Thank you." Natalie picked up a pen, ready to take notes. "Could you tell me about Jack's life insurance policy? What the amount is and how the payout will be processed?" No matter how she worded it, to her she sounded like the greedy wife, anxious to cash in on her husband's misfortune.

Mr. Murray coughed. "Of course. The policy was for five hundred thousand dollars."

The amount was less than Natalie remembered. Still, she was grateful for Jack's planning. She knew from her parents' meager policies that insurers paid quickly and she could certainly use the money for living expenses. At his pause Natalie pushed through her uneasiness. "How do I arrange for payment?"

"Oh, you don't have to do anything. We received a copy of the death certificate and have issued the check."

Making a note on the pad, Natalie supposed the mortuary had supplied the death certificate. "So the check has been sent?" Maybe it was at the post office today.

"Oh, no. It was picked up."

A chill crept up Natalie's spine. "Picked up? By who?"

"Well, by Mrs. Hildegard Clayton, the decedent's mother."

Why had Jack's mother picked up their life insurance check? "Oh, I see. I thought it would come to me since I'm the beneficiary."

"I'm sorry, Mrs. Clayton. I believe there was a change in beneficiaries sometime back." A tight knot seized her throat, causing her voice to squeak. She asked what change and heard pages shuffling. "Yes, here it is. The date of the change is January 11 of this year." Mr. Murray's voice quieted. "I'm sorry. I'm afraid you were deleted and Hildegard Clayton was added as sole beneficiary."

Addison entered the room and must have seen the stunned look on her face. She mumbled an explanation to him, and he took the phone receiver from her. Through a growing buzz, she heard him request a copy of the insurance forms and the change authorization. Then he asked what he needed to do to get the information released for the investigation, thanked the man, and hung up the phone.

Natalie grabbed a crutch and hobbled into the living room and fell onto the couch, head spinning with the information. Jack always promised he'd take care of her, make sure she had enough to live on if something happened to him. Why had he changed the policy without telling her?

January 11th. She tried to recall that date, but nothing special stood out. Christmas Eve two weeks before with Jack's mother had been a disaster. In the middle of dinner, Hilde had started in again on how Natalie was a sorry excuse for a wife and how Jack would be better off without her. Finally, Natalie couldn't take it anymore. She slammed out the front door and stood on the icy sidewalk in front of the stark Colonial Revival brick structure of which Hilde was so proud. Natalie expected Jack to come out and take her home, but he never did. She'd thought of nothing but getting away from Hilde's stinging barbs and hadn't stopped to retrieve her coat from whatever closet the maid hid it in.

After twenty minutes in the freezing wind, she rang the door bell, then waited on the step in humiliation while Hilde's maid checked with her mistress to see if Natalie could come back in. Jack informed her he had no intention of leaving, and she'd never forget the smug satisfaction on her mother-in-law's face as, for the remainder of the evening, she fawned over her son and pointedly ignored Natalie.

Had that incident caused him to change his policy? Was it her fault for not trying harder to get along with his mother?

Natalie snapped back from the awful memory as she realized Addison had spoken. "I'm sorry. What did you say?"

He knelt down beside the sofa and captured her with his brown eyes. "You need to call Jack's mother."

"What for?" She'd rather step in front of a bus.

"Well, you can't afford the funeral expenses. With the insurance settlement, it's only right she pay for them, not you." His gentle voice washed over her like a needed balm, making complete sense.

Yet she couldn't face another interaction with Hilde Clayton. She shook her head in response. The woman had proved over the last eleven years she didn't have a sympathetic bone in her body toward Natalie. A minimum wage job for the next ten years to cover the funeral expenses sounded like a far better alternative than a conversation with Hilde.

Jack pursed his lips before speaking. "How about this? What if we treat this as part of the investigation and I listen in on your conversation?"

She shook her head again. It wasn't going to happen. "I'll wait for the crime lab to release the cash. And I'll be going back to work as soon as my foot heals a little more."

"Natalie, it's not just about covering the funeral expenses. We need to figure out who is trying to kill you. The old adage 'follow the money' is true more times than not. I need to hear her reaction. Could you do it for me?"

She considered his request. Another talk with Jack's mother was sure to be painful and spite-filled. But if it helped Addison, maybe there was hope to get her life back and get out from under the constant threat she felt. Finally, she dropped her shoulders in defeat and went back to the kitchen bar phone while Addison got the portable phone from his bedroom.

"Won't she know where I am by Caller ID?" Natalie asked, feeling like a condemned prisoner seeking a last minute stay of execution.

Addison gave a little shake of his head, dashing her hopes of a reprieve. "Caller ID Blocking. All cops have it as protection for their families."

Natalie's shoulders slumped as she dialed the number from memory, for what she prayed would be the last time.

"Clayton residence." The voice of Annabella, the maid, contained the same stern tone as her employer.

"Hello, Annabella. This is Natalie Clayton. I wonder if I could speak to Mrs. Clayton for a moment?" She heard no response except the sound of the receiver slamming the hard surface of a table. No 'Just a minute' or 'Hold on, please.' Even the hired help held nothing but disdain for Jack's wife. She squeezed her eyes shut, blotting out Addison standing nearby with the portable to his ear.

A cold voice came on the line. "This is Mrs. Clayton."

Taking a deep breath, Natalie spoke. "Mrs. Clayton, this is Natalie. I need—"

"Natalie who?"

Her eyes popped open along with her mouth and she stifled the urge to strangle the woman right across the phone line. Addison's eyebrows lifted. Forcing an unnatural calm, she answered. "Natalie Clayton, Jack's wife."

"He had no wife."

"I, uh…" Natalie glanced to Addison who returned an encouraging nod. "Look, I don't want to argue with you. It's just…, well, I spoke with Jack's insurance agent today and he said you received the check for his life insurance." Silence filled the line. "I was wondering…well, you see, the house burned down and I need some…"

"I'm sure it was your fault." Hilde Clayton's interruption caught her off guard.

"What?"

"I said I am sure the fire was your fault."

Natalie couldn't believe the innate meanness of the woman, but forged ahead.

"No, actually it was arson." Her reply came out a little stronger than she planned.

"Where are you staying?" Hilde's voice had softened to a tone Natalie had only heard the woman use with her son.

This was new. Hilde showing concern for Natalie? She caught the shake of Addison's head, but she had no intention of informing her mother-in-law of her whereabouts.

"I'm, um, staying with a friend."

"Just what is it you want? I'm very busy." Meaning she had no time for Natalie. Nothing new there.

Another nod from Addison. "I need financial help to cover the funeral expenses."

"No."

"But I…"

"No. You say you're his wife? Then it's your responsibility to pay for his funeral."

The headache returned in force. "Yes, but you see, Jack withdrew all the money from our checking account and I don't…"

"You stole that money."

The accusation surprised Natalie. Hilde made no secret she didn't approve of Natalie, but that wasn't a crime. An accusation of stealing was altogether different. "No," Natalie said, letting some of her own backbone show. She was through kowtowing to the woman. "Jack took the money…"

"How dare you accuse my son. You've been stealing from him all along."

"Mrs. Clay—"

"You've stolen from him from the day you trapped him into marriage with that faked pregnancy."

"I didn't—"

"He worked hard and you constantly spent and squandered his money."

"Squandered?" Fury rushed up her throat, coloring her skin along the way. "I never—"

"Don't call me again." The line went dead.

Addison took the phone from her hand before she could hurl it through the living room window. She dug her fingernails into her palms, fighting against screaming, but not tears. Too many tears already and she wearied of being the victim, the defenseless downtrodden wife.

How dare Hilde accuse her of squandering their money. Jack outspent her twenty to one, even rationalizing his fancy Porsche by saying he needed it for his business image.

But the problem remained: how could she cover the expenses of the funeral, let alone the back house payments?

She felt a warm hand on her back as she lay her head down on the kitchen bar. The cool tile countered the heat of embarrassment. However, neither the warmth of the hand nor coolness of the surface held any answers.

77

- 16 -

Addison excused himself to head back to the station after Natalie assured him she would be fine. He shook his head. The phone call with Hilde Clayton had been brutal, but after a few minutes of rest, Natalie had sat up with renewed determination and assured him she'd be fine.

Turning onto the expressway choked in late afternoon commuter traffic, Addison drummed a beat on the steering wheel, running facts of the case through his head.

Before being pulled off onto other cases, Arnie had found out from the doctors that Jack Clayton's heart attack and death several hours later had come from natural causes. Clayton had no prior history of heart disease, but was known to be sedentary, had high cholesterol, and his father had died from a heart attack. The physicians said they saw dozens of cases like it each year. No mystery there.

However, the closing of the savings account and draining of the checking were another matter. They spoke of planning, premeditation. But by whom? Until he heard from the crime lab on the bank withdrawal signatures, he couldn't be sure who was telling the truth. He wanted to believe Natalie, but her signature had been on the savings closure same as Jack's. The countering fact that someone tried twice to murder her spoke strongly in her favor.

Addison gave up on the expressway and turned onto a side street, and then picked up Riverfront Drive. Of course, Natalie could have hired someone to make it look like attempts on her life. She hadn't personally been attacked, only those two women around her. But what motive could she have? If she did take the checking and savings money, somehow cause Jack's heart attack, and then arrange for the attacks on the women and arson, what would she gain? Causing Jack's death if she thought she'd gain the life insurance money Addison could understand —he'd seen it a dozen times in his years in police work. Still, Natalie's surprise at the beneficiary change seemed genuine. And why the attacks on Donna Montgomery and the other woman in the hospital? Why the arson? He shook his head. No, that didn't fly. From all accounts, Donna Montgomery had been a true friend to Natalie, and he was convinced Natalie was the intended victim.

His cell phone rang and he pressed the answer button. "Conner."

"Hey, partner. You ever coming back to work today?"

Addison grimaced. He'd spent so much time on this Clayton case the extra workload fell to Arnie. "Sorry, bud. On my way. Stuck in traffic." Traffic on Riverfront had come to a sudden stop. He turned onto a narrow side street, then into the alleyway behind a strip mall, dodging empty beer cans and bags of trash. "Be there in a few minutes."

"Good. Crime lab boys and girls said they'd have the signature analysis back about five o'clock. Thought you'd want to see that."

"Definitely." He glanced at the radio clock. Three-thirty. "I didn't think they'd get to it for a few days." The crime lab had a notorious backlog.

"Yep. Guess they had a handwriting teaching session with a bigwig from Detroit and used the Clayton forms as a real-life case study. One of the techs volunteered to bring them over. Said she didn't want to get called on in front of the group." Arnie chuckled.

"Okay, sounds like we're finally getting a break. I have to tell you, this thing's got me going in circles." He maneuvered around a skinny dog that stood dumbly in the center of the alley, crossed the side street, and continued into the next alley.

"Yeah." Arnie sighed. Addison knew his partner had put in a lot of hours this week, and the weariness showed in his voice. He hadn't said anything about Addison's extra time with Natalie...not yet, anyway. But Addison still felt guilty for not pulling more of the load.

"Arnie, you want a double-E?" If he cut two blocks north, he could swing by Killer Koffee—named for its proximity to the city jail—and pick up Arnie's favorite espresso.

"Amigo, you do that and I'll make sure Corinne sends in some carrot cake tomorrow."

"Deal. Then I'll see you in about ten." He punched the call end button and dropped the phone onto the seat. Corinne's desserts were famous in the department. He'd be sure to arrive at work early.

The Conners' telephone rang and Natalie picked it up after she heard the beginnings of a message by the auto insurance adjuster. He explained that since both cars were lost at the same time, the company had aggregated the claim. Jack's Porsche still had a sizable loan, but her paid-for, ten-year-old Honda retained a good value. Bottom line, after paying off the loan, she would receive a settlement of $4,350. He could have a check ready tomorrow.

Natalie hung up the phone and thought about her options. It wasn't a lot of money, but she hadn't expected even that much. Except for attending Donna's memorial service tonight, nothing held her in Steerman. She had no place to live, and her boss, J.D., would have surely fired her by now from her job—she hadn't called into work since before Jack's burial. Nor did she want to. The thought of returning to Emerald Title with Donna no longer there had no appeal.

She crutched around the kitchen, suddenly anxious to do something for herself instead of waiting. Grabbing her scarf, she tied it with determination, and went out the front door.

The steamy day quickly soaked her back with perspiration as she hobbled to the end of the block and turned the corner, but the exercise felt good as she pursued her goal. Six doors down, it sat where she remembered when Addison drove her home. She turned up the driveway and stopped at the older Jeep Wrangler. Sunlight bounced off the bright yellow paint, creating luminescence against the dark green hedge. Inside the windshield, a red-bordered For Sale sign read "94 Wrangler, 6-cyl, automatic, AC, power steering, power brakes. 129K mi." It didn't state a price.

Natalie moved around the vehicle, checking out all sides and finding no dents. Big tires looked ready for off-road trails. The phone number on the sign made her wish she'd brought a pen and paper.

"Help ya?"

Natalie turned at the gravely voice to find a man standing on the walkway to the house. He was mid-sixties, had gray hair, a matching shaggy beard, and wore a battered green John Deere cap. The toothpick in his mouth flicked from side to side as if he might be irritated, but he had kind eyes.

"Yes. I'm interested in your Jeep."

"Pretty banged up."

"The Jeep or me?"

The man looked her up and down, then the corner of his mouth twitched up slightly. "Jeep's okay." He removed the toothpick and tossed it toward an open trash bin sitting by the garage.

"It's an automatic transmission?"

"That's right."

"I learned to drive on my dad's old Jeep."

The man stuck out his hand. "Name's Walter. Walter Thompson." Natalie shifted her weight and grasped his work-rough hand. She introduced herself and moved aside as he stepped up to the Jeep and ran his hand along the yellow hood as if tending a thoroughbred. "Got some miles on her, but the engine's real strong. Always regular oil changes and tune-ups. Paint's only two years old."

Walter opened the driver door and pointed out the newer, high-back seats, and tilt steering wheel feature. "That might come in handy with your cast and all."

"How much are you asking?" She feared the price would be out of her range. The tires, paint and interior were in excellent shape. But at ten years old she didn't want to over pay. And the canvas top had tears in the rear corners.

"I'm askin' $4,000." Walter rocked back and forth on his heels, hands in the front pockets of his faded jeans.

She'd hoped the price would be lower than that, but any less for a car and she'd probably be buying junk. Car repairs later could eat up even more. The only possibility was the $9,000 from the safe deposit box, if Addison could get it released from evidence soon enough.

"Why are you selling it?" Natalie's father taught her to ask the question about anything she bought used. Not that the person selling was always honest.

Walter's countenance sobered and the bill of his cap pointed to his boots. "Don't need it anymore." After a pause, he spoke so softly Natalie had to lean forward to hear. "Belonged to my son. Kept it real nice for him while he was gone."

Natalie didn't know what to say, so she turned to the vehicle and inspected the rollup windows. She almost didn't hear Walter's next words, so softly were they spoken.

"He was killed in an army training accident." Walter turned away and took interest in the hedge separating his driveway from the neighbor's.

"I'm sorry." She hadn't asked for intimate details, but Walter seemed to want her to know for some reason.

A woman came out the front door. "Walter?" She stopped when she saw Natalie. "Oh, I didn't know you were talking to someone."

Natalie smiled at the woman and introduced herself.

Walter returned from his reverie. "She's interested in Billy's Jeep."

"Oh." The woman smiled. "Our Billy was a good boy. We want his Jeep to go to a good person. Are you a good person?"

"Well, I…" What a strange question. "I like to think so."

"Billy believed God watched over him everyday. He said he could depend on God no matter what." The woman cocked her head to one side, as if sizing her up before asking her next question. "Do you believe in God?"

This was getting weirder by the minute, and Natalie wondered if she should back away and go find another used car. The last thing she needed was to get involved with some religious nutcases who thought God should determine who bought a Jeep.

She'd never been interviewed when buying a car. And what did her belief—or lack of belief—in God have to do with purchasing the Jeep? Cautiously, she took a couple of steps back down the driveway, intending to thank them and make a retreat.

Still, she felt an unusual conviction to be honest with these people. They didn't seem like crazies. She stared at the cracked concrete.

"I, uh…I'm afraid I don't know God that well." The new skin on her face and neck tingled in the high sun and she yearned to get back to the cool house.

"That's okay, dear." The woman stepped close and took Natalie's hand in her own, gave it a firm squeeze and looked her right in the eye. "All in due time."

Natalie turned away from the strange couple, mumbled something about the price being a little steep for her and she'd think about it, then hurried down the sidewalk. She tried not to run.

Natalie sorted through the last of the bag of mail, throwing away the junk mail and keeping bills for cable TV and one of Jack's VISA cards. The last envelope from the bag contained no return address and had Natalie's name typewritten in the "to" area. She slit the flap and pulled out a single folded piece of paper. At first sight of the neat handwriting she snatched her hands from the paper and let it fall to the table. The writing was Aunt Rowena's. And Aunt Rowena had been dead for six months. Without touching the paper, she leaned forward and read the words.

Dearest Natalie,

I'm now in heaven where I belong. I've waited my whole life to get here, and how I wish I could tell you about it, but you'll have to come see it for yourself one day.

You're only receiving this because you didn't come to the funeral. Now, please know I'm not faulting you for missing it. No, not at all. I understand—probably more than you know. You would have attended if you were allowed.

Allowed? How could Wena know she hadn't been allowed to go?

Natalie, I'm writing to let you know the day might come when you need to leave Missouri. Even as I write these words, I know it's going to sound like I'm a silly old woman, but please bear with me. In my prayers this morning, God put this on my heart. He said to tell you that if you leave, don't tell anyone where you're going. Now dear, I'm not entirely sure what that means. I just have to trust that you know.

I'm sorry, Natalie. I always planned to be around longer, but life has a habit of slipping away. I don't mean to sound like I'm complaining, because I'm not. I've had a wonderful life.

If there is regret in its end, it's leaving you. Take care of yourself. Seek the important things in life and grab every moment. Don't let it slip away.

Love,

Rowena Riley

P.S. Natalie, don't miss out on heaven. Nothing in this world matters as much.

Natalie sat in stunned silence, hand trembling on her lips. The postmark date was six days ago and it had been mailed from her aunt's hometown. She picked up the note with trembling hand and re-read it twice, then returned it to the envelope, placed it on the table, and smoothed it with her hands.

How could her aunt know about her danger? The handwriting was Rowena's; she'd recognize the back-slanted, looping style anywhere. Could Rowena have had some kind of premonition about the attacks?

Natalie crutched into the kitchen with restless energy. Anger at Jack for his imposed limitations churned her blood. She should have insisted on going to Rowena's funeral. Even her aunt had seen through Jack's smooth exterior to his controlling nature, that was obvious by the letter. Had Natalie been the only one blind to it?

No. If she was honest with herself, she had seen the problems early on in their marriage. He'd changed after their wedding. But every time she'd wanted to talk about it, he'd twisted her words somehow, making her arguments sound stupid and spiteful. Eventually she'd given up and let him have his way in everything. He'd have gotten it anyway.

But now the years of bottled anger flooded to the surface. All the years of missed opportunities. The things they could have done together. Wasted. She cast about for something to do, something to eat.

Anything.

She spotted the anemic Creeping Charley in its hanging pot and lifted it down to the sink. The poor plant had nearly crept its last, and needed water and serious trimming. Rifling through the drawers, she located kitchen shears and set to work snipping back the leggy growth.

The click of the front door announced Mandy's arrival from a day with friends at River Beach.

"Hey." Mandy dropped her beach bag on the breakfast table.

"Hey, yourself." Natalie forced a smile, but Mandy picked up on her mood immediately.

"What's up?" The girl came around the bar into the kitchen, but kept a safe distance from Natalie's flying scissors. "Whoa, easy there."

Natalie glanced up from her manic work and sighed. "Sorry. I got carried away."

Mandy fingered the remaining stubs of the plant. "It looks good. I like short cuts." She gave Natalie a lopsided grin and fingered her spiked hair. Natalie giggled. Mandy giggled too, and soon they were laughing out loud. Natalie dropped the scissors on the counter and hugged the girl, so much taller than herself.

"Thanks. I haven't laughed like that in a long while." She wiped away tears—happy ones for a change—and pushed the hair back from her eyes, conscious of how it looked without the scarf. "I'd better get some water onto this plant or it'll die from shock."

Mandy headed for the refrigerator. "I'm getting some milk. Want some?" She opened the door and took out the plastic jug.

"No thanks." Natalie pulled a glass out of the cupboard and turned on the faucet. As she put the glass under the stream, a large hairy spider sprinted across the back of the sink. Natalie screamed and jumped back. The glass shattered in the sink.

Above the sink the window shattered with a pop, and behind her she heard an "Ugh" and a crash. She turned at the sound while wondering how the broken drinking glass and the window were connected. Mandy lay sprawled on the floor on her scattered beach bag contents, the open container of milk glugging white across the ceramic tile.

"Mandy!" Natalie hobbled forward, but something slammed into her right side, twisting her around. A searing burn radiated from her arm. The single crutch tangled in her legs, and she grabbed for the refrigerator handle as she fell. She heard another pop as her head smacked the refrigerator. Pain radiated through her forehead and her fingers slipped off the handle. The kitchen spun and her face struck the hard floor.

The cold wet surface seeped into her consciousness and momentarily brought her eyes open. Mandy lay face down next to her. Blood oozed from the girl's shirt and curled into the white milk in a hideous strawberry swirl.

- 17 -

Addison walked into the office and handed Arnie the double espresso, taking his own to his desk. His partner closed his eyes and took a long sip.

"Ah, man, does that taste good or what? Sooo much better than the rat poison here. Thanks." Arnie leaned back in his chair and closed his eyes, balancing the coffee on his leg.

"Tough afternoon?" Since the captain split them up to cover the increasing workload, they never seemed to catch up. Arnie had been racking up the hours and his wife wasn't happy about it.

"Four new cases."

"Ouch." Addison scanned his desk for messages, picked up two new files and took a sip of his own coffee as he opened the first one and read through the officer's report. It was a commercial burglary involving an electronics warehouse. Fortunately, only four TVs were missing from the inventory, but the owner wanted a full investigation and was anxious to talk to a detective.

Ninety minutes later, Addison hung up the phone from talking to the second report's victim and began revising his scribbled notes from the call. A radio squawked in the dispatch room they shared with the uniforms. He idly glanced through the glass to where Gladys once again reigned in front of her calendars, radio mics, and computer screens. Gladys had joined the force fifteen years ago and ruled the desk like a cross between a protective mother hen and an irritated drill instructor. She tolerated no horsing around, but had a heart of gold. Bought off by regular bribes of Corinne's double chocolate chip brownies, Gladys tended to look the other way where Arnie was concerned.

Sharon stopped by the dispatch desk as the radio squawked again, obviously interested in the excitement of the moment. Gladys spun from the phone to the keyboard, then punched the mic and leaned close. Addison took serious interest when the captain ran from his office to Gladys' desk and leaned close in an animated exchange. Sharon backed up a few steps, hand covering her mouth. Then Gladys, the captain, and Sharon turned as one to stare at Addison with expressions of clear horror.

Out of the corner of his vision, he saw Arnie's chair snap upright. Addison's gut wrenched into a hard knot and he came halfway out of his chair. His cell phone rang and he dropped his Styrofoam cup, splashing brown liquid across the desk. The caller ID on the tiny screen showed Mandy's cell.

"Mandy!" Addison barreled through his front door to be stopped by a uniform.

"Sir. Sir." The massive cop blocked his path like a St. Louis Rams linebacker. "You can't go in. EMTs are already here. Plus, it's a crime scene."

Addison bounced his chest against the bulky patrolman. "That's my daughter in there. Get out of my way!" The cop licked his lips and spread his arms wide, either to show he meant no harm or to keep Addison out.

"Listen, man. I've got a daughter, too, and I know you got to see her. But stand over here by the breakfast table, okay?"

Addison took a breath and forced himself to stand down. He let the cop lead him to the breakfast nook so he could see around the bar into the kitchen. Mentally he knew they were all doing their jobs, taking care of the victims, preserving the scene, but the father in him wanted nothing more than to run to his daughter and take her in his arms.

"How is she?"

The cop gave a slight shake of his head. "I don't know. They got here fast." The atmosphere buzzed with multiple radio broadcasts, and codes Addison knew by heart blurred into nonsensical noise.

Two white-shirted EMTs blocked his view of Mandy and he was

shocked to see two more huddled in the small kitchen, bending over Natalie who leaned against the refrigerator. New concern surged through him. He'd forgotten about her when the call came in about a shooting. Her matted blonde hair stuck to the side of her face, dripping white and red from the ends. Her eyes were closed and her head rolled slightly to each side as the paramedics worked on her.

The sirens-blaring, high-speed ride across town left him twitching with adrenalin and worry. He clenched his fists to stop the shaking. The big cop held out something in his latex-gloved hand. Mandy's cell phone.

"This was clutched in her hand when we got here. Looks like she hit the speed-dial for your phone before she passed out."

Addison squinted at the tiny screen. 'Detective Dad' and his cell number filled the display.

Before he could ask the EMTs about her condition, Arnie, who had insisted on driving, rushed through the living room and gripped his partner's shoulder. "I just checked with the guys outside. Shooter got away. A neighbor saw a man sneaking around in your back yard with a handgun and called it in. Lucky the black and white was only a few blocks over on another call."

Lucky? Addison stared at his daughter's still form. Who could call this lucky? Mandy and Natalie lay in pools of blood on his kitchen floor. He ran his hand across his face.

God. What is happening?

"Addison. How's Mandy?" He opened his eyes to find his captain facing him.

He shook his head. "I don't know." The EMTs' hands flew, ripping open bandages, snaking IV lines, while constantly talking to the hospital by radio.

"We'll get this guy. We're canvassing the neighbors. We'll find something."

Addison nodded. A uniformed officer rolled a gurney into the house and they all helped shove the breakfast table and chairs deep into the nook to make room. The EMTs gently lifted Mandy onto the unit, then raised it to height for the short journey to the waiting ambulance. As they maneuvered it around the counter, he stepped forward and grasped his daughter's limp, sticky hand. Her skin appeared white, and blood saturated what was left of her favorite lime tee shirt. Most had been cut away, and a large pressure bandage covered her upper chest. She'd be mad about ruining her shirt.

Tears dripped off his chin. He hadn't even known he'd been crying, but he didn't wipe them away. This was too much like the final time he'd held Elizabeth's hand. He couldn't bear to lose Mandy too.

Please, God.

His eyes found Natalie over the counter. They'd cut her shirt open and were bandaging her right side. Her eyes were open and he raised his brows in a silent question. She nodded and mouthed 'go.' He nodded back and started to leave, but then he turned back. Natalie no longer looked his way, but behind the pain, her blue eyes held a determination he'd not seen. He turned once more and ran to the ambulance.

- 18 -

Frustration surged through Natalie's veins. There was no way she wanted to spend another night in the hospital, but she had no other choice. The E.R. doctors said her impact with either the refrigerator or floor had caused a large knot on her forehead, but no concussion. Her headache gave credence to their words. All she wanted was for people to leave her alone and let her rest, yet Natalie hated the feeling of helplessness the hospital gave her. Not that being away from it seemed any safer.

The bullet had passed exactly between her right arm and chest, searing a surface path through skin on both, but doing no serious damage. Still, it stung like fire...something she was getting used to. Natalie grimaced as the nurse cleaned and smeared anti-bacterial salve onto the bullet tracks, and then covered them with loose bandages.

After a review of the x-rays of her skull, they said she was lucky. One nurse said Natalie's guardian angel was on the job. But if that were true, what about Mandy? Had her angel been on a coffee break?

Pain throbbed in her skull with every movement. She concentrated on remaining still as the nurse finished up. Inquiries of everyone who came in the area yielded no information about Mandy.

This whole thing made no sense. Why would someone try so hard to kill her? What had she done? There could be no doubt now someone was after her, tracking her even to a police detective's home. It was crazy. She owned nothing, had zero left to take.

But other people kept getting in the way and getting hurt—or killed.

Natalie had to do something. No one else could be hurt because of her.

Weariness and pain medication settled over her as an orderly wheeled her bed from the E.R. to the ward. Fluorescent ceiling fixtures and fire sprinklers blinked by in hypnotizing repetition. At the entrance to her room a uniformed officer tipped his hat as she passed. She grabbed his other hand and made him promise to update her on Mandy as soon as he heard anything. He assured her he would. She closed her eyes, glad to know he watched over her.

The orderly clipped the call button and TV control to her pillow and checked her water pitcher. Natalie fought to stay awake to find out about Mandy's surgery, but her body refused the direct order, lethargy pulling her eyelids down, shrinking her world to the immediate smell of pine cleaner and the occasional clatter of a cart in the corridor. She drifted off with the two realizations that tonight was Donna's memorial service, and Mandy was in surgery, another victim of this killer.

The casters of a passing food cart rattled Natalie awake. Antiseptic mixed with scrambled eggs and coffee—how could anyone think it appetizing? She squinted in the bright sun peeking between the vertical slats on the window.

Gingerly, she rotated her neck and found the headache gone. A touch to her forehead revealed only a minor bump. She swung her legs over the side of the bed and sat for a minute, waiting for any dizziness to develop. It stayed away. She lowered to the floor, mindful of her cast left foot. The ubiquitous IV drip made a trip to the bathroom urgent and she hobbled to the door, supporting herself on the rolling IV stand.

As she pulled the door closed, strong déjà vu gripped her. However, this time she was in a private hospital room and a guard sat on a folding chair outside, giving some comfort as she perched on the cold toilet seat.

When finished, she washed her hands at the sink and surveyed the new damage to her body. Harsh light from the bathroom fixture illuminated mercilessly. She examined the tender bump, located where her forehead met hair. If the situation weren't so serious, she would have laughed at her appearance. While most of the burns had peeled and showed new pink skin, her hair still hung in jagged chunks. The new lump, darkening with spider web capillaries, added a macabre element. Too bad Halloween was still two months away. All the kids on the block would run screaming.

She washed her face, then hobbled to the doorway and asked the guard about Mandy's condition. An orderly delivered her food tray while the cop told her Mandy came through surgery fine and was in recovery, still listed as serious. The bullet traveled through her upper chest, missing the lung and bones. She was a lucky girl.

Natalie rolled the IV stand back into the room and sat on the bedside chair. Luck. There was that word again, and it played in Natalie's mind as she ate a tasteless breakfast of toast, applesauce, eggs and sausage. From what she knew, luck was something that happened to people without any volition on their part. Was Mandy lucky or unlucky? Was the fact she wasn't dead indication of God's protection? Natalie didn't know the answers.

One thing she did know: whoever was after her wasn't giving up. If that hideous spider hadn't caused her to jump, she might be dead right now. That was bad. But even worse, her situation had brought danger to Mandy and Addison. Mandy could be dead. A shiver whipped through her.

It was time to make her own luck.

Pushing away the half-eaten food, she called to the guard and asked if someone could retrieve her purse, makeup, crutches, and some clean clothes from Addison's house. She told him where to find everything. After a short call on his radio, he said one of police volunteers would bring them over within the hour. She sighed. Everything was borrowed, even the purse—one of Elizabeth Conner's that Mandy had saved.

She settled back and stared out the window, planning her next move.

At 9:00 AM. Natalie called her auto insurance agent. "I know you said you could have a check ready for me today, but I have a favor to ask."

- 19 -

It was late morning when Terry Kerslake, the auto insurance adjuster, and Natalie turned onto Addison's street. Natalie immediately spotted two news vans in front of Addison's house, still several houses down the block.

Quickly, Natalie pointed to the nearest house on her side. "Here it is. You can drop me off right here. This one with the rose trees."

Kerslake pulled into the curb. "Would you like me to help you to the door?" He started to climb out.

Natalie gave him a smile. "Oh, that's not necessary. I can manage fine." Kerslake looked dubious, so she increased the wattage of her smile. "Really, I'm not as bad as I look." His reaction said she'd lost her marbles.

She opened the door and slid out quickly before he could insist, gritting her teeth against the pain. She turned back to him. "Thank you so much for all your help. I really appreciate it." She grabbed her bag of items and adjusted her crutches—thoughtfully brought to the hospital by the police volunteer—and waved. As he drove away, Natalie slowly walked a few steps up the path toward the strange house, hoping no one was home. She stopped when she saw Kerslake's car turn the corner, then she turned around and worked her way back to the sidewalk, turning away from the news vans and the house with yellow police tape. It would be a long way around the block the other direction, but she couldn't go near the house.

So much pain and suffering. First Donna, then the woman in the hospital, now Mandy. It was time to stop endangering others.

The crutches chaffed her new bandages under her right arm, and sweat dripped down her back when she finally rounded the corner onto the street. The yellow Jeep sat unmoved, the For Sale sign in its window. Was it only yesterday that she stopped by? Natalie pushed the doorbell button, thankful for the shade of the porch. Potted geraniums lined the brick area, giving off their unique scent. The door opened and Walter peered through the screen.

"Well, you're back."

"Who is it, Walter?" His wife poked her head around the man's shoulder. "Oh. Natalie, wasn't it? Please come in."

Walter pushed the screen door open for Natalie and took the paper sack holding her makeup and extra medicine from the hospital. She crutched into the cool interior.

The homey room testified to the couple's Early American tastes, and included a maple dining room table and several antiques. Knickknacks, mostly roosters and pigs, lined the shelves of a hutch.

Walter's gruff voice pulled her from further observation. "Looks like you've been in another fight."

"Walter, mind your manners." The woman pinched his arm. "Don't you mind him, Natalie. Come over here and sit. By the way, I don't think I gave you my name. I'm Rowena."

Natalie jerked up, remembering the letter. "That was my aunt's name."

"Really? Don't find too many with that name these days." Rowena settled herself in the spindly rocking chair opposite the sofa where Natalie sat. Walter stood nearby and they waited for her to speak.

"I know I must look a sight. I'm staying around the corner at a police detective's house and—"

"You're staying with Addison and Mandy?" Rowena's eyes lit up. "Why, what a coincidence. We go to the same church. Did you know Elizabeth?"

Natalie closed her mouth and shook her head. "No, I didn't. I needed a place to stay after someone attacked me—that was the first time—and Addison offered his home. They've been wonderful."

Rowena straightened the hem of her apron. "Elizabeth was such a dear. She and Mandy used to bring over cookies. Don't you remember that, Walter?"

Walter issued a grunt that passed as a yes.

Natalie dropped her gaze to the sculpted carpet. "I'm afraid my misfortune followed me here. You heard the sirens yesterday?" They shook their heads.

Walter cleared his throat. "We were gone last night and this morning, visiting my sister in St. Louis. We just got back about an hour ago. What happened?"

"A man tried to kill me. I got off lucky, but Mandy got hurt pretty bad."

"Oh, my!" Rowena grabbed Walter's hand and clutched it to her.

The couple wanted to know how Mandy was doing, so Natalie told them as much as she knew, and then got to her point. "Evidently this man isn't going to give up, and I can't put anyone else in danger. I want to buy the Jeep. I'm leaving town. Today. Now. My aunt—Rowena—left me a cottage on the Pacific coast. It's the only place I can go. But it's far enough I hope whoever is doing this won't find me." She stopped herself, not sure why she felt compelled to share her life story with these people.

Walter perched on the edge of a recliner, flicking his toothpick from left to right and back.

Natalie licked her lips. "I don't have a lot of money, but I'm prepared to offer you $3,600. Cash." She looked down again, but caught the raised eyebrows in the couple's silent communication.

Walter broke the silence. "I'm afraid we can't accept that."

Despair pressed Natalie into the soft cushion. They wanted the full $4,000, leaving her only three hundred fifty dollars. With the license transaction for the vehicle and traveling expenses, she wouldn't have anything left. She might not even have enough for gas for the trip. There was no telling when she would get the money from the safe deposit box. With a sigh, she rose to leave. So much for making her own luck.

Rowena rose and reached for her hand. "What Walter is saying is we won't accept your offer. But we want to make an offer to you. Would that be alright?"

"I, well." Natalie looked from one to the other and blew out her breath. "Well, honestly the $3,600 is a stretch. I can't go higher."

"Oh, that's not what we mean." She spoke to her husband. "Walter, why don't you go get the title and keys for Billy's Jeep?" Walter stood and headed down a hallway.

"Wait," Natalie said, looking from one to the other. She didn't want to commit to anything. Not if it emptied the slim envelope in her purse. She'd have to look for another car. Perhaps she could use their phone to call for a taxi to a used car lot.

Walter paid her no heed and Rowena pulled Natalie toward the front door. "Here's our offer. Do you remember when I asked if you were a good person and whether you believed in God?"

Natalie nodded, wariness creeping back in. Walter joined them, paper and keys in hand and he nodded once to his wife. Rowena drew in a breath.

"Our offer is $2,000 for the Jeep. Full price."

"I...what? I don't understand. Not that I don't want it at that price, but..." Natalie held tight to the woman's hand.

"There is only one condition." Walter's words chopped off her exuberance before it could begin. No one gave you anything for free. Even Jack's monthly allowance came with strings attached. She tried to retrieve her hand, but Rowena held tight as Walter cleared his throat.

Here it comes.

- 20 -

"What do you mean she's gone?" Addison thrust his face toward the police officer named Jefferson. "You were supposed to be guarding her."

The uniformed cop bent forward until they were nose to nose. "Yes. I was keeping anyone from coming *in*. I didn't know she was going to sneak *out*."

Addison turned away and threw his arms up in frustration. No one had suspected Natalie would leave. She'd just been shot, for goodness sake. He checked his wristwatch. One o'clock. He'd been with Mandy through the surgery, and then sat all night in an uncomfortable side chair, falling asleep just before sunrise. Then there was a scare with an infection and he couldn't leave to check on Natalie. Now she was missing.

He didn't think anyone had taken her. The officer had left Natalie's door for only a minute at her request. When he returned, the bathroom door was closed and the officer heard the fan running. He'd assumed she was inside. She must have snuck out using the stairwell at the opposite end of the hall. Her clothes were gone, so she'd planned it. Where would she go? She had no money. How did she get away from the hospital?

Addison ran back to the critical care unit to check Mandy and found her sleeping soundly after the last pain meds. He left the hospital and drove home.

It was too early for the five o'clock news vans and live broadcasts, so the street was quiet. Police tape covered the house and Addison checked the seals and found them intact. Natalie hadn't been here. The crime lab investigators were coming by later to do a final check and remove the tape. He knocked at the houses on either side to see if they'd seen anything, but his neighbors weren't home. Defeated, Addison drove back to the hospital. Unless Natalie showed up tonight, it was a good bet they were back to a family of two. She'd run—somewhere.

Natalie wound her way through the afternoon traffic in her new Jeep, smiling at the vision of Walter and Rowena waving goodbye from their driveway. She shifted her purse on the passenger seat, uncovering the snapshot Rowena had pressed into her hand as they helped her climb behind the wheel. "Take this so you'll know we're praying for you everyday." In the photo, the couple stood smiling, arms around each other, the four presidents of Mount Rushmore in the background.

Walter's rough warm hand had closed on hers as he transferred the Jeep keys. "Take care. No more fights now, you hear?" He winked and gave her a hug,

She whispered 'thank you' in his ear and smelled Old Spice. Happy tears ran down her face as she nodded agreement at Rowena's directive to call them, a promise she aimed to keep.

The Jeep turned easily on its big wheels. Natalie loved sitting up high and the feeling she could roll over anything in her way. This was a *vast* improvement over her Honda.

Natalie braked as crossing arms for train tracks descended ahead, glad she was the first car. Diesel locomotives surged past, lumbering freight cars following more slowly, it seemed. Although already loud through the Jeep's canvas top, she rolled the window down to hear the power of the engines, the clickity-clack of the wheels, and the non-synchronized clang-clangity-clang of the warning bells.

As a little girl, she'd always been thrilled at train crossings, wanting to be close, but frightened by the size of the rocking, noisy behemoths and the occasional hobo staring out from the open door of a boxcar. When eleven or twelve, she and a friend had stopped on the sidewalk just as a train passed. They dared each other to get closer, giggling over the thunder of the railroad cars. The quaking sidewalk beneath their feet was enough to keep them a safe distance, but it felt like she could touch the stenciled, rough sides.

Suddenly, Natalie realized this train was headed west, on a journey so like herself—to unknown places. What *did* lie before her? Everything she'd known was here in Steerman, Missouri, but now most of that was gone, history. Except for this week's friends.

"The condition is you allow us to pray with you. Pray for you. Will you do that?" Walter's quiet words still shocked her. She had been ready for... well, she didn't know what she'd expected, but praying for her definitely wasn't it. Receiving gifts wasn't something she was used to. For the second time in three days, someone had held her hands and prayed for her by name. What did that mean? Why now, at thirty-nine years old, her life coming apart at the seams, did God keep popping up?

The train cars flew past now as it picked up speed. Through the open window, she felt wind from the rocking cars and, with a sudden final whoosh, the last car rocketed past, dragging the noise with it as the clickity-clack retreated and the bells fell silent. The crossing arms rose and cars behind her started their engines. She followed suit and accelerated across the tracks.

Finally on the road, she sighed in relief. The killer—whoever the man was—didn't know of her new car, nor did he know her destination. *If you leave, don't tell anyone where you're going.* A frown of regret creased her face as she accelerated up the onramp to Interstate 70. Though the danger diminished with each rotation of the tires, those same tires took her away from Addison and Mandy. Their love and acceptance soothed her even now. If only there had been a way to let the friendship develop with time. The last goodbye had been eye contact with Addison across the bloody kitchen floor.

She shook her head. Her emotions were raw and she was thinking stupid, as Aunt Rowena used to say. When she stopped for the night, she would call Addison. Perhaps she could talk to Mandy in the hospital, too. She hadn't heard any more about the girl's condition than the officer told her this morning.

Natalie ached inside for the pain she'd brought down on Mandy and Addison. The look in his eyes when he'd rushed into the house... A father's love for his daughter. Mandy *had* to be okay.

Yes, she'd call tonight. It wouldn't be enough, but it would have to do. She couldn't go back and endanger them again. And she should apologize for sneaking out on the guard at the hospital, telling him her call button had broken and asking him to fetch a volunteer.

Natalie set the aftermarket cruise control Billy Thompson had installed, then rolled her shoulders and settled in for the long drive. Today had turned out well despite waking in the hospital. Mr. Kerslake had been surprised, but agreed to bring the settlement in cash instead of a check. And, after explaining her predicament, he'd been a dear to pick her up at the hospital and drive her to Addison's. The dash clock read one fifteen. She could make Kansas City in about four hours. If Walter and Rowena hadn't insisted on feeding her lunch, she might have tried for farther, but the bad night's sleep in the hospital limited her range, and she needed to buy a few clothes. One tee shirt wouldn't do.

Houses quickly gave way to open space as she headed into the afternoon sun. As open land increased and fences diminished, a sense of freedom rose from the asphalt through the humming oversized tires. It twined around her legs, seeped into her lungs and exited in a deep cleansing breath. Maybe escape from danger caused the feeling, or simply the age-old allure of the Wild West, but for the first time in a very long time, Natalie felt free.

From her parents' home, to life with Jack, someone else had always set expectations for her. She realized now how passive she'd become, letting others do the thinking and deciding. Her parents picked her college, even though she wanted to go away to another school with some high school friends. Jack chose her two cars, dismissing her wish for a sportier model this last time. His placating tone ended the discussion.

"The Honda is more sensible for you. You'll be happier with it."

What would Jack say about buying a totally impractical Wrangler 4x4? She laughed out loud and stroked the dash. Vinyl though it was, it belonged to her. She'd picked it out and bought it all on her own, without Jack's interference.

Guilt washed over her for thinking ill of Jack. He wasn't a bad person. She'd simply failed to stand her ground for what she wanted in life. The canvas top flapped mightily at sixty-five miles per hour, nearly drowning out the thrum of the off-road tires. Yet to Natalie, pointing the glistening yellow hood toward the unknown gave a release to her spirit she'd never known.

Addison spent most of the day at the hospital, only leaving during meals and then again at seven thirty when Mandy's eyes drifted closed. He pulled out of the hospital parking lot and turned toward the office rather than his empty home.

The night sergeant at the dispatcher desk greeted him and asked about Mandy. After a few minutes, Addison headed for the darkened offices and plopped in his chair. Piles of folders glared at him, demanding attention he was too exhausted to give. One envelope caught his eye: the crime lab report on Natalie Clayton's signature. He tore it open and read the brief paragraph. The withdrawal slip had been signed on a rough surface, like an embossed checkbook cover, so it made the comparison difficult. Conclusion: inconclusive. Either the signature was genuine or a very good forgery.

He tossed the letter on the desk and spun his chair toward the window. Ribbons of white and red lights traced paths on the twilight expressway. Everyone going somewhere, traveling to a destination, a goal.

Perhaps Natalie was in one of those cars. Even she had a plan of some sort, whatever it was. What plan did *he* have? He raked his fingers through greasy hair and barked a laugh. He couldn't keep Natalie or his own daughter safe, couldn't even keep up with the piles of work. So much for all *his* plans. For the first time since Elizabeth died, Addison seriously contemplated major change. Anything to get out of this rut. Natalie had been a distraction for a few days, but if she didn't return, the days ahead loomed long, monotonous, unbearable.

Addison walked to the break room and grimaced at the first sip of truly awful coffee. How anyone could make coffee this bad... Arnie would say the perp should be put behind bars. He stared out the window at the darkened landscape, drinking without tasting.

It wasn't that the work wasn't interesting. He loved partnering with Arnie, sifting through evidence, putting bad guys behind bars. Over the years, they'd done a lot of good work here in Steerman. Still, there was something missing.

Church provided a solid basis for support, and those friendships had kept him sane when Elizabeth died. But with her gone, and now with this shooting compromising the safe-haven of his home, well...what really held him in Steerman?

Maybe he should give his brother a call. Ben had a good listening ear, and Addison needed to tell him about the shooting and Mandy.

He glanced at the wall clock, shocked to see it was a quarter after nine. He'd been here an hour and a half and hadn't accomplished a thing. Picking up the nearest three folders, he stuffed them in his briefcase and headed for the door.

Ben's new phone number was in his desk at home.

The inexpensive motel room had one thing going for it—relative cleanliness. The rattling air conditioning unit poured musty air into the concrete cubicle, similar to the hospital room in its sterility. A cabinet with askew fake bamboo doors held a 19" television. Above the double bed hung a painting of a cowboy astride his horse, surveying Arizona cactus country.

Natalie perched on the worn bedspread and pulled labels off her new clothes. Those she wouldn't wear tomorrow she packed in the new nylon duffle. The last item out of the shopping bag was a pre-paid phone card. With a sigh, Natalie steeled herself and dialed the Conner home. The nightstand clock read 8:12 p.m. After several rings, the answering machine picked up.

"Hi. This is Addison…and this is Mandy…and we're not home right now. Please leave a message." Beep.

She tried to speak, but the lump in her throat choked back the words. After coughing a couple of times they came out in a shaky whisper.

"Hi. This is Natalie. I'm sorry I missed you. And I'm sorry I left without saying goodbye. But I knew I'd put you both in danger and I needed to get away. I, uh…I'll try you at the hospital, Mandy. Otherwise, I'll call again or when I get to…to where I'm going." *If you leave, don't tell anyone where you're going.* She managed a shaky goodbye, then grabbed a tissue, wiped the tears, and took a shuddering breath. Hearing their warm, cheery voices reminded her of Scrabble and popcorn. She called information for the hospital number and dialed it. The receptionist routed her call to Mandy's room.

"H'lo?" Mandy's sleepy voice squeezed new tears from Natalie's eyes.

"Hi, Mandy. This is Natalie."

Tarz's truck splashed through mud and rolled to a stop beside the 1960s single-wide trailer. He switched off the engine and listened to rain drumming on the steel roof. For a moment he crossed his arms on the steering wheel and put his head down. It had been a miserable day and a half.

The Clayton woman had been lucky again, depriving him of finishing the job. It'd been a risk to try it in the daytime, but the old lady was on his case every day. 'The election's coming, the election's coming.' Yeah, yeah. What did he care?

Well, he cared to get paid, that's what. He stared through the cracked windshield at his new home, illuminated by the pickup's single headlamp.

Ha! New. What a dump. He lived in a dump because of Natalie Clayton.

He swore and pounded the steering wheel until his fist hurt, then he kicked open the door and slogged through mud to the three by three porch. He hunched his shoulders, trying to stay dry while he wrenched open the screen door and fiddled with the cantankerous door latch.

The first thing he smelled was dog pee. The forty-pound mutt jumped on his legs and yapped incessantly as Tarz trudged across cracked linoleum to the kitchen counter, leaving a trail of mud. Two yellow puddles covered most of the tiny kitchen's floor.

He rounded on the dog and kicked, but the hound dodged and snapped at his leg. That was enough.

Tarz seized the dog's collar, the one his sister had given him, and dragged the animal across the floor, wiping up the mud as the dog fell and slid. Tarz kicked open the screen door, sending it flying into the yard. He wrapped his hands around the dog's throat and lifted him up to eye level.

The animal's eyes shone in the glow of the yellow bug light and reflected fury and fear. The dog twisted, teeth grazing Tarz' wrist as his sharp toenails raked Tarz' chest and stomach. Tarz swore and pushed the animal away. It dropped to the porch on all fours, head lowered, a guttural growl emanating between sneering lips. Tarz backed up a step. The dog's head dropped a bit more and he advanced, hate-filled eyes never leaving Tarz's face.

"Whoa, easy there, fella," Tarz held his palms out. He backed another step into the trailer. "No need to get all bent out of shape now, is there? Haven't I always taken good care of you?"

Spittle dripped from the bared teeth, landing on the muddy floor. Maybe Tarz should get some duct tape, chain the mutt to the steel post in the yard. Let him spend the night in the mud and rain. The mutt needed a bath anyway.

Or he could get the gas can from the shed and give the dog a *hot* bath. Fire and water. That would be a sight if anyone were around in these hills to see it. Well, *he* would see it, and that's all that mattered.

An idea came to him. Tarz growled, "Where's my gun?" The mutt's ears perked and its head came up. Tarz shaped his right hand like a gun, pointed it at the dog's head. "Bang. You're dead." The dog dropped on its side, then rolled onto its back, legs in the air. Not a muscle moved.

Tarz knelt down, but the animal didn't so much as twitch. Finally he whispered, "Okay," and the dog jumped to his feet and leaped at Tarz, tongue reaching for his face and tail beating the air. Tarz laughed and scratched behind the pup's ears.

"Guess we'd better clean up this mess and get you and me something to eat, eh fella?"

After Tarz had mopped up the urine and mud, he tossed some meaty bones into the food bowl, then clamped the opener on a can of beef stew. As he twisted the handle, he imagined tightening a rope around the throat of the Clayton woman. She was wrecking his life. If she hadn't escaped this time, he'd have his payment and could move from this hole of a trailer. Tarz wrenched the metal handle harder. The can slipped from the teeth and careened across the counter and onto the floor, spraying stew juice all the way.

With a growl of his own, Tarz kicked the rolling can, throwing chunks of carrot, peas and beef onto the cabinet. Before the can clattered to a stop, the dog was licking up the savory liquid. Tarz's dinner.

"Leave that alone!" Tarz swung his foot at the dog's head, but the mutt danced back, eyeing him warily as it retreated toward the still open front door. "Yeah, you'd better leave, you worthless—" Tarz charged and the hound whirled and was out the door in a flash, disappearing into the curtain of rain. Tarz stopped on the porch, hands gripping the 2x4 railing hard enough to leave marks. Rain dripping from the roof edge and splattered on his boots. "And don't come back!"

Tarz grinned into the night. "You're a lucky dog. You always have been, ever since that night at Nick's office. You remember that little buddy?" Tarz felt the grin fade to blank.

"Lucky dog." Tarz went in the trailer and shut the door.

- 21 -

Near noon on the third day, the weak auto air conditioner no longer kept up with the soaring temperatures in western Colorado, so Natalie shut it off and lowered the windows. Hot, dry air rushed in and whipped her new haircut, one too short to blow in her eyes. She'd stopped at a beauty shop in a small town and asked them to even it out. One thing led to another and...well she now looked more like Mandy. Some of the burned patches needed weeks to grow out completely, so one of her new scarves covered her head most of the time, but she liked to leave it off while driving because of the heat.

At the next fuel stop, Natalie unzipped the plastic back and side windows, effectively transforming the remainder into a safari top. She leaned into the back to store the plastic windows, and the rays of the sun slanted in the vacant window and highlighted what looked like the edge of a book under the back of the passenger seat. She limped around to the passenger door and pulled the seat forward, revealing a thin book wedged under the seat slide mechanism. A tug freed it and she turned it over in her hands. The book's title seemed to glow and she ran her fingertips over the embossing.

Holy Bible.

Gold letters of the owner's name adorned the lower right corner: Billy H. Thompson. Walter and Rowena's son.

Reverently, she fanned the pages, stopping when she noticed yellow underlining. She found page after page of verses underlined in several colors, along with handwritten notes in the margins. Orange highlighting caught her attention and she stopped to read the words.

"You will be secure, because there is hope; you will look about you and take your rest in safety. You will lie down, with no one to make you afraid…" Job 11:18-19

Natalie closed her eyes. These words conveyed importance to a young man who no longer lived, a man who put his life in danger in the military, but who obviously used this dog-eared book extensively. She longed for the things spoken in the verses—hope, security, safety, rest—held the warm leather to her chest for a moment, eyes closed, and then placed the Bible on the seat with the picture of Billy's parents. She would send it to Walter and Rowena as soon as she got settled.

It was in Cedar City, Utah, at the end of the twelve-plus hour drive, that Natalie began to cry. Tension released like a spring stretched tight for too many years, then let go all at once. The tears caught her by surprise. One moment she lay by the motel pool on a plastic lounge chair observing the stars in the hot night sky, and the next moment the heavenly sight turned into a slurry of fuzzy points running together.

A mom, dad, and two children splashed in the cool water, batting a red and blue beach ball between them. Their squeals and laughter filled the courtyard. Sudden regret at all she'd missed overwhelmed her. She wished her relationship with her parents had been warm and full of hugs like the family in the pool, where the boy of six or seven imitated his dad, while his older sister took after mom. Natalie ached for the laughter that never was in her childhood of serious adults.

Embarrassed by her emotion, she turned toward the shadows. For years she had fooled herself, saying having children wasn't important, her marriage to Jack would improve, and—the biggest deception of all—that she was happy.

Lies.

The young family gathered their toys, towels, and flip-flops, then marched off to their room, leaving only a trail of water as a testament to their passing. Would her life be like those water drops evaporating on the warm concrete, here for a while, then quickly gone? She had no family and no friends to remember her. No one to pass down traditions or possessions to. Natalie's joy at newfound freedom dissipated at the awareness of being utterly alone under the broad canopy of stars.

She stood and, but for the cast and bandages, would have dived into the pool, swimming lap after lap until the ache in her arms and legs overshadowed the one in her heart.

- 22 -

The chill Utah morning retreated in the presence of the rising sun as Natalie left the hotel office and climbed into her Jeep. Tangy high desert sage filled the air. She'd skipped dinner last night in what, in daylight, she recognized was a depressed mood. But this morning her appetite returned in strength, so she searched the pioneer downtown area until she spotted Jessie's Diner, a literal hole-in-the-wall, sporting an 1850s brick façade and a flickering neon sign promising good food. The empty parking spot in front of the restaurant sealed the deal.

Forty minutes later, Natalie emerged with stomach stretched taut from eggs, buttermilk pancakes, and an exquisite hash brown and sausage fry. A paper bag contained a leftovers container of homemade chunky applesauce, complete with plastic spoon provided by Jessie herself. Natalie pushed her crutches into the passenger seat and leveraged behind the wheel with a groan. If she didn't get this cast off soon and begin exercising, she'd gain some serious weight.

Natalie followed the signs to the I-15 onramp. Tonight she'd arrive at her destination and figure out what came next.

A few minutes down the road, Natalie passed the sign for Zion National Park's Kolob Canyon Visitor Center, next exit. She'd always wanted to visit some of the nation's parks, but Jack hadn't been enthusiastic about taking vacations. As Aunt Rowena always said, 'Now's the time.' Decision made, Natalie took the exit and halted at the stop sign. She patted Billie's dash. Somewhere on the trip she'd named the Jeep in honor of its former owner. Now Billie was her companion on this journey.

She spent the next two hours driving the Kolob Canyon Road, stopping at points of interest, and ogling majestic red sandstone cliffs. At the end of the time she reluctantly headed back to the freeway, vowing to return someday for a real vacation.

Addison opened the front door for Mandy and supported her arm as she entered the house.

"I'm okay, Dad."

"I know, but I don't want you falling or anything—at least not until you've healed up." He grinned as she flashed her 'thanks a lot' glare, and then reached to close the door, but not before scanning the street, searching every car, tree and hedge. They still hadn't caught the guy who shot Mandy and Natalie. He was out there—somewhere.

"You fixed the window."

He found her standing in the kitchen, examining the pane above the sink. Glazier's putty still smeared the edges. His eyes cut to the magnet covering the bullet hole in the refrigerator door, then to the two holes in the wall below the cupboards. He thanked God again that the shooter used a .22 caliber gun. Although they were powerful enough to kill easily, at least the small bullets didn't do quite as much damage as a .38 or 9 millimeter. He turned to find Mandy following his gaze. "Uh, you want to lie down?"

"Not hardly. After three days in that hospital bed, I'm ready to talk to my friends. Can I invite someone over?" She cast him her best pretty-please.

As much as he wanted things to be back to normal, life wouldn't be the same with a killer loose. So far, Arnie and he had no reason to believe anyone other than one man was responsible for all the attacks. Although all seemed directed at Natalie, he had to be careful. Plus, no parent he knew would let their child come to the Conner house right now, and he said so to Mandy.

She put up a little fuss, but understood and went into her room to glue her ear to the phone. Being a gunshot victim put her at the top of the popularity list, and for a middle school student that mattered.

The doctor had assured him she would be fine for school's start in a week. He ran his hand over his unshaven face, wondering if *he'd* be ready for her going back to school. Would she be safe there?

Shaking himself out of the reminder at how close he'd come to losing Mandy, Addison found a putty knife and patching compound in the garage and went to work on the bullet holes.

Natalie hadn't called since that first night. He'd listened to her message three times, hoping for some clue as to where she'd fled. Mandy didn't remember too much of Natalie's call, except she had bought a car and was heading out of state. He hoped she trusted him enough to tell him where, though it wasn't too difficult to figure it out, provided she followed through with auto insurance, had her mail forwarded, or contacted her bank about the house mortgage. Addison had feelers out.

He smoothed the filler and stepped back to admire his work. A coat of paint and it would be as good as new. He only wished he had something to patch the other holes in his life.

With her last ounce of strength, Natalie twisted the steering wheel and guided the Jeep onto the gravel road toward the ocean. Moonlight reflected off the water in the distance, sparkling like a field of undulating diamonds. She steered around three huge cypress trees at the bend in the driveway and pulled to a stop along side the familiar dark cottage. The dash clock—1:20 AM in her new time zone—blinked out as she shut off the engine and lights. Although the cabin blocked the view of the sea, sounds of waves crashing on rocks immediately eclipsed the ticking of the cooling motor.

Easing her stiff body from the car, she lowered herself to the ground and stretched. This last leg of the trip had been nearly sixteen hours, but she hadn't wanted to make another overnight stop. Goose bumps rose on her arms in the briny onshore breeze. After days of hot driving, and a whole summer of hot sticky days, the cold night air along the coast felt refreshing. Nevertheless, she grabbed her bag and hurried to the cabin.

The doormat yielded the key, just as the management company had promised, and Natalie unlocked the door and flipped on the light switch. She dropped her duffle inside and surveyed her new home.

Originally built as the Perilous Point lighthouse keeper's cottage in the late 1800s, its construction utilized the same soccer-ball sized river rock that formed the light tower base. Walls were a foot thick in places, and the windows were tall and narrow with a gothic arch at the top.

While undoubtedly good at minimizing heat loss during the cold, windy winter nights along the California coast, they didn't let in much light except in direct afternoon sun.

The interior smelled of pine cleaner and furniture polish. Even though still August, Natalie shivered in the chilled interior. The rock fireplace, situated in the center of the house, provided the only heat, but she wasn't about to light it. She shuddered, more at the memory of fire than from the cold. Open flame she could do without.

Red and white checked curtains fluttered above the kitchen sink, and Natalie quickly moved to close the window undoubtedly left open by the management company to air the place out. Years of paint buildup on the small double-hung sash fought her. She finally managed to get it shut, though the lock wouldn't engage.

She turned on the oven and opened the door to let the heat escape into the room, then filled the battered teakettle and placed it on a front burner. She left the minuscule kitchen in search of an electric space heater. Besides the living room and kitchen, the cabin contained an add-on bathroom set off the kitchen, and one bedroom with an open alcove to hang clothes. A beaded curtain separated the kitchen and bedroom. As a girl, she'd been fascinated by the long, colored strands, how they swung and clicked with each passing. She'd wanted to hang some in her room at home, but her mother had flatly refused. Sometimes Natalie wondered how her mother and Rowena had ever been sisters.

A broom closet off the kitchen dashed her last hope for a heater. She'd have to buy one in the morning.

Natalie drank some hot tea as she pulled back the covers on the double bed in the bedroom and kicked off her sneakers. Her eyes began to droop as she washed up. She fell onto the lumpy mattress, drew the heavy quilt up to her chin, and instantly fell asleep.

- 23 -

Persistent knocking rescued Natalie from another disturbing dream about the fire. Her t-shirt stuck to her damp back as she padded to the only door. Since there was no peep-hole, she had no choice but to open it.

An elderly woman in a billowing blue flowered muumuu swept into the room and enveloped Natalie in a fierce hug.

"Oh, it's so good to see you, Natalie. It's been *years*." She pushed back and looked Natalie up and down, her expression changing to one of horror. "Good heavens, girl. What in the world happened to you?" The woman turned Natalie's head side to side. "You look terrible."

"Good to see you, too, Millie." Natalie smiled at Millie Trafford's trademark honesty. "It's kind of a long story."

"That's why I'm here, dear." With a flourish, Millie settled herself on the sofa and pointed first to Natalie, then to a chair opposite. Natalie gently combed her fingers through her hair and obeyed the seating instruction, noting the clock by the door read 7:12—in the morning. So much for a good night's sleep. Yawning, she leaned back in the overstuffed chair and told Millie her story.

When finished, Millie squinted at her through horn-rim glasses while fanning herself with a six-month old Reader's Digest. "My goodness. So, you think this man is *still* trying to kill you?"

"I couldn't stay and endanger anyone else." She rose and walked to the small kitchen where she leaned on the counter to take the weight off her foot. The last few days had strained the break, probably prolonging the healing.

"Natalie, it wasn't your fault your friend died and that young girl was wounded. You didn't do anything wrong."

Natalie wished that were true. But something she'd done had prompted the attempts on her life. If only she could figure out what.

"Are you staying here in Perilous Cove permanently?"

Natalie nodded. She filled the old teakettle with water and placed it on the burner to heat. "There's nothing to go back to." That reality had hit her during the trip. She'd never driven so far, certainly not alone. But acknowledging it was a one-way journey with nothing left behind made her a little queasy, like driving over the crest of hill too fast where the bottom drops out. Free and weightless, yes, but also unattached, waiting to come crashing down, out of control.

"It's not so bad here, you know. Darryl and I fell in love with Perilous Cove the minute we drove into town. Let's see…that was in 1957, I think." Millie heaved herself to her feet and joined Natalie in the kitchen. "Hard to believe he's been gone almost fifteen years."

Natalie remembered Darryl Trafford as a big, jovial man with a ruddy complexion. Her aunt, Wena Riley, and Millie—great friends for decades—became even closer after Darryl's death. Since Wena never married, her friends and Natalie's family were the objects of her affection.

Tea bags in hand, they settled at the two-person kitchen table. Millie reached out, grabbed Natalie's hand and searched her eyes. Natalie met her gaze, breath caught in her throat, afraid of the unasked question. It was too personal, too private, too—

"You didn't come to Wena's funeral."

The accusation stung because it was the truth. Natalie cleared her throat. "I, ah…" No excuse seemed sufficient. Natalie's father had been an only child, so Rowena Riley, as Mother's only sibling, had been Natalie's only aunt. "I should have come."

"What stopped you?" Millie's tone held no condemnation, only curiosity. Natalie withdrew her hand. Millie harrumphed, drawing Natalie's gaze as the woman spoke one word. "Jack."

How could Millie know Jack had forbid her to come? She'd begged and cried for two days, but he told her to 'forget the old woman.'

"But Jack, she's my only aunt. I need to be there."

"Well, *she* won't know you're there. And you don't know anyone in the town. It's a waste of money to fly clear across the country for a one-hour funeral."

"I *do* know some of the people." Natalie couldn't believe he'd refuse her the money to go.

"Say…" Jack's countenance brightened considerably. "Is her house worth anything? Do you think she left it to you? We could sell it and use the money."

Rowena Riley had once confided that everything would go to Natalie, but her aunt also solemnly instructed Natalie not to tell Jack. Natalie hadn't understood Wena's request at the time and had been upset by it. But seeing his gleeful attitude at the thought of an inheritance made her glad she'd adhered to Wena's mandate.

"No." Natalie grasped frantically for an answer. "She lived in an old, run-down, tiny cottage. Anyway, it goes back to the state of California at her death as part of the lighthouse property."

Jack's crestfallen face confirmed her decision to lie, but it left her heart cold. She had determined right then to call her aunt's lawyer back and make sure no communication about Rowena's estate came to their house.

"It was Jack, wasn't it?" Millie's question broke Natalie's reflection. She nodded, unable to meet Millie's piercing gaze.

Millie leaned back. "Wena never liked him, you know. Honey, that's why she set up the trust to maintain this house for you. She knew Jack would take control of it if given half a chance."

A sigh escaped Natalie's lips. "I wanted to come." Since their marriage, she'd been out to visit Wena only once. At the time, Natalie had been disappointed Jack had refused to come. Now she was glad he'd never been here, never seen the town, the cabin, the lighthouse, or the beautiful ocean. She'd called her aunt every month for years, buying pre-paid cards and using the phone at work so her husband wouldn't find out.

"I know you did." Millie patted her hand.

A comfortable silence stretched between them as they drank their tea, broken only by the soft whir-tick of the black and white Kit-Cat clock hanging near the broom closet. Its tail swung back and forth once each second.

The chair creaked as Millie rose.

Natalie stood too and took their cups to the sink. She turned to Millie. "How did you know I was here?"

"Heard you drive in last night and I saw the Jeep parked outside while on my morning walk. Pretty cool ride you got there."

Natalie smiled. "Thanks."

"Everyday I walk past here down to the lighthouse and back. Figured it must be you." Millie's home stood another hundred yards inland and uphill along the ridge, making her Natalie's nearest neighbor. Her driveway access road passed by it. "Especially since I sent Wena's letter."

Natalie's mouth dropped open. "*You* sent it?"

"Of course I did, just like she told me to. Said, 'If Natalie doesn't come to my funeral, wait six months and send this.' Then she handed me the letter, all sealed and stamped."

Tears stung Natalie's eyes, and Millie enveloped her in another hug and rocked her back and forth. After a few minutes, Natalie broke away and blew her nose.

"What now?" The old woman's gentle voice soothed Natalie's frayed nerves.

"Have you told anyone else I'm here?"

"Nope. Haven't seen anyone this morning."

"Good." Natalie blew out a breath. "Here's my plan."

- 24 -

"Steerman Police Department. How may I direct your call?"

"I'd like to speak to Detective Conner, please." Natalie pulled her jacket tighter against the damp wind whipping loose newspapers by the front of Brodie's Hardware. She propped the pay phone receiver in the crook of her neck and replaced the phone card in her wallet before it blew away.

"Conner." His sharp answer caught Natalie off-guard and she dropped the receiver. Her grab for the swinging set bounced it against the phone booth pole before she snagged it.

"Sorry, I dropped the phone." Natalie's wallet fell to the ground and she strained to reach it while tethered to the metal cable.

"Who is this?" Addison's voice held more than a little irritation. She retrieved her wallet and pressed the receiver to her ear.

"It's Natalie. Natalie Clayton."

"Natalie. Oh. Hi. I...uh...how are you doing?"

The softening of his voice gave her confidence. "I'm okay."

"I hoped you'd call."

"You did?" She'd missed his warm brown eyes, the way the left side of his mouth lifted first when he smiled.

"Of course. Mandy asks every day if you called again."

"How is she?" It had only been a week since she spoke to the teenage beauty in the hospital, but she missed her terribly. How had they become so close in only a few days? Addison filled her in on Mandy's injury, homecoming, and her resulting popularity.

116

"I'm so sorry she got hurt. I never—"

"It wasn't your fault." His confidence gave her strength. "Can I ask where you are?" Addison's warm tone soothed her nerves.

"You can't tell anybody."

"I won't."

"Promise me. I have to stay hidden." Her heart began punching at her chest.

"I promise you, Natalie, I'd never tell anyone. At least not anyone outside the immediate investigation, and only then if they have a need to know."

She drew in a deep breath. If word of her location slipped out, she might be facing the killer again. Her body shuddered, but it wasn't the cold. His promise would have to do.

"Natalie. I'll protect you until we catch this guy. Trust me."

She did trust him. But he was a couple of thousand miles away. She wished he were here with her right now.

"I'm in Perilous Cove, California. Just a small spot on the coast." A dreary place right now. Although still summer, heavy fog curled among the boats in the harbor and crawled up the street, wrapping every surface in misty dampness, including her head and jacket.

"I know it well."

His answer shocked her. "You...you do?" He laughed at her surprise.

"I grew up at Storm Lake, a few miles inland from Perilous Cove. We used to drive down to the beach in the summers. But it's been a long time since I visited."

The beach was north of the lighthouse point in the next little cove and faced northwest. Calm in the summer, Aunt Wena had told stories of ferocious winter storms attacking from the Northern Pacific. The summers when Natalie had visited her aunt included many picnics to the beach.

They talked about the town and he asked questions about the church on the hill, the lighthouse, and the hot dog stand. Natalie turned and sought out the tiny hut built on the wood planks where the dock began. She wasn't sure if its name, Bird Dog, denoted the addition of chicken to the menu, or was a tip of the hat to the line of seagulls squatting and pooping on the roofline. Diners beware.

She explained about inheriting the cabin and the trust fund Rowena created to cover the taxes and upkeep.

"I'm changing my name."

"Because of the man who tried to kill you." It wasn't a question.

"*Trying* to kill me. I don't want him finding me."

"We'll find him first. You're a long way from him now."

While she had confidence in his detective abilities, she knew they might never find the clues to the man's identity.

"I'm working with a legal service in Mission Peak to file the papers."

"This seems like a strange question, but what's your new name going to be?" Humor tinged his voice.

"Samantha Riley. Samantha is my middle name, and Riley was my Aunt Rowena's last name as well as my mom's maiden name. They were sisters. Seems like a good combination." She never used her middle name and it sounded awkward, even after a couple of days of practice. Maybe she'd shorten it to Sam.

"Interesting. There's a woman around the block named Rowena. She and her husband go to our church."

Natalie smiled. "Walter and Rowena Thompson."

Surprised colored Addison's response. "How in the world did you know that?"

"Remember the yellow Jeep they had for sale?" The wind picked up and shook droplets loose from the top of the phone booth. Natalie wiped them from her nose.

"Their son's Jeep? Sure, I... Wait. You bought Billy Thompson's Jeep? Well I'll be." His startled laughter warmed her chilled body. "I noticed it wasn't in their driveway, but I never connected the dots."

"And you call yourself a detective?" Her teasing surprised her. She realized she was copying Mandy's easy relationship with her father and it felt good. He laughed harder at her joke.

"I wondered how you'd gotten away from here. I did track down your auto insurance agent, but he didn't know you'd bought a new car."

Natalie explained she hadn't called yet since she knew the company would cover a new vehicle for a few days. She would register and insure it when her official name change came through. The legal service promised three to four weeks. Except for occasional trips to town like today, she'd parked the Jeep in the decrepit one car garage behind the cabin and hoped the sagging roof didn't collapse before her insurance coverage began.

"Samantha Riley," Addison said, apparently trying it on for fit. "I like it." He agreed the name change was probably a good idea. A pause followed before he asked how he could reach her. She didn't have a phone installed yet.

"No cell phone either?"

"No. The coverage isn't very good in town, and it's non-existent at the cottage. PC isn't exactly on the technology grid yet." She promised she'd get a phone number and an answering machine.

"Call me in three days, okay? Let me give you the toll free number." He rattled it off and she repeated it back to memorize it since she didn't have paper or pen.

"Addison, I've got to go. I'm at a pay phone and it's starting to rain. It's freezing here and I'm getting soaked. My cast will dissolve."

"Natalie...I mean Samantha—boy, this is going to take some getting used to—I'm really glad you called." He paused before adding, "Mandy and I are praying for you every day."

"Uh, thanks." Walter and Rowena promised the same daily prayers. Four people praying for her, and she didn't even know if God existed. Weird.

They said goodbye and Natalie replaced the receiver in the holder. The click of the switch seemed to give the silence and chill permission to invade, chasing away the warmth of the conversation.

Natalie climbed the hill on the side street where she'd parked, counting the days until she could lose the cast and crutches. She drove north, then turned left on the road leading past Millie's house to her cabin.

A smile curled her lips at her newfound ability to make Addison laugh. Jack never had much of a sense of humor, and in response to her teasing simply stared at her blankly before turning away. She'd missed so much. She swiped the wetness from the corners of her eyes and told herself it was caused by the biting headwind.

At her cabin, she shut the door against the rising gale and secured the new deadbolt. The cold front had moved in suddenly and she stared longingly at the dead fireplace, then turned away in frustration. Not yet. It was too soon to deal with fire. With a sigh, she clicked the small space heater onto LOW—she'd found out the wiring and fuses needed upgrading before they could handle higher settings—and tucked the sofa quilt around her legs, shivering at its initial frigid touch. A gust rattled the pane in the west-facing living room window and moaned around the stone walls. Dust settled on the floor. Tomorrow she'd buy window putty.

- 25 -

Addison wadded up the last of his sandwich in the wrapper and tossed it in the trash, then paced to the window. Nothing had changed in the parking lot since he'd looked ten minutes ago. Heat still rippled off the black surface and vehicles. The hot summer brought out the worst in people. Young punks roamed the streets looking for trouble. This summer had been especially bad and he looked forward to the cooler days of fall. Nothing like a freezing ice storm to quell the crime rate. Running a hand through his hair, he spun and started out of the room, nearly toppling Gladys who was just coming in.

"Whoa, cowboy." Gladys backed up a step.

"Sorry." His response came out sharper than he intended and Gladys' eyes narrowed. He dropped his gaze and forced himself to take a deep breath. "What have you got?"

She held out four files, each at least an inch thick. "Captain needs you to go through these old cases."

The date on the top one was from seven years prior. "Cap doesn't think we have enough to do?" He didn't attempt to hide the irritation in his voice. He'd been here until eight-thirty last night and then taken work home. Every night was the same now.

"These are more of the fallout from the DNA lab scandal. Appeals have been filed and new trials are almost guaranteed. We're going to have to brief the district attorney's office on the evidence." Gladys' voice softened and she squeezed his arm. "Overworked and underpaid?"

His lips turned up at the corners. "Something like that. Sorry about snapping." He tossed the folders on one of the piles with a sigh.

"Want some advice?" Gladys leaned on his desk and regarded him with a serious look.

Addison frowned, knowing he was going to hear it whether he liked it or not. He dropped into his desk chair and lifted his arms wide in a let-me-have-it invitation. Gladys didn't give advice flippantly, so he'd better give a listen.

The woman pursed her lips and leaned forward. "You're ruining your life, Addison."

"Hey, that's not fa—"

"Correction." Gladys cut him off with a gesture. "You have no life, so I guess you can't really ruin it." She crossed her arms and scowled at him.

He pushed forward in his chair and indicated the stacks of files across his desk. "We're working as fast as we can, and now Cap is piling on even more. There's no way we can keep up." Unable to sit, he stood and paced the tiny space behind his desk.

"You've been overworked before. Something's different this time." Gladys pulled his side chair up and leaned forward. She was in for the long haul.

"Meaning?"

"Meaning your priorities are going off track." The older woman ran a hand along one of the stacks. "My suspicion is Mandy's getting short shrift." She paused and skewered him with her eyes. "Am I right?"

Addison stopped pacing and plopped into his chair. Slowly he nodded. "Yeah, you're right."

For the next ten minutes they talked about the pressures of the job and never-ending cases. Then Gladys interrupted him with an "Ah-ha."

"What?" Addison's eyes narrowed at the smug look on Gladys' face, not sure he wanted to hear her revelation.

"You're lonely." The woman leaned back and examined her short fingernails.

"Lonely?"

"Yep."

"What in the world are you talking about? I have Mandy, friends from church. Lord knows I'm around everyone here twelve hours or more a day. I've never had so many people in my life. I don't have *time* to be lonely."

Gladys rose and almost bounced to the door where she stopped and turned. "It's been two years since Elizabeth died?" She didn't wait for his affirmative answer. "Most men don't make it that long before getting married again." She winked, swirled—even in her bulky uniform with utility belt and gun—and flounced to her desk, casting one knowing glance over her shoulder.

Addison became aware his mouth hung open, so he clamped it shut and turned away from the doorway. Where had the loneliness and marriage idea come from? Sure, he'd thought about dating, finding someone special he could get to know, someone who shared his values, who liked to laugh. Someone who looked at him in that unique way Elizabeth had.

That right there was the trouble. He and Elizabeth had a great marriage. They'd grown close in so many ways over the sixteen years they'd been together, nearly eighteen if you counted dating and engagement.

Addison wandered over to the coffee station and poured himself a cup, testing a small sip to make sure it wasn't the awful stuff. Not too bad. He strolled to the window above the parking lot. A young uniformed officer and his girlfriend or wife stood by a car, talking and laughing. She reached out and drew her fingers down his arm as they spoke. Then they moved together and he kissed the blonde woman tenderly. After a moment, she separated, laughed, and climbed into the car, then waved goodbye as she backed out of the space and drove away. The officer turned and, with a big smile planted on his face, jogged to the building.

Elizabeth and he had been twenty-four years old when they'd met, twenty-six when they married. In many ways they'd discovered life together: financing a house, dealing with deaths of parents, job changes, moving, having a baby and raising that beautiful young girl, finding their faith, learning how to sustain and deepen their love. It wasn't easy to replace a companion like her—maybe impossible. And for the past two years he hadn't wanted to even think about it. But now…he thought of Natalie—Samantha—and smiled again at how she'd made him laugh on the phone this morning. But she was clear across the country now, making a new life for herself.

Shoulders drooping, he turned away from the window and stared at the piles of folders on his desk, which somehow hadn't grown smaller during his musing. Pulling the top one in front of him, he opened it and reviewed the notes about a robbery. No suspects, no fingerprints, no witnesses, just some blood on the broken rear window of the store. Ten minutes later, as he filled a legal pad with questions and follow-up items, the captain stuck his head in the door.

"Addison, I need you. We've got a child abduction from the playground at the Riverside Park. Doesn't look like parent involvement."

"Amber alert?" Addison tossed the folder aside and grabbed his coat off the tree.

"Already in the works." The captain stood back so Addison could exit the office and they hurried down the hallway. "I need you to get to the park and interview other kids and parents before they head home. Mitchell is there, trying to find out names of anyone who already left. Ballisaro is handling the Amber alert, and I'm preparing a statement for a press conference. Call me as soon as you find out anything."

"Will do, Cap." The captain slapped him on the back as Addison rushed out the precinct door, piles of folders momentarily forgotten. This was what he loved about the job—making a difference in people's lives.

As he jumped into his car he glanced at his watch. Mandy expected him home early today. He'd promised to take her shopping for school clothes since they hadn't had time last week. Addison pulled out of the parking lot into traffic and flipped the switch for the flashing lights to clear the way. He couldn't help thinking this little girl at the park was only a few years younger than Mandy as he mashed the accelerator. He navigated through a busy intersection and sped down the boulevard, dialing his daughter's cell number as he drove. The shopping trip would have to wait.

- 26 -

Natalie didn't see much point in clearing out Wena's possessions since she'd brought nothing of her own, but she did fill a trash bag with old magazines, saved grocery bags, and most of a huge accumulation of cleaning rags that spilled off the shelf in the small closet. Then she brought another bag to the overflowing bookcase in the living room. Natalie ran her finger down the rows of volumes, scanning the titles. Perhaps she could find a clue to Wena's happiness and contentment.

A two-foot section of shelf held dozens of books about the sea, ocean animals, the history of Perilous Point, the lighthouse, and one unusual item—a large forged skeleton key fully six inches long and weighing nearly a pound. Wena had utilized it as a bookend, but Natalie wondered what kind of lock needed a key this large? She lowered herself to as close to a cross-legged position as her cast permitted. Two spiral-bound albums on the lower shelf had handwritten titles on the spines. The first was labeled "Life," and the second, thinner one "Genealogy." Intrigued, she pulled the second volume out and leafed through the pages.

There were family tree charts and newspaper clippings of weddings, births, and funerals, dating back several generations. Rowena had traced Natalie's family back through her dad and mom to the middle 1700s. Many pages were photocopies of public records. Several envelopes had the return addresses circled with _SAVE_ scrawled beneath.

Natalie turned the page and was surprised to see _Clayton_ written in Wena's shaky hand across the top of a single sheet of graph paper.

Hilde's name, with her maiden name of Ernstrom, appeared first, but it wasn't her marriage to Lawrence Clayton.

A line connected Hilde to a son born before Jack. No given name, just "Male - Baby Crane" and a date of birth—three years before Jack's. No marriage was recorded, but the father's name was noted as Frank B. Crane of Arkansas. Natalie did some mental calculations: Jack's half-brother—if he still lived—would be fifty years old. Hilde was sixty-five years old at her last birthday.

With a start, Natalie realized her mother-in-law would have been an unmarried fifteen-year-old when she gave birth to her first son. Hilde had married Jack's father, Lawrence, two years later at seventeen, which had seemed very young when Natalie first learned that, but things were different in the fifties. Jack had come along only a year later. So the two boys were three years apart in age.

According to Wena's neat pen, the boy's father had raised him. That comment was dated two months before Wena passed away. Where was the brother now? And why hadn't Hilde ever mentioned him? Natalie wondered if Lawrence Clayton had known about his wife's first child.

The next page showed Jack and Natalie's wedding date, and held a familiar snapshot of Natalie in her wedding dress alongside Jack, strikingly handsome in his black tux. She'd sent the photo to Wena, but now, looking at it, she wondered why she hadn't chosen a different picture? No one would describe this shot of Natalie as radiant. She had a glazed, empty look, and Jack, though not dour, lacked enthusiasm. In fact, he looked a little bored. She couldn't remember—perhaps it had been taken at the end of the day when they were both tired by the activities.

And why *couldn't* she remember? Brides were supposed to recall every detail of their wedding day. But not this young woman who looked lonely on her most important day. Natalie touched the photo. Eleven years ago—separated from the present by death, fire, and half a continent.

And disappointment.

A gasp escaped Natalie's lips as she read the next entry. Under their names, Wena had written "Baby Clayton - girl," with the date of birth listed as four days after the wedding. Natalie traced the letters with her fingertips as tears filled her eyes. She'd never seen any record of her lost child. Every time she mentioned it to Jack, he dismissed it, unwilling to admit his daughter had existed, even if for not quite four months. Even Natalie's mother had said it was better to forget what couldn't be changed.

On Natalie's one visit to Perilous Cove after her marriage, she'd sat at Wena's tiny kitchen table and told the story of the baby, the miscarriage, and the end result that she would never have any more children. Rowena held her while the tears flowed, silence broken only by the soft swishing of the Kit-Cat clock's tail. Her aunt had deemed the baby significant enough to record in her genealogy book.

"Thank you, Aunt Rowena." Natalie brushed the corners of her eyes.

Hilde's comments had been much harsher. After they'd returned from the honeymoon, Jack's mother suggested he get an immediate annulment. Now was the time to "get out of" the marriage, to "get rid of" Natalie. She'd made sure Natalie overheard every word. A shiver crawled up her spine and raised hairs on the back of her neck.

Natalie flipped the page, shutting off the memories, but the next was blank, as were the rest of the pages in the book. She turned back to the page listing Hilde's first son. Wena must have used the town's library computer to search out the information.

A seagull screeched outside. Natalie slid the book to the floor and shifted her body to lean against the bookcase, stretching out her cramped legs.

Jack had never mentioned a brother. Maybe no one knew except Hilde. With her political career, that could make sense, especially if there had never been a marriage. Hilde had lost the last gubernatorial election by only a few percentage points. It was widely believed she had a good shot at unseating the growingly unpopular incumbent in next year's campaign.

The public liked Hilde—she promised all kinds of things critics claimed were completely impractical—but the woman had made plenty of enemies along the way, both in her commercial real estate business and in politics. Revelation of an illegitimate son—even one born so many years ago—would give her opponents a juicy scandal. Hilde could never allow that. At sixty-five years old, she was seasoned and experienced, but at seventy she might be deemed too old. This could be her last shot at the four-year governor's term and, Natalie knew, her mother-in-law would stop at nothing to win that prize.

Natalie returned the book to the shelf and pulled out the other, thicker volume. The first pages held pictures of Rowena Riley's childhood, memories captured forever on glossy, scallop-edged squares of paper. Natalie ran her fingers over black and white images of Rowena and her younger sister, Natalie's mother. In two photos, Natalie's grandfather, a man she knew only through pictures, held both girls, one foot propped on the bumper of an old car. The second photo had him helping the girls with a fishing pole on the bank of a stream. A posed family portrait showed Natalie's grandmother—a young woman in a polka dot dress—standing demurely by her husband. The girls, perhaps six and eight, knelt in front.

The continuing timeline of pages showed Rowena on a horse, at high school graduation, and several photos of Natalie's parents' wedding with Rowena as maid of honor. Natalie's dad stood stiffly, young and thin in his tuxedo, with the same forced smile she remembered. He was never comfortable in front of a camera. She missed her parents so much.

The next brittle page held a 5x7 color print of the young couple, holding Natalie as a baby. They sat on the familiar red sofa, later relegated to the den, but here it was new and unworn.

The first awareness of tears was when they splashed on the open album, soaking into the dry black paper. Natalie hurriedly wiped them off with the sleeve of her shirt, then swiped her eyes. Her grandparents, her parents, her aunt, her husband. All gone except Natalie Clayton—now Samantha Riley. It all stopped with her. No babies to carry on the family legacy. No birthday parties, first dates, high school graduations, or weddings.

Only funerals.

The beamed wooden ceiling of the cabin blurred as Natalie leaned back against the bookcase. Where was the hope in life when the only future was death?

Part Two

- 27 -

"Hi, Sam. The usual?"

"Yep. Make it a small, okay?" Natalie boosted up onto a stool and swiveled to the bar. Even after nearly three months, it still felt funny to answer to Sam or Samantha Riley, but that was her legal name now. Other than Millie, no one in town had known her as anything other than Samantha Riley, Rowena's niece.

White-haired Conrad Langworth—Connie to his friends—ran the best and only coffee bar in Perilous Cove. Little wider than the double doorway along the quaint storefront row, the Last Drop interior looked like a mini saloon. The front of the store was just wide enough to hold three small tables with two chairs each. A narrow bar with stools began about halfway back and ran to the rear wall. Behind the varnished wood surface, Connie roamed the slim enclosure, finessing the machines that lined the wall.

"Have a busy day planned?" Connie slid an extra large steaming latte in front of her. She opened her mouth to protest its size and he ignored her by studiously scanning the rest of the customers before settling down for some conversation.

"Thank you." She caught and held his eye until he blushed and retuned a small smile while polishing a portion the spotless countertop. By her own effort, people in town didn't know much about her. But somehow Connie knew of her chronic money shortage. He never charged her more than the price of a small.

"Don't mention it."

Maybe Millie had said something.

Connie's music tastes were as varied as his coffees. Today, Sam recognized Allison Krauss's bluegrass stylings, one of her favorites. Tomorrow could be jazz. His easygoing manner made him perfect for the job of barista, combining coffee expertise with the counseling capability of the best bartender. Rumor was he'd saved more than a few marriages with well-placed advice. She marveled how he appeared as if he'd forgotten to shave his white whiskers every day, achieving a Hollywood-actor-meets-small-town persona. He'd become one of her first friends in Perilous Cove.

Sam sipped the steaming brew, which contained Connie's signature pinch of nutmeg. While the coffee flavor was predominant, it always reminded her a little of the holidays. "Oh, this is so good. I need it today. Tour group going out at nine o'clock with Captain Tom."

Tom Borah's boat, Fin Finder II, held up to twelve passengers. Her job consisted of preparing snacks and tour guide narration while they cruised the rocky coast looking for whales and other sea life. November was early in the migration season, but two grays had been spotted last week. Plus, there were always dolphins, sea lions, and otters to keep the passengers entertained.

"So, you're the lackey?"

Sam shot him her best stern expression. "That's lackey first class to you, mister."

"Yes, ma'am." Connie gave a mock salute.

"You ever been out on a whale watching boat, Connie?"

"Nope."

"Maybe it's time you went."

"Not me. Only time I went out, some buddies talked me into a half-day fishing excursion. One of 'em got sicker than a dog. Heaved his breakfast all over the deck and off every rail for four hours before we came back in." His grin deepened the crow's feet, but shed some of his sixty-plus years, revealing some of the boy inside. "I vowed never to go out on a boat again."

"I sure hope we don't have that today." She took another sip. The job had fallen into her lap when Captain Tom's daughter, Amy, got pregnant with her first baby. Morning sickness plagued her right when Tom needed a crewmate for this year's tour season. Fortunately for Sam, Amy had scripted the narration, so Sam had picked it up quickly and loved the job. Rowena's nature books had helped. Never had she thought of trying such a thing, but it felt a perfect fit for her new life. This was her third tour trip.

Sam asked about Connie's grandkids and he produced the latest photo of young Caleb, a cherubic two-year-old who, even at this young age, resembled his grandfather.

Connie never inquired about her past and she silently thanked him for it.

Sam felt a hand on her back and turned to find Maxine Young leaning over to catch a glimpse of the photo.

"Oh, Connie, isn't he a doll? He looks just like you. Doesn't he, Sam?" Maxine squeezed her ample frame between the stools, lapping well into Sam's space. The woman wasn't huge, but she could play Mrs. Claus during the Christmas play with little makeup.

A glance at the clock told Sam she'd better head for the boat, so she slipped off her stool, which was quickly commandeered by the other woman.

Connie leaned around Maxine. "Be careful out there, Sam. Radio says there's a storm front coming down today. You warn Tom." Connie poured her remaining coffee into a to go cup, topped it off, and handed it to her. "Gonna get cold."

"Thanks. I'll dig out the extra blankets." She waved over her shoulder and pushed through the door, ringing the bell above her head.

The biting November air stung Sam's cheeks as she stepped down the wooden planks of the boat dock, but she loved the rawness of the coastal climate. She felt so alive and vital, her existence in St. Louis felt drab by comparison. Although she'd visited Aunt Rowena here, she'd never considered living near the sea. Now she couldn't imagine anything else. It felt right, down deep inside.

The wind blew offshore this morning, carrying sweet wood smoke from chimneys of homes sprinkled upslope from the harbor. The oak, eucalyptus and pine—both fresh and burned—mixed with fishy harbor smells in a rich soup unique to Perilous Cove, or so she liked to think. Later this afternoon when the weather front arrived, the wind direction would reverse and sweep onshore, clearing the air, slamming waves onto the breakwater rocks, and imparting bouncing enthusiasm to all the boats in the small harbor. Sadly, for many of the craft, it was the closest they got to any real action. Sometimes, on the wilder days, Sam imagined the boats straining to be free, like caged animals eager to run and play.

She stopped at the Fin Finder II and turned back toward the picturesque cove. It amazed her how quickly this small village had become her home. The colorful building housing the Last Drop had been there since the street was oiled gravel, and upstairs Mildred Ettlebaum still taught sewing to young girls, a task she'd begun as a mere girl herself at the brink of World War II. Now a tradition and rite of passage, moms still brought their little girls to sit under Mildred's gentle tutelage, just as they themselves had done years before, and some of their mothers before that. The "Little Ladies," as Mildred referred to them, learned as much about proper manners as how to make a tight stitch or judge the quality of thread and yarn. She celebrated the completion of each class with a dress-up Victorian tea party.

Next door stood T.J.'s Deli with tables on the front patio. The small deck above the deli held three tables and was a prime spot during good weather, giving a birds-eye view of the action on Harbor Street. The two-story Royal movie theater anchored the north corner, complete with time-worn neon lights adorning a simple marquee, a free-standing ticket booth, and seating for an optimistic fifty-five. A local theater group shared the stage with occasional art films.

Around the corner was the PC Post Office where junk mail already arrived addressed to "Mr. Sam Riley." She had no idea where they'd gotten her name, but it worried her a little. If the advertisers could track her this quickly, could she remain safe from the man who'd tried to kill her? Almost two thousand miles from Steerman, Missouri, but it didn't feel nearly far enough. Sam glanced toward the mouth of the breakwater where the untamed Pacific Ocean began. She couldn't go any further.

Seagulls squawked overhead, startling the dark thoughts from her mind, and she grabbed the rail of the boat to step aboard.

"Sam!"

Sam turned and squinted through the ships' riggings for the source of the shout. She spotted ten-year-old Starfire Trafford running along the shore, crimson ponytail flying. The girl had one speed: flat out.

Star pounded down the dock, skidded to a stop and bent over, hands on her knees, panting in exaggerated exhaustion. "Can I come with you?"

A smile tugged at Sam's mouth, and she covered by placing her finger on her lips and staring loftily above Star. "Let's see...did I hear someone ask, '*May I please* come with you?'"

"May I *puh-lease* come with you?" The proper wording was somewhat countered by Star rolling her eyes.

Sam gave into the grin. "Don't you have school? Today's Friday, you know."

"The teachers have an in-service day. I'm off!" The girl picked up a box of supplies Tom had left and started to carry it aboard. Sam put her hand out to stop her.

"Hold your horses, Star. I don't know where Captain Tom is, and it's not up to me, you know."

"I saw him go into the marine supply a few minutes ago." Star stood taller, as if that might make up the crucial difference.

"There may not be room depending on how many guests we have." The boat was only licensed to carry fifteen people including crew. The girl's shoulders sagged and Sam immediately felt bad. She brushed stray hairs from the girl's freckled cheek. "Let's find Tom and then call Grandma Millie. She's the final say-so."

Star sat the box down and jumped in a circle. "Let's go, let's go."

As they walked back to shore, Sam hip-bumped Star producing an instant giggle. "You know we both answer to your grandmother, so it's best to keep on her good side." Star returned a huge grin and Sam tugged her ponytail.

Star's parents—Millie's only son, Roy, and his girlfriend—had been a disastrous match from the day they met at a seedy bar in nearby Mission Peaks, making one bad choice after another. The only good thing they'd produced was this wonderful little red-haired girl. But toddler Starfire hindered their fun, so one day they dropped the three-year-old off at Millie's with promises to be back in an hour. One month later, after a burglary for drug money, Roy attempted to outrun police in a high-speed chase on I-5 through central California. The final rollover crash near Bakersfield ejected Star's mother, killing her instantly. Millie's son survived to face a dozen charges, including three counts of felony hit and run for clipping cars on the freeway, burglary, and manslaughter. Now serving a long prison sentence, he'd signed papers giving Millie full custody of Star.

Sam and Star found Captain Tom haggling prices with Hank at the marine supply store. Every time Tom would make a verbal point, his dog, Blew, would raise his head and give a half-hearted growl at the store owner, then lay back down across Tom's feet. The dog's antics didn't seem to be helping the price negotiations, but it entertained several observers.

Tom gave the go ahead for Star to ride along, so they called Millie from the pay phone in front of Brodie's Hardware. As Sam had expected, Millie encouraged Sam to spend as much time as possible with Star.

"You're good for her—and she's good for you."

They returned to the boat as the first passengers arrived. Two couples were from Sweden, with others from Idaho, Arizona and California.

Sam handed Star a clipboard and assigned her the job of guest check-in and getting them onboard, while Sam prepared snacks in the galley. Juice and bagel quarters made up the first snack. Halfway into the tour, when they turned homeward around noon, she would fix sandwiches on sour dough rolls, chips, and butter-toffee popcorn, a favorite of Tom's. Blew waited alertly at her feet in case a morsel should fall to the deck. She pointed her finger at him. "No begging, Blew. You know the rules." Her comment produced a raised ear and soft whine, brown doggy eyes glued to her finger. She flicked a chunk of turkey in the air and Blew snatched it before it hit the floor. She could have sworn the old mutt smiled at her before dashing outside to let the passengers scratch his head and back.

A deep rumble from the engines vibrated through the deck and Blew jumped the stairs to join Tom in the cockpit. Sam hurried onto the dock. When Tom backed the boat up to slacken the tether, she untied the stern line and tossed it aboard. Then she unlooped the bow line and hopped aboard as Tom eased away from the dock. What would Jack think of his wife jumping onto a moving boat?

In the cabin, Sam switched on the PA system. "Welcome aboard Captain Tom's Whale Watching Excursion, ladies and gentlemen. My name is Samantha Riley—you can call me Sam—and I'll be narrating our tour. Up above is Captain Tom, a thirty-two-year veteran of these waters, along with his whale-spotting dog, Blew." A loud "Woof" echoed from above, generating laughter from the group.

"Assisting us today is Miss Starfire Trafford, a fifth-grader from Perilous Cove Elementary. She's very happy her teachers have in-service training today." Several passengers laughed and kidded Star as she served the snacks. She was a natural with people and more sure-footed than Sam on the shifting deck. Together they instructed everyone about safety procedures and location of life vests, as well as how to use the boat's toilet, called the head. Star polished the lenses on the binoculars available for passengers.

The Fin Finder II's engines revved as they rounded the protective breakwater and swung north along the cliffs. They passed Perilous Point and its lighthouse. Tom kept the boat well away from shore where waves crashed on half-hidden rocks and threw impressive sprays of salty foam high on the cliff. Sam automatically sought out her cabin, partially hidden up the ridge from the lighthouse tower.

Her cabin. How strange to think less than three months ago she had lived in St. Louis with her husband. So much change it made her head spin. Some mornings she awoke disoriented, only relaxing when she recognized the pounding of the waves and the sound of the Cyprus trees sifting the wind.

A hundred feet north of the lighthouse, Verde Falls splashed a thin stream of water thirty-five feet down the cliff to the rocky beach. Verde Creek ran not too far from her cabin and, with the bigger winter rains, the creek would flush the algae from the small pond perched on the flat area only ten feet from the edge. Every summer when the water warmed, kids would hike along the edge and, with backs to the sea, dive into the deepest end of the pool. Worried parents who didn't want their children hiking along the cliff's slippery edge in bare feet commissioned a security fence around the pond, but enterprising teens soon had an opening cut into it. The fence ultimately served a useful purpose, though: it became a convenient drying rack for towels.

Sam flipped the pages of her tour book and pulled the microphone from its hook. She read the text of her narrative about pelicans, seagulls, and other birds, trying to sound natural and spontaneous, while keeping an eye out for otters, sea lions and dolphins.

"Grays are the most often seen whales along California's coast since they travel close to shore. Their twelve thousand mile round-trip, from Alaska to Baja California and back, is one of the longest mammal migrations in the world. Pregnant cows depart Alaska in October headed to Baja's warm lagoons in December, where they give birth."

One of the women asked about the whales' birth process and Sam skimmed her fact sheets for the answers. Then one of the men spotted an otter swimming and diving among the shore rocks. Tom slowed the boat and Sam flipped to the otter pages.

"Sea otters are members of the weasel family, which includes minks, badgers, skunks and wolverines. They depend on their dense fur to stay warm in the cold water, and spend large amounts of time grooming. Parts of a sea otter's body are covered with up to a million hairs per square inch, while we humans have about 100,000 hairs on our entire head."

"Not my head." One of the men pulled off his cap to reveal his shaved dome and everyone laughed.

Tom invited anyone who wished, to step up to the pilot's cabin. He even let Star steer the boat when they slowed to observe some sea lions on rocks. And though the air turned colder, everyone went to the rails when five dolphins swam by not forty yards from the boat.

High, wispy clouds scudded across the sky, foreshadowing the weather front and possible rain, but Tom assured the group they would be tied up at the dock before it got rough. True to his word, they turned toward home port as the sky darkened and wind picked up. For the return trip, most of the passengers chose the comfort of the interior cabin, though three of the men remained on the open stern deck, searching the water for telltale blows of southbound whales. Eventually they came in, cheeks and noses reddened from the dropping temperature.

Sam and Star served the sandwiches with hot cider and coffee, and took pictures for groups of friends. Tom said part of running a great tour boat was making everyone feel right at home, even if, like today, they didn't spot any whales.

As they disembarked, Captain Tom handed out discount tickets for coffees at the Last Drop and encouraged everyone to try the clam chowder or fish and chips at Maxine's.

Chilled to the bone, hot chowder sounded divine to Sam, but she had to watch her money. She'd blown too much of her eating out budget on coffee at the Last Drop, so a can of soup from her pantry would have to do. Even that sounded good as she tightened the hood of her parka against the rising wind, grabbed a blanket from the boat, and looked for Star. She spotted the girl on the dock, using leftover sandwich scraps to entice Blew to shake hands.

"Come on, kiddo. Let's get home before our feet freeze to the dock."

Hip to hip with the blanket tugged tight around them, Sam and Star trudged up the low hill to their homes. Star regaled her with stories of her fifth-grade teacher, Mrs. Beetle, and for an instant Sam imagined them as Samantha and Starfire, mother and daughter.

She dismissed the thought quickly before the pain began again.

- 28 -

"Are you going to eat that other half?"

"What?" Addison, pulled from his west-coast thoughts, looked up at his partner.

"The other half of your sandwich." Arnie pointed to the neglected Italian sub. "Are you going to eat it?"

"Oh. No, go ahead." Addison shoved it across the plastic table outside Subway. Aromatic bread-baking steam billowed from the building vents, designed to entice anyone passing by. Today it did nothing for him. Cars whizzed past on Steerman Expressway a couple dozen feet distant, swirling wet mist from the morning's light rain. He and Arnie should have eaten inside, but the place was jammed with at least fifty high school students, all talking on cell phones and listening to MP3 players at the same time as eating and shouting at each other. Yet it was fatigue, not the noise, which kept him from a move to the drier interior.

"Hey, it's starting to rain. Let's get back in the car." Arnie gathered up the sandwich and trash. Addison followed him, sliding into the passenger side of the vehicle. Rain splattered the windshield and ran down the glass. The last few days' weather matched his mood: gray and dismal.

"Any progress on the Clayton case?" Arnie finished the last bite, tossed the wadded paper into the back seat, and started the engine. He backed out of the parking space and turned the car toward headquarters.

"Not much. The fire team confirmed arson in their report a couple of

138

weeks ago."

"No surprise there."

"Nope. But the evidence didn't link to anyone specific."

"What about the life insurance?" Arnie switched the wipers to high as the sky opened up.

Addison and Arnie had been working a dozen new cases and had split them up to save time. The Clayton case was now his alone. "I finally tracked down the agent who sold Jack Clayton the policy for Natalie. The guy changed companies and then left on vacation, so it took awhile. He said both Claytons came in and signed the forms."

"Uh, huh."

"Only thing is, Natalie says she never signed it, didn't know anything about it. I'm waiting for the insurance company fraud unit to get me the application form so a handwriting expert from the crime lab can compare the form's signature to Natalie's." He glanced at his watch. "I need to bug them again. I'll call them when we get back to the office. I've had so many other cases I haven't followed up the way I should."

"I hear you there." Arnie braked as a driver cut into the lane in front of him. "For two million bucks, didn't the insurance company require a physical?"

"Yes. And they have the test results. The blood type matches Natalie. But again, she said she never had the physical."

"So, someone stood in for her?"

"Looks like it. Unfortunately, they don't keep blood samples, so there isn't any DNA to compare with Natalie's."

Arnie whistled. "Two million bucks'll make some people do crazy things."

"Got that right."

"She still in California?"

"Yeah." Addison stared out the streaked side window as Arnie pulled into the parking lot.

Arnie popped the keys out of the ignition, cracked the door, and then put his hand on Addison's arm. "You okay, amigo?"

Addison blinked. "Sure. I'm fine." But if he was so fine, why did it feel like a piece of his life was missing? Why were many of his thoughts centered on the petite blonde woman who stayed in his home for only five days, but still haunted its halls?

Though he tended to think of her as Natalie, Mandy had immediately adjusted to "Sam," and talked to her at least once a week by phone, and those were only the times Addison knew about. To keep from going broke, he'd upgraded Mandy's cell phone plan to include nationwide long distance.

He opened the car door and they sprinted through the hard rain. At the building entrance, Arnie held the door for him. Inside, he shook the water from his head and pulled off his wet coat. Someone had cranked up the heat. That, and the pungent odor of stale coffee and burned microwave popcorn, nearly drove him back outside.

He pushed open the door to their office and cracked the window for some fresh air. Before he could sit down, his cell phone rang.

"Conner."

"Eees theeis Monsieur De-tec-teeve Cone-or?" The nasally French accent—a poor attempt at Inspector Jacques Clouseau—pulled a laugh from him.

"You are *so* bad at imitations."

His brother's voice reverted to its normal deep tones. "You never were any good, either."

He laughed at Ben's feigned offended response. "Yeah, but I knew enough to stop trying."

It was Ben's turn to laugh. "So, little brother, how's it going?"

Ben tended to cut to the chase and Addison liked that. They'd talked on the phone twice in the last month, and Addison was relaxing into the renewed connection with his brother. He gave Ben a rundown on the latest with Mandy, plus his poor excuse of a life lately. "Sorry. Didn't mean to dump." He straightened pencils in his holder.

"Hey, it's okay. Got your message this morning. What's up?"

Addison told him his idea and Ben wholeheartedly agreed. After finalizing their plans, Addison reluctantly hit the end call button. He sank deeper into his chair and stared at the desktop, covered in files, each representing a hurting individual or family. So many needs. The momentary lift he'd gotten from talking with Ben fled in the wake of his workload.

As if by its own volition, his hand reached for the dog-eared folder labeled 'Clayton' in red tape on the tab. He opened the cover and leafed through the pages of photos of Donna Montgomery, the burned house and crime scene, Donna Montgomery's funeral, and a picture of Jack Clayton, provided under threat of subpoena by his mother. The exchange at her front door still stung.

"I'll not do one thing to help that woman," Hildegard Clayton had told him that day.

Addison opened his notebook. "You're referring to Jack's wife, Natalie?"

"She was no wife to my son. He despised her." The woman's bitterness caused him to step back from the front door of her home, as if it might contaminate him somehow. He was glad she'd refused him entrance.

Finally, Hilde Clayton had produced a photograph of Jack standing beside her in a garden setting. She thrust it at Addison, demanded a receipt for the photo, and then slammed the door in his face.

Addison replaced the photo in the case folder, noting Hildegard Clayton's adoring smile for her precious son. He shook his head, unable to fathom the woman's motivations. Obviously she'd worshiped her son and hated her daughter-in-law. Did she blame Natalie for Jack's death? And if so, could Hilde be involved in some way? Maybe he should call Natalie and ask her more about Hilde Clayton.

He went to the restroom, then stopped on the way back to say hi to a couple of patrol officers. When he rounded the corner to his office, he spotted Sharon leaning over his desk, leafing through a folder. She had one arm wrapped around her now obviously pregnant belly, and her face had that special glow he remembered so well with Elizabeth. Yet most of the time Sharon's countenance held a sadness that seemed to wipe the joy away. He'd felt sorry for her since Gladys had told him Sharon's married boyfriend had dumped her. He'd tried to be more caring and she seemed to be responding. She'd stopped by his desk or caught him in the hall several times in the past two months, asking about Mandy, his cases, his church.

"Hi, Sharon. Can I help you with something?"

Her head snapped up and she flipped the folder closed. "Oh, Addison. Hi." She brushed some errant strands of blonde hair behind one ear. "There are some evidence updates for the Cavanaugh file. Leroy needs it."

She stepped back at his approach and he glanced at the file she'd been viewing. "That's the Clayton file, Sharon."

"Oh, it is?" She gave a little laugh. "I can't see anything without my glasses these days."

Addison sorted through a ten-inch stack, pulled a thick green folder from the middle, and held it out to her. "Here it is. I finished my comments this morning, so I won't need it back."

Sharon moved closer and her hand brushed his as she took the file. "Thanks, Addison. I really appreciate your help."

She stepped closer still and the backs of Addison's legs pressed the edge of the desk. He hadn't noticed how tall she was until now when she met him nearly eye to eye.

"Uh, no problem, Sharon."

She dropped her gaze shyly, and then looked up from under her long lashes. "I appreciate your friendship, too." Her free hand touched his arm. Its hairs snapped to attention and ran uphill to the back of his neck like an army unit on double-time.

He scooted sideways along the desk, but she matched the maneuver.

"Addison, if there's anything I can do for you, you'll tell me...won't you?"

"I..." He wished he'd opened the window wider as sweat trickled down his collar.

His phone beeped and he checked the display. A text from Mandy. A glance at his watch confirmed his fear. Three-thirty. He'd promised to take her shopping this afternoon for the pre-Thanksgiving banquet at church Sunday night. Where had the time gone? Morning chaos and a late lunch, that's where.

"Sorry, Sharon. I, uh, have to go." He pointed to his phone while sliding sideways from between her and his desk. "Emergency." Emergency shopping trip. Never had shopping sounded so good. He grabbed his files and dropped them in his bottom desk drawer.

"Arnie." He spotted his partner at Gladys' desk in the hall. "I'm outta here." Gathering his coat and wallet, he ran for the door, glancing back to see Sharon still standing by his desk, a pouty smile curving her lips, and Gladys ping-ponging looks between the two of them, eyebrows raised. He groaned and knew he faced a full police interrogation from the dispatcher next week.

The call to Natalie would have to wait. He punched in Mandy's cell number as he went, excited to tell her he had a surprise for her.

- 29 -

The trap door next to the stove had captured Sam's curiosity since she'd arrived at the cabin. Today was the day to see what treasure it concealed. She worked a butter knife into the recessed finger-pull, digging out years of floor wax, and pried it up so she could get her finger under it. Standing, she tugged at the cover, glued shut at the edges from years of mopping.

After several mighty heaves, it broke loose and she cautiously lifted it open on creaking hinges and leaned it back against the wall. A musty breeze billowed into the kitchen, promising another opening somewhere in the blackness. Nothing crawled out, but spider webs draped the opening, causing a shudder to run through her body.

"Eeeww." She grabbed the broom from its nail by the bathroom door and swatted the sticky webs away.

The opening measured about two feet wide and five feet long. Steep wooden stairs of heavy planks descended into darkness. There was no way she was going down there, but curiosity sent her in search for a flashlight. She found one in a junk drawer beside wooden matches and candles. She turned it on. The weak glow grew brighter as she worked the switch on and off a few times to clean the contacts, but it was still marginal. She made a mental note to buy new batteries at the hardware store.

Sam got down on her hands and knees and directed the light into the hole. A rough-cut railing, worn smooth by decades of hands, framed one side of the stairs. Halfway down she spotted a light switch, one of the ancient round units with a T-shaped knob you twisted to turn it on and off. She still didn't want to go down so, grabbing the broom by the wrong end, she poked at the switch. The broom handle kept slipping off the small knob. Why couldn't they have put the switch at the top? Or even better, in the kitchen?

Ten more attempts had her sitting cross-legged and wiping sweat from her brow.

This is ridiculous. What would Wena do? "Come on, Sam, let's get to it." Wena always charged ahead, unafraid—or at least unwilling to let fear stop her.

Courageous was not a word Sam would have used to describe herself in the past, but given the events of the last three months, perhaps she was becoming more like her aunt. And perhaps courage was less about being afraid than it was about being willing to step out. Living alone forced one to take on challenges. She stared at the black rectangle. Like this basement.

Using the broom to clean each plank, Sam crept down three steps before she could reach the switch. Giving it a firm twist to the right, she was rewarded with a solid 'click.' Weak light from a bare bulb suspended from a floor joist chased back the shadows somewhat, yielding a glimpse of a hard-packed dirt floor in a room roughly ten by twelve feet. From the direction of the stairs, the room extended along the back of the house, under the added-on bathroom. Sam pointed the flashlight into the far corner and spotted the water and drainpipes for the tub and toilet.

She brushed the low ceiling with the broom as far as she could reach, then cleaned two more treads and took another step down. A workbench stood against the westerly wall furthest under the house. Several moldy cardboard boxes sagged on it, covered in so much dust everything took on the same tan color. The end of the bench held a large chest with a rounded top like a treasure chest she'd seen at Disneyland on the pirate ride. A large lock secured the box, hiding whatever might be inside.

Rusty garden tools hung from nails along one of the floor joists. The east wall held a jumble of haphazardly stacked clay pots along with a seriously deteriorated half wine barrel. Natalie shook her head. Why would Rowena keep such a thing?

Two final step cleanings and she stood on the earthen floor. Again she swept the ceiling as far as the broom would reach. She'd always hated spiders, ever since one of her babysitters had read Little Miss Muffet to her as a child, acting out the motions of the spider. To this day she had no idea what curds and whey were, but just the mention gave her shivers.

The hanging light bulb flickered twice, flared, and went out, plunging the cellar into near darkness. Sam swung the yellow flashlight beam back along the bench and inhaled sharply as the light caught two beady eyes —staring right at her. A gigantic rat sauntered around one of the boxes and sniffed in her direction. Then crept to the nearest edge of the bench, as if trying to get closer.

"Ahh!" Sam lurched up two steps and smacked the back of her head on the edge of the opening. Her hand flew to the radiating pain and she watched the flashlight bounce down the stairs and blink out, returning the rat to his realm of darkness. Now he could be anywhere.

Wielding the broom before her as a weapon, Sam hurried up the stairs and slammed the trap door into place, stamping it with her foot for good measure. A cobweb slipped off her head and dangled in front of her face, and she did a heeby-geeby dance, brushing madly at invisible eight-legged crawly things, at her shoulders and back.

"What are you doing?"

The voice was right behind her and Sam screamed and lurched into the table, sending napkins and a cup of coffee to the floor. Star Trafford stood in the doorway, eyes wide.

"Don't you ever knock?" She hated the cutting tone of her words even as they left her mouth. The girl's eyes instantly teared and she bolted for the open front door.

"Star!" Sam cast aside the broom and sprinted after the girl. "Star, wait." Sam caught up with her by the big cypress near the end of the driveway and grabbed her sleeve.

"Let me go." The redhead fought off Sam's hand and backed against the huge trunk.

"Star. I'm so sorry." Tears streaked the poor girl's cheeks. Sam sank to her knees a few feet away, dimly aware of the sharp driveway shells cutting into her jeans. She dropped her head, unable to look at the scared girl. "Oh, Star. I'm so sorry I snapped at you. I was scared and I took it out on you." She felt tears run down her own cheeks and she raised her head. Star stood against the tree, arms spread wide like she was protecting it rather than drawing strength from its girth. When she spoke, her voice shook.

"What were you scared of?"

"A big rat in my cellar."

"A rat?" Star sniffed and wiped her nose on the sleeve of her sweatshirt. "How big?"

"As big as a cat."

"A rat as big as a cat?" The corners of her wide mouth turned upward in a slight smile.

Sam nodded and opened her arms. Starfire took a tentative step away from the safety of the tree and then ran to Sam's embrace. She rose, hugged the girl tight, and buried her face in her hair, inhaling shampoo and sea air. They remained under the cypress, holding each other, gently rocking to the wind singing in the upper branches.

After a few minutes, the cold forced them to move. Sam pulled back and stroked the girl's silky hair. "Come on. Let's go back to my rat-infested cabin and I'll fix us some hot cider."

Star shook her head. "I can't. Grandma sent me to get you. She's not feeling good."

"Again? Okay, let me get my coat." Sam ran back and retrieved her coat from the hook by the door, then they hurried to Millie's.

Tomorrow she'd hire an exterminator. Or a big game hunter.

"Dad, no way! California for Thanksgiving?" Mandy practically tackled him when he picked her up for shopping.

"I talked to your Uncle Ben and he said to come on out."

Mandy screamed again, grabbed his hands and swung him in circles. Her enthusiasm made him feel even guiltier for staying detached from Ben. He smiled as Mandy happy-danced around and dug in her backpack for her cell phone. She'd begged him to go to California the last two holidays, but he just couldn't.

Mandy found her phone and punched a speed dial key. "I'm calling Sam," she threw at him. She bounced on her toes, grabbed her jacket, and checked her hair in the hall mirror, all while keeping the cell phone glued to her ear. Addison was continually amazed at her bursts of energy, followed by the need for twelve or more hours of sleep every Saturday...unless there was a shopping trip planned. He held the door open as they headed for the car.

By the time they'd backed into the street, Mandy had clicked off the cell and her shoulders slumped. "She's not home. And she *still* doesn't have an answering machine."

Addison had run into the same problem calling her about the case. "She doesn't have a lot of money and I think she's just being really frugal. It was a stretch for her just to get the phone installed. Hey, I've got an idea. Maybe we should buy Sam an early Christmas present?"

"Like an answering machine?" Mandy pursed her lips. "Earrings or a cute short jacket from Forever 21 would be better." She turned to face him. "Can we get both?" The gleam in her eyes made him wary. Ever since Sam left, Mandy had been subtly suggesting he call her, write her, or go visit. Although this was a trip to stay with Ben, Sam was only a few miles away, and he knew Mandy would want them to get together several times. Was he ready for that?

"Dad, where are you going? You passed the mall."

Addison took a right at the next corner. "I, uh, was just going in the back entrance." He turned into the driveway and cruised down the rows of cars, pointedly ignoring his daughter's smirk. "It's not as busy back here."

"Uh, huh."

She always got the last word.

30

Sam kept her arm tight around Star as they watched the receding ambulance. Although Millie had improved after the EMTs arrived, the doctor wanted her in the hospital for observation. She'd been white as a ghost when Sam and Star had arrived at the house, and Sam immediately called 911.

"Come on, let's get your things and we'll drive to the hospital."

Inside Millie's house, Sam stood in the living room while Star used the bathroom and got her jacket. The décor was typically Millie and leaped beyond all conventional boundaries. An antique writing desk stood next to modern sculpture pieces so bizarre Sam wasn't sure what they were supposed to be. Works from a few local artisans filled some of the space, but most were from Millie's own talented hands.

Specializing in mixed media art, Millie wove complex tapestries of brightly colored seascapes and harbor scenes together with bits of dried seaweed, shells and driftwood. Tables and floor held pottery and hanging baskets with shells woven into the hemp cording. Handmade rugs in a variety of shapes and colors warmed the cherry hardwood floors. In anyone else's home, the items would clash and repel each other. But somehow it all worked here, perhaps held together by the force of Millie's personality. Opposites wouldn't *dare* clash if Millie Trafford put them side-by-side.

Sam had toured Millie's garage where shelves held at least a hundred ceramic creations, everything from sea lions to eagles, bears to ballerinas. An ancient kiln, installed by Darryl before he died, occupied a rear corner of the crammed space, leaving barely enough room for the car.

The house itself was a California craftsman style, complete with wide front steps, a deep porch with covered roof supported by tapered pillars, and multi-paned windows overlooking the harbor. Darryl and Millie had purchased it in the sixties and remodeled it top to bottom. Its location at the top of the bluff commanded magnificent southwest views across Perilous Cove and to the vast Pacific beyond.

Star's hand slipped into Sam's and squeezed tight. "I'm ready."

"Okay." Sam sighed and cast about. "Uh, keys. We need keys for the house." She turned toward the kitchen, but Star tugged her hand.

"I have them."

They walked behind Sam's cabin to her one-car garage where she swung the double doors open and climbed into the Jeep while Star waited outside. The narrow space was tight even for the small Jeep, so she always parked far to the right. She turned the key and pumped the accelerator twice like Walter had suggested. Billie hadn't been driven in a week and the engine cranked for several seconds before sputtering to life. She backed out and waited while Star closed and latched the doors, then got in.

Mission Peak Hospital was about forty minutes away, and the oversize tires sang happily on the pavement in stark contrast to the weight pressing Sam's heart. Millie had been sick a lot lately, but today had scared Sam good.

Millie hadn't given away her age yet, but she had to be pushing eighty…at least. What if she was seriously ill, dying? Although Sam had other friends in town, Millie alone knew Sam's secrets, the only person who shared her history. An occasional sniff from Star broke the silence.

"We should pray." Star sniffed again and looked at Sam as if expecting her to lead the way. Sam kept her eyes on the road, checked the rearview mirrors. She couldn't pray while driving, even though there were only four cars visible on the two-lane road. Prayer wasn't something she knew anything about anyway. And did it even work? Did God listen? She hadn't seen much evidence of God's care in her own life.

Sam forced an overly cheery smile toward the slim girl. "Maybe you could pray while I drive?"

"Okay." Star closed her eyes and prayed for her Grandma Millie to get well, that God would take care of her and bring her home fast. Then she prayed for her daddy in prison, asking God to take care of him and make him into a good person.

Sam wiped her eyes repeatedly so she could focus on the road. Then Star surprised her.

"God, thank you for Sam. I don't know what I'd do without her. Please keep her safe from the bad man. Amen."

Sam guided the Jeep to the side of the road and stopped.

"What's the matter?" Star turned in her seat, searching the road for a problem.

"Nothing." Sam sniffed and reached for the box of Kleenex she kept behind the seat. After blowing her nose and wiping her eyes, she pulled Star close.

"That was a beautiful prayer, honey. Thank you." Sam grabbed more tissues from the box and used the mirror to repair the damage to her makeup. Then she took a deep breath, checked the side mirror, and pulled back onto the road.

Sam should be mad at Millie for telling Star about her past, but Millie probably wanted her granddaughter to be aware of the danger. If the killer ever found out where she lived, no one around her would be safe. That could never happen. If he found her, she'd run again and hide. She'd never put anyone else in danger again.

At the hospital, they sought out Millie's doctor, finding him at one of the nurse's stations. Dr. Alejandro Navarro's Spanish good looks shocked Sam every time she saw him. Antonio Banderas had nothing on this guy. He'd been to Millie's house three times in the last month, and lived on Simpson Creek Road, not far from Perilous Cove. Millie teased that the only reason he came around was to see Sam.

"Ah, my sweet Starfire. How are you doing?" The doctor drew Star's hands to his lips as he bowed. Sam covered her grin at Star's wide eyes. Would the good doctor have performed the chivalrous kiss if he'd seen Star swipe her nose on the back of that same hand an hour ago?

Then Dr. Navarro turned to Sam. She found herself placing her hand in his.

"Samantha. Beautiful as always." Without taking his black eyes from hers, he brought her hand to his lips, and lingered...only for a moment, but what a moment. Heat coursed through her hand, up her arm, and down her spine to her toes before he released her. As he turned to Star,

Sam let out the breath she'd been holding. It was all she could do not to shiver.

"Should we go see your grandmother?" The doctor secured Star's hand in his own and led her down the hospital hallway.

Sam followed at what she hoped was a safe distance, letting her cheeks cool and berating herself for her reaction, especially when Millie lay in a hospital bed. Alejandro Navarro was confident and too handsome for his own good...or hers. She'd buried her husband barely three months ago, and here she was, getting all fluttery over a man, albeit a handsome doctor.

Dr. Navarro turned into a doorway where he urged Star ahead to see her grandmother, then waited with Sam.

"Is she going to be okay?" Sam kept her voice low so Star wouldn't hear.

His deep, rumbling, "For now," did nothing to give her confidence.

She glanced up at him, then followed his gaze to the old woman and the young girl. Millie's perpetual seaside tan was gone, replaced by a translucence that blended into the stiff white hospital sheets. When had she lost her color? Although she'd been sick before, Millie had brushed off Sam's concern with an 'I'll be fine.' But there had been other trips to the doctor in recent weeks, as well as Dr. Navarro's house visits. Millie always asked if Star could stay with Sam.

For the first time she noticed how Millie's thin white hair contrasted with Star's red tresses as the girl sat on the bed, holding her grandmother's hand and animatedly sharing her school day. Millie's face showed a mixture of contentment and sadness that Sam couldn't decipher. She didn't want to think about the meaning.

After a few minutes, she and Dr. Navarro entered the room, and he invited Star for an ice-cream cone in the cafeteria. As they passed Sam, the doctor caught her eye and nodded over his shoulder toward Millie and mouthed 'Talk' over Star's head. Sam watched them walk away on the gleaming tiles, took a deep breath for what was to come, and moved to the woman's side.

"Hello, dear." Millie smiled and took her hand. An IV line snaked from a bag of clear liquid and dripped regularly. A heart monitor beeped and displayed her pulse and blood pressure. All-too-familiar hospital smells conjured unwanted memories of Jack's brief stay in ICCU. She hated it.

Millie had always seemed larger than life, attacking everything with a head-on vigor envied by all. Sam decided to use the same direct approach.

"What is it, Millie? What's wrong?"

Millie sighed and her clear gray eyes glistened with sudden moisture. "I'm sorry, Sam." She dabbed her eyes with a tissue. "I'm dying."

Sam dropped her chin to her constricting chest, every exhale replaced by immeasurable heaviness as if the air itself contained lead. She shook her head. Please, no more death.

"It's okay, Sam."

"Okay? How can you say it's okay?" Anger welled up with her tears. "It's *not* okay." It wasn't fair. Nothing in life was fair. Everyone who meant anything to her was dead, dying, or far away.

Wasn't life meant to be happy? She wanted joy, peace, safety. Was that too much to ask? Sam rubbed the bridge of her nose. Just for a little while.

"Look at me, dear." The sudden strength in the old woman's grip brought Sam's head up. "I need you now."

Sam was certain she knew the question in Millie's mind. What she didn't know was the answer.

The driveway shells popped and crunched as Sam steered to a stop in front of the cabin's garage. Weariness pulled every molecule of Sam's being. She'd taken Star with her on two whale watching excursions today, then they'd driven to the hospital again.

"Should we sleep at your house again tonight?" she asked Star. Although Millie had improved greatly, the doctor wanted her to stay over Saturday night.

"Can we stay here at your cabin?" Star bounded out of the car to open the wooden doors. She pushed open one door and propped it open with a brick to hold it against the cold wind. Then she opened and held the other door.

Sam pulled into the garage and climbed out. With the headlights off it was pitch black, and she squeezed carefully out of the tight space, brushing along the Jeep to avoid nails in the wall where tools had once hung. She needed to find a hammer and pull them.

"I've only got the couch to sleep on, you know." Star loved the cabin, and had stayed with Rowena many times.

They hadn't eaten dinner, but Sam had pasta and sauce. She unlocked the cabin door and Star darted inside, tossing her backpack on the couch before Sam could even turn on the light.

"Whoa, it's freezing in here. Can we start a fire?"

"No, I'd rather not. I'll get the space heater out of the bedroom." She headed through the kitchen.

"I can get the wood. There's plenty stacked out by the corner." Star hopped up and down.

Sam stopped. She hadn't lit a fire since she'd moved in, though several nights had been in the low 40s. Not bone-chilling by Steerman standards, but the rock walls of the cabin oozed cold like a refrigerator, and the wind found every gap in the window frames. Her little heater couldn't keep up. She'd had the fireplace professionally inspected, but…

"Please, please, please?" Star continued to hop in anticipation. "I can do it. Gramma lets me start them almost every night."

Sam stared out the tiny kitchen window into the black night. This ten-year-old wasn't afraid of fire, and Sam knew she shouldn't be, either. She rubbed a patch of skin on her left hand, still lighter in color than the surrounding area, and turned back to the dancing girl.

"I, uh…no, I'd rather not." Sam watched the enthusiasm drain out of Star like water down a drain. She felt bad for disappointing her. "Maybe another time."

"Fine." Star's clipped retort stung as she shrugged into her coat and made for the door.

"Where are you going?"

"Home. At least it's warm there. It's always freezing in your house."

"Wait." Sam ran to the open door as the girl marched up the driveway, then spun around, hands in the air.

"I don't know how you stand it." Star dropped her arms, turned, and trudged up the incline toward Millie's.

"Star, please. Come back." But the girl continued without a backward glance, her crunching footfalls gradually swallowed in the evening fog.

Sam turned on the porch light, then eased the door shut and leaned her head against the battered wood. Who was she kidding? She had no idea how to parent a ten-year-old. Should she go after her now or wait until later? Did Star want to be alone, or was she begging for attention? If Sam had children of her own, she'd know what to do by now.

Star was probably petrified about losing her grandmother, although Millie hadn't told her the seriousness of her illness yet. But the girl was smart and picked up far more than people gave her credit. Sam saw Star's astute reading of people on the Fin Finder II. The girl instinctively knew when to offer someone something to drink, a pair of binoculars, or when to guide them quickly to the head.

Sam turned, slid down the door to the floor, and leaned her head back. The cold, soot-blackened fireplace mocked her weakness. What would Wena do? Wena would start a fire in a heartbeat. Pile on the wood. Probably throw on some gasoline to get it going quicker. Sam let out a heavy sigh. But that was Superwoman Rowena, not Samantha Riley. Even if she had taken her aunt's name, Sam didn't automatically gain Wena's spunk.

31

"*Still* no answer." Mandy snapped her cell phone closed and checked her watch for the third time in a half hour. "She can't be working on the boat in the dark."

Addison glanced over at his daughter, who, in the light of the dash gauges, looked at least eighteen tonight instead of fourteen. Her raven hair sparkled with silver glitter, and tastefully applied blue eye shadow complemented her cobalt blue strapless evening dress. Long silver and blue earrings—called shoulder dusters, she'd informed him—produced a slightly exotic look, which was, he'd also been told, exactly what she intended.

Oh, boy.

Mandy had been the hit of the Thanksgiving banquet. No sooner had they reached the threshold to the church fellowship hall, than Mandy's gait transformed from young-girl skipping enthusiasm to the elegant glide of Grace Kelly mixed with the sophisticated sway of Sofia Loren—a deadly combination. Mandy had exuded poise and confidence, and Addison had spotted half a dozen boys with their mouths hung open as he'd escorted his daughter into the church's multi-purpose room.

The decorating committee had remade the utilitarian space. Gone were the institutional fluorescent lights, hidden above miles of crisscrossed crepe paper streamers. Large artificial trees dotted with white Christmas lights forested the walls, and round tables with what must have been a hundred flickering candles bathed the room in a warm holiday glow. Cinnamon and pumpkin spiced the air, and the tantalizing aromas of turkey and stuffing floated from the buffet tables.

After dinner, Addison stood talking with a group of other dads, but his eyes watched Mandy interact with the other kids. With the girls, she was engaged, but tended to listen rather than jump into the middle of the topic. It was with the boys he noticed his daughter's completed transformation from middle school student to sophisticated woman.

With Mandy's height plus high heels, she towered over the middle school boys, but it put her eye to eye with several high school boys, all of whom had taken notice. Five of them surrounded her in a loose circle. "Holding court" popped into Addison's head as he watched her speak to each young man, sometimes inclining an eyebrow to something he said. Often when she asked one of them a question, her fingers would brush his arm. The guys lit up brighter than all the Christmas lights on the trees.

He'd watched his wife interact with people that same way: smooth confidence coupled with warmth, care, and interest. It was an irresistible combination. When Mandy excused herself and swayed away, the boys all gaped. Although she couldn't see their reactions, he saw the left side of her mouth quirk in a self-satisfied smile. He shook his head. He was in big trouble. How had she learned this stuff? It had to be genetic.

Addison heard more than one girl remark to Mandy she looked "amazing." And she did. She *was* amazing. After tonight he'd need a baseball bat by the front door to scare off the boys. Maybe he'd openly clean his gun when boys came by.

They reached the house and he turned the car into their driveway and punched the remote for the garage. "I wish your mom could have seen you tonight."

Elizabeth had died right as Mandy began to bloom into a young woman. His wife had missed so much in the last two years, and he missed sharing these special times with her. There was more he wanted to say. How beautiful his daughter was, how elegant and graceful, but the words stuck in his throat. Mandy reached over and squeezed his arm.

He drove into the garage and lowered the door behind them before getting out, not to keep out the bitter cold, but to be safe. It paid to be cautious.

"I think I'll wear this to school tomorrow," Mandy said, twirling in the gown.

"And I'll have to send SWAT in to break up the riot."

"Aww, Dad." She took his arm and laid her head on his shoulder as they walked from the garage into the kitchen.

"Time for bed, young lady." He gripped her shoulders and guided her toward her room. "School tomorrow and then we fly out Tuesday at 4:50."

"I've got to get hold of Sam. I'll try her again after I wash up. Then you try her tomorrow from work, promise?" She turned to make eye contact, ensuring a solemn oath.

"I'll call her. Now, off to bed." He hugged her goodnight, and held on a little longer than normal, painfully aware he couldn't hold on forever.

Sam closed the door to Millie's house and started down the hill. It was after ten and, though she should be exhausted from the day, she stopped at her cabin to get the book and her new flashlight before continuing down to the lighthouse.

Star's temper had evaporated with the Sunday dawn. She woke Sam and informed her it was time to get up for church. But Sam had promised Captain Tom she'd do a morning run for a group of tourists in for the holiday week. Gray whales had been spotted twice in the last few days and all the visitors were antsy to get a look.

With Star's help, they located a family to take her to church, feed her lunch, and keep her until Sam returned. In the afternoon, Sam and Star drove Millie's ancient Chevy four-door to Mission Peak to bring her home from the hospital.

Once Millie was settled in her bed, Sam left to do grocery shopping for everyone. The afternoon and evening were filled with overloaded laundry from both houses and fixing dinner. By the time she helped Millie "get a proper bath" and assisted Star with a homework assignment on Thanksgiving traditions, Sam was more than ready for some solitude.

The path to the lighthouse wasn't difficult, but there were some steep sections of timeworn stone steps. Rusty railings made the going easier. A rare November Santa Ana wind charged off the hills, carrying scents of grasses and sage, and raising the temperature into the upper sixties even at this time of night. With all moisture blown far out to sea, stars shone like diamonds scattered against the obsidian sky. Usually ocean mist or a distant fog bank created a wide demarcation between sky and sea, but tonight, stars gleamed down to the water's sharp horizon. A high, half moon painted a sparkling highway across the water, right to the foot of the cliff.

Sam left the flashlight off and, aided only by moonlight, circled the base of the tower and ducked under the railing. Two jumps down was her favorite rock, a relatively flat block of dark granite the size of her Jeep. She tucked her sweatshirt under her bottom to insulate the cold stone and dangled her feet over the edge. More large rocks slanted at a steep angle, plunging into the silver water.

Until three months ago, her life in Steerman had been wholly predictable. A steady job, a good friend, a husband who…well, she was no longer sure what Jack had felt for her—or her for him for that matter. She didn't have one picture of them together, or even of him alone. All had been burned. Her previous life was fading just a little, the memories not quite as distinct, as if her new surroundings and life were overlaying the old. Maybe that's the way it always was, why time healed.

Had she and Jack been in love? She pinched the bridge of her nose, remembering the weeks leading up to their wedding, the ceremony. She couldn't recall feeling swept off her feet or all lovey-dovey. Getting married had seemed the right thing to do at the time. Would she do it again the same way?

Sam blew out a breath. She didn't want to go there. Probably no one would do things the same way if they had the chance for a do-over. Best to focus on the future. But now, just when she thought she had a slight grip on things, her life was spinning out of control again.

Millie was dying…said she had maybe a few months to live before the cancer took her. She refused to discuss the specifics of her illness, only saying she had decided not to continue the treatments that made her so sick.

"I'm an old woman, Sam, nearly eighty-one. I'll hit that milestone if I make it to January 22nd. No guarantees there, though." Millie's laugh shocked Sam.

"Don't talk like that, Millie, please. I can't bear it."

"Sam, honey, come here." Millie scooted over and motioned her to the bed. Sam crawled up on the bed and leaned her head on the old woman's shoulder. "Listen. We all die—some sooner, some later. I'm one of the later ones, but no one escapes forever. It's all part of God's plan."

Sam picked at pills on the chenille bedspread. "God's plan sucks."

They lay quietly for a while until Millie spoke softly. "You're scared, aren't you?"

She nodded, unable to think about Millie gone from this house. Everything about it testified to her life. Her art covered walls and tables in vibrant color, the color of life and vitality.

"Starfire is, too. And for that I'm truly sorry." Millie shifted higher against the headboard. "I want to show you something. Hand me my Bible there on my nightstand."

Sam retrieved the book. Its cracked cover reminded her of Billy's Bible. It still sat on her living room table. When she'd called Walter and Rowena to say she found it, they asked her to keep it and read through their son's margin notes and underlined verses. She'd gotten as far as Psalms.

"Now, where are my glasses?" Millie found them in the pocket of the sweater she wore even in bed, and began flipping pages in the book. Finally she mumbled to herself and looked up at Sam. "You remember that old song about 'To every thing there is a season'?"

"The Byrds. I had their album." Sam smiled at the memory of the treasured vinyl record, full of clicks and pops from constant play. It had been one of her first. What had become of it?

"Weird name for a group, but they got those lyrics right out of the Bible, did you know that?

Sam shook her head.

"Look here." Millie handed Sam the book and pointed to the words with her finger. "Read."

Sam read. "To every thing there is a season, and a time to every purpose under the heaven: A time to be born, and a time to die; a time to plant, and a—"

"Okay, that's enough. You get the point, don't you, hon? We all have a time in life. I've had a good *long* time. Now, I'm not anxious to leave you and Starfire, but I *am* anxious to see my Darryl in heaven." Millie painfully adjusted herself again in the bed, then pointed to the book. "Take that home and read it again. And read verse eleven a bunch of times. Do it for me, okay?"

Sam had promised to read the verses, but refused to take Millie's well-loved Bible, saying she had one of her own.

Waves slapped the rocks below as Sam clicked on the flashlight and opened the Bible to Ecclesiastes chapter three. She almost didn't need to read it since she'd played the song so many times on her record player.

The words in Billy's Bible were slightly different than Millie's, but the meaning was the same. When she scanned down to verse eleven, it was one not in the song's lyrics.

"He has made everything beautiful in its time. He has also set eternity in the human heart; yet no one can fathom what God has done from beginning to end."

She reread it, then turned off the flashlight, pondering the meaning. The passage clearly talked about God, but what did it mean that he set eternity in the hearts of men?

A glimmer of silver in the moonlight caught her attention and she focused on the spot a mile or so out. A cloud of spray, then another, marked a pod of Gray whales migrating south. She sighed as the silent beasts moved beyond the slice of moonlight into the vast darkness. They had purpose and a destination. The cows headed to Baja to give birth. Then, in the spring they would turn north for a summer of raising their young and feasting in the bountiful northern Pacific.

What did she have?

Sam rested her elbows on her knees and watched the swells rolling in, one after another, some bigger, some smaller. They began somewhere far out in the Pacific and traveled thousands of miles to dash themselves on the rocks below, quietly tonight, but sometimes in thunderous crashes that inundated this rock and threw water halfway up the lighthouse tower.

She realized her life was much the same as these swells. She'd traveled two thousand miles, running from danger and uncertainty, only to land on these same rocks. Just as the waves couldn't go any further, neither could she. There was nowhere else to run. She only hoped her life wouldn't be smashed on the unforgiving boulders like these waves. And if God had some kind of grand plan—that "no one can fathom what God has done from beginning to end" thing—she had no idea what it could be.

- 32 -

On Monday morning, Addison hung up the phone after his fifth attempt to reach Sam, irrationally angry with her for not having an answering machine. They were flying out tomorrow afternoon and he had mountains of work to complete before leaving. Cap had grudgingly given him the time off for the holiday, but that didn't mean he could slack off for one second. He did wish he could connect with Sam. Now that he'd made the decision to go, he felt like a giddy high school kid at the thought of seeing her.

Dummy. He shook his head and pulled another thick file off the foot-high stack. In the next hour, he filled ten legal pad pages with an outline summary of the investigation and the evidence used to convict one Malcom Foley of rape and attempted murder. The DA's office already had the trial transcripts.

Arnie worked across from him at his own desk, searching through file after file until he broke for lunch and to run down another case. "See you later, partner," Arnie called as he left the room. Addison kept working.

These were the last of the DNA review cases and Addison had a briefing appointment at the District Attorney's office tomorrow morning. After finishing the reviews, Addison pulled his keyboard close and began typing up summaries for each case.

Someone in the hallway yelled goodnight and Addison glanced at the clock, shocked to see it was five fifteen. Sharon approached with three new folders and an apologetic smile. Her purse hung over her shoulder and she had her coat on, ready to go home. It didn't look like Addison would be so lucky.

He stood to stretch his aching neck and shoulder muscles as Arnie hurried into the room.

"Hey, partner. Got good news." Arnie waved a red folder at him and tossed it on his desk.

Addison arched an eyebrow and flipped open the cover.

"A finger print from the garage of the Clayton home showed up in a burglary in Easton three days ago. Lab boys and girls matched it today when they ran it."

Addison quickly read through the faxed lab report while Sharon and Arnie chatted. The print had been lifted off an ice pick found behind a toolbox in the corner of the Clayton garage. The arson report had concluded the ice pick had been used to puncture the gas tanks. Arnie continued his briefing.

"Guy's name is Tarz Broderick. Alias Ned Crane. Lives in Arkansas, down by Pine Bluff."

"Have they found him yet?"

"That's the good news. He's in the hospital in Easton right now. He tripped a burglar alarm and the police arrived at the house before he left with the loot. Fell from the second story balcony off the master and whacked his head on the sidewalk. Bad concussion."

"Let's go." Addison grabbed his coat and they ran past Sharon for the door. On the drive to Easton, he called Mandy to let her know he'd be late and that he hadn't been able to reach Sam. Arnie called the Sergeant at the Easton PD to let them know they were on their way. The Sergeant arranged for one of their detectives to be present at the hospital.

They hit rush hour traffic at its worst and crawled through the streets of Steerman and then Easton. Addison pounded his palm on the steering wheel in frustration. Even with the strobe light flashing on top of their unmarked car, the traffic clogged the narrow downtowns of both cities. The drivers who bothered to take note of the flashing beacon often had nowhere to go to get out of the detectives' way.

An hour and thirty-five minutes later, Addison turned into the parking lot of Easton Hospital, only to be greeted by several other police cars, fire trucks, ambulances, and other police vehicles, their lights flashing, too.

"Oh, boy." Arnie unsnapped his seatbelt and jumped out. "This can't be good."

Addison clamped his jaw at his partner's typical understatement and followed him through the tangled barricade of emergency vehicles.

To the right, in a cordoned off area away from the building, they saw dozens of hospital workers with patients in beds or wheelchairs, some clinging weakly to IV stands, their thin gowns gaping in the back. Police officers ran from the building clutching armloads of blankets and towels, and began distributing them to the staff and patients, some of whom were barefoot. Ground fog obscured the more distant street lights, and Addison estimated the temperature to be in the low forties.

He and Arnie entered by the main doors of the building. An officer with hand on his gun checked their ID and pointed them to a gray-haired man in uniform standing in a group at one side of the lobby. As they approached, he acknowledged them with a nod, but continued his instructions to the other officers. Arnie and Addison stood back until he finished and the men had hurried off in several directions.

The gray-haired man introduced himself as Lieutenant Paulson. "You're here to see Broderick?" With their nods, the man sighed and waved them to the lobby seating area. Two men with face shields and Bomb Squad written on their heavy jackets came out one hall and headed down another.

"Bomb threat?" Arnie asked.

Paulson nodded. "Call came in about forty-five minutes ago. Anonymous caller, of course. From a payphone in Steerman."

Steerman. Addison had a bad feeling about the whole situation. "Find anything?"

"Dozens of staff backpacks, hundreds of boxes of supplies." He rubbed his face. "Do you have any idea how many cardboard boxes there are in a facility this size?"

Easton's hospital was at least twice as big as Nickerson Memorial in Steerman. Last year, Addison had participated in the hospital's emergency preparedness drill, which included a bomb search. It had proved daunting to search every room, storage closet, AC vent, bathroom, stairway, and office, as well as have dogs sniff all the cars in the parking lot. This job was a whole lot bigger.

"The first units responded in three minutes. By that time...well, it wasn't chaos by any means, but staff had patients in the halls, elevators, and stairways, herding everyone to the exits." He paused and his glance flicked from Addison to Arnie and back. "Somehow in all the confusion,

Broderick disappeared."

Anger boiled in Addison's gut. This was their first significant connection to someone suspicious in the Clayton case and these guys let him get away? "Weren't you guarding him?"

Tendon's bulged in Paulson's neck at the implied accusation and he growled, "Of *course* we were guarding him."

Arnie's soft question cut through the tension. "Can you tell us what happened?"

Paulson relaxed a bit and explained what they knew. The guard at Broderick's door had hurried to help an elderly patient who had fallen a few yards away. She'd broken her arm in the hurry to get out of the building.

"He was only away for a couple of minutes until a nurse and doctor took over. When he looked in the room, Broderick was gone." Paulson told them an APB had been issued, but many of the city's police were here at the hospital. Besides searching for a bomb, they'd checked every room for the fugitive, but without luck.

Ten minutes later, Addison and Arnie were in their car headed back to Steerman.

"Lucky break for Broderick, that bomb threat."

Addison glanced at his partner in the car's dim interior. "Yeah, right. Real lucky."

"What?" Arnie's eyebrows rose in mock surprise. "You think maybe it wasn't a *coincidence*? Like maybe he had outside help?"

Addison snorted at the rhetorical questions. The obvious conclusion brought a new potential threat. If Broderick was the murderer in the Clayton case, he likely had an accomplice they hadn't known about. That meant Sam could be in double the danger.

"Penny for your thoughts." The soft, male voice came out of the night, a whisper just above the beat of the surf.

Sam sucked in a breath and dropped the flashlight, which bounced into a crevasse and winked out. "Who's there?" Her voice trembled in the frigid air. She'd come back to the lighthouse rocks tonight after another long day of back-to-back whale watching tours and helping Millie and Star. But last night's relative balmy warmth had given way to more typical November weather, and she clutched her jacket tight at her throat.

A dark form moved to the rock next to hers, but she couldn't make out a face in the cloud-obscured moonlight. "I'm sorry I startled you, Samantha," said the slightly accented voice. The shape moved to the rocks below and, after some fumbling around, a light clicked on, illuminating the face of Dr. Alejandro Navarro.

"Dr. Navarro. What are you doing out here?" Sam tried to slow her breathing. The cold air burned her throat. For one horrifying moment, she'd pictured the killer's mug shot—Tarz Broderick, as she knew him now from the overnight envelope Addison had sent. Revitalized nightmares interrupted her sleep, and she exercised more each day to wear out her body. If it had been him tonight, she'd rather jump into the churning sea than stay here on the rocks.

"One could ask the same question of you, I suppose." He smiled and handed her the flashlight.

Sudden panic gripped her. "Did something happen to Millie? Is she all right?" Sam scrambled to rise, but he motioned her back down.

"No, no. Millie's fine. I just left her." He pointed toward the rock beside her. "May I?" She hesitated, then nodded and scooted over. The flat surface wasn't large and she felt his body heat through her jeans.

"Dr. Navarro, I—"

"Please, call me Alejandro." His deep voice rumbled warmth that seemed to push back the night chill. "What were you reading?"

Sam looked down to the book in her hand and clicked off the flashlight, for some reason embarrassed at being caught reading the Bible. "Oh. I, uh...Millie wanted me to read some Bible verses."

"Ah, yes."

Sam sensed his understanding nod. Maybe he was a Christian like Millie. "Do you read the Bible?"

He paused before answering. "I did, once."

He didn't elaborate. She didn't know him well enough to ask more. They sat in silence for a few minutes, listening to the crashing waves thirty feet below. On the incoming tide, the waves reached further up the embankment with each passing minute, throwing an occasional spray high enough to touch their faces.

Sam licked her lips and tasted salt. "I don't understand it very well."

He offered no comment, only a 'hmmm.'

She smiled. "Did they teach you that at doctor school?"

"What?"

"The 'hmmm.' You're very proficient." The parting clouds allowed enough moonlight to see his spreading grin.

"I received an A grade in that class."

Her laughter turned to a squeal as a large wave peppered their clothes and faces. Alejandro took her cold hand and rubbed it between his two warm ones, and then he helped her to her feet. She shook water from her hair and jacket.

"We'd better head back before the next set," he said, and guided her up the two large rocks to the concrete walkway circling the base of the lighthouse. Alejandro tucked her arm through his and covered her hand with his own as they skirted the tower.

He began talking as they slowly climbed the steps toward her cabin. His family had come from Spain and Portugal, settling in California around 1900. His grandparents worked on cattle ranches, eventually buying their own spread. Over the years, they added to their holdings and, when Alejandro's father grew up, he took over the biggest of the enterprises and expanded even more. They now ran over three thousand head of livestock.

Alejandro was the first in his family to graduate from college. While his two brothers took over the running of the ranch, his mother pushed him toward medical school. She wanted a doctor in the family and now proudly bragged to all the ladies at her beauty shop about her handsome son the doctor.

They reached Sam's cabin and walked to the door on the uphill side. The weak porch light pushed back the night in a yellow circle, and the building sheltered them from the onshore wind. Though they had stopped, Alejandro kept her arm tucked in his.

"You never answered my question." Sam felt his thumb rubbing small circles on the back of her hand. His touch, though intimate, didn't bother her. What *did* bother her was the memory that Jack hadn't touched her like that for years. Maybe never.

"What question was that, Samantha?" Alejandro's smile hovered only inches above. She loved the way he extended the last 'a' in her name, adding a beauty to it lost in the more typical chopped-off pronunciation.

"Why you came down to the light house tonight," she reminded him.

"Oh, yes, that question." He smiled and released her arm, only to capture both her hands in his—Bible, flashlight and all. "I sometimes come down here after a long day. The ocean gives one a sense of life and vitality, don't you think?"

She nodded.

"But that's not the only reason I came tonight. I have to confess that I stopped here at your cabin first. When I didn't find you at home, I decided to look for you at the lighthouse."

"Look for me? Why?"

"I wanted to invite you to my family's ranch for Thanksgiving dinner."

"Oh." Sam's heart speeded up and her palms became damp. She hoped he couldn't tell. His invitation caught her off guard. She hardly knew the man and wasn't sure she wanted to begin anything. Thanksgiving day sounded like a date, and she was still morning the loss of her old life. Plus, she needed to stay and help Millie. There was no way she should go.

"I, uh, well I'd love to, but I—"

"I invited Millie and Starfire, too. They're coming."

She looked up in surprise. "They are?" Then a smile touched the corners of her mouth. "Do you invite all your patients?"

He shook his head.

Sam gazed up into the dark pools of his eyes. They held no humor now, only intense seriousness.

"I hope you will join us."

Sam licked her suddenly dry lips. "I...well, I...uh." She looked down at their hands until she felt him give a little tug.

"Will you?"

- 33 -

Tuesday began at dawn for Addison as he and Arnie were assigned the investigation of a barroom knife fight that ended up with one person in critical condition. Interviews with the bartender, grouchy hung-over patrons, and the barely conscious victim, led to an arrest mid-morning. They found the suspect snoring loudly in his pickup, parked in the littered alley behind a liquor store. Empty cans from a six-pack were scattered across the rubber floor mats. His inebriated state required a four-man carry to the waiting patrol car. Addison and his partner were glad they didn't have to drive him to the station—those molded plastic rear seats served a purpose when the cleaning crew got the cars.

Addison hurried through the remainder of his work, triaging files into piles of those that could wait as opposed to those needing immediate attention. Arnie had agreed to cover for him during the holiday. At the last second, he sped across town to pick up Mandy.

"Did you reach Sam, Dad?" Mandy tossed her backpack into the back seat and slammed the door. Their suitcases were already in the car, so Addison headed straight to the airport.

"No. I didn't have a moment to even try her."

Mandy rolled her eyes and gave him her 'Da-ad!' response, then dug out her cell phone and punched the numbers. A moment later she closed the phone, shoulders sagging. "Still no answer. Where could she be? I haven't talked to her in almost a week."

"Probably working. Remember she said the whales were showing up off the coast, so the tours will be filling up. We'll keep trying her right up until we board the airplane."

Sam had always been easy to reach, and now nothing, day or night. Tomorrow was Wednesday and they had a full day planned of visiting relatives and friends at Storm Lake. But maybe they'd have better luck contacting her.

Sam pushed through the door to the Last Drop and slumped into a vacant stool at the counter. From the other end of the counter, Connie spotted her and held up a pot of regular coffee, questioning with his eyebrows. She nodded, not willing to wait for anything he'd need to concoct, mix or blend.

"Tough morning?" He produced an extra large mug for her and filled it to the brim. She took a grateful sip before answering.

"The worst. Rough seas, two very seasick tourists, and a seven-year-old boy who overflowed the boat's head with a whole roll of toilet paper."

Connie chuckled, replaced his coffee pot on the warmer, and leaned on the counter. "And that, young lady," he pointed a stir stick at her, "is why I don't go out on tour boats." He rubbed his white stubble and launched into one of his famous stories, this one about a cross-country car trip as a boy where their family dog had gotten sick in the back of the station wagon. By the time he finished, she was laughing so hard she'd all but forgotten her own queasy stomach.

The noon crowd had cleared out of the Last Drop and only one of the tiny front tables was occupied. Captain Tom had another run in an hour, and she told Connie she had to go find something to eat. She didn't want to climb back on the boat with an empty stomach.

"Wait right here." Connie ducked into the back room and reappeared with two Styrofoam cups and a container from Maxine's. He peeled back the lid and revealed thick, creamy clam chowder.

Sam sat up straight. "Connie, that's *your* lunch. I can't eat it."

"Shush. Maxine always doubles my order." He winked. "I think she has a crush on me." Connie filled the two cups and passed her a spoon.

The first bite caused Sam to close her eyes in ecstasy as the chunky soup rolled across her tongue. "Oh, man. That is *so* good." Maxine always used fresh cream and butter from a local dairy farmer. Sam could almost feel the cellulite spreading to her thighs, but she scooped another spoonful.

"Oops, almost forgot." Connie reached under the counter and pulled out a container of oyster crackers.

Sam took a handful and sprinkled them on the soup. After another bite she waved her spoon at him. "You're the best, Connie."

"That's what Maxine says, too."

She laughed with her friend, and shared her own story of how Tom's dog, Blew, whined and jumped into his owner's lap when the head overflowed.

When they scraped the bottom of the soup container, she thanked Connie again and said she wanted to check on Millie before the next excursion.

The wind whipped her hair and reddened her cheeks as she hurried along Harbor Street, inwardly amazed at the friendships she'd developed in Perilous Cove. Since the beginning of her marriage, friendships had been few and far between. Jack said he dealt with people all day and he wanted peace and quiet at home. She couldn't remember the last time they'd had anyone over for dinner. Yet, in the three months she'd lived here, she'd become friends with several people, enjoyed dinner at their houses, laughed together, and had people on whom she could depend if needed.

She suspected Millie instigated some of the invitations and drop-offs of an occasional casserole or zucchini bread, especially during those early weeks as she healed from her injuries—both visible and hidden. At first, it had been uncomfortable for her to accept gifts from complete strangers, but she'd grown to realize caring for others was normal for this small town and she longed for the day when she could reciprocate.

Of course, there were some in town who seemed to distrust her. Kitty Epstein frowned at her every time they passed on a sidewalk or met in a store. And Sam had seen the woman whispering to her friend, Helen something-or-other, while tactlessly inclining her head in Sam's direction. Even Captain Tom's wife, Trudy, had given her several hard looks when she'd shown up at the house once. Maybe it was the chopped hair or the fading burn scars and broken foot. Whatever caused the suspicion or outright dislike, she supposed *some* small town people would also be small-minded. Although maybe that wasn't too different in larger cities too.

As she hiked up the hill toward Millie's, wind buffeted the grass and shrubs along the path to Millie's, blowing fine sand along the ground. Beyond the bluff, whitecaps marched on the steel-gray sea, and she gazed longingly at her cabin down the point. She secretly hoped the afternoon tour group would cancel, freeing her to curl up under a quilt in the cabin. She sighed, weary from late nights and double tours during the days. At least Tom had declared Thanksgiving a day off.

- 34 -

As nasty as Wednesday had been, Thanksgiving Day was glorious. Alejandro had offered to drive Sam to the ranch when he'd picked up Millie and Star—but she said she'd like to drive out a little later, so asked for directions. She'd pretended not to notice the slight frown on his handsome face. The man could be a bit pushy at times.

Sam spent the morning catching up on laundry for the three of them, and between loads she went for a run. There was a 10K coming up on the first of December and, although she'd never been a runner, on a whim she had signed up. The last three weeks had been killers, but her body felt stronger than ever before.

Doing well against the other competitors wasn't particularly important. Testing her limits mattered more, so she ran every morning, rain, fog, or shine. Mostly it was fog, and she would return to her cabin soaked to the skin. But she was up to four miles a day, and some days she did that twice.

While waiting for a load to dry at Millie's, she walked down to the Last Drop to visit with Connie before he closed for the day. Town was quiet and, after a few minutes, Maxine came in with her homemade rum cake.

"The secret," Maxine's chuckle shook her generous curves, "is three parts rum to one part everything else. That way they don't remember if it tasted good or bad."

The three chatted over coffee and the scrumptious cake, so rich, Connie said, it should be illegal. Sam agreed, feeling a little woozy after the heaping portion. Maybe all the alcohol hadn't baked out like it was supposed to.

At ten o'clock Sam backed the Jeep out of the garage and folded the ragged top down. Dust and water splotches marked the vehicle's hood, evidence of leaks in the garage roof. She'd have to call someone to fix it. Of course, since she didn't have money to hire anyone, maybe she'd have to do it herself. There could be a toolbox hiding in the cellar of the cabin—if she could get up the nerve to search down there. She had yet to call the exterminator and, as far as she was concerned, the basement was the rat's domain.

Though sunny, there was a chill in the air, so she pulled on her hooded parka to keep the wind off her neck. The Jeep chugged and bucked until it warmed up. She found a radio station playing salsa and tropical music as she pulled out of the driveway.

Sam turned north, then east as she followed the directions written in Alejandro's strong script. Fortunately he'd made his typical doctor scrawl neater than usual, and she didn't have trouble reading the several road names as she drove inland on narrow country trails, climbing into the foothills on deserted back roads. Probably most families were already together, cooking up feasts and playing games.

Coast live oaks dotted the hills and pastures on each side, their hunter green foliage standing out against the tan grasses or plowed fields. Many of the stately trees were draped with mistletoe or Spanish moss. Poison oak in its fading crimson guarded the trunks. That and the occasional maple or poplar was the moderate west coast's feeble attempt at autumn colors.

At one curve she braked to let a group of wild turkeys meander across the road. The large birds were thinner and taller compared to their store-bought, unlucky cousins, and were in no hurry to let her pass. Two large males sported featherless red heads with fleshy caruncles. Though they didn't seem the least concerned about her idling vehicle, the males' eyes never stopped scanning the surrounding ditches and brush, keeping watch for foxes, wildcats, or coyotes.

Sam pushed back the parka and leaned against the headrest, letting the sun warm her face. She closed her eyes, watching the sun-dappled shadows move on her eyelids as the light filtered through overhead trees. The air smelled of moist grass, crushed leaves, wood smoke, and rich earth. She'd never owned a convertible, and one nice thing about having the top down was all the smells.

She loved her job as tour guide. Maybe she'd grow tired of it in a year or two and want a break, but it was great right now. She'd seen a position advertised for a guide at the nature museum in Blue Rock Harbor that intrigued her. A large outcropping of tide pools covered the shore at the base of the museum, making it a regular destination for tour groups and school field trips. She smiled at the thought of working with a team of people who loved nature, again wondering why she'd wasted years of her life working in office jobs.

Finally, the last of the turkeys ducked through the barbed wire fence on the other side of the road and she drove on, watching for half-hidden road signs and indicated landmarks.

The entrance to Alejandro's parents' ranch was unassuming, marked by a simple sign on a timber crossbeam on two tall poles: Casa Navarro. After winding up a long driveway, which looped around a steep hill, she wheeled the Jeep into a graveled parking area beside a dozen other cars and pickups.

White puffy clouds dotted a cobalt sky, giving dimension and perspective to the fantastic view from Alejandro's family home. Broad, rough-hewn plank stairs led up to a porch fully ten feet deep and as wide as the front of the house. Instead of knocking on the arched door, Sam walked along the covered porch, trailing her hand along the log railing, polished smooth by many generations of family and visitors.

California's famous golden hills and scattered oak trees stretched as far as she could see. The elegant adobe house stood on a terraced hill and faced southwest, garnering the warmth of the weak sun. After three months of the sea's comforting background noise, she was struck by the whispering silence. Crickets, the soft swish of grass, and an occasional meadowlark were the loudest sounds. A screech drew her attention to a red-tail hawk soaring high above. Squinting, she could make out its russet tail.

"Did you know their eyesight is eight times stronger than ours?"

Sam jumped sideways. "Alejandro. Do you always sneak up on people?" He had a way of invading her personal space that felt just a little uncomfortable, but she hoped the tone of her words didn't sound harsh.

"I'm sorry, Samantha. I didn't mean to surprise you. I heard you drive up." His smile seemed relaxed, and his dark eyes stared down at her. No.

They smoldered. She'd always wondered how the male characters in romance novels could have smoldering gazes. Dr. Alejandro Navarro was the poster child for the look.

She turned back to the hawk and watched as it swooped behind a distant oak. Alejandro's hand covered her own where she leaned on the railing.

"I came to ask if you would like to go riding with Starfire and me. Also, my sister is anxious to get back in the saddle."

Sam didn't want to lead the man on; she had no desire to date anyone. But she had to admit, he had a certain magnetism that drew her, and she liked his gentle, gracious manner, passed down, no doubt, from his parents.

Plus, there was that whole smoldering gaze thing he had going. Finally she nodded.

"Let me introduce you to everyone before we go."

He had arrived early and situated Millie in a comfortable chair near the bustle of the kitchen where she could interact with the women. Dinner was scheduled for two, and a whole team of family crowded the massive kitchen to help Alejandro's mother prepare the dishes. In five minutes, Sam met two-dozen brothers, sisters, aunts, uncles and a raft of cousins of all ages. She'd never keep them straight. However, she noticed Star already seemed to know everyone.

Glorious smells made her stomach rumble. Kids crowded around a credenza loaded with tortillas and six kinds of homemade salsa. Sam managed to snag one of the warm tortillas and stuff it in her mouth before she let Alejandro lead her down the gravel path toward the barn.

The first hundred feet was shaded by a wide arbor, encased by thick grape vines holding the last of their autumn leaves. Here and there shriveled bunches of dark purple grapes hung from the branches.

"As kids, we used to sit here in the cool shade on a hot day, picking and eating our fill." Alejandro fingered one of the clusters. "Did you know that even on days well over one hundred degrees, grapes remain cool as long as they are still on the vine?"

She *did* know that, but didn't reply, rather let him lead her toward the barn.

Star's excited laughter greeted them before they reached the wide barn doors. Inside, the odor of sweet hay permeated the warm air, and they found Star with Alejandro's younger sister, Pilar, and her daughter Rainya.

"Where are the rest of the kids?" Sam expected the dozen other grandchildren and cousins to be clamoring for horseback rides.

"One of the ranch hands hooked up a wagon behind a tractor for a hayride to the pond. We'll meet them there." Pilar lifted a saddle from its rack and swung it over the back of a huge brown horse, then expertly fastened the straps and buckles.

Sam's riding experience was limited to a couple times in college and, had she known of the hayride before, might have opted for it instead of the horse. But Star's enthusiasm was contagious.

Soon they were all mounted and Pilar led them out of the back of the barn and through a corral. Rainya and Star followed next with Alejandro and Sam bringing up the rear. For the next few minutes they wound around hills, through barbed wire gates, and alongside plowed fields. The November rains had been enough to dampen the dust, but not to create mud. The high sun warmed the air so that Sam pulled off her sweatshirt and tied it around her waist.

The side-to-side swaying and the creaking leather fit perfectly among chirping birds and occasional dashing squirrel. The tangy sage and dry grass made her nose itch, but the smells drew her close to the land as much as the salt air connected her with the sea. Although very different from each other, each reminded her of life's vitality, its preciousness. Something to be held tenaciously. When she thought how close she'd come to...

A cloud blocked the sun and a shiver ran through Sam.

"Cold?"

Sam looked across. Alejandro had been watching. Was he so observant to notice her slightest discomfort? What woman wouldn't want a man tuned to her every need? How long had it been since someone had cared for her so? She answered with a smile, and tilted her head back as the sun reemerged.

Pilar broke into a gallop, and the two girls followed in quick pursuit. The horses were ready to run and Alejandro and Sam surged ahead. Surprised by the power of the beast under her, Sam held tight to the saddle horn and eyed the ground speeding by far below. The thunder of five horses' hooves mixed with the girls' shrieks and laughter, but Sam's concentration was focused on staying in the bouncing saddle that seemed at odds with her body and pounded her relentlessly. Alejandro edged in front of her horse. He reined his steed to a walk and Sam's thankfully took the hint and fell into step. Alejandro fell back alongside.

"Sorry," she apologized. "I'm not much of a rider."

Alejandro smiled. "Pilar practically grew up in the saddle and rode all over these hills until she moved to San Jose a few years ago. When she visits, she rides as much as possible. Rainya, too."

"Did you ride a lot?" Although she'd met at least twenty-five of his family members, she still didn't know the man beside her.

"Cattle ranching requires constant patrols, so we often rode seven days a week, checking fences and herds. We used vehicles as well, but if the weather was good, we took the horses. It gets in your blood." He paused to observe the two girls far ahead. "Star is a natural."

"I wonder if she's ridden before?"

He grinned. "This is her first time."

Sam slumped in the saddle. How did he know that? Again she felt like an outsider, skimming along the surface of the lives surrounding her. She'd grown so detached from family and friends, she'd forgotten how to get to know people. Well, that wasn't completely fair, but it still felt that way sometimes.

Thirty minutes later they reached the pond, a two-acre body of water surrounded by gentle hills. Alejandro helped her down and she stretched stiff joints. Though glad to be on foot again, it felt as odd to walk as it did stepping onto the dock from the Fin Finder II. Strange that a ride on a horse and a boat had similarities.

Star and Rainya were already running to join the other kids in their contest to see who could throw rocks the furthest out into the water. Sam resisted the urge to tell Star to be careful with the rocks, something Sam's mother would have done. Sam always hated that, especially when Mom did it in front of friends. Besides, she wasn't Star's mother.

"You're frowning."

"Am I?" She ducked her head. "Just old memories."

"Bad ones." It wasn't a question.

"Not all bad. Are you always so observant, or is it a doctor thing?"

He responded by stroking his chin and muttering his best doctor's "Hmmm," and she laughed at the seriousness of his expression.

The ranch worker who had driven the tractor offered them coffee from a thermos, and Alejandro led her to a bench near the shore where they watched the children make up new games. Two ranch dogs had come along for the ride and romped happily among the kids. It was only a matter of time before one of the kids tossed a stick into the water and the dogs leapt in to fetch it. They paddled to shore and much doggy shaking and squealing followed as water flew.

Sam had been an only child, as was Star. What would it be like to grow up with five brothers and sisters like Alejandro had, plus cousins galore? She'd never known this free-for-all play with a family group.

Pilar grabbed a cup of coffee and strode toward the bench in her calf-hugging, brown leather boots. She possessed the beauty of a model, complete with luxurious black hair, a tall curvaceous body, and a flawless olive complexion. She settled beside Sam and tilted her face to the sun. Without opening her eyes, she asked Sam what she did for a living.

"Well, right now I'm a guide on a whale watching tour boat."

Pilar's lifted a brow and she turned one eye to Sam. "Now that's something you don't hear everyday." She closed her eye again. "Tell me more."

Sam told of her experiences these last few weeks, of the whales migrating south, of the otters, dolphins and seals. It was the first time she'd explained her job to a stranger, and she realized how proud she was of what she did as well as how much she'd learned.

Of course she'd talked to people in Perilous Cove about her work, but it was familiar to them. They lived by the sea, and the tour industry brought a lot of income to the small community. Pilar asked about the animals, and Sam tried not to sound like she was reading from her narration notes. Alejandro asked questions of his own and the time passed too quickly. A sharp whistle by the ranch hand alerted them it was time to head back.

As much as Star wanted to ride again, she wanted to experience everything. Eventually she and Rainya traded with two boys, and the girls climbed into the hay wagon. When Sam's rear settled onto the hard saddle, she wished she'd thought of that, too. She looked around, wondering if it was too late to change, but Alejandro swung into his own saddle and turned his horse after the other three. With a sigh, Sam followed, feeling every fall of the beast's four hooves. She'd never again complain about Billie's rough ride.

Thanksgiving at the Navarro homestead was a wonder. Sam lost count, but at least thirty-five people eventually crowded into the ranch house dining room and adjoining screened porch. Open French doors connected the rooms and provided the perfect setting for family and friends. Ages ranged from five to ninety-three, the oldest being Alejandro's maternal grandmother.

Sam watched the table interactions with interest. Cousins traded stories, adults asked questions of young people and gave attention to their answers, and everyone laughed while passing overflowing dishes. There was no kids' table. Star sat next to one of Alejandro's elderly aunts and had the woman laughing over something she said. The woman tousled Star's red curls, freed today from her de rigueur ponytail.

Several people offered toasts to family and friends: for births, marriages, and in one case in memory for a cousin who died. They celebrated their family and all its growth and changes through the years. Spanish and English seemed interchangeable, often in the same sentence, but no one had trouble understanding the intent.

Sam's childhood had been so different it seemed she must have grown up on another planet. On the rare occasion families did gather, kids were relegated to a card table in the kitchen or another room away from the adults, and asked to 'go play' while the grown-ups talked. It wasn't unfriendly, but it lacked the warmth and generational connectedness of the Navarro clan. Around this table was one of Sam's dreams: being married and part of a large family.

Jack's family had been far worse than her own, and she shivered at the memories. Formal dinners held little conversation. Long silences filled by clinking silverware and muffled throat clearing into ironed linen napkins. Meals were served by mute maids—no passing of dishes allowed.

Anything unusual elicited a glare from Hilde, and Sam had nearly been afraid to eat for fear she would use the wrong spoon or her trembling hand would overturn her crystal water goblet like she had during their first dinner with Jack's parents. That foible had brought a blistering reproof for her clumsiness from Hilde. But Jack's lack of defense hurt her much more than the woman's words. He had simply grunted and continued eating as one of the staff mopped up the mess.

Alejandro whispered in her ear. "Is anything wrong?"

Sam saw the concern on his face and shook her head, forcing a smile. "No, nothing's wrong." Under the table he separated her damp, clenched hands and took one in his own.

She loosened her jaw and rolled her shoulders as Alejandro's brother stood to offer a toast to his grandmother and his parents. His tribute was one of honor and thanks for their legacy, a shining example for these families who loved each other, through good and bad times. He kissed each of the three on the cheek before raising his glass high. Tears ran from Sam's eyes as she touched her glass to others around her and sipped. The three family heads basked in the honor. There was no embarrassment.

Sam swallowed past the lump in her throat. Would anyone pay her a tribute like this someday? Would she have a family surrounding her? Maybe not as many as this crowd, spilling into two large rooms, but at least someone who loved her?

Or would she be alone, eating a microwaved turkey dinner in a freezing cabin?

- 35 -

"Let's drive to Perilous Cove, Dad."

Addison grinned at Mandy's impatience to see Sam, but had to admit he was as anxious as his daughter, though for another reason. He didn't want to cause her concern, but their inability to connect with Sam worried him. Once Mandy and Sam had begun talking by phone, never more than a few days passed without a call one direction or the other. He glanced at his watch and saw it was nearly nine thirty and they'd just finished a leisurely breakfast at Ben's.

"Okay."

The resulting whoop from Mandy brought Ben from the kitchen just as she ran by and up the stairs.

"Something wrong?"

"Nope." Addison rose from the couch. "We're going to drive down to Perilous Cove and see if we can locate our friend, Sam Riley. Will the Bronco make it that far?" The ancient Ford had been in the family since the late 60s, and now—due to rust—sported more fiberglass than metal. His brother had maintained it pretty well, fixing things along the way.

Ben grinned at him and pushed up the bill of his Evinrude cap. "Friend, huh?" Addison opened his mouth to counter, but Ben launched ahead with a description of the Bronco's idiosyncrasies. "Sure it'll make it—probably. No, I'm sure it will. Just give it three or four pumps of the gas pedal when it's cold, only one if it's hot. If it won't start, try wiping out the distributor cap, that always works...usually." His brows furrowed in sudden concern. "You do have roadside assistance don't you?"

Addison shook his head and couldn't stop a grin. Ben never changed. However, with the Bronco his words held an element of truth, so Addison made note of the specific instructions.

"It needs to be driven. Good for it. Blow the carbon out, you know?"

Probably more like shake the carbon out.

Ben pulled his jacket off the coat tree. "I'll go get it ready. Meet me out front." He went into the garage from the kitchen and Addison heard the sound of the garage door opener.

Mandy hopped down the stairs with her shoes and jacket and they opened the front door.

The Bronco roared to life and belched a cloud of black smoke before settling down. Ben backed it out of the garage and handed it over to Addison. Mandy climbed in the passenger side. Her door clanged shut and the window crank fell on the patchwork carpet. She cut a glance at Addison.

Over the noise, Ben called to him through the driver window. "By the way, when you get to the long hill heading down to Perilous Cove, watch the brakes don't overheat. Wouldn't want to hear you drove into the bay." He waved and turned toward the open garage bay.

"Dad, was he serious?" Mandy stared dubiously at a nest of wires hanging below the dash. A red and yellow pair snaked across the center hump and disappeared under the seat. The radio knobs were missing and the windshield had a crack in one corner. Outside, smoke billowed up from underneath and enveloped them in a cloud. "Is this thing safe?"

He laughed as they pulled out of the driveway and turned onto the road circling the lake. "Mostly." He'd forgotten how good it was to be with Ben.

As they drove over the mountains and down to Perilous Cove, Mandy talked non-stop about how great yesterday's Thanksgiving dinner had been. He knew it wasn't about the food. It was about family. All their relatives were here in California and he and Mandy lived halfway across the country. It felt far away, and it was. Now that he'd reconnected with Ben, he had an intense desire to spend regular time with him. It would be good for Mandy, too, and he regretted the time missed these last two years since Elizabeth's death.

They came to a steep downhill section and he down-shifted the Bronco, letting the engine slow the car instead of the brakes, which, he'd discovered, had a sharp pull to the right. As he let out the clutch pedal, an ominous clunk sounded from underneath and Mandy shot him another look. He grinned in reassurance. That clunk had been part of this Bronco experience for as long as they'd owned it and it never seemed to get any worse.

Ten minutes later they pulled into Perilous Cove and cruised slowly down narrow Harbor Street, past old building fronts and quaint gift stores. Mandy spotted several places she wanted to shop. They drove north through town and then turned left onto Perilous Point Road. Sam's cabin sat at the edge of the slight downhill slope of the point.

"I can see the lighthouse." Mandy pointed to the tower, which stood a couple hundred feet beyond and downhill from the cabin. She jumped out of the Bronco as soon as it stopped and made for the front door. Her knock brought no response, so she tried again and called Sam's name.

"Doesn't look like she's home. Let's check the garage." Standing separately off to the right of the cabin, the single-wide structure was constructed of aged barn siding and sported sagging double doors. Except for the dubious roofing, it looked sound. Addison cupped his hands and peered through the crack between the doors. In the dim interior he made out a yellow Jeep. "Her car's here."

Mandy surveyed the area. "Maybe she walked to town. It isn't very far. We might have passed her in one of the shops."

Addison headed around the cabin to the water side. "Since we're here, let's walk down to the lighthouse." They climbed down the series of ramps and steps to the structure and circled the stone base to the far side where they had an unobstructed view of the Pacific Ocean.

"Wow, what a view." Mandy shielded her eyes with her hand. Large swells marched from the distant horizon to the base of the rocks, erupting in crashing, dramatic sprays. A stiff wind blew face-on, and mist from the breakers dripped from the rusted safety rail.

"Don't lean too hard on that railing." Addison gave it a shake and it wobbled a few inches, rattling the corroded bolts in the bottom flanges.

"Maybe you could get a job out here, Dad. You're good at fixing things."

Addison shot her what he hoped was a quelling look. This was her third job suggestion for him since they'd arrived.

Mandy held her hands up, palms out. "I'm just sayin'...." But her grin communicated more than the words.

They hiked back up the stairs to the cabin and knocked again, but

Sam didn't answer, so they climbed into the Bronco and drove down to the town. Addison parked in one of the angled spaces and they stood on the sidewalk in vain hope of finding Sam exiting one of the stores. After a few minutes, he pointed to the coffee shop and they pushed through the door into the steamy interior. Fragrant vanilla, cinnamon, and cocoa scents combined with dozens of coffee flavors to turn the warm interior into a veritable soup. A couple of glass cake servers held a variety of scones and cookies.

The white-haired man behind the counter flashed perfect teeth.

"What can I get for you folks on this cold November day?"

Addison laughed at that. The temperature outside was in the low 60s and several tourists wore shorts and windbreakers. Typical California winter. Nothing like Steerman. Mandy ordered a mocha concoction mounded with whipped cream, and a platter-sized chocolate chip scone that looked like it contained more chocolate than flour. When Addison asked for regular coffee, she gave him such a hard time he relinquished and changed to a double espresso.

"Has the town changed much, Dad?" Mandy sipped her frothy concoction, then dunked a wedge of scone and sucked off the liquid.

"Nope, not too much. More cars."

The man behind the counter joined their conversation. "Town's busy this week. Lot's of people come stay during the holidays. Where are you from?"

Mandy explained they were from Missouri, but were staying with her uncle and looking for their friend, Sam Riley, but she wasn't at home. At this, the man's eyebrows lifted slightly. Addison asked if he knew her.

"Yep, I know Sam. Saw her this morning. She's out on a whale watching tour now." He checked the clock on the end wall. "Should be back in a couple of hours. Depending on how cold it is, she'll stop in and grab a cup now and then. Excuse me a minute." He moved down the bar to wait on another customer, and Addison and Mandy relocated to one of the tables for two by the front window so they could have a better view of the boats in the harbor. A few people prepared their boats and left the safety of the harbor for the open sea, but most of the vessels were secured for the winter, snug under fitted snap covers.

The storeowner pulled another chair over and sat down at their table. He introduced himself as Connie Langworth. Addison held out his hand. "Addison Conner. This is my daughter, Mandy."

Mandy spread blackberry jam on the scone, as if it needed more sugar. "I thought there'd be more big boats here."

Connie twisted to look out the window. "Most of those are at Blue Rock Harbor south of here. That's where the fishing boats go out from, and even most of the tour boats. But we have a few here in our little harbor. In addition to the boat Sam is on—that'd be Captain Tom's Fin Finder II—we have two other tour boats. Looks like they're all out today." He turned back to Addison. "Would you like to leave a message with me for Sam? I'd be sure to give it to her."

Mandy wrote out a message with lots of exclamation points and hearts, and included their cell phone numbers plus Ben's house phone. They finished their coffees, said goodbye to Connie, and headed out.

Priority one for Mandy was hitting the shops along the old street, so Addison gave her some money and they set a rendezvous time. Then he walked down to the marine store to check out the boating and fishing supplies.

Sam winced as a particularly hard bump jarred her bottom against the galley stool. She shifted, trying to find a more comfortable position. Who knew a couple hours horseback riding could be so memorable?

As she assembled the finger sandwiches for the trip back, she hummed along with a Beach Boys tune playing softly on the boat's radio. Sunlight streamed in the portside windows and Sam made a mental note to wash the salt spray off them when they got back to the harbor.

One of the passengers asked Sam this morning if it got boring doing tour after tour on the same route up the coast and back. She answered that every trip was different...and it was. While this morning had sun, who knew what this afternoon would bring? Everything changed: the wave size and direction, the color of the water, height of the tide, wind, sun, temperature, smells, and the wildlife. How could any trip be boring when each revealed endless variety? And that variety brought vitality Sam had never experienced in Steerman.

Two sharp barks sounded from the cockpit and Blew bounded down the steps and out the door to the back deck. Sam dropped a cover over the food and grabbed her narration notebook. Blew stood on his hind legs, front paws on the starboard rail, tail wagging happily. Everyone gathered around him and pointed toward two sea otters romping among the shore rocks.

Sam didn't need to open the book this time, and spent the next ten minutes telling the guests about the otters' feeding and cleaning habits. As the otters receded in the distance, four dolphins came along side and played in the boat wake, entertaining everyone. The gray-skinned creatures seemed to sense another animal on the craft, and chattered in response to the dog's barks as he raced back and forth along the rail. Eventually the dolphins made an abrupt left turn and headed out to sea toward some distant shoals, leaving Blew barking a goodbye. As Captain Tom brought the Fin Finder II about for the homeward leg, the tourists gathered around Blew and took each other's photos, memories of the whale-spotting dog.

Sam was pleased she'd memorized much of the narration and facts. They'd seen gray whales several times now, and she didn't think she'd ever grow tired of watching the magnificent beasts rolling silently through the water. Today they'd had good views of a pod of five whales heading south about a mile offshore. The northern migration in spring hugged the wave line as mothers protected their newborn calves from the great whites that prowled these waters, but the southern route each fall was further out. Star said they observed the rules of the road just like cars, swimming on the right side of the ocean road.

As Sam finished up the sandwiches and served everyone, she wished Star could have come to help today, but the full tour precluded another crewmember. Besides, Millie needed someone to be with her—not that the woman would admit it. Her good-natured stubbornness brought a smile as Sam tore open a bag of caramel corn and dumped it in bowls.

Twenty minutes later, the Fin Finder II slowed, made its turn around the tip of the breakwater, and entered Perilous Cove. Seagulls squawked and circled the rocks of the protective barrier, fighting over some bit of food. One of the passengers tossed a piece of sandwich into the air and two-dozen birds whirled toward the boat. Sam didn't think the tourists would be so amused if the large birds dropped a tidbit of their own.

Captain Tom slowed even more and brought the boat smoothly to the marina docks and their slip. Sam jumped out and looped the stern line over the dock cleat, then she pulled the boat tight against the bumpers and secured the bow, twisting the rope and pulling it snug three times like Captain Tom had showed her. Blew leaped over the side before Tom opened the door through the gunwale, and pranced around, sniffing all significant spots.

The passengers filed out, scratching Blew's head one last time and thanking Tom and Sam for a great trip. As the last one walked away, Sam turned back to the boat to grab a sack of trash.

"Sam!"

She turned at the shout and squinted through the tangle of boat masts and rigging, trying to spot Star. A girl ran down the dock ramp and for a moment Sam waved, but then dropped her hand. The girl's hair was all wrong. Instead of red ponytail, this girl had spiky raven hair. And she was much taller than Star. Behind the girl, a man trotted down the ramp. Even at this distance, she recognized the blond hair and physique of Detective Addison Conner.

Something poked her in the side and she looked down to find Tom's elbow.

"Your mouth's open."

She snapped it closed, angry at her reddening cheeks. Maybe he'd think the cold air caused it. Only it wasn't that cold.

"Friend of yours?" The twinkle in his eye told her she hadn't fooled him. He was probably itching for a juicy morsel for his wife's so-called sewing circle. Not much sewing went on at those get-togethers. Trudy Borah had a reputation for being—as Millie tactfully put it—a rumor communications specialist. Sam blasted Tom with her best 'don't-go-there' glare.

Mandy arrived, grabbed Sam into a spinning hug, and squealed in her best middle-school voice, "Look at your hair. It's just like mine!"

Sam swore the girl had grown another inch or two and said so.

"Only three-quarters of an inch. But then it's only been three months." Mandy bounced up and down.

Sam turned toward Addison who stood smiling a few feet away, hands jammed in his faded jean pockets and looking like a bashful schoolboy in tennis shoes and worn sweatshirt. His surfer-blond hair was longer and had a just-out-of-bed look that caused her stomach to go funny. She'd forgotten how good-looking he was.

"Hi."

"Hi."

"Doesn't Sam look great, Dad?" Mandy tucked her hand around Sam's arm.

Captain Tom stepped up and introduced himself, causing Sam

another round of embarrassment for forgetting all about him. She countered by introducing Blew who woofed a greeting, then rolled on his back and wagged his whole body when Mandy bent to pet him.

"I'll take care of the boat," Tom winked at her. "You go ahead."

Sam retrieved her backpack from the galley, and the three of them walked together toward Harbor Street.

"I've only got until 1:30. That's our next tour." Sam glanced at her watch and saw it was nearly noon. "And I need to check on Millie."

At Addison's suggestion, they bought sub sandwiches from T.J.'s Deli, and then climbed into the Bronco. It rattled so much when he started it, Sam wondered if they'd make it up the short hill, but it lurched ahead with vigor when he applied the gas. They parked at Millie's.

Star opened the door as they stepped onto the porch.

"Hi, Sam." Curiosity crossed her face as she spotted Mandy and Addison.

"Star, this is Addison Conner and his daughter Mandy. They're from Missouri."

"Did you say Addison Conner?" Millie's voice rang out from inside. "Come in, come in."

They trouped inside, Addison bringing up the rear. Millie struggled to her feet from her lounge chair, pushing aside a colorful quilt. "For goodness sakes, close the door so you don't let all the heat out."

"Yes, ma'am," Addison said, a smile playing at the corners of his lips.

Millie stood, hands on hips. "Well, I'll be. Addison Conner."

"Hello, Millie." Addison crossed the room and gave the woman a big hug.

Sam stared from one to the other in complete surprise. "You two know each other? How?"

Millie let Addison help her back into the chair before answering. "I used to baby-sit this little feller, he and his brother both. They were a handful, those two." She laid her head back, exhausted from simply standing.

Addison introduced Mandy. At Millie's insistence they broke out the sandwiches and sat around the living room to eat. Mandy, who took a great interest in the babysitting revelation about her dad and uncle, pulled a chair close to Millie and asked for all the details, which the old woman was only too happy to oblige.

Sam found herself smiling around bites of her sandwich as she listened to stories about Addison's childhood. Millie had taken on babysitting for a number of local children, including some up at the lake where she drove twice a week. She did her own artwork while kids played with clay, watercolors, or whatever medium she was into at the time. Parents got used to giving the kids baths after being with Millie.

"And who can ever forget when you two ended up in jail?"

"Jail?" Sam and Mandy echoed at the same time.

"Oh, Millie. I'd hoped you'd forgotten that one." Addison smiled in embarrassment.

Mandy turned her sights on him. "Tell. All."

Sam joined in. "Yes, *Police Detective* Conner. Please do tell us about being in jail." His face turned a satisfying shade of red.

"Oh, it wasn't much. Ben was sixteen and I was fourteen. He'd just gotten his drivers' license and we drove down here to the Cove." He gestured toward the yard. "In that same Bronco. We decided to climb to the top of the lighthouse. Of course it was locked so we couldn't go up the inside stairs. We got a long rope out of the back of the Bronco and tied piece of angle iron onto it, intending to snag the upper rail of the lighthouse and climb up like in the movies. But we couldn't throw it high enough. In those days, you could drive right up to the base of the tower, so Ben moved the Bronco and then climbed on top. He swung the rope around and around and let go with a mighty heave—and struck the glass of the lens room, shattering it into a million sharp pieces that rained down."

"Wow. Did you get cut?" Mandy's eyes were wide.

"I ran like crazy and Ben jumped off the Bronco and broke his ankle. Fortunately, none of the glass got him. But the light station keeper did. He happened to drive up right then and called the sheriff who carted us off to the hospital and juvenile hall in Mission Peak."

Now Mandy's tone took on a familiar teasing. "And what was your punishment?" Her dad looked decidedly uncomfortable.

"Oh, well. We don't need to get into *all* the details." He stood and began gathering sandwich wrappers. "Besides, Sam has to get ready for the next tour." He turned to her, pleading in his eyes.

Sam pointedly looked at her watch, then smiled sweetly at him. "Oh,

I think I've got some time, yet. Please, go on." She winked around him at Mandy who promptly high-fived her.

"Yes, Addison." Millie propped her chin on her hand and raised her eyebrows. "I think it would be a good lesson for the young people to hear about the consequences of your crime."

Addison lowered into his chair. "Uh, well...we spent a night in the hall—after Ben got his ankle cast at the emergency room. We paid to replace the broken glass, and had ten weekends of raking the beach and picking up trash. Ben milked that ankle the whole time, making me do most of the work."

"That sounds like Uncle Ben," Mandy said.

Addison made to stand again, but Millie interrupted.

"Might as well tell them the rest, young man."

All eyes ping-ponged from Millie back to Addison.

"Oh, yeah. I forgot. We had to use buckets to empty the portable bathrooms at the dock and carry the waste up the hill to a dumping station."

A chorus of 'ewees' and gagging sounds erupted from Star and Mandy, while Sam burst out laughing. Eventually, Addison began laughing, too.

"Ben had the worst of it, though. The pails kept sloshing on his cast. He had to have it replaced twice because of the smell." This brought a whole new round of responses, and Millie dabbed at her eyes as she laughed.

Sam watched the scene before her, thinking it wasn't unlike Alejandro's family, but on a smaller scale. Three generations in this room —though not all related—good food, stories and laughter. Not the same as yesterday's huge ranch gathering, but...

The yearning for a family welled up, bringing Sam to the point of tears. All the other times she'd felt this, she'd smashed it down, hidden it away with other unreasonable hopes and dreams, unwilling to live in the pain of reality. But this time the feeling wouldn't leave. It carved out a space in her heart and set up camp. She drew a shaky breath and Mandy glanced her way. Sam ducked her head with a forced smile and fled to the kitchen, pretending to straighten up while turned toward the small window and blinking rapidly. Would Jack's mother have warmed to her if she'd been able to have children? It was something she'd never know, never wanted to know with Hilde. But now—

The phone rang and Star ran to answer it. After a moment, she took it to Millie. "Grandma, it's for you."

Sam retrieved her coat from a bar stool and shrugged into it. She had fifteen minutes to get back to Fin Finder II for the afternoon tour. She heard Millie answer a couple of yes's and no's, then give a groan. Sam looked up and saw the color leave Millie's face. The phone dropped from her hand and clattered to the wood floor. Sam ran to her side and took her trembling hand.

"Millie? What is it?" The woman only stared, eyes streaming tears. But these weren't tears of laughter.

Star ran to her grandmother's other side and hugged her, crying in fright. Sam put her arm around the girl's bony shoulders and held grandmother and granddaughter, not knowing what to do. Addison grabbed up the phone and spoke into it while turning away. Sam couldn't make out the conversation. He carried the phone to the kitchen table and wrote on a pad of paper. Mandy stood at his side and held his arm, as if suddenly afraid to leave the security of her father's strong presence.

Sam heard the phone bleep off and Addison caught her eye, motioning to the other side of the room. She gave Star a squeeze, stroked her hair, then steadied herself on the arm of the recliner and got to her feet. The furrow between Addison's eyes said the news wasn't good.

Suddenly she knew it had been Alejandro on the phone, giving Millie bad news. She couldn't breathe as she walked across the room. Although Millie knew she was dying, she'd counted on making it to her January birthday at least. This wasn't good.

"What did the doctor say?"

Surprise showed on Addison's face. "Doctor?"

"Wasn't that Millie's doctor?"

"No." Addison's voice was a whisper. "It was the prison warden where her son, Roy, is incarcerated."

"Star's father."

Addison rubbed a hand over his face. "I figured that was the relationship, although I wasn't sure." He looked tired again, whereas only a few minutes ago his laughter had made him appear ten years younger.

Sam squeezed his arm, drawing his attention, yet fearing the answer. "What is it?"

"The warden said there was a knife fight in the laundry room." Addison's voice was low, and he faced away from Star and her grandmother. "Roy took a knife to the chest. He died before they could get him to the infirmary."

Mandy pulled closer and Sam slipped her arm around the girl's waist. They turned to the two women across the room, one old and one so very young, hanging onto each other in comfort. Sam took a deep breath, knowing she would be the one to tell Starfire her father was dead.

- 36 -

Addison stood on Millie's front porch, breathing in briny sea scent and watching Sam and Star walk arm-in-arm toward the lighthouse. Too many times in his years on the police force, he'd had to inform someone of a parent's or child's death. No matter how old the victim, death was always a shock, stealing life not just from the deceased, but from everyone around as well. He shook his head. Poor Millie. Sam had told him about her terminal illness. Now this. And all of it coming down on the shoulders of a young girl.

Roy Trafford had lived a rough life. He'd been a year older than Addison and attended different schools, but as they grew older, they'd met here and there. Ben had warned Addison to stay away from Roy, that he was trouble. Ben had been right.

And now it ended—breaking a mother's heart and shattering a young girl's romantic notion that her dad might come home someday. A tragic waste.

A new silver Dodge Ram truck pulled into the drive and rolled to a crunching stop. A tall, dark-haired man got out and walked toward the house. He wore a camel, thigh-length suede coat with brown leather patches at the elbows, dark pants, and highly polished shoes. Even from the porch, Addison detected a masculine aftershave on the breeze. This guy had taste and the expensive clothes to match.

Addison stepped down onto the walk. "Can I help you?"

"I'm Alejandro Navarro, Millie's doctor." He extended his hand and gave a firm shake, exuding confidence and strength. Sam had called him, alarmed at Millie's weakened condition.

"Yes, of course. Come in." Addison introduced himself as a family friend. "My daughter's keeping Millie company." He led the way up the stairs. "I didn't know doctors still made house calls."

Navarro smiled, revealing perfect white teeth set against his dark complexion, five o'clock shadow showing early in the afternoon. A half-inch scar stood out on the underside of his chin. "Millie has been a friend for many years. And I live nearby."

"Her bedroom is right—"

"Yes, I know the house." The doctor stepped around him.

"Well alrighty, then," Addison mumbled to himself. He shoved his hands in his jeans, feeling casually dressed after the encounter with the doctor. That suede coat probably cost more than he made in two weeks.

Mandy came down the hallway. He put his arm around her and they went back out to the porch to sit.

"Did Sam leave to tell Star?"

He nodded and noticed her eyes were red. She was silent for a few minutes, staring at the ocean. He followed her gaze and saw a pair of pelicans beyond the breakwater. The brown birds circled, riding the wind, looking ungainly even in the air with their dangling legs and S-shaped necks. Then one folded its wings, stretched out its neck, and dove straight down, plunging below the surface. It surfaced immediately, tossed its head back, and extended its throat to swallow the hapless prey in one gulp. He didn't think Mandy was really watching.

"I remember when you told me about Mom." Mandy still stared out to sea. Her lip quivered. "That was so hard." Her shoulders began shaking and he knelt on the hard porch and wrapped her in his arms. Mandy buried her face in his neck and sobbed, gripping his back, reliving her own pain, but also knowing what Star was experiencing right now.

Tears stung his own eyes as he remembered walking away from Elizabeth's body in the hospital room—away from his wife for the last time—and toward his waiting daughter. Although she'd known her mom was going to die anytime, getting the words out to tell her was the hardest thing he'd ever done. And while he'd had to attend to Mandy at that time, to be there for her, it still felt wrong to leave his wife. Disloyal. He'd wanted to stay in the room, hands fisted in the sheets still warm from her body. At least until she grew cold. It had never seemed right to leave Elizabeth while she was still warm. Never right.

Mandy took a deep breath and sat back to wipe her eyes. "I have to get some Kleenex." She went inside and Addison wiped his eyes. A moment later the door opened and the doctor stepped out.

"Millie's okay…well, as good as she can be, anyway. I gave her a mild sedative." He put his hands in the pockets of the suede jacket, and then looked closely at Addison. "I take it you know about her illness?"

Addison nodded and faced into the stiffening wind, letting the briny cold dry his eyes. "Sam told me." He told Navarro the details of the phone call from the warden, and that Sam had initially assumed it was the doctor. She'd later confirmed Addison's suspicions Millie was terminally ill.

Navarro nodded and looked around. "Where are Samantha and Starfire?" The names rolled off his tongue with the smoothness of a Spanish heritage Addison could only admire.

Addison pointed to the lighthouse. The doctor surprised him by stepping off the porch and striding purposefully toward the tower.

Samantha. He'd just begun to get used to "Sam." He'd never known anyone who'd changed first names. It was odd, especially since all his files at the station referred to her as Natalie. He felt as if he was dealing with two different people: different names, looks, places.

Somehow Sam fit, though. So did Samantha. Her new haircut, outdoorsy job, and cabin for a home, gave her such a new persona that a name change seemed natural if not outright required. Making such a change while remaining in Steerman would have been weird. But here on this windblown bluff it made all the sense in the world.

A few minutes later, Sam, Star, and the doctor rounded Sam's cabin, trudging slowly up the hill. Starfire walked between the two adults who both had their arms around the slim girl. The doctor's arm stretched behind Star to Sam's waist, and Addison suddenly wished he'd accompanied Sam and Star. He went inside, not wanting to appear an observer, but when he reached the kitchen area, he couldn't help watch through the front windows.

The trio stopped in the front yard and huddled in a small circle. Star wiped her eyes and nose with the sleeve of her sweatshirt and Sam stroked the girl's hair. Navarro took Sam's hand and spoke directly to her for a moment, then turned to Star. The girl hugged him and he wrapped an arm around her, not letting go of Sam's hand. Then he leaned toward Sam.

"Dad? What are you looking at?" Mandy came into the room.

Addison spun away from the window. "I, uh...I was just watching Sam and Star say goodbye to Dr. Navarro."

"Oh." Mandy looked out the window. "He sure is handsome, isn't he?"

"Is he?"

"Better watch out he doesn't steal Sam away."

Addison turned to his daughter, expecting to see narrowed teasing eyes and a smirk. But instead, her face was dead serious. A million thoughts raced through his head and he opened his mouth, but he had no idea what to say to this young woman beside him. She grabbed his hand and squeezed it, then went out the door and down the stairs. He watched as she spoke to the group and shook hands with the doctor before he climbed into his truck and drove away. Then Mandy took his place on the opposite side of Star as they came up the stairs.

Addison wished he had her boldness, sureness. That was a trait she'd inherited from her mother, not him. Elizabeth had shined in any social situation.

They first met at La Fiesta in Santa Barbara when he visited a friend, Blake, who attended the university there. During summer, Blake had met a girl at a bookstore who wanted him to meet her at one of the celebrations on State Street. While Blake searched the sidewalks, restaurants, and plazas for his mystery girl, Addison finally grabbed a vacant seat on one of the benches lining the street and watched the jousting crowds.

Lowrider Chevys cruised the boulevard, festooned with lights, chrome, and pavement-scraping tailpipes. More convertibles than he ever knew existed clogged the street, and people dodged between bumpers in an endless jaywalking stream. Police ignored all but the most flagrant infraction.

Music filled the evening air and everyone had friends and places to go—except him. Finally bored, he started to rise to go find Blake when a group of girls stopped in front of him, blocking his exit as they argued about what to do next.

One girl with long, silky black hair spotted him. He wasn't sure how it happened, but four of the girls entered the adjacent store to shop while she took a seat beside him, introduced herself as Elizabeth, and struck up a conversation. He never saw Blake again that night, but he and Elizabeth covered the streets, danced to Mariachi bands in plazas lit by colored lanterns, and even found time to slip away to the quieter beach area for a walk to the end of Stearn's Wharf. She held his hand on the way back to town. They talked for hours. It had been a magical night, and he missed her every day.

Now he was a big, bad policeman, but a ninety-eight pound wimp when it came to relationships. He never knew what to do next.

There was no denying the special friendship Mandy had forged with Sam, even with a couple of thousand miles separating them these last three months. She missed her mom, and for some unexplainable reason, Sam fulfilled that unique relationship of friend and parent figure in a way no one else had.

Although he hadn't dated, Addison made sure Mandy had female companionship with women at their church. Ellen's mom, among others, had taken special interest in her. They'd gone shopping together, had lunches. While Mandy always had fun and enjoyed the times with the women, she had instantly attached herself to Sam in a way unlike anyone else. Addison couldn't deny the depth of the connection, and frequently spotted non-verbal communication between the two—quick glances, smiles, a casual touch—like they had radar that picked up on the same things.

When the three came into the house, Star ran to the bedroom to sit with her grandmother. Mandy and Sam moved around the kitchen, preparing ingredients for a pot of soup. With their short, black hair they looked like mother and daughter. Had Sam cut and dyed hers as a disguise or to look more like Mandy? She glanced his way with those blue eyes, saddened by the pain of the day, but communicating thankfulness at his and Mandy's presence.

He pulled out a bar stool, intending to sit opposite them and join in the conversation, when his cell phone rang. He answered it and could tell it was Arnie, but the sound was watery and garbled, and then he lost the call. His cell phone display alternated between one and no signal bars. He picked up Millie's phone and called the station on the toll free number.

"Hey, Arnie." He carried the handset outside and dropped into a rickety wicker chair.

"Compadré. How's that fine California weather?"

Addison laughed. "Cold at the moment, but nothing like Steerman, I bet."

"Got that right. Had to use Corine's hairdryer on the car door lock this morning."

"What's up?" Arnie hadn't called to talk about the weather.

Sam and Mandy finished up the soup and put it on the burner to simmer. Then Sam gave Star some money and encouraged her to take Mandy down to the town for coffees at the Last Drop. Millie was fast asleep under the effects of the sedative.

Sam had only had a couple of private minutes with Millie after the shock of the warden's call. The old woman had clutched Sam's arm in a desperate grip and whispered, "We need to move up the timeframe." At that point, Star had come into the bedroom, still unsure of what had happened that so upset Millie.

Sam had called Captain Tom—he persuaded his wife, Trudy, to fill in for the afternoon tour—then she'd taken Star to the lighthouse to tell her about her dad. That had been tough. Alejandro's arrival had been a godsend for Sam.

Now, seeing the fragile stability she'd built up crumbling, the low throbbing of a headache pressed behind her eyes, and she pinched the bridge of her nose, squeezing it back. There was no time for self-indulgence—there was too much to do.

It was unfair to Mandy to send Star off with her after the news of Roy's death, but Mandy jumped at the chance, and Star seemed glad to go, too. Although Sam had no personal experience, the girls appeared to be bonding like sisters.

Sam checked her watch. She'd asked Tom not to tell Trudy about Roy Trafford's death until they were out on the boat. That would mean the whole town wouldn't know about Roy's death until at least four thirty-one, one minute after the boat docked and time for Trudy to reach a phone. Of course that didn't take into account anyone Trudy might have already called on the boat's radio.

Star had been upset by the news, but she'd been more scared because of her grandmother's reaction. The last time the girl had seen her dad and mom was when they dropped her off at Millie's when she was three years old, so she remembered them only through pictures of her dad.

Sam didn't know if it was good or not, but there were no photos of Star's mother.

Roy had never called from prison, nor had he answered any of his daughter's letters, and Star had written a bunch. He hadn't wanted Millie to come visit. Maybe it was his way of distancing Star from his failures as her father. Sam liked to think the man had at least some redeeming quality, but probably he was more concerned with living his life, such as it was. In doing so, he'd missed a relationship with a wonderful little girl. Idiot.

Millie had filled the role of both parents and was Star's entire family. Now Millie wanted Sam to take over that role. As much as she desired a family, she had to ask herself if she had what it took to be a parent?

Sam fell into the overstuffed chair in the living room and leaned her head back against the red flowered upholstery. Her eyes roved the eclectic artwork and sculptures, a lifetime of collection. Probably not valuable pieces, but they were uniquely Millie. In a few months at best, Millie would be gone, and only things, useless things, would remain.

Except for Starfire Trafford.

The weight of responsibility pressed Sam deep into the chair cushions. She felt like a small girl herself, staring out at an oversized world, one of overwhelming responsibilities. Millie provided friendship and a family substitute she relished, needed. Millie would be leaving her, too; just like her parents, just like Jack. Leaving her alone to make all the decisions, to provide financially for them both, to raise Star into a young woman. It was so much to figure out. She had run from danger in Missouri seeking safety in this small town. Now the danger came in the form of responsibility. And she'd have to do it alone.

Alejandro wanted a deeper relationship with her. That was evident in the way he sought her out, hinted, found excuse to touch her arm, her back. The very confidence of his actions sometimes felt like pushing, and it made Sam skittish.

To be fair, the good doctor knew none of her secrets. He didn't know she'd been a married woman less than four months ago. Didn't know her only friend was murdered in the downstairs guest room. Nor did he know of the attacks on her life and continuing threat. Alejandro only knew the new Sam Riley, not *her*, including all she'd been as Natalie Clayton. And she wasn't ready to share those things just yet. He'd noticed the fading burn scars, but her external wounds had largely healed before she'd met him. The internal ones still hurt.

From long talks with Millie, Sam recognized now that Jack had been a controller. Eleven years of that had squelched her personality and individuality until she lost who she had been. Millie said Rowena had discussed it with her many times, prompting the deeding of the cabin to Sam in case the time came when she needed to escape, to regain herself. The circumstances for Sam's flight had been quite different than Rowena imagined, but the need was the same.

Alejandro's presence confused her journey. Maybe recovery was a better word. Sam needed more time. But time was in short supply now.

A frown pulled at her mouth. She turned her head so she could see out the front window where Addison sat, the sleeve of his shirt just visible. Odd that his presence didn't cause her to feel that pressure. He never crowded. Perhaps it was that shy approach, his quiet strength. He was so unlike any cop she'd imagined from television or the few she'd met in person. Heaven knew she needed strength like that right now. The reality of the upcoming months terrified her. How could she fulfill Millie's desires?

Sam leaned forward, pressing the heels of her palms into her eyes, rocking in the chair. After a few minutes, the door opened, and moment later a hand closed on the back of her neck. She let herself be pulled into Addison's strong embrace, eyes closed, head against his chest. He smelled of outdoors, the sea. He didn't speak, just held her for a long time, gently massaging the taut muscles. How did he know it was exactly what she needed?

But soon he would go home to Missouri, and she would be alone to face the tough times ahead. Who would hold her for a lifetime?

Mandy and Star volunteered to clean up after dinner—well, Mandy volunteered and convinced Star to help. Sam owed Mandy for that one. She checked on Millie, still resting in her bedroom, then headed out toward the porch, grabbing two large quilts from the hall closet on the way. Addison said he had news from Arnie on the investigation and wanted to talk in private.

"Thought you could use this." Sam handed him a quilt. He draped the thick blanket around his legs. Multi-colored chickens and eggs decorated the fabric. She probably should have given him the one with tractors and wagons, but that one was her favorite.

"Thanks. It's pretty cold out tonight." He watched as she cocooned herself. "We could go to your cabin if you'd prefer."

Sam shook her head and gave him a smile. "Might be warmer out here." He stared at her for a long moment. He seemed comfortable with quiet, not having to fill a void. For a while, they listened to the sounds of the outdoors: whispering wind through the cypress, low waves on the rocks below the bluff, the occasional swish of a car on Highway 1, two hundred yards east and uphill of Millie's house.

"It's not unusual for fire victims to be skittish around open flame, you know." Addison kept his eyes trained across the cove toward the southwest. "Sometimes it takes months before they're able to relax."

Sam studied his profile. A breeze teased the shaggy hair at the back of his neck and over his ears. He could use a haircut. She sighed, wishing they could talk about simple things. Today had been tough enough already. "What did Arnie say?"

Addison turned and studied her, as if assessing how much more she could take. "The Arkansas state police located Broderick's school records and found information on his father."

She tensed under the quilt, no longer cold, not sure she felt anything. "Have they talked to him? Does he know where his son is?" Addison shook his head.

"The father died in a suspicious fire thirty-five years ago. His name was Frank Broderick Crane."

Disappointment shoved Sam into the chair. Another fire. Another death. The facts were too hard to comprehend. Had the son killed the father? If so, he'd been doing this what...three and a half decades? Addison answered her next question before she asked.

"No mother was listed in the school records. People in the community remembered Crane as suave on the surface, but meaner than a snake underneath. The police dug through their old records. Dad had a rap sheet listing multiple assaults. Charges were dropped for attempted murder when the victim suddenly recanted and left the state."

Sam rubbed her forehead. Crane. The name had a familiar ring. Where had she run across it?

"The son, Tarz, was fifteen at the time of his father's death. He bounced around in foster care for the next three years, never lasting more than a few months at any one place. Arnie said they'd only been able to locate one of the foster parents so far, an elderly lady named Collinwood who remembered him very well."

Addison stopped and reached for her hand. She slid it from the warmth of the blanket, and he wrapped his larger hand around hers. Sam feared his next words, whatever they were. He cleared his throat.

"Mrs. Collinwood had to take one of the younger kids to a dentist appointment one day. When she came home, she spotted smoke coming from the back yard. Tarz had a fire going in the pit barbeque. The family dog…" Addison stopped and looked away for a moment.

Sam's heart stuttered and she couldn't seem to get enough air. Oh, no, no, no.

"The dog was on the ground, tied with duct tape, still alive. Tarz was going to put him on the grill."

Sam swayed, unable to take in yet another horror, but Addison shook his head at her expression.

"The lady was pretty gutsy—threatened him with a shovel and he backed down. The Department of Children and Family Services removed him from the home and placed him with a family used to dealing with extreme cases. Broderick attended weekly one-on-one therapy sessions for two months, then group sessions for three more. According to the records, he was a model client, never missing a session and even helping in the groups."

Sam took a tentative breath, then a deeper one, not taking her eyes off Addison. There was more to this story.

"On Broderick's eighteenth birthday, he disappeared from that last foster care home, not even waiting for the birthday cake his latest foster mom baked for him."

Sam leveled her gaze at Addison. "What else."

He swallowed before answering. "Seven years later, Mrs. Collinwood's home caught fire in the middle of the night. She was no longer doing foster care, so there were no kids there. She got out safely. But they found that same family dog in the living room where the fire started. The dog may or may not have been dead when the fire started."

Despite Addison's warm hand, hers was cold as stone. "Did they catch him? Surely she pressed charges?"

He shook his head. "During the time of the fire, Broderick had a job as a regional sales rep for a plumbing company in Tennessee. Traveled a lot. He had a credit card receipt for a motel in Knoxville where he stayed regularly on his route. And the manager said Broderick checked in around seven o'clock that evening and checked out right after breakfast the next day."

"Tennessee borders Arkansas on the west," Sam said, recalling her junior high geography, "but Nashville is a long way across the state."

Addison nodded. "Arnie did some calculations before he called me. It's over an eight-hour drive round trip, closer to nine, really. But it's doable...for someone who's determined."

Sam knew Tarz Broderick was exactly that. "He's not going to give up. Ever." She felt Addison squeeze her hand, but it brought little comfort. Broderick was worse than she'd imagined. Seven years. Could she hide out for the rest of her life? And what kind of existence would that be for Star?

A more horrifying thought pierced her brain like a flaming arrow: what if he went after Star in five, ten, twenty years? If he ever discovered the girl's connection to Sam...

No! She couldn't let that happen.

"Sam?"

Maybe she should run again, go north. Canada, or Alaska. She could buy a gun and learn to shoot.

"Sam?"

She looked at the man next to her. Would Addison take Star and raise her with Mandy? He'd invited Sam into their home when he knew her even less than they knew Star. The girls were like sisters, weren't they? Star would be safe with him.

Suddenly, Sam knew that wasn't true. Broderick had shot Mandy in Addison's home. Yes, he'd been trying for Sam, but would he leave them alone? He knew where they lived. It might be months or years, but he was relentless.

Sam pulled her hand away from Addison's, aware it was shaking as she clasped it across her mouth. There was no safety anywhere.

- 37 -

"We *have* to stay, Dad."

"Mandy, we've been over this. The funeral isn't until next Sunday and we fly home tomorrow morning. You can't miss a week of school and I can't miss work." Addison drove the Bronco up the grade Saturday afternoon, away from Perilous Cove. Away from Sam, Starfire and Millie. The machine coughed and sputtered, jerking and surging so Addison had to slow at times and baby the gas. On all the other trips the old Ford V-8 had run well, but today it, too, seemed reluctant to leave the cove.

"Then we'll have to come back," Mandy said with a determination he'd come to fear. He glanced at his daughter and saw the profile of his wife, right down to the set of her jaw. She stared straight ahead, but her eyes weren't on the road. He sighed.

"I don't think that's a possibility, hon. I have to work on Saturday to make up for the time off."

Mandy turned in her seat. "What good is a vacation if you have to work extra to make up for the time you're gone? You've got plenty of vacation days saved up. You told me you did."

She was right. He *did* have a lot of vacation due, more than five weeks worth. In fact, he'd lost a week due to departmental accrual limitations. But he'd learned that just because he had it, didn't mean he could take it, not with the current workload. The mere thought of the files awaiting him sent a wave of exhaustion coursing through him and he slumped in the seat. Even with Millie's sickness and her son's death, the last few days had been a welcome break and, if he admitted the truth, he didn't want to go back. He wanted to run away from the responsibilities. But he couldn't tell that to his fourteen-year-old daughter.

"Star needs me," Mandy stated. "And Sam needs you."

He shot her a look. "What do you mean by that?"

"She's all alone, Dad. She needs you." Mandy turned to the side window and watched raindrops dance their way across the glass. She mumbled something, but the noise of the Bronco drowned it out.

"What did you say?"

Mandy answered without turning. "I said, *you* need her. And so do I."

Frustration welled up in Addison. How could his daughter know his needs? Plus, they really didn't know Sam all that well. They'd spent less than ten days total with her other than phone calls. She'd had a rough marriage—maybe abusive. He mentally kicked himself, realizing he'd forgotten to ask about that. Besides, for all he knew, she was already dating the dashing Dr. Navarro.

Bitterness crept into his reply. "What do you expect me to do, Mandy? Quit my job and move out here to see if something works out?"

She turned toward him with red eyes. "I don't know," she yelled and waved her arms. "Why not? It's not like you love your job anyway. You're gone all the time, then come home with hours of work still to do. Life's too short to waste it where you don't want to be." More quietly she added, "We learned that with Mom." She turned to the door and exhaled a heavy sigh.

Addison took a deep breath and regarded his daughter out of the corner of his eye. She rarely let fly with her emotions like this. Since Elizabeth died, she'd been so strong that at times he wondered who supported whom. This was a new side of her. Or it could be just some kind of teenage thing. He didn't know much about women. But one thing he had learned in his sixteen years with Elizabeth—when a woman expressed strong emotion, he'd better take note. Therefore, he chose his words and spoke softly.

"I can't just quit and leave."

She sighed again and spoke quietly, regaining her control. "I know it's not that simple. I just know I miss Mom. And I love Sam. And Starfire, too." Mandy turned toward the window once more and said almost too soft to hear, "She's like my little sister."

Love? Mandy remained quiet for the rest of the trip to Ben's, but Addison's thoughts roiled. His daughter's connection with Sam was far stronger than he'd imagined. Mandy had spent quite a bit of time with Star, too. As soon as Star learned Mandy had also lost her mother, the two became inseparable. When he and Mandy had driven back to Perilous Cove today, the two girls had spent most of the time together.

Addison rubbed his chin, realizing that for Mandy the same instant connection had occurred with Star as it had with Sam. The kids seemed to have it all figured out, but the adults had no clue what to do. Of course kids didn't have to deal with the reality of jobs, bills, commitments, and places to live. It all boiled down to who they liked— or loved.

He cared for Sam, too. He wasn't sure what it was, but something about her drew him. She was both terrified and hardened by the news about Tarz Broderick, and he respected her ability to cope with the threat from such an evil man. Addison couldn't help wonder what Sam's next move would be, but she hadn't confided in him.

And, although he hadn't said anything to Mandy, he'd felt a loss at saying goodbye today that left him empty. Wherever Sam's hand had touched him, it left radiating heat. He rubbed the place where she'd squeezed his arm today.

But most of their time together so far had revolved around murder and death, a shaky foundation for any relationship. Still, he wished with all his being he could grant Mandy's request and camp out at Ben's for another week.

Today, Sam had talked about the difficulty of Millie's request. The original plan had been that, upon Millie's death, Sam was to take Star. Now with Star's father dead, Millie wanted Sam to initiate immediate adoption proceedings, before Millie died, skipping a guardianship arrangement altogether. Millie had asked Sam to contact an attorney on Monday. As much as Sam loved the girl, it was a huge responsibility, made more difficult by her own pain of loss and the knowledge that Tarz Broderick was somewhere out there. Addison didn't envy her the decisions she faced.

He slowed the Bronco for a tight corner as they climbed toward the lake. Maybe the one thing he could do was make some progress on the case. When he returned to the office, he vowed to light a fire under all the evidence folders and review everything again. He had to figure out Broderick's motive for this relentless pursuit. It was likely related to the life insurance money. As Arnie said, two million dollars will make people do crazy things. With Jack Clayton, the primary beneficiary, dead, his mother was listed as next in line for payout if Sam was killed. Could she be involved somehow? It didn't seem likely. Yes, she was a nasty person, but all the evidence so far pointed to Jack. His business problems gave him motive. The withdrawn cash could hire a hit man, which screamed opportunity. It looked like a solid plan had been in place and Clayton's heart attack had just been unlucky timing—for him.

Sam had to get that policy cancelled, but the process was complicated. For one, the policy was paid a year in advance. But keeping Sam's whereabouts secret was the biggest hurdle. The insurance company wanted her current address and phone, which she obviously didn't want to give them. And even the company wasn't quite sure how to handle Sam's name change—it hadn't come up before. What name would Sam use to sign the cancellation letter, and what would they accept? Everyone Addison called at the company said they were "checking on the proper procedure." They seemed to have plenty of procedures for checking procedures.

One thing he knew for sure: he didn't like Sam living out here alone with Broderick on the loose. He set his jaw; he'd check with the captain about getting a couple more days off next weekend, but wouldn't say anything to Mandy until he was sure it would work out. And he'd ask Ben in private about returning next weekend.

Addison glanced at his daughter as she leaned against the Bronco's cold side window. She was right—she needed Sam.

And just maybe, so did he.

- 38 -

Captain Tom had two full whale watching tours on Sunday, and Millie had insisted Sam go ahead with them and to take Star for the afternoon one. A friend had come to stay with Millie. Sam was glad for the work. She needed the money.

All hope of finding the missing funds from her bank account had vanished when Addison revealed more about Tarz Broderick. Police had located his bank account, and records showed a deposit of fifteen thousand dollars in cash the day after Jack died. It appeared Jack withdrew the cash and paid Broderick to kill Sam, but unlike a check, there was no way to prove the cash was Sam's. The money was gone forever. She was on her own.

Although the ocean tours were busy, the narration and duties were now routine for Sam. Even in the midst of the activity on the boat, she had time to think and wrestle with her problems. Too much time, really. She picked up a pair of binoculars and swiped their already clean lenses.

Star was uncharacteristically quiet when she came aboard for the 1:30 tour, and sat for several minutes combing her fingers through Blew's thick winter fur. The dog was happy to oblige and laid his head in the girl's lap, only moving to nudge her back to activity when her hand stilled.

Sam knew the death of the girl's father had shaken even the small hope of one day having a normal family. Not that Star had pie-in-the-sky ideals of the perfect family, but Sam suspected a deep-down little-girl wish had evaporated with the warden's phone call.

Star hadn't said anything about Millie's terminal illness, but the girl was sharp. She had to know by now her grandmother was dying. All the girl's dreams were shattering.

Sudden understanding coursed through Sam as she watched the girl and dog: Star faced the same loneliness Sam experienced. Both their families were gone, or soon would be. It wasn't only the present loss, but the missing future, too. The lost family gatherings, the children, grandchildren, traditions and memories.

She studied the red-headed girl. Were the two of them together enough to forge a mother-daughter relationship? Sure, they wouldn't be alone if they had each other, but together didn't a family make. Sam knew firsthand how lonely being with someone could be.

At a shout from starboard, Blew rocketed out the door. Excited passengers pointed to a pod of whales. Star listlessly followed, standing back slightly from the group, as if already disconnecting from those around her.

Sam rose from the galley stool, pulled on her jacket, and stepped onto the rear deck. Frigid salty spray drifted from the bow of the boat, covering them all in a glistening sheen. Standing behind Star, Sam wrapped her arms around the girl. Star's head came back against her chest and Star's hands clasp Sam's. Maybe having each other *was* enough. She'd been so worried about whether she could become a good mother she'd missed the simple need of this young girl for someone, perfect mother or not, to just be there.

It wouldn't be easy. They both carried hurts and losses. Money would be tight. But for the first time in as long as she could remember, Sam understood that life wasn't only about the leavings. It was also about the coming togethers. Star's ponytail tickled her chin and Sam let the boat's rocking action become their own.

The Monday and Tuesday after Thanksgiving proved quieter than most for the police precinct. Gladys said all the criminals were Christmas shopping with their stolen money. Arnie, on the other hand, speculated the light snow and freezing temperatures kept the low-lifes indoors. Whatever the reason, Addison was thankful for the extra time to wrap up two cases and make progress on several more, including the Clayton file.

Tarz Broderick hadn't surfaced since he escaped the hospital in Arkansas. The local detectives reported rumors of a woman, ex-girlfriend maybe, but no one had a name. It seemed Broderick had worked for several years as a long haul trucker and had moved around the country quite a bit. But the more recent history put him in Missouri and Arkansas. The locals were checking with street sources in Arkansas where Broderick had been linked to a suspicious warehouse fire. He also had three known aliases. Transaction monitors were in place on his one bank account and credit card they knew about.

While the week was professionally productive, it proved personally uncomfortable. Sharon had cornered him twice in hallways and once in the parking lot, asking about his work and Mandy, while physically inching closer. Addison found himself scouting rooms before entering, and was tempted to carry a mirror for checking around blind corners. He felt torn between wanting to be polite to the woman and his rising desire to flee.

Though her questions seemed innocent, he'd noticed a hard edge to her personality that sometimes slipped out in a biting remark—never to him, but to others in the office. As a detective, he knew it neither fair nor smart to judge a person on their looks, yet her thin lips, pinched mouth, and set of her eyes reminded him of old Bette Davis films where she played the shrew.

Sharon seemed to find him attractive, or at least available, and he wasn't sure how to dissuade her without hurting her feelings. Best to avoid her until she lost interest.

Tuesday afternoon ended with a lost Alzheimer patient. Fortunately, a uniform found the man in an alley a short distance from his home. When Addison returned to the precinct, everyone had gone home for the night. A note card with his name lay in the middle of his desk blotter and he ran his finger under the tab.

Dear Addison,

I know we don't know each other very well yet, but I've always felt a special connection to you. That's why I want to ask you for a huge favor.

The note continued, but he glanced to the bottom where he saw Sharon's signature, then read the rest. Then he re-read it.

In disbelief, he dropped his head into his hands.

Sharon wanted him to be her Lamaze coach!

- 39 -

Wednesday morning Addison decided to talk to Gladys about Sharon, but when he rounded the corner leading to the dispatcher's desk, Sharon occupied the space. She smiled shyly at him and informed him Gladys was out sick with the flu. Sharon had fill-in duty, and rose to her feet as she asked what she could help him with.

He said never mind, and beat a hasty retreat into his office. He would have to wait until next week to talk to Gladys.

At eleven o'clock, a courier delivered a padded envelope and Sharon brought it to him.

"Anything interesting?" she asked as he slit it open and slid out a video tape.

"Maybe. Bank surveillance video." Addison spun his chair and popped the tape in the TV with built-in VCR on the corner table. The screen lit up and black and white figures jerked across the screen, time separated by a two seconds between each frame.

Sharon leaned close behind him, placing her hand on his shoulder. Her perfume—something overly floral that reminded him of the three streetwalkers he and Arnie had busted last week—displaced the air in his throat. He wondered if he could open the window.

"I didn't know we had a bank robbery," Sharon said, pressing against him.

Addison concentrated on the flickering images. A digital clock in the lower right showed the time and date. Addison fast-forwarded until the clock read 10:00 AM, the bank's opening time. An employee unlocked the door and several people entered.

"We didn't." He studied the images for no more than a minute until one looked familiar. "Ah." He retrieved the photo of Jack Clayton from the folder and held next to the screen. "There he is." Addison clicked the pause button, freezing Clayton. At his side walked a blonde woman in a long coat and large sunglasses. A scarf covered much of her hair and was tied under her chin Jackie Onasis style.

A choking noise compelled him to turn and look at Sharon. Her right hand clamped her mouth and her left dug into his shoulder painfully. Her round eyes cut from the screen to his, then she turned and fled the room, causing Arnie to dodge sideways in the doorway as he came in.

Arnie slipped his hip onto the corner of Addison's desk. "What was that all about?"

"I have no idea. We were just looking at this video." He massaged his sore shoulder. "Morning sickness?"

Arnie rubbed his chin. "Maybe. But Gladys told me Sharon was past that now." He gestured toward the screen. "What's this?"

"Video from the bank when Jack and Natalie Clayton"—he did air quotes with his fingers for Natalie's name—"closed their savings account. I just found them on the tape. Anything look unusual to you?"

Arnie studied the screen for a minute while Addison rewound and ran it forward a couple of times. "I would say that's a woman trying very hard not to be recognized."

"My thoughts exactly." He rewound the tape and ran it through again, searching the woman's features for anything that might help.

"Stop right there," Arnie said, and Addison hit pause. "How tall was Jack Clayton?"

Frowning, Addison leafed through the folder until he came to Jack's personal information. "Driver's license says six-one." He regarded his partner. "What are you getting at?"

"Natalie's how tall?"

"Five-three," he said immediately. Arnie burst out laughing and Addison realized his mistake.

"Didn't have to look *that* one up, did ya' buddy?" Arnie slapped his leg, then did a drum tap on the desk edge.

Addison felt redness rising up his neck and across his face. "It's because I'm more familiar with her...I mean, not familiar *with* her, but it's...uh...because of the similar sizes between her and Donna

Montgomery. From the case. You know."

Arnie laughed all the way around to his desk and fell into his chair, shaking. "Whatever you say."

Addison turned back to the video to avoid his partner. Though it was intended as good fun, he'd never been comfortable talking with anyone about his feelings...except Elizabeth. Sure, he and Arnie joked a lot and were pretty good friends. But talking to him about Sam didn't seem right. He ran the video ahead and caught the couple exiting the building twelve minutes after arriving.

Arnie spoke from his desk. "Figure it out yet?"

Whatever Arnie saw, Addison didn't get it.

"Notice her shoes?"

"Shoes?" Why was Arnie asking about shoes? Addison ran the tape until they had the best view. He squinted at the grainy picture. "Uh, they're dark, perhaps black, brown, red. No heel."

"Yep."

"What?" Addison turned to his partner. "You mean no heel?" Sudden understanding spun him toward the TV. "She's too tall."

"Way to go, detective."

Excited, Addison ran the images forward and back. "If Jack's six-one, this woman must be at least five-ten or eleven. So it can't be Sam."

"Who's Sam?" Arnie asked, leaning across his desk, a puzzled look on his face.

They'd been working so many separate cases, Addison hadn't told him of the name change and had always referred to her as Natalie for the case. He filled him in on how Natalie Clayton became Samantha Riley.

Arnie rapped a pencil on his blotter. "Well. Since I discovered this pivotal piece of evidence for your case..."

"Hey, I would have gotten it."

"Maybe, maybe. But since I got it first, I think the least you can do is buy me lunch."

Addison scratched his chin and checked the clock. "Okay, I guess I do owe you something." He ejected the tape from the player, stacked it on the Clayton file, and dropped them both into his bottom drawer. "Grab your coat. I've got a pile of work before Friday's flight."

Arnie stopped midway into running his arm into a sleeve. "You going somewhere?"

Addison winced and pushed him toward the door. "I'll tell you on the way." When Arnie found out Addison was California bound again, he'd have to buy dessert too.

- 40 -

Sam ducked her head under her parka hood and tightened the drawstring. The thick cotton sweatshirt had been plenty warm this morning, but the afternoon seas sported a thick crop of white caps, building wind, and occasional showers. While she personally didn't think the weather fit for man nor beast, the tourists and whales disagreed. Eight adults, four children, and one dog lined the rails, watching a pod of five gray whales roll leisurely through the rough water. Of course the weather didn't bother the beasts. They were already wet.

"Hey, ya' dumb whales. Come over here. I dare ya'."

"Bernard, get down from there."

Sam looked over to see a mom pull on the belt of a chubby ten-year-old. Chubby was kind—the kid was built like a bowling pin. She shook her head as the boy pulled away from his mother's hand and climbed back onto the railing. The brat had been nothing but trouble since coming aboard. First he'd spilled a whole pitcher of sticky punch when he'd pushed one of the other children so he could get to the front of the line. Then he'd managed to lock the door to the head—with no one inside. Captain Tom had to stop the boat to get it open. The kid had been disrespectful to everyone. Even Blew gave him a wide berth.

Sam hurried over. "Bernard. You need to step down right now. It's not safe for you to be up there." When he ignored her, she gripped his arm and spoke with her most authoritative voice. "Get down. Right now."

Bernard threw his elbow back and caught Sam across the face. She tumbled backward across the wet deck, tripped over a bench, and went down hard. She heard Bernard's mom speaking to her son.

"Bernard. That was uncalled for. Please come down and apologize to the lady."

Sam rolled onto her back and let two of the men help her stand. It wasn't just the wallowing of the slow-moving boat that caused the world to tilt. The men guided her to the bench.

"Hey, ya' dumb whales."

She looked over and saw Bernard up on the rails.

"What do you want us to do?" one of the men asked.

Sam thought for a moment. Both men had video cameras in their hands. These were paying customers. It wasn't fair to involve them in the problem.

"Nothing. Let's leave him alone and hope he doesn't fall overboard." She smiled at them. "Go ahead and keep filming. This is a rare opportunity." She shooed the men back to the rail where the whales were closer than before, then looked toward the stern where Bernard played king of the world. His mother cut an embarrassed glance her direction and gave a small shrug and pitiful smile.

Carefully, Sam maneuvered into the closed cabin of the boat and dropped onto a stool. This trip would soon be over and she could say a permanent goodbye to Bernard. His poor mother wouldn't be so lucky.

The whale pod peeled off toward deeper water, and Tom brought the boat about and opened the throttles. Rain and wind chased them down the coast as they raced toward home. The cold front had passed and was now ahead of them.

Tom had cut this one a little close, she thought, as the swell height increased and the hull slapped each steel-gray wall. Sam served partially full cups of coffee to everyone as the suddenly frigid air drove them inside. Everyone except Bernard, who ran back and forth across the deck like a wild man. His mother looked miserable as she tried to corral him. Finally, she came and stood inside the cabin door and watched the boy through the glass. Her cheeks were beat red, and her graying hair stuck out in all directions. Sam took her a cup of coffee, which she gratefully accepted.

"I'm sorry about what happened earlier. I don't know what gets into him sometimes."

Sam figured it wasn't anything a good spanking wouldn't cure. But maybe it was too late for that. She opened her mouth to reassure the woman when, through the streaked glass, she saw Bernard disappear over the stern rail.

Sam didn't have time to think. She screamed, "Man overboard!" toward the cockpit, then slammed through the door, grabbed a life preserver, and dove over the stern. She hit the water headfirst, but the speed of the boat was still faster than her dive. Instead of going under, she tumbled backwards along the surface like a fallen water skier. Water sluiced down her arms, neck, and up her pant legs. It was too early in the season for the temperature to be at its lowest, but it was still bitterly cold. Finally she righted herself, spit out salt water, and began swimming.

The wake of the boat had smoothed the churning seas, but now they rushed back, turning the surface into a maze of valleys and peaks, each wave tip blown into a froth of spray by the increasing wind. Desperately, Sam wiped water from her eyes and searched for the boy in the gathering gloom.

"Help!"

Sam angled left and spotted him sliding out of sight behind an advancing swell. She stroked as hard as she could up the swell, thankful for all those summer swimming lessons in junior high. The sweatshirt that had felt so comfortable in the cabin dragged at her arms like lead, making it difficult to even lift them out of the water. She kept going.

Somewhere behind her, Tom would be turning the boat, but at full throttle it could take three or four minutes to slow, turn, and get back to them. By that time, the boy could disappear in the chop—faster if he couldn't swim.

Cold sloshed down her neck, sapping her body heat. At first the water felt warmer than the air, and it was. But mid-50s wasn't warm for very long. Sam struggled to move each arm.

Kick. Remember to kick!

The voice of her junior high swim instructor came to her. Kicking had always been her weakness, and the instructor constantly harped on it during the lessons. While she concentrated on her arms and breathing, her legs would drag listlessly. She couldn't afford that now. The life ring impeded her arm movement, so she focused on her kicks.

The initial surge of adrenaline waned as each crest slapped her in the face with stinging needles.

There!

Bernard was less than thirty feet away, gasping and sinking. His hands slapped the water. Clearly he wasn't a swimmer, and Sam renewed her kick as she pushed the ring in front. A toot of the Fin Finder II's horn sounded encouragement, and the bright beam of a searchlight swept across Bernard, then settled on him—just as he slid beneath the water.

Sam let go of the life ring and dove under water, angling toward the spot the boy's head had disappeared. Sound became muffled beneath the surface, and she forced her eyes open in the stinging salt water, searching. The intense beam brightened the water to tropical green, and she spotted Bernard sinking slowly ten feet below. Three strokes and she grabbed the back of his jacket and kicked for the bright surface. Her lungs burned for air, and with each kick, the surface seemed farther away. Their clothes weighed a ton. If she didn't do something, they'd both die.

Sam stopped kicking and wrapped her legs tightly around Bernard. Then she stripped the sweatshirt over her head. Her t-shirt came off with it, leaving only her bra. She pushed the thirty-pound lump of clothing out of her way and again started for the surface.

Every kick and stroke was one of desperation. Her lungs were going to burst, but she didn't dare let any air out. Without it, she'd be less buoyant. Ringing built in her ears, and even in the cold water, the top of her head prickled with heat, the same sensation she had in Dr. Mason's office when she'd fainted after a tetanus shot at age nine. She wasn't going to make it.

Maybe she should let go of the boy, surface for air, and dive again? No!

God. Please help!

The light seemed inches away. If she could only reach the light…

Sam pulled Bernard up her body, pushing from beneath as she kicked frantically. Suddenly, the boy rose out of the water, leaving Sam free. She kicked again trying to gain the last few inches to freedom, but the air exploded from her lungs and she swallowed seawater.

She clamped her mouth shut as her lungs convulsed and tried to cough up the invading liquid. She reached for the light, but her shoes and pants pulled her toward the bottom of the sea.

A body hit the water right in front of her. Blew's white-brown fur swirled as the dog dove beside her. She grabbed a handful of the hair and Blew turned upward.

Remember to kick.

Icy wind hit her face and she sucked a huge lungful of the sweetest air in the whole world. She coughed up salt water and swallowed more as waves slapped at her.

Strong hands caught and lifted her into the boat. She lay panting on the deck, staring up into the bright beam from the top of the boat. She'd reached the light.

Two women bundled her with coats. Their warmth reminded her body of the cold and she began shaking head to toe. For some reason, hard as she tried, she couldn't focus on the activity around her. Everything blurred and shifted. Voices shouted about an emergency, then she felt the deck vibrate against her back as the powerful engines throbbed. Blew licked her face. His raspy, hot tongue was the last thing she remembered—that and the light.

Addison shed his coat as he entered the station building and headed for his office. He'd spent his lunch hour running errands and looked forward to the sandwich in his cooler. As he passed the break room, another detective waved him in.

"Hey, Conner. You gotta see this! I heard about it on the radio. It's just coming on again."

At least ten people crowded around the wall-mounted TV, tuned to one of the national news shows. The picture changed and the camera switched to a talking head.

"We've all heard of animals rescuing people, but here's a story of an animal rescuing the rescuer. Reporter Amy Ivanhoe at our local affiliate in Mission Peaks, California, filmed this report last night with a follow-up this morning."

The screen filled with a night shot of a reporter standing on a boat dock. She wore a heavy pea coat with the collar turned up against the driving rain. Bright lights shown on a boat behind her.

"What could have been a terrible tragedy is being hailed a heroic rescue, both by man and beast. Or, in this case, woman and dog. It all started about four o'clock this afternoon when a ten-year-old boy fell overboard in rough seas while returning from a whale watching tour. The woman tour guide dove in to rescue the boy while the boat turned around. She pushed the boy to safety, but then, when she got into trouble herself, the captain's dog jumped in. According to the other passengers, the boy would have died had the woman not located him underwater. And the woman might have died except for some quick action by a very special dog."

While the reporter spoke, the film cut to a view of the boat speeding to the dock. Fire Rescue personnel ran down the planks, followed by the bouncing camera. Men helped a wobbly, blanket-wrapped boy onto the dock where the EMTs laid him on a stretcher and clamped on an oxygen mask. The video switched back to the reporter.

"The tour guide is one"—the reporter checked her notebook —"Samantha Riley, a fairly new resident to this small village of Perilous Cove. And the hero dog is a locally renowned whale-spotting hound named Blew, appropriately spelled B-l-e-w."

Addison sank into one of the chairs and whispered, "Please don't let there be any pictures of Sam. Please."

The video switched again as a gurney rolled up the dock. Addison recognized Sam in a semi-reclining position, smothered under a mountain of blankets. She had a ski hat pulled down over her ears, and an oxygen mask covered her face. Addison let out a breath. No one could recognize her if they didn't already know her new identity.

The reporter continued on with more of the details of the rescue while the video looped over and over. Addison stood up. He had to call Sam and make sure she was all right. He started to exit the room, but the next scene on the television stopped him.

The network talking head said, "Amy Ivanhoe filed this follow-up report just a few minutes ago." She turned toward the studio monitor.

The video switched to daytime and showed the same reporter in different clothing. She walked toward Sam's cabin as a handheld camera filmed over her shoulder and knocked on the door. Addison held his breath again.

"There doesn't appear to be anyone home this morning at this hero's house. It's possible she's staying with friends after yesterday's ordeal... oh, wait. There she is!"

The camera spun in the direction of the reporter's pointing hand and caught Sam walking down her driveway. Sam stopped, hands in pockets, obviously perplexed to find the news crew in front of her cabin. Bright lights obliterated the shadows of the tall cypress and washed across her face, causing her to throw up her hand.

Addison slumped into the chair again. Sam had no hat or mask to hide her facial features this morning.

"Samantha Riley?" The reporter ran to Sam and shoved the microphone in her face. The bouncing camera followed, then steadied. "Can you tell us what it feels like to be a hero this morning?"

The reporter's bubbly personality contrasted with Sam's astonishment. Addison watched the emotions play across her face, anger quickly changing to fear. Sam ducked her head and mumbled that she didn't want to talk about it, and then she pushed past the reporter. The camera tracked and zoomed as Sam ran into her cabin and slammed the door. The camera pulled back from the zoom and showed the cabin with the lighthouse beyond, then panned left for a shot of the harbor while reporter Amy Ivanhoe pontificated at length about the humble hero who lived next to a lighthouse in Perilous Cove, California.

"It's me," Tarz growled, then shifted the cell phone to his left hand so he could drive with his right.

"Where have you been? I haven't heard from you in days. I—"

"Can it, sis. You think my life's been easy? I've been chased out of my home by lousy cops, had to leave my cute little dog behind, and I'm livin' out of a fifteen-year-old beater Chevy more rust than metal." He'd changed the license plates for some from the Piggly Wiggly parking lot, then added a new registration sticker he'd pealed off a car at the airport long term parking lot. As air swirled around his frozen feet, he wondered why he'd bothered. No one would report this trash heap as stolen; they'd be afraid the police would tow it home. Tarz laughed and slapped the cracked steering wheel.

"What are you laughing at?"

"Nothin'. You got anything for me?" He glanced at the gas gauge—the needle read an eighth of a tank. He needed a job. Not work, just a job. Except for the advance, he hadn't been paid for the Clayton hit since the woman was still out there somewhere alive and well. Even a simple fire would hold him for a while. A box of matches rode shotgun on the passenger seat. He always had a box with him even if he had no money for food. His sis was in a position to uncover potential customers, and that meant gas money and eats. Her whiny voice cut into his thoughts of a warm fire, and he wasn't talking about one in a fireplace.

"Have you seen the TV news lately?"

Tarz cursed. "I'm living out of a stolen car. Does that sound like I have a cable hookup?"

"Okay, okay. Don't yell at me." She took a shuddering breath.

Tarz stared out the cracked windshield at the lush Arkansas countryside and tried to calm down. He had to treat her with kid gloves. She'd always been like that. Technically, they weren't related. She was the daughter of his father's second wife and eight years younger than Tarz. But they shared a common background with the old man, one best forgotten. Tarz' own scars were bad enough. But hers…

"This is good news, Tarz, really good. Have you heard of Perilous Cove, California?"

- 41 -

After a week of tours, caring for Millie, and working with several people to plan Roy Trafford's funeral, Sam turned Saturday's tours over to Trudy and spent the morning cleaning her cabin and washing clothes at the Bay Wash Laundromat a block behind Harbor Street.

At ten o'clock she finished the last load of clothes, parked the Jeep by the cabin and opened the back to retrieve her laundry basket. The crunch of tires on shells caught her attention. For a moment she feared it was another reporter, though the story had died quickly as the fickle new juggernaut shifted focus on some other hapless victim. She breathed a sigh of relief as the familiar Bronco rattled to a stop and she recognized Addison and Mandy.

Mandy's door opened before the car settled, and the girl grabbed Sam in a fierce hug. In a barrage of words only capable by a teenager, Mandy told her about her crazy week at school. Then, after practically pushing Sam and Addison together, Mandy ran off to find Star.

For a moment, Addison and Sam stood looking at each other in awkward silence, the towering Cyprus trees shushing overhead. Then she glanced down to find her underwear lying on the top of the clothesbasket. She'd bought the lacey red set on a whim, spending more than she'd intended, but beguiled by something Jack would have deemed excess. She whirled toward the cabin door, hiding the basket with her body.

"Would you like some coffee?"

"Sure. That would be nice."

Sam hurried into her bedroom to hide the underwear-festooned basket and take a few deep breaths. The walls of her tiny cabin squeezed closer as the detective's broad shoulders filled the kitchen doorway. His hair, windblown during the drive over, made her fingers itch to comb it straight. Had it only been a week since he and Mandy were here? It seemed longer, shorter—she didn't know.

Sam tackled the simple act of making coffee, but it became a daunting task. She was too aware of him leaning against the counter, studying her in silence. The carafe clattered against the sink and she sloshed water on her shirt. His hand covered hers as she reached for the paper towels.

"On second thought, let's forget the coffee. How about we go for a walk?"

Sam nodded to his brown eyes, not trusting her voice.

The wind hit them as soon as they stepped out the door. Another weather front was due this afternoon, followed by a bigger storm on Sunday. The local forecasters warned of heavy rains, giant surf, and strong winds. But the temperature hadn't yet dropped and she settled for a light jacket. Addison grabbed a sweatshirt out of the Bronco and tied it around his waist.

He turned her off the driveway and down the lower path, which descended along the bay side of Perilous Point and switchbacked down the steep bluff toward town. She'd only been this way once before with Star, but since then the dirt path had been eroded in several places by water runoff, leaving two to three foot cuts in the steep hillside. Addison stepped across these, then reached back for her hand to help her hop across. After the last one, he didn't let go.

Native grasses and brush dotted the slope, clinging to rocks and other roots to keep their tenuous hold. Tiny yellow and red flowers poked out among the rock. In several spots, small slides of gravel and rock covered the path, and in one place a trickle of a spring wept into a muddy pool.

After walking for ten minutes, they had descended to where the breakwater joined the base of the bluff, and the path toward town widened to a flat thoroughfare. Locals and tourists alike made regular use of this access to the rocky breakwater to fish and watch the waves.

They walked toward town along the edge of the bay, overlooking moored cabin cruisers, crusty fishing boats, sleek sailboats, and dinghies, Sam acutely aware of her small hand in Addison's large one. It felt good, natural, and completely disconcerting. Jack had rarely touched her in public, and she couldn't remember the last time they'd walked holding hands.

The further she got from Jack's funeral, the more she realized there were a lot of "the last times" she couldn't remember. Had their marriage really been so dry, so stagnant? Could she have done more to please Jack and bring a spark to their relationship? She'd been so blind, so used to the way it was, that she couldn't imagine how it could be.

Addison abruptly stopped walking. "What's wrong?"

She'd been squeezing his hand too tightly, and she forced a smile and shook her head.

The call of a circling gull brought his head up, and she examined his profile. Today he wore faded jeans, a chambray work shirt and tennis shoes, so different from his detective attire. He appeared completely at ease, and his face had lost the stress lines she remembered from Missouri.

He led her onward, and several times he seemed about to say something, only to turn toward the bay. Finally, she stopped, and the tug on his hand brought him around to face her. The main street of town lay a hundred yards ahead; the aroma of coffee from The Last Drop swirled on the breeze.

"What is it, Addison?" Now he looked like a ten-year-old called to the principal's office.

"Ahhh, I…" He glanced down and placed his other hand on hers and she did the same. But he didn't say anything, simply rubbed the back of her hand. A pink blush crept up his neck.

"Addison, if we keep standing here like this, people are going to think we're pledging undying love or something."

His eyes followed her nod toward the town and people walking along the boardwalk. He dropped her hands and stepped back, shoving his own in his pockets. "Oh. Sorry."

Sam felt bad for his embarrassment. She slipped her arm around his waist and hooked her fingers in a belt loop and smiled. "It's okay. Come on. I'll buy you a really *good* cup of coffee. Not like the stuff I make."

He laughed and his arm draped across her shoulders, casual, natural, speaking silent words of safety and security, a message she hadn't heard in many years.

- 42 -

Addison and Mandy treated Ben to Sunday brunch at the Deep Blue restaurant at the lake's marina. Then at three o'clock, Addison fired up the Bronco and he and Mandy drove down to Perilous Cove for Roy Trafford's funeral.

Heavy rain swept across the sloping parking lot of PC Community Church, driven by gusty winds off the gray, white-capped sea. The church sat on the hill overlooking the village and, on days with much better weather, commanded a magnificent view of the harbor and ocean beyond. The white clapboard siding, needle-like steeple, and gothic side windows declared its 1892 construction by New England merchant seamen drawn to Perilous Cove.

The weather today would do a northeast sailor proud. Predictions grew more dire by the hour. On the drive down, the car radio announcer warned coastal residents to prepare for up to eight inches of rain beginning this afternoon, almost unheard of in desert-like California. But coupled with high surf, wind gusts of sixty miles per hour or more, and dropping temperatures, the result could be a hundred year storm. As if a portent of the hours to come, the radio station faded to static after the final forecast.

Addison followed Mandy up the broad front steps where they huddled beneath the deep portico and waited until Sam, Millie, and Star arrived with Dr. Navarro. Across the parking lot, an American flag snapped in the wind while its rope clanged a bell-like staccato against the hollow galvanized pole. Organ music drifted out the open doors in odd defiance of the wind, bringing human comfort against the face of raw nature.

"There they are." Mandy pointed to Navarro's four-door crew cab pickup. The doctor parked next to the stairs, and Addison and Mandy met them with umbrellas. They virtually carried Millie inside.

A center aisle divided the wood pews, which stood in short rows on the wide-planked floors. The dark benches gleamed with decades of rubbing, and the rich scent of polish filled the warm room. They settled Millie in the front row.

She insisted Addison and Mandy sit in the row with her, and it took some shuffling before they were all arranged. Millie sat on the aisle with Starfire beside her. Dr. Navarro was next and maneuvered Sam next to him. After Addison's embarrassment yesterday with Sam, he hung back and let Mandy sit next to her, taking the end seat for himself.

He had no idea what to say to Sam. Yesterday, he'd wanted to talk to her about his feelings, not getting into deep things like love or anything, but at least laying it out on the table. But how to begin? She was still so close to the pain of losing her husband as well as her best friend, Donna Montgomery. He well knew it took time to heal and he didn't want to rush her. As they'd walked yesterday, the closer they got to town, the more nervous he'd become, and...well, it wasn't a moment to remember, that was for sure. He was grateful now as a gust of cold air rattled the gothic window at his side and pushed past the crumbled glazing, cooling his reddened neck.

As a distraction from his thoughts, Addison turned to observe the rear of the chapel. Guests filed in, dripping water and shaking umbrellas in the tiny foyer. Many came forward and offered Millie and Star hugs and whispered condolences. Tears ran down Star's freckled cheeks and he hurt for the girl's loss. The simple casket in front of the church brought a sobering reality, even if she didn't remember her father. Mandy turned to him, gave his hand a squeeze, rose and stepped around Sam. She bent and spoke to the doctor and he and Sam scooted down so Mandy could sit next to Star.

Addison's own eyes watered as his daughter pulled the younger girl close and exchanged glances with Millie. Mandy was growing into a remarkable young woman. Today she wore a turquoise blue sweater over a white skirt. She'd combed her black hair softly back with just a hint of gel. Stones set in silver Navajo earrings matched the blue of the sweater. If only Elizabeth could see the grace and beauty of their daughter.

But he was most proud of the way she saw need and cared for others. He ducked his head and brushed his eyes. Funerals reminded people of the shortness of life and the necessity to enjoy the journey every minute, every day. He vowed to tell Mandy how proud he was of her. And he promised himself to talk to Sam too.

A hush settled like a soft blanket, and old wood creaked as people shifted on their pews. The pastor stepped to the pulpit and began the service.

Since moving to Perilous Cove, Sam had attended church a few times with Millie and Star. But she didn't know what to expect at a church funeral service, so she sat quietly with her head bowed. Her parents' service had been at the mortuary, as had Jack's.

The closed casket below the pulpit invited unwanted memories, and she shifted on the hard bench, its lack of comfort echoing her own unease. Maybe that was the whole point of funerals and church: to cause unease in the common person's everyday life and provoke change.

She shook her head. No, that wasn't fair. Down deep she knew God wasn't cruel. But did he really care about individuals? Surely with a whole universe to care for, he'd hardly have time to be involved with each one of them. With her.

Sam had always envisioned life as a never-ending cycle of weddings, births, and funerals, but it seemed like her world was suddenly filled with far more of the latter than anything else. After the weddings of her college friends, she'd lost touch with them and the subsequent births of their children. Jack hadn't encouraged her to stay in contact, but she couldn't lay all the blame at his feet. She'd used his lack of enthusiasm as an excuse to decline the baby shower invitations, each birth announcement a cruel reminder of her own inability to know the joy of sitting in a celebration circle, opening presents of miniature outfits, watching others coo over her baby. That was never to be.

She ran her hands through her damp hair and took a cleansing breath. Millie blew her nose in a tissue and Sam glanced down the pew. People always said it wasn't right that parents bury their children, and Sam couldn't imagine what it was like for Millie to lose her son.

Sam's own loss felt both raw and oddly distant at the same time. Had it only been three months? In that time, everything in her whole life had changed. She lived in a different state, city, and house, owned a different car, had none of her old things, and her work was something she'd never imagined. People called her by a name she sometimes still failed to respond to right away. Yes, her personal grief seemed like a year or two distant…at least.

But it wasn't the pain of Jack's funeral that surfaced as frequently now, rather his betrayal. Could Jack have wanted her dead in order to collect on life insurance? It seemed impossible. After eleven years of marriage, could he be so cold, so unfeeling? Able to hire a hit man?

A shiver shook her, and she forced another deep breath. Sandwiched between Addison and Alejandro, she should feel safe, but the palpable testosterone tension between the two men only added to her discomfort. If not for Millie and Star, she'd bolt for the nearest exit. Instead, she shelved her personal life and concentrated on the present.

A small table to the left of the casket held three photos of Roy. The first showed a towheaded boy of about seven. He stood feet together on top of a crooked wood fence post using his arms to balance and looking like a swimmer readying for a high dive to a pond below. A mischievous grin split his face, revealing his missing front teeth. In the second picture, a slightly older Roy sat on top of a dusty red Farmall tractor, again with a wide grin. His hands gripped the steering wheel, pretending to drive while Millie, young and beautiful, smiled up with pride. Sam could almost hear the boy making engine sounds as he twisted the wheel from side to side.

The last picture captured a pensive Roy, gazing out the front window of what Sam recognized as Millie's home. Now in his mid-twenties, he was dressed in jeans, tee shirt, and a studded leather motorcycle jacket. The blond hair had turned darker and shone with some kind of gel. It looked like he was trying for James Dean as the rebel, a feat Roy easily pulled off due to his bad-boy good looks. It was a beautiful, artistic portrait done in black and white. Sam had spotted the resemblance to Star in the previous pictures, but this final shot introduced a hardened young man, all traces of the little boy gone for good.

What turned a cute kid into a young adult bound and determined to destroy himself and bring agony to loving parents? Had Roy suspected his life would burn out early? Would he have changed if he knew his fate, or would he have continued down the path toward the cliff?

She glanced sideways at Star, whose freckled hand clutched Mandy's. If someone as strong and good as Millie had such struggles with her son, how did Sam have a chance with Star? What if the girl followed in her mother and father's footsteps? What if Roy's criminal behavior somehow carried on through his genetic code? Looking at Star's freckled face, it was inconceivable she'd stray like her parents. But if she did, could Sam handle the pain and disappointment?

Tarz slapped his face and rolled down the window. The cold, wet air shocked him awake—at least for a minute. He'd driven twenty hours straight, but didn't remember the last hour. The wipers smeared streaks across the bug-encrusted windshield, doing little to improve his vision, while at the same time lulling him to sleep with their steady rhythm. Rain soaked the cloth upholstery of the seat, but he ignored it.

The '95 Honda Civic he'd procured in Denver purred beneath him, and Tarz thanked the Japanese for designing the most popular stolen car. Once over the California line, he'd stopped in Barstow at a huge outlet mall and did a three-way trade of license plates so he'd have a fresh California set. It would take the cops a long time to straighten out the mess. Meanwhile, he looked like any Golden State driver.

He checked his map one more time as a sign for Mission Peak, 58 miles, came into view, and blew out a deep breath. Nearly there. Grabbing the package of No-Doz, he popped two tabs and chewed them, gagging on the bitter taste. He needed his wits and couldn't take time to stop for more coffee. Besides, his stomach felt like the bottom had been eaten out by the acid. He snapped a Rolaids tube open and dropped in some of those, hoping they didn't diminish the stimulant.

Tarz fiddled with the radio, skipping through stations until one caught his ear. He smiled and settled into the seat. Perfect. A good omen.

He sang along with The Mamas and the Papas, belting California Dreaming out the open window toward the furious sky.

"Say your prayers, Natalie Clayton, it's showtime."

- 43 -

Sam covered the casseroles, salad, and dessert they'd eaten, left at Millie's by the church ladies. The outpouring of care from the small congregation amazed her. The women had braved hard rain and fallen tree branches to bring the dinner by after the church service. No one had done that for Sam's parents' service, or for Jack's.

In the living room, laughter had replaced weighty sorrow as Millie and Addison reminisced about Roy's younger years. Star lay snuggled into the big chair beside her grandmother, grinning at stories she'd never heard about her dad. Sam knew Addison's feelings about Roy Trafford. As a cop, Addison dealt with Roy's type all too often. She loved the way he put aside his law enforcement career and helped the two women remember the best parts of the man's life.

The pastor had read a quote during the service: "Every man deserves to be remembered for his best moment." They were giving Roy that honor now.

But while the old woman had a smile on her face, her gray pallor worried Sam. Millie needed rest. The graveside service had been postponed two days due to the weather, and she would need her strength for that ordeal. Sam knew how draining it could be to lower a loved one into a dark hole. Even with Jack's treachery, planning her murder for the insurance payout, Sam recalled the numbing finality of the internment. She hadn't stayed while they lowered Jack's coffin and covered it with dirt, but her chest had compressed on the way home with Donna as she imagined the workers completing their job.

Millie's eyes closed, but the corners of her lips turned upward as she listened to Star, Mandy, and Addison. Maybe, Sam thought, this was rejuvenation in itself. There would be too few of these family times in the days to come, so Sam decided to let her rest where she was awhile longer.

The enchiladas were still too warm for the refrigerator. Sam set them on the counter to cool, and put the teakettle on to boil. Rain peppered the window over the sink like a fistful of gravel thrown against the pane. Actually, it had let up a little, but now the wind and unstable air behind the initial front barreled down on them. Distant thunder rumbled and the wind howled louder as if it feared what was to come.

Sam shivered. It wasn't cold in the house, but the blackness beyond the glass seemed more ominous than any previous night, harboring a malevolent force bent on destruction. She jumped as a hand touched her shoulder, and gasped in a breath before she caught Addison's reflection in the window.

"Are you okay?" His deep voice soothed some of the tension. As she turned to face him, he slid his hand down to her lower back. Its warm weight penetrated her sweater. She relaxed back against the counter and nodded. The window shook like someone wanted in. Or some*thing*.

He glanced at the window. "Quite a storm out there."

Sam rubbed her arms. "It's eerie, almost alive. Like it wants us."

Addison chuckled and moved his hand in light circles. "You've been reading too much Stephen King."

But she hadn't. That was the thing. "Broderick's out there somewhere, looking for me."

"Let's take a break from that right now."

It hadn't made sense the second and third time the killer had attacked her, either, but logic hadn't stopped him. And with his history, his childhood…

Drops splattered the window, pressing into the glass. As a girl growing up in the mid-west, storms had fascinated her. She would sit for hours in the middle of the night, arms on her windowsill, watching lightning and counting the seconds for the thunder to arrive. Sometimes she tracked the intervals with paper and pencil. She loved storms. But this…

"I'm heading into town for a few minutes," Addison said. "I need to call Arnie for updates, then I want to call Ben and tell him we're not coming home tonight. I'm afraid the road will have mudslides and downed trees." As if to punctuate his decision, wind shook the house and howled around the corners. Sam moved closer, not wanting him to go. He put his other arm around her and pulled her into his warmth.

"If your cell won't work here, just use Millie's phone," she said, laying her head on his chest. She listened to his heartbeat as his hands moved up her back. It felt perfect.

"I tried her phone a few minutes ago. It's dead. Probably a tree limb knocked down the line. Hopefully the phones in town work or maybe I can get a cell signal up by the church." He stepped back, reluctance written across his face, but with it, resolve.

A man of duty. Sam wished the world would leave them alone, if only for a little while. As Addison told Mandy where he was going, Sam picked up the kitchen phone. She might as well have been pressing one of Millie's ceramic art pieces to her ear.

Addison donned his heavy jacket, and then headed out the door into the semi-darkness. Mandy and Sam watched him sprint through the downpour to the Bronco, then heard him crank it several times before the engine roared to life. She was glad for the old truck's four-wheel drive.

Mandy followed Sam back to the kitchen to finish the clean up. "I guess we'd better work out the sleeping arrangements for tonight."

Other than the occasional night here with Millie and Star, or Star at Sam's cabin, she had been by herself every night since fleeing Steerman. She'd gotten used to it, but couldn't say she liked it. Yet the thought of all of them sharing the three-bedroom house sent color creeping up her neck, Addison's touch on her back a few minutes ago fresh in her mind. So much had changed. And while she desired it, it was all very new.

"I should just stay at my place, it's—"

"No way," Star interrupted as she brought her empty glass into the kitchen. "Your cabin is drafty and freezing, and it'll be ten times worse tonight in the storm. We'd have to take you to the hospital with hypno… hypno…"

"Hypothermia," Mandy finished for her.

Sam folded her arms. "I have my space heater."

The girl mimicked Sam's stance. "The only way to heat your place tonight is with a roaring fire in the fireplace."

Sam glanced at Mandy who gave a slight shrug. "Star told me about your…reluctance to have a fire." Her face softened and she put her hand on Sam's rigid shoulder. "I understand, Sam. I haven't forgotten."

Sam searched Mandy's eyes and saw only care. The girl had seen the results of that night: the painful burns, the singed hair. Sam gave an involuntary shudder, remembering the horrible nightmare at Addison's house. Being alone tonight sounded like an awful idea.

Together, they figured out a plan. Mandy would share Star's room, Sam would take the spare bedroom she normally did, and Addison could have the large sofa in the living room.

Sam went to the front door and cracked it open. Wind tore through the treetops, stripping needles and cones, and raining them down on the yard like missiles, but the rain had diminished to a sprinkle. Okay, she admitted, it was horizontal rain, but at least it wasn't pouring. She shoved her arms into her jacket and zipped it up.

"You're not going out there?" Mandy came beside her to look out.

"I've got to run down to my house to get my overnight stuff and clothes for the morning. Looks like a good time to make a dash for it. What do you think?" The girl looked at Sam like she was nuts, but reached for her own jacket.

"I'll come with you."

Sam put her hand on Mandy's arm and smiled. "Stay here. No sense both of us getting wet. I'm going to run for it and won't be five minutes." She cinched down the drawstring for the hood, tunneling her vision.

"You're sure?" Mandy didn't sound convinced. "We could wait for Dad to get back."

"Oh, I forgot," Sam said, turning back to Mandy. "I need to check on my Jeep. The garage roof has a few leaks and so does the Jeep's top. I have a tarp I can throw over it for tonight. I'll be back in ten minutes tops."

She slipped out the door and jogged down the walk to the white shells of the driveway. Fifty feet from the porch, Millie's big driveway floodlight disappeared as the rain began again.

Sam pounded down her curved driveway, shoes crunching the shells that kept her from living in mud. Distant lightning provided the only illumination, but its irregular strobing did little to drive back the night. She negotiated the turns by memory, glancing off two bushes and narrowly avoiding one tree. Raindrops—condensed high in the old cypress limbs—fell as giant water bombs, adding to the increasing downpour. The sharp tang of sea salt filled each labored breath.

Cold rivulets seeped around her hood and snaked down her neck. The dress slacks she'd worn to the funeral wrapped her legs like a wet second skin, and water ran into her flats. She'd grab her stuff and run back up the hill. A hot shower at Millie's sounded really good.

The wall of her cabin loomed, barely visible in the dark. She landed with a thump against its reassuring solidness and scurried to the shelter of the three-by-three porch overhang and her doorway. She gasped a few lungfuls of air as she turned the knob.

The inky interior made the outside darkness seem like daylight, and her wet shoes snagged on the oval rug. Her instinctive flip of the light switch yielded no change. A toppled tree probably took out a power line somewhere. There might not be electricity for hours—or days as Millie said was sometimes the case. She sent up a prayer for Addison's safety, wishing he hadn't gone out.

Sam shrugged off her coat and hung it on the wall peg beside the door. She could hear it dripping and slid the rug over to protect the planks. The cabin's air felt like it had come straight down from the arctic. Rain beat down on the roof, determined to find a way into her house.

Sam trailed her hand along the wall to the kitchen, fumbled along the counter, and found the junk drawer where she kept matches. She struck one along the box. It broke and fell away. She retrieved another one and tried again. This time the match flared to life, impossibly bright to her straining eyes. A fat emergency candle lay in the open drawer, and she set it on the counter and touched the match to the wick. As the match died away, the wax string surged to life, pushing back the darkness a few feet, at least.

Sam tossed the spent match in the sink. She had yet to buy a replacement flashlight for the one she'd dropped in the cellar. An involuntary shiver shook her shoulders at the thought of the confined, dark space beneath her feet.

The candle cast a feeble light in the bedroom, its light absorbed by the room's dark paneled walls. Sam set it on the dresser while she gathered her duffel bag and clothes. In the bathroom she tossed in her toiletries. Her dry tennis shoes were by the door.

In each room, she held the candle high and checked for water spots on the ceiling. Although rain drummed on the roof, the interior was dry.

So far, so good.

Sam hurried back through the kitchen, gearing up for a wet trip to the garage and then another uphill to Millie's. As she passed the window above the sink, a brilliant flash of lightning turned night to day.

Silhouetted against the six-paned glass was a man.

Addison couldn't get a cell signal anywhere in town. He tried the pay phone in front on the hardware store, but the line was just as dead as Millie's. He figured the whole town was out. The wind had increased dramatically, turning over wooden benches along the harbor and scattering the outdoor furniture at the deli.

He dodged a rolling garbage can and jumped back in the Bronco. Maybe a little farther south on the highway.

The road uphill out of town was littered with rocks and tree limbs. Rain came in torrents, washing muddy rivers down each side of the road, picking up speed as it rushed toward the ocean. But overall, the highway seemed in good shape. He passed only two oncoming cars during his drive. Everyone who had sense was holed up someplace safe and dry. And warm.

Ten minutes south of town, his cell phone beeped and he pulled over at the next turnout. It was too dark to see the ocean, but Addison heard the thundering roar of the waves crashing on the shore rocks. He loved watching the surf during storms. As teenagers, he and Ben would drive down to the beaches whenever a big front came in. Once, they set up a dome tent on the sand. Only when the wind threatened to launch the tent airborne—with them inside—did they wad it up and run for the car. Tonight held no sense of adventure.

Addison checked the cell signal: one bar. Maybe it would hold. He pressed the speed dial for Arnie's phone. Crackled ringing sounded, nearly drowned out by the rain hitting the Bronco's steel roof and hood.

"Hey, partner," Arnie's distorted voice came through the tiny speaker. "How's sunny California?"

Addison barked a laugh. "Unbelievable at the moment." A pickup truck surged by going south, sending water sheeting over the parked Bronco.

"What's all that noise? Sounds...you're under water."

"Almost." He told Arnie about the storm front making landfall. The volume of the phone was set as high as it would go; he strained to hear over the storm and increasing static.

"…news. State…ported…arge…to a ca…"

"Say again, Arnie. You're breaking up."

"…police said…charge on…card."

"Did you say credit card? A charge? Arnie?" Addison checked the display. No signal. The call had dropped.

He started the engine and drove south another few minutes before the phone showed two bars. He pulled over and called Arnie again.

"Arnie, can you hear me better?" Ball bearings pelted the truck's steel top.

"Addison? You disappeared on me."

"I think cell towers are down. Land lines are." He prayed this connection would hold. "What have you got?"

"Bad news. State police tracked a credit card charge at a Barstow, California gas station. Then an ATM cash withdrawal on the same card a few minutes later. The card is registered to Ned Crane, one of Tarz Broderick's aliases."

Addison's stomach tightened. California. Was Broderick heading their way? "How long ago?"

"Six hours. They didn't find it right at first—some kind of delay with the bank's processing."

"How far—"

"Is Barstow from Perilous Cove?" Arnie interrupted. "Only about five hours."

Broderick could be in Perilous Cove right now. Maybe in one of those cars he passed. He reached for the ignition key.

"He used the card again in Paso Robles. That's only—"

"I know where it is. He's close or already here." Addison pounded the steering wheel in frustration. He should have called earlier.

"It gets worse, partner."

Addison turned the key and pumped the gas. The engine roared to life. "I've got to get back Arnie."

"I know, but wait a sec, Addison. You need to know this. Broderick has a sister."

What did he care if Broderick had a sister? He needed to get back to Mandy, Sam, and the others.

"We caught Sharon sneaking your Clayton file back into your desk.

After an hour of interrogation, she broke down and confessed. Her married boyfriend that got her pregnant was none other than Jack Clayton. And she was the woman in the bank video." Arnie's voice took on a hard edge Addison rarely heard from the easy-going man. "Addison, she's Broderick's half-sister. She called him two days ago and told him where Sam is and about her name change. He's coming for Sam."

"Arnie, call the local police out here. Or the Highway Patrol. Sheriff's office. Anybody you can get. Tell them to come. I've got to get back."

"I'm on it, partner. Be safe."

Addison tossed the phone on the passenger seat and spun the steering wheel. The four tires sprayed gravel and mud as he hung a U-turn and floored the accelerator. The wipers did little to improve visibility, but he didn't back off until he reached seventy. He planted the left front tire on the center line, following the curving road as much by the feel of the raised reflectors as by sight.

God, let me get there first.

Flashing red lights ahead appeared from the curtain of rain. He slammed on the brakes, sliding on the wet pavement. Frantically, he twisted the wheel left to avoid the stopped car, then right to correct for the sideways slide. The Bronco rocked to a stop, nose facing the right-hand ditch, awash in water. Not ten feet from his driver door, illuminated by the other car's headlights, a tree stretched across the road.

Addison dropped his head on the steering wheel for a moment. Then he flipped up the hood of his coat and opened the door just as a man ran up, cursing at Addison for driving like an idiot.

- 44 -

The candle bounced off Sam's foot and rolled across the room, its light snuffed out by the fall. She heard it ricochet off a chair leg, but her mind was furiously processing what she'd seen. With the lightning's instant fade, oppressive darkness closed tight, and once again her eyes strained to gather in any light. But there was none. She dropped to all fours and felt for the candle. Light became a physical need.

Who was the man? Addison would have knocked, as would Alejandro. If it wasn't a friend, that left ... She couldn't finish the thought.

Rain pelted the roof of the cabin, drowning out—literally—all other outside sounds. Maybe he would go away. Maybe, in the flash of the lightning, he hadn't noticed her anemic little candle.

Hope dissolved as she heard the squeak of the front door hinges. She hadn't locked it. A blast of wind and damp air scurried across the floor, then she heard the door click closed. If this *was* a friend, he would have said something.

As quietly as she could, Sam backed toward the bedroom. Maybe she could prop a chair under the doorknob, or push the dresser against it. She tried to ignore the wet footsteps squeaking on the hard floor and backed faster. A few more feet. She would slam the bedroom door shut, wedge her foot against it, and pull the dresser in front of it. She could do this. She—

"Going somewhere?" The gravelly voice pinned her as securely as the blinding beam of his flashlight.

She struggled to breathe and jumped to her feet, caught in the light. She grabbed one of the kitchen chairs as a weapon. They were well made —evidenced by many years of withstanding Millie's one-time considerable bulk—but they were also heavy. Before she could lift it, the man batted it aside and brought the flashlight down on her head.

Pain spiked through her skull like lightning bolts, burning paths to her neck and shoulders. She collapsed on his large boots, slimy with mud. He'd taken a path to her house other than the shell-covered driveway. Now he tracked mud across her just-mopped floor. Sparks of light danced before her closed eyes and she couldn't seem to move.

Rough hands yanked her to her feet and slammed her against the wall. Aunt Rowena's Kit-Cat clock shattered, and a jumble of plastic parts clattered to the floor. It had been Sam's favorite item in the cabin and, as a little girl, she'd sit at the table and count the tail wags as her aunt chatted away and baked cinnamon rolls for breakfast. That was the first time Sam had counted all the way to one hundred.

"Good girl, Natalie. You should be rewarded with a nice, treat. Does that sound good?" Aunt Rowena asked, holding a plate of the buttery rolls.

A hard backhand snapped her from the safety of the memory, and blood rather than cinnamon filled her mouth. Sam reached for the man's face and gouged at his eyes, eliciting a curse and a blow to her stomach. She doubled over, trying to suck in air with lungs that no longer worked.

"Let's go." The man gripped the back of her sweatshirt and propelled her across the room toward the door. He didn't pause for her jacket, and they plunged into heavy rain and wind.

Sam's legs quit working without oxygen, and she sagged to the ground. In seconds the water plastered her hair against her head and ran icy rivulets down her neck and back. The cotton sweatshirt failed to keep her either warm or dry. A rough hand circled her bicep and pulled her up and forward. After a few feet, Sam was finally able to get enough air to speak.

"Who are you?"

A grunt and shove was his response.

"Tarz Broderick?" Sam spit the name out along with rainwater. The man stopped and turned on her.

"Well, well. Pretty smart, aren't you."

"Where are you taking me?"

"Not far. Just far enough." His vise-like grip slid to her wrist and yanked her ahead. She had no choice but to stumble along, barely keeping her feet as she tried to clear her spinning head.

In the blackness, Sam couldn't be sure which direction they headed. Water blurred her vision as fast as she wiped it away. As bright as the flashlight had seemed inside the house, its beam did nothing to push aside the unleashed storm.

Sam tripped on the rough ground and fell headlong into a muddy puddle. The man dragged her along in it for several feet before stopping and lifting her to her feet. She knew it wasn't because he felt sorry for her —it was easier on him to have her walk.

Dim flashes grew in brightness and Sam realized they were nearing the lighthouse. She recognized the distant roar of the diesel generator in the power shed concealed in a small grove of trees off to their right, its noise nearly swallowed up by the impossibly loud waves crashing on the rocks. The generator was wired to start up automatically in case of a power failure, feeding electricity to the light tower.

The uphill side of the tower had sheltered them from the worst of the wind, but as they circled left around the rock foundation, the full force of the onshore storm slammed into them.

Forecasters had predicted fifty mile per hour winds with gusts significantly higher. For once, they'd gotten it right. Sam and the man caromed between the steel pipe railing and the lighthouse foundation, but still Broderick forced her on, the bones of her wrist grinding together beneath the man's hand. Rain stung Sam's face like hundreds of tiny needles, blinding her and filling her mouth every time she tried to speak.

As they rounded to the seaward side of the walkway, waves sprayed over their heads, salt mixed with fresh, and all of it icy cold. Flashes of light strobed the angry water below. The tide was higher than she'd ever seen it, only a few feet below her favorite rock, but the swells and waves were even higher.

Broderick threw her against the railing, grabbed her sweatshirt and jeans in his fists, and began lifting her above the steel bar.

He meant to throw her into the sea.

Sam gripped the scaly metal in desperation and wrapped her legs around his. With her free hand, she sought his face again and dug her nails into the flesh. Her thumb found his left eye and she felt her nail plunge deep into the socket.

Broderick's scream cut through the night. Suddenly freed, Sam fell onto the steel pipe, teetering toward the oncoming waves. She tried to twist to safety, but she tumbled backward and landed with bone-jarring impact on the sharp rocks a few feet below. A wave drenched her and sucked at her with awful power. She dug her fingernails into a crevice, tearing skin, but hanging on as her feet swung free in the retreating water.

Sam had to get back on the walkway before the next wave dragged her out to sea. But Broderick was still somewhere near. In the light's next pulse, she saw him sitting against the lighthouse base with his hands over his face. The gale precluded any need for stealth, Sam held her breath, grabbed one of the steel posts, and swung her legs onto the concrete walkway. She got to her hands and knees and crawled away from the man. Sam knew the light station grounds well enough to evade him, even with his flashlight.

She'd just pushed to her feet when something struck her in the neck and she collapsed. He swore at her and threw her back the way she'd come. Dazed, Sam clung to the railing and tried to wipe water from her eyes with the muddy sleeve of her sweatshirt. The flashlight bobbed around, then steadied, and the man shone it on his jacket pocket. In the next instant, Sam saw what he pulled free. He pointed a pistol at her.

She had no chance to escape.

"Why are you doing this? What do you want?" Her shout seemed lost in the tumult around them, but the man heard. In the next light beacon pulse she saw his cruel smile.

"I've got what I want. You."

"Why?" Sam pressed her back against the cold steel.

"Money. Why else?" The man laughed and took a step closer, bracing his feet as wind whipped his clothes like a flag on a pole. "Plus I don't like it when a job isn't complete. You're a loose end and ruining my professional reputation."

Sam had no idea what he was talking about, but she knew he wouldn't stop until he killed her. She had to run. Gathering her strength, she let go of the railing and heaved right. A blast of wind twisted her away as the gun cracked. She crashed to her knees and spun around, grasping at the guardrail to keep from being blown over. The wind had knocked the man back against the lighthouse wall. The flashlight wobbled and pointed skyward, catching his face in its beam.

Now was her chance. She jumped to her feet and made one stride before slipping on a pile of seaweed. She splayed flat out on the rough concrete, her palms burning where the skin tore away.

"That's far enough."

Sam looked up at the man above her, into the beam of the flashlight. At its edge she made out the barrel of the gun.

A wall of water crashed down on them, washing Sam into the man's legs. He fell on her, knocking her breath away. Underwater, she could hear the sizzle of the froth before the wave receded and allowed her to gasp a shallow breath.

The flashlight had disappeared, but in a flare of lightning, Sam saw the glint of metal in the man's hand. She rolled away and heard another report from the pistol. Shattered stone sprayed her neck and scalp, but her skin was numb with cold. Another wave drenched them with hundreds of gallons of water. From all her days watching the ocean from these very rocks, she knew large waves came in sets. Several big ones were followed by a period of relative calm. Were there more on the way?

The next pulse from the lighthouse showed the man standing, clutching the rail, his gun rising toward her. Behind him, a gleaming mountain of water towered twenty feet above. Sam had time for one quick breath before it fell. The gun spit fire at her.

The chaos of the storm disappeared in the muffled underwater world of bubbles, foam, and swirling grit. Sam's ears popped with the pressure, and salt water surged between her closed eyelids, stinging and threatening to tear out her eyeballs. As the wave threw her about, she banged her head, back, and legs on the craggy cliff. A brief weightlessness caught her, and she wondered if this was what daredevils going over Niagara Falls felt—right before dying on the rocks below. Then another crushing weight slammed her against the rocks. Pain radiated through her back and hip, nearly forcing a scream from her clinched lips. But she kept it in as the water dragged her away for another try.

During the last storm, Sam had met some surfers sitting out the gale in The Last Drop. They told her of being caught in what they referred to as the washing machine, tumbled along the bottom, sandblasted by sand, and thrown onto the beach—only to be sucked back out for another round. Now she knew it first hand.

As best she could, she protected her head with her arms and concentrated on holding her breath. The rocks at the lighthouse base were the size of refrigerators, with angular edges and rough surfaces. If the waves pounded her against them, she'd be dead in no time. But she could do nothing except wait it out like the surfers said.

Her left side burned, but she had no time to press against the pain. Lungs screamed for air, but even if she could swim against the current, she had no idea which way was up. Swirling blackness came from every direction, and she felt her spine wrench as the water bent her legs over her back like an acrobat. Precious bubbles escaped from her mouth as she screamed in pain. Still the churning continued.

And then she knew. It would end here. She'd run as far as she could. Thought she'd reached safety. But this place proved to be as perilous as its name. How foolish to believe God cared about her as Millie said. Millie lay dying. Star would remain motherless. Addison and Mandy were lost to her. And Sam's whole life had amounted to nothing.

Bright pinpricks of light raced across her vision, then narrowed into blackness even as she felt the water lifting her higher and higher.

- 45 -

With bloodied fingers, Tarz pulled his body over the rocks and reached for the rusty post of the lighthouse railing. He breathed a sigh of relief as his fingers closed around the rough steel. Waves thrashed against him and knocked him to his knees. He couldn't rest. He forced himself up onto the concrete walkway where he lay panting for moment. Blood ran from a gash on his forehead, and he rolled onto his stomach and coughed up salt water along with most of a bloody front tooth.

"Man, I must have swallowed a gallon of that stuff." He'd lost his flashlight, but at least the woman was gone. His left eye stung like fire. He swore at the woman and all the trouble she'd brought him—and his sister. But he'd gotten her. Natalie Clayton was no more.

Another wave drenched him. He'd done his job. Now he had to get out of here before the sea got him too. He tucked the gun in his pocket and, on hands and knees, crawled along the curving path until the lighthouse sheltered him from the ocean. He got to his feet, swaying, and held the stone wall. His left ankle throbbed where he'd smacked it on the rocks, but he could put weight on it okay.

Tarz limped up the hill, past the cabin, on up the road, skirting the next house where candles flickered in windows. He finally reached his car where he'd left it parked behind some bushes along the main road. Rain stung his eyes as he dug in his pocket for his keys.

"What miserable weather. Why couldn't Clayton have run to Miami?" 'Course, with his luck, there'd probably be a hurricane.

His fingers poked through a hole cut into his trousers. The keys were gone. In disbelief he thumped his head on the unsympathetic metal of the car roof. Then he turned toward the house with the candles.

Tarz blinked in the candlelight, bright after the utter blackness outside. The room danced with vibrant color reflected from amazing art pieces. He scrutinized the room beyond the young girl who'd answered the door, and found an old woman ensconced in an overstuffed chair. She didn't move. The skin of her face sagged like melted yellow wax. It was the redheaded girl he'd have to worry about. Piece of cake.

"I'm sorry I'm such a mess. I'm dripping water all over your lovely floor," Tarz said, giving them a close-lipped smile, but the old woman, sick as she was, didn't seem to buy it. "My car broke down and I fell in the dark. Broke my tooth." He fingered the jagged stump.

"That must hurt," the redheaded girl said, her face scrunched up in sympathy.

"I was wondering if I could—" A clatter came from his left.

"Is Dad back?"

Tarz turned at the new voice, coming from a doorway off the kitchen toward the back porch. A flashlight wobbled through the kitchen and a woman came in wearing a hooded sweatshirt. She keyed off the flashlight with one hand and raked back the hood with the other.

Tarz went dead still. She wore the same short black hair as the Clayton woman he'd just killed. He'd only seen her in the glare of his flashlight, but this girl was a dead ringer. His hand involuntarily reached for his gun before he stopped himself. She wasn't Clayton. He willed his heart back to normal and reapplied his smile.

In less than a minute, he'd convinced the young woman to pour him a cup of coffee. He'd no sooner gotten his jacket off than headlights flashed across the southern windows as a vehicle pulled into the side driveway and around to the porch. The younger girl ran back to the door and peered out through yellow and red lace curtains.

"It's your dad, Mandy." She yanked the door open and fell back at the torrent of rain, wind-blown leaves, and icy air. Napkins blew off the dining table and fluttered around the kitchen like blue butterflies. Tarz stepped behind the door, making it look like he was just getting out of the way.

The man came through the door and fought it closed against the gale.

He turned to the light and removed his hood. Tarz recognized him instantly as the detective from Missouri.

"The phone lines are out everywhere. I had to..." The detective's voice trailed off as he glanced at Tarz, then did a double-take. The man's eyes narrowed in recognition, but his arms were still caught in his half-off jacket sleeves.

Tarz pulled the pistol from his pocket and swung without hesitation, catching the cop full on the jaw and knocking him to his knees. He struck the back of his head with the heel of the gun and the man toppled face first to the wet floor, arms still tangled in the jacket.

He ignored the screams in the room until he was sure the cop wasn't getting up. A body landed on his back and fingers gouged his face, ripping his cheeks. He spun and slammed back against the wall. The Clayton look-alike released her grip with an "Oof," and fell in a dazed heap next to her father.

"Enough." He pointed the weapon at the screaming younger girl and the old woman who struggled to rise from her chair. He backhanded the girl, knocking her to the floor. "Shut up, Red. Find me some duct tape."

Ten minutes later, he had wrists of the detective and older girl taped behind their backs. The cop hadn't moved, but the dark eyes of the girl flashed with anger. She'd be trouble.

He smiled at her. "I see you recovered from your bullet wound."

"Who are you?" The girl was more angry than scared, but that would soon change. He admired her spirit. It would make the coming necessities more...interesting.

He knelt down and leaned close to her face. "Don't you recognize me from your back yard?" He held up the pistol and pointed it at her. "BANG!"

She jumped satisfactorily, and he let the pistol swing down to his side as he stood.

"You." Her voice was quiet now, in respect for him. "You shot us." The windows rattled in the wind as if punctuating the accusation.

The telephone ringing startled him. The lines were back up. The old woman reached for it and Tarz swung the gun toward her.

"Let it ring." After ten rings it went silent. The cop stirred and moaned, and his daughter scooted closer to him.

Tarz paced the small room, thinking of what to do. The cop had recognized him the minute he'd walked in the door. And the other three had gotten a good look at him. Even if he took the old woman's car, they'd have the authorities after him in short order.

Then his eyes fell on a red and blue box of matches on the kitchen table, evidently used to light the candles. Like old friends, they called to him. Ohio Blue Tips. So rare now, he hadn't seen any in several years. These people had no idea how precious these were. He slid the cover off and ran his fingertips across the rough sticks with the beautiful dark and light blue ends. The wood turned red where it soaked up the blood from his raw hands. He'd marked them, now, and they were his. They whispered instructions to him.

"Use me." "I'm the one." "No one needs to know you've been here."

He could disappear in the storm. His mother would help him get his tooth fixed and take on a new identity. The old witch owed him that much. It was her fault he was in this mess. And she owed him the money for finishing the Clayton job.

Tarz lifted a single stick and lovingly drew its head along the strip on the box cover. Bright flame erupted in a cloud. His nostrils burned when he breathed in the pungent sulfur. It soothed his soul, sharpened his senses, gave him strength. He now knew what to do.

The phone gave a half ring again and shook him from his moment of peace. The device went silent. He dropped the burning match. It burned for a few seconds, then fizzled in the damp carpet. Crews were probably working on the telephone lines. But up or not, someone might soon come checking on the old woman. This house lay too close to the road leading to town.

The cop, still face down on the floor, now stared up at him, dulled eyes only half-open. The old woman's gaze was filled with pain. Red crouched at her chair and clung to the woman's legs. He swore under his breath. He hated having to do the kid. The older girl's eyes held defiance and she struggled against the duct tape. She would be easier.

Thunder shook the house. Tarz replaced the cover on the matchbox and zipped it in his pocket where it would stay dry, then he turned to the group. "Okay, everyone up. We're going on a little nature walk."

- 46 -

Sharp pain trampled Sam's spine like stampeding cattle, and rain slashed her face and ran into her mouth. She rolled over and gagged up both fresh and salt water, wincing at more pain from her left side. Resting on the jagged rocky surface, she gradually became aware of one simple fact: she was alive. A thundering wave rained droplets on her head, enveloping her in a fog of tangy salt mist. She needed to move.

But where was she? Except for lightning flashes and the lighthouse strobe, darkness covered everything like a thick wool blanket. Sand and salt rubbed the inside of her eye sockets and she wished for clean water to wash the grains away. Instead, she closed them tight and tried to move her eyeballs as little as possible, letting tears flow to cleanse as much as they could.

Gravity alone showed her the way to go. She reached bleeding fingers to the rock above and pushed to her feet. Burning pain in her side drew her hand, and she felt a warm wetness seeping into her cold clothing. She couldn't tell the extent of the wound. There were more important things.

Sam wrapped her fingers around the next rock and pulled, wincing in pain, but making it up and over the granite boulder. The wind pushed her the last few inches and she panted from the struggle. At any other time she would have appreciated the wildness of the storm, the fierce fragrance of the sea, the wondrous power of the waves. Tonight she longed only for safety.

As she rested, she thought of that worm at her husband's burial service, pulling itself up and over the edge of the grave. If that little worm could crawl up several feet, she could make it to the top of these rocks, however far it was. Of course, the worm hadn't had a bullet wound in its side. A wave broke at her feet, bathing her in icy water and pulling at her clothes. She clung to the rock until it receded.

Lightning flashed and she caught a glimpse of the lighthouse towering above. Inches away lay the steel railing and safety. But safety, she had learned, was fleeting. Where was the man with the gun?

God, you got me this far. Please, help me the rest of the way.

Sam levered herself onto the concrete walkway and crawled away from the churning sea.

Sam limped from the lighthouse to her home, each step pumping more hot liquid out of the hole in her side. Rain pelted her back, and the only light was the tower's strobe and lightning.

The path to her house wound along the harbor side on the right, but Sam went left. Broderick was here someplace. He was too tough to give into the sea. She wasn't giving him another shot… Sam shook her head at her unintentional joke, then sank to her knees beside an old woodpile several yards from the house.

So tired. She rested her head on her hand.

What would Broderick do? The man was a certified nut, but he was smart. And he didn't give up. If he thought there was a chance she'd survived the gunshot and ocean, he might wait in her house, expecting her to come back here.

Using the logs for leverage, Sam pushed to her feet and slowly circled the cabin about thirty yards out, being quiet even in the midst of the crashing storm. The heavy rain made it difficult to see details, but the ocean-facing windows were dark. She could go behind her garage and through the brush along the creek. It would be tough going, but at least she wouldn't have to worry about meeting Broderick. Then she could come out behind Millie's and go in the back door.

Sam rounded the left side of her cabin just as a bobbing flashlight revealed huddled figures approaching the far side, feet crunching on the shell path.

"Get in there," a man's voice growled.

Tarz Broderick.

He was herding the group toward her cabin door. Sam dropped to the ground behind a tilted wheelbarrow and peered around its dripping edge. Mud and water ran into the neck of her sweatshirt, but she kept her head on the ground and paid no attention to the minor discomfort, instead squinting at the people.

Mandy, wrists taped in front, helped Addison who had blood running down the side of his face. Star supported her grandmother who looked about to collapse. Millie needed to be in the hospital.

A hundred ideas raced through Sam's head. She could sneak around behind Broderick and club him with a chunk of firewood, or run to Millie's and call for help. Or just rush him with the baseball-sized rock under her right hand. She had risen to her feet when she saw the gun shining in the ring of light from the flashlight. It was no good. Broderick would just shoot her dead and then hurt her friends.

She dropped down again, but crawled forward several feet until hidden behind a mound of topsoil Rowena had planned for a garden. Sam wished her aunt were here with her, telling her what to do. But Sam was on her own now, and her life was as shattered as the Kit-Cat clock on the kitchen floor. Millie promised God would help when everything looked bleak.

"Okay, God," she whispered at the wind, "now would be a good time."

She scooted forward until she could see the little porch.

"Now, do as I say and you won't be hurt," Broderick chuckled.

In a construction style long abandoned, the door on her cabin opened outward. He herded the group inside, shoved the door closed, then rolled two half wine barrels against it. He wedged a third behind the other two. Sam used them as flower planters and they were full of wet, heavy potting mix. No one inside could force the door open.

She shrank back as Broderick crossed in front of her toward her garage. Two bushy trees blocked her view. Had he gone into the garage? Maybe he was stealing her car. He could have it as long as he left them alone. A new wave of rain descended, blurring her vision, but she could see well enough to know Broderick hadn't returned.

The cabin door again drew her gaze. Maybe when he left she'd be able to move the barrels, but she wasn't sure. Cramps knotted her left thigh, and she stretched it behind her. Each time she bent her leg, the charley horse returned. She desperately wanted to lay down somewhere dry. A nice fire sounded good. She'd let Star build one as soon as they could find some dry wood.

After a few minutes he still hadn't returned, so she rose to her feet. At her first step, her foot caught on an exposed root, dropping her face-first into the mud. In a spinning haze of pain from her wounded side looked up and saw Broderick returning, carrying the flashlight in one hand, and the yellow five-gallon jerry can from her garage in the other. Sam swiped mud from her eyes and peered from her hiding place. A spasm jerked her leg, and she grunted against the knotting pain. Broderick stopped, then turned toward her. He set down the can and shone the flashlight across the wheelbarrow, then the dirt pile.

Sam pinched her eyelids shut and willed herself one with the muck. Her hair was black and her clothes dark, but her eyelids brightened when the beam of the light slid across them. Could he see her laying here? Rain pummeled her back, and muddy water sucked her wounded side. She didn't dare move, not even a breath. Finally she could stand it no longer and peered through squinted eyes. The man was gone along with her dizziness. If she hadn't tripped, he'd have caught her for sure. Was that God's way of helping her? She had no idea.

She slid forward until she could see the front of the cabin better. He wasn't anywhere in sight. Again she began to get up.

Don't move. Trust me.

Sam froze. The warning hadn't been spoken aloud, but didn't lack urgency. She sank back and waited, feeling strangely less alone in the wet violence of the night. So she waited. Broderick came into view. He'd found three old mason jars from Rowena's boxes in the garage and she watched as he filled them with gasoline, then stuffed rags into the tops. He soaked the rags and, in the meager protection of the overhang above the door, lit the first, then the second, then the third.

Horror flooded Sam even before the man backed up and hurled the first one through the living room window. Flames leapt through the opening and she heard someone scream. It sounded like Star.

Terror raged through her as she thought of those inside. They were the ones she loved. All that mattered in life. No, God. Please!

Rescue them.

How? How could she get to them? The fire. It would burn her as it had before.

She saw Broderick hurl another bottle against the front door and it erupted in flame, curling up under the porch overhang and steaming the drops of rain as they fell from the edge.

The final bottle flew toward the kitchen window, but broke on the narrow rock sill. Fire cascaded in a waterfall down the stones and lapped at the shrubs.

She had to get to them. But how? The windows were too small to get through. Perhaps Star could squeeze through if Sam could break out all the glass. But what about Millie and Mandy? And Addison. Tears poured from her eyes as she realized all she wanted in life was perishing before her.

As she stood to her feet, Tarz Broderick stepped slowly backward from the cabin. His right hand held the pistol, and his left was stretched palm out toward the building heat. Blinded by his fire, he couldn't see her hidden in shadow. But she could see his face clearly. And she saw pure, twisted glee. He'd never leave. He'd wait there with the gun, reveling in the thrill of the fire until they were all dead.

Sam turned and ran downhill toward the lighthouse as fast as her broken body would take her.

There was one chance.

- 47 -

Tarz reflected in the beauty of the fire as it engulfed the living area and brightened the other windows. The thought of it consuming the four lives within filled him with wonder. Even during his most vivid dreams he'd never imagined four at one time. It was almost as though their life force would be his, would transfer to him at the moment of their passing. He spread his arms wide, feeling the heat of the flames on his wet clothing, his hands, his face. This was his work, his masterpiece. He longed to remain and feel their life energy released.

But sadly, he couldn't linger. Even in the storm, it wouldn't be long before someone noticed the fire, especially as it reached the roof and broke through. The rain might knock it down, but not before all inside were long dead.

Reluctantly, Tarz turned away...and nearly ran headlong into a woman standing behind him, clutching an umbrella.

"Well, hello...mother."

"I told you never to call me that."

"Yes. You did." Though he kept his tone light, ancient fury bubbled acid into his throat. Always meddling. "Come to check up on my work?"

"Work?" Her shrill voice sliced through the howling wind. "I sent you here to kill one woman. And now I find you killing four others? I saw you. I was watching from right over there." She pointed toward the garage. "You're a worthless excuse for a man, let alone any son of mine."

Wind whipped the umbrella inside out and, while she wrestled with it, Tarz stepped forward and slapped her hard, knocking her to the

254

ground. The wind threw the umbrella into the bending trees. In the flashlight's beam, he saw panic ripple across his mother's face before it switched to anger.

"How dare you strike me, you—"

"You're still doing it." He gripped the front of her designer raincoat and yanked her to her feet. "Comparing me with your precious Jack." She pushed away from him.

"You stupid oaf. Every job I send you on, you screw up."

She drew her hand back to slap him, but he shoved her away. Instead of falling this time, she only stumbled. Fear flickered in her eyes as she glanced at the gun in his hand. *Yes, old lady. I'll use it.* She took off at a run, first toward the garage, then making a sharp left downhill toward the lighthouse.

A crash in the cabin drew his attention and he turned. The beautiful light called to him.

Stay here with us. You know you want to. Dance with us. Watch as we do your work.

A groan of longing escaped his lips. His hand rose toward the flame, feeling its scorching power. He pivoted in a full circle, letting the light warm all sides. If he stayed a little longer, the life-force of those within would be his.

Staaa-y.

Reluctantly, Tarz dropped his hand. He had to catch his mother. He shone the beam around the night and caught a flash of movement on the path to the lighthouse. He raised his pistol but she disappeared in the closing storm. He cursed and set out after her, dodging a woodpile and small shrubs.

On the lawn in front of the lighthouse door, Tarz found her sprawled on the slick grass. She'd tripped over a flowerbed, and now tried to crawl out of the circle of his light.

"It ends here, mother." He spat the word like a curse. "I'm tired of trying to please you. Nothing I do is good enough. Maybe that's what attracted you to my father, eh? Kindred spirits with a common goal of stomping on ole Tarz?"

"You're crazy." She licked her lips and her eyes darted around, as if seeking rescue—or escape. "I always loved you, respected you."

Tarz feinted at her with a yell. To his delight, she screamed and he grinned. Rain dripped from a cypress overhead, drops smacking her raincoat like marbles on a plastic tarp.

"Leave me alone. Let me go and I'll pay you twice what I promised." Her plaintive whine gave him courage. No longer was she the one wielding the power. Dear half-brother Jack was gone, and still she wouldn't give Tarz the respect he was due. But now he was the one in charge. He held the gun. He'd make her kiss his shoes, beg for her life. Then maybe he'd haul her back to the cabin and throw her into the fire, just like Shadrach, Meshach, and Abednego in his favorite Bible story.

He shook his head. No. As satisfying as it would be to watch her burn, he needed her body in one piece. For easy identification.

She rose on her knees to run, and he kicked her in the side. She rolled across the lawn in front of the lighthouse. Again she scrambled to get up and he tripped her, laughing at her pitiful efforts at escape. He wished this could go on and on.

"Jack's gone, mother. So is your husband. I'm all you've got left. When they find you dead, all your money will go to me, and I'll spend it any way I want. Sure, people will talk about you. In fact, you'll be famous. The public servant, governor wannabe, found dead on a lighthouse lawn in California." Horror contorted her face, and he laughed.

He put his index finger against his lips, as if contemplating. "Hmmm. I guess we'll need to buy you an appropriate tombstone. How about one that reads, 'Here lies Hilde Clayton, Finally at rest, Gone forever, Wicked Witch of the Midwest.'" He threw his head back and laughed long and loud, tears and rain slipping into the collar of his jacket.

In defeat, his mother rolled onto her back and stared up at him, clutching her precious designer purse to her as if it could shield her from his anger. Stupid woman. He *should* drag her back to the burning cabin and throw her into the inferno—a practice run for her descent to hell.

"Now I'm calling the shots, mother." He laughed again, holding up the gun. "Get it? *Shots*!" Her expression told him she wasn't amused. Too bad, but it *had* been funny.

"Well, it's been nice knowing you. Say hi to dear old daddy Frank. He lifted his gun and curled his finger around the trigger.

Something kicked him in the chest, and he stared dumbly at his pistol. Then he noticed a burning above his heart. He stared again at his mother where she reclined in the muddy grass. Smoke curled from a hole in the bottom of her purse. She pushed the bag aside, revealing a chrome revolver in her right hand. Another crack and his head snapped back. He registered spinning, falling—waiting for the landing. But it never came.

Lightning and the flash of the lighthouse strobe painted a cartoon-like mural on the lawn, where characters moved in jerky stop-action like some college dorm play. Frozen at the entrance to the lighthouse, Sam recoiled as the woman shot Tarz Broderick a second time, the anemic pop of the bullet nearly lost against the backdrop of nature's violence. The man twisted as he fell and landed face-first with a small splash on the scraggly lawn. He didn't move.

Sam let out a deep breath. He couldn't hurt her anymore. But who was the woman? Sam had only picked up a few words over the raging wind and booming storm, but it sounded like the man had shouted "mother."

The woman got to her feet, right arm extended, weapon sighted on the prone form. When the body remained still, she lowered it to her side. Sam took a step forward. She wanted to run to the woman, thank her for saving her life. Then ask for help in saving everyone in the burning cabin.

But Sam hesitated. There was something... The woman's thin frame, the way she adjusted her purse.

A brilliant, sustained bolt lit the area like a movie backlot. Raindrops sparkled like diamonds, frozen in the pulsing flashes. The woman straightened her spine and lifted her chin. Sam sucked in her breath. It couldn't be!

A fraction of a second later, a dozen cannons exploded, nearly knocking her off the step. The noise seemed to shake the very clouds, and they released instant torrential rain. The woman across the lawn disappeared behind a curtain of water.

Hilde Clayton. That chin lift was a signature Sam knew too well. But why would Jack's mother be in Perilous Cove? Had this man been her son? And she'd shot him? Was this the brother Rowena had noted in the genealogy pages?

Sam couldn't wait around to find out. Where was that key? John, the current light station keeper, kept one around the door somewhere. She'd been searching for precious minutes. Shoving aside a flowerpot, she found the brass key stuck in a crack. John kept the padlock well-oiled, and the key turned easily. She pushed open the thick wooden door.

The sheltered interior felt warm in comparison to outside, but it couldn't be over forty degrees. Her teeth chattered and she pressed her left elbow tight against her aching side. The blood flow had slowed, but energy still seeped down her pant leg. An emergency lamp, mounted ten feet up on the wall above the door, bathed the chamber in dim, pulsing yellow light, but it seemed bright as the sun to Sam.

The room muted the storm, but rumbling thunder reverberated in overlapping echoes from the high reaches. Ornate cast iron stairs curved up one wall, making a half revolution of the tower before disappearing through a heavy timbered floor fifteen feet above. A second floor lay above that before a ladder completed the journey to the trap door and the light above. John had given her a tour three weeks ago on a crystal clear day. The spectacular view from the top gave the impression she could see the curvature of the earth.

Four medium-sized wooden crates lined one wall. One had been opened, the top propped against the side. Probably replacement bulbs for the signal light. A stack of two-by-fours, a red metal toolbox, a small table with two chairs, and a wall calendar made up the sparse furnishings.

Sam hurried across the round room to an elaborate wrought iron gate mounted under the staircase. Leaping dolphins and twisting seaweed decorated its surface, and any other time Sam would have stopped to admire the decades-old craftsmanship. Instead, she inserted the same key and unlocked the mechanism. She yanked on the heavy gate. Lighter than it appeared, it flew open and banged against the wall. She shot a glance toward the open lighthouse door, hoping the clash confined itself to the three-story interior. Would Hilde notice the noise or the lighted opening? Sam couldn't worry about that now.

Before her, stairs descended into pitch darkness, and Sam hurried down the ten stone steps into a dank tunnel. She wished for a flashlight. On her tour, John had shone a powerful beam into the tunnel, but they hadn't gone in. Sam stepped forward, tracing the left wall. Smooth river rock stones the size of basket balls undulated under her fingers. Her right she kept in front of her face, wary of more injuries as she hurried along. She couldn't afford to be tentative.

The main tunnel turned slightly. She'd always had exceptional spatial orientation and knew her cabin now lay straight ahead. The floor of the tunnel remained flat for seventy-five feet or so as it passed under the lawn, then she stumbled at the sudden incline as the shaft angled shallowly upward.

John loved history. During her tour, he'd recounted how, two weeks after the attack on Pearl Harbor, the Japanese had sunk the SS Montebello oil tanker just offshore from Perilous Cove. Then two months later a sub shelled an oil refinery north of Santa Barbara. Panic swept California as fears of another aircraft attack fueled the rumor mills. It became the Coast Guard's mission to fulfill their name. They constructed the tunnel from the cabin to the lighthouse so coast watchers could move back and forth without being observed by enemy aircraft. Ultimately, no Japanese planes reached California, and after the war the tunnel was forgotten.

Spider webs caught Sam's face and hair and she swatted them away. Water dripped steadily, and in some places it poured in like a mini waterfall, slipping down her collar like an icy snake. Already she could smell smoke, and she began to sweat in the freezing air.

- 48 -

Mandy was in the tiny kitchen scrounging for a knife when the first flaming bottle crashed through the living room window and shattered on the coffee table. The room exploded in flames. Blinded by the sudden light, Starfire screamed, fell into her grandmother and knocked her down.

"Star, get back." Mandy grabbed her arms and pulled her off Millie and away from the fire. Then the two of them helped the old woman to her feet. They retreated to the kitchen where Mandy's dad lay collapsed on the floor. He'd been disoriented and had vomited twice on the forced march to the cabin. From her first aid training, it sounded like a concussion.

Another thump sounded against the front door, and Mandy could see a surge of light around the edges of the ill-fitting portal. Another ball of flame erupted right outside the kitchen window, but the glass didn't break.

Smoke filled the small cabin quickly. Books on the shelves caught easily and the fire spread through the living room with frightening speed.

Mandy searched around, but there was nowhere to go. Keeping low, she grabbed a pot from the counter. She placed it under the sink faucet and turned it on. Water trickled from the spout at an agonizingly slow speed. It took a minute to fill it halfway. Mandy threw it toward the fire causing a momentary sizzle, but the flames recaptured the inches in seconds.

"Star. Get pots and fill them in the bathroom. We have to stop the fire." Even as she issued the command, she knew it was hopeless. The fire licked up the dry knotty pine walls of the living room and spread to all the curtains. If only the windows were larger—but Sam had told her they had been built narrow to keep the cold out, not as a way of escape.

A crash sounded behind her. Star had turned over a small rolling cart and was clawing at the floor.

"What are you doing?"

"Help me, Mandy. We can hide in the basement." Star's fingers tugged at the small ring in the floor. The rectangular outline of a trap door was visible in the flickering light.

Mandy grabbed a butter knife and pried at the crack. The door lifted an inch and fell back. They tried again. This time, when the trap door lifted slightly, Star thrust her fingers in the gap and held on long enough for Mandy to pull up the door and lean it against the wall. Below was a black square of night.

"There are a few steps down to the floor, like six or something," Star explained, then ran to her grandma. "Come on, grandma. I'll help you."

Mandy's eyes watered from the smoke and she couldn't get enough air. Burning embers from the books now swirled around them like crazed fireflies, and they batted the sparks from each other's clothes.

First they helped Millie down the steps, Star in front and Mandy leaning down supporting from above. Then Mandy spun her dad around on the floor until his legs dangled into the hole. Fire crawled from the living room carpet to the edge of the linoleum, sending up oily black smoke only a foot from his head. She grabbed his belt and wrestled him further until he slipped into the hole. Mandy tried to hold onto him, but he was too heavy. His body rattled down the steep stairs and dragged her headfirst after him. Her recently healed shoulder banged on the rough steps before she landed in a heap on top of her dad.

Her left wrist hurt like crazy, but she was more worried about her dad. She untangled herself and rolled to the side. Hard-packed dirt gave off a musty odor. She got her bound hands underneath her and pushed up to a sitting position, then bent to examine her dad, assisted by the flickering light of the fire above. Star scrambled past her and up the stairs. The next instant the trap door slammed shut, casting them in cold but blessedly cool blackness.

Besides the absolute darkness, the other thing Mandy noticed was the sudden muffled silence. In the midst of the escape effort, she hadn't realized the roar of the blaze. How long could they last down here before the flames burned through the wooden floor? As she listened, the roar got louder by the second and her gaze instinctively lifted to the black ceiling. They'd bake alive in this dirt-floor oven.

Mandy felt the girl brush past her as she descended the stairs. "Star, is there a way out of here, an outside door or something?"

"I don't know. I don't think so." The girl's voice took on a high-pitched timbre, bordering on hysteria. "I just knew it was here. Sam told me she was going to hire somebody to clean it out, that it was all nasty and had rats and stuff, but I don't think she ever did." The girl moved away.

Mandy shivered and felt her own panic rising. She prayed someone in town would see the fire and send help. People in small towns were supposed to watch out for each other, weren't they? But with the storm raging, most people were probably holed up behind closed drapes, tending a nice, safe fire in their fireplaces. There was nothing safe about the blaze inches above their heads.

Mandy touched her dad's face. She felt his breath on her palm.

"Dad? Can you hear me?"

Something off to one side crashed to the floor.

"What are you doing?"

"I'm looking for a flashlight," Star replied. More noise, like items shifting on shelves, was followed by a triumphant shout. "Found one!"

A yellow glow identified Star's position ten feet away. Star clicked it on and off a few times, each time gaining a little improvement.

"Shine it on my dad." Mandy huddled closer to him, coddling her left wrist to her side as much as the duct tape would allow. The weak beam settled on her dad's head and she saw new cuts and blood. His eyes were closed. Oh, man.

Millie's feeble whisper came from where she sat against one stone wall. Star swung the light toward her where it showed her leaning listlessly.

"What did you say, grandma?"

"There's...a tunnel..." Millie's words were slurred and she obviously fought for consciousness. "To the lighthouse." The woman's head lolled and she fell silent. No amount of shaking by Star brought her around.

"Look around, Star. Maybe it's hidden behind a box or something."

Mandy pushed to her feet and shoved boxes around on the shelves. "Did you see a knife anywhere? I've got to get my wrists free."

Shattering glass drew her attention and she saw Star holding a piece of broken dinnerware in her hand. "Will this do?"

The sharp edge of the plate sliced through the tape, and in seconds Mandy's hands were free. The sudden release caused her to cry out in pain, and she tucked her left wrist across her stomach for protection.

The beam of the flashlight dwindled as quickly as their hopes. The basement was only a few feet on each side and there didn't seem to be an opening anywhere. Smoke sifted down through cracks in the floor above them, forcing them to the ground in search for clean air. Their only hope was that the fire department would arrive and put out the fire before it burned through.

"Mandy, down here. There air's fresher." In the last glow of the flashlight, Mandy saw Star lying in front of the shelves, pulling aside an antique wooden Pepsi crate, filled with dusty glass bottles.

Mandy joined her. The air *was* better. But as she took a few welcome breaths, the ceiling began to glow in spots and embers dropped on her dad. He startled awake as his sleeve burned through to his skin. Mandy batted them away with her hands and half-helped, half-dragged him away from the foot of the stairs.

"Mandy, look!" Star pointed to the thin trap door. "What are we going to do?" The wood was yielding to the inferno and Mandy watched it curl and disintegrate in several spots.

Millie coughed, licked her lips, then issued one command: "Pray."

- 49 -

Sam slipped on the mossy incline and fell hard on knees already scraped raw from a half dozen previous falls. It seemed like hours had passed since she saw the killer set fire to the cabin, but she knew it had only been ten or twelve minutes. But how long could Addison, Mandy, Millie and Star hold out, trapped in a burning house? Were they dead already? She couldn't stand the thought.

She struggled to her feet and pushed forward, keeping her feet spread as much as possible to avoid the trough of slime. Smoke burned her nose and she wiped at it with her wet sleeve. She kept her eyes tightly closed and fought the compulsion to open them as she inched ahead. They were no help in this tunnel of endless midnight.

The lighthouse acted like a huge wind funnel: one second smoky air swathed her face, causing her to choke and cough, then the next brought a breeze at her back, clearing the air.

She was close. There wouldn't be this much smoke if not. Even so, Sam wasn't prepared when she cracked her head on a low archway. Gingerly, she lowered to her knees, crept forward, and felt in the dark. Was there a door to the basement of her cabin? John hadn't explained that, and Sam hadn't again ventured into the creepy space from her side to find out.

Her hand stopped against rough wood. Surveying with her fingers, the wood-covered opening measured about two feet wide by four feet high. Sam shoved and one piece gave way in silent rot. Sam crumbled away piece after piece. No wonder the rats had easy access to her basement. Shuddering at the thought of a furry body with sharp teeth, hoping the smoke had chased them far away, Sam pushed her arm into the gaping hole as far as she could. She screamed when something clamped her fingers.

Terror snaked up Sam's body, fingers to hand to arm to shoulder. She reared back, yanking her hand to safety. Or at least she tried to. Something encircled her wrist and she succeeded only in scraping her arm against the solid upper boards of the door. Sam sucked in a breath and prepared for another heave when a muffled voice sounded through the hole.

"Wait. Help us." Star's plea was quickly followed by Mandy's repeat, and Sam sighed, willing her racing heart back to a more sedate two hundred beats per minute. When she could get enough air she squeezed the other hand and leaned close to the breach.

"Star, Mandy! It's me, Sam."

Working together, they battered down the rest of the disintegrating door, then the girls emptied the shelves and lifted the boards off the frame, clearing the previously concealed entryway. Sam stepped through into her own basement.

The dim flashlight was eclipsed by the burning opening where the trap door had been. Sam threw her arm across her face to block the incredible heat as embers rained on the dry wood stairs. The fire's intensity created an updraft, sucking clean air up the tunnel and clearing the smoke. But the roaring beast thrived on the new oxygen like a blacksmith's forge and bellows. The danger now was the whole floor would collapse. They had to get out. Now.

The three women assisted Millie into the tunnel, the effort reviving the old woman enough to help.

"You girls get Millie to the lighthouse," Sam directed the girls. It would take them both to navigate the slippery floor.

Mandy shook her head. "I'm not leaving my dad." She turned toward him, but Sam grabbed the girl's wrist. Mandy yelped and cradled it against her stomach.

"You're hurt," Sam said, and slid her hand up Mandy's arm.

"I think it's broken. This evil man—"

"Shhh. I know." Sam hugged her. "I'll get your dad, Mandy. I need you to help Millie and Star. Be careful—the tunnel's really slippery."

Mandy nodded and moved through the low arch where Millie and Star waited. The cool wind suddenly reversed, sucking acrid smoke and burning embers down through the hole in the kitchen floor in a swirling, deadly light show.

Sam dove for Addison where he lay unmoving. He was already on his back, so Sam slipped her arms under his and put all her weight into pulling him across the dirt floor. Pain stabbed her side. She felt warm blood seeping into her shirt, but ignored the injury and dragged the detective a few more inches.

His body warmed Sam's cold hands, and it reminded her when he'd helped her out of the car and into his house. That day, his hands had spread warmth along her ribcage and embarrassed her. By offering her shelter he'd taken her to safety. Now it was her turn to do the same.

Addison Conner was impossibly heavy at two hundred pounds, but the grit covering the dirt surface acted like tiny ball bearings, assisting her effort. She dug her heels into the clay and scooted him inches at a time.

A heavy timber near the trap door crashed down in a cascade of sparks. Sam saw the refrigerator teetering above, then it toppled sideways and rolled down the stairs. She jerked Addison halfway through the tunnel opening as the white box flew by inches from his feet and smacked the opposite wall, breaking open and spewing milk, eggs, and produce across the floor.

Wind now flooded the tunnel with hair-singeing heat and choking smoke. She had to get out from under the house in case it all collapsed. There was no clean air to breathe, no respite to garner strength. Soot coated her mouth as her lungs starved for oxygen. Sam lurched backward, dragging Addison fully onto the sloping tunnel floor.

Within a few feet, the slime began, and this made the going easier. On her way up, she'd cursed the slippery surface, but now she thanked God. With each pull, they slid several feet. By the time they reached the level tunnel under the lighthouse lawn the air was cool and clear and Mandy had returned to help her. They each took an arm and dragged Addison's dead weight the rest of the way to the bottom of the stairs leading up to the interior. They rested there for several minutes. She leaned her hands on her knees and drew in the clean air, coughing with each exhale from her raw lungs. Six inches of water pooled around them, with more sluicing across the tunnel floor every second. The tunnel ceiling had never been constructed to be waterproof.

A low moan came from Addison's lips. Mandy sat on the concrete with his head cradled in her lap.

"He's waking up, Sam." In the light of the opening above, Sam saw Addison's eyes flutter, then open. She couldn't make out if they focused. His hand came to his face and he winced at the bleeding gash on his temple. Sam knelt next to him.

"Addison. Can you hear me?" He nodded once and she breathed a sigh of relief. "We need to get you a few stairs up to the lighthouse. Do you think you can help us? You're too heavy to carry."

He licked his dry lips. "Yes." It was a whisper, barely there, but it warmed Sam's heart.

She gripped his hand and, with Mandy's help, raised him to a sitting position. After a couple of minutes, he got onto all fours and began crawling, one by one, up the stone steps.

Mandy went in front while Sam bent over his side, her arms around his chest. His muscled runner's body felt strong, firm under her hands, but each step gained required rest. His muscles tightened under her fingers before each new upward push.

Sam lifted as much as she could from her awkward, bent over angle. He probably could have done just as well without her help, but she relished the heat of his skin under her hands. This man wasn't a quitter.

After what seemed like an interminable time, they arrived at the flat floor of the lighthouse chamber. Outside, the storm still raged, thundering echoes reverberating about the interior. Mandy moved to her dad's other side, and together they assisted as he crawled beyond the iron gate and collapsed face down. Mandy found a roll of paper towels and slipped it under his head as a pillow.

Only then did Sam turn around and look for Star and Millie. They were on the opposite side of the room. The old woman sat in one of the chairs at the small table, head back against the wall, eyes shut, white vapor condensing in the frigid air with each shallow breath. Star knelt at her grandmother's side, one arm on the woman's lap, but she wasn't looking at Millie. Sam followed the girl's eyes to the lighthouse doorway where a slim, cloaked figure stood, holding a deadly chrome pistol.

"Hello, Natalie. I saw you on TV. I almost didn't recognize you."

The hood of the coat completely hid the woman's face, but there was no mistaking the bitter sarcasm, more acidic than all the smoke Sam breathed in the last fifteen minutes.

"Hil—"

Sam saw the muzzle flash and an explosion cracked beside her right ear. She dove left and came up against the rock wall. Hilde advanced, gun extended and trained dead center on Sam's chest. She stopped a few feet away.

"Shut up, you piece of trash." Spittle glinted as it sprayed on the 'p.'

Sam eyed the pistol. Hilde could have killed her, but she'd evidently meant the shot as a warning. "What do you want?"

The woman pulled herself up another inch, if that was possible. The hood slipped a little, enough for Sam to see the woman's scowl.

"That's easy. I want you." The cruel eyes darted around the suddenly small chamber. "But I wasn't expecting so many to have to deal with."

Sam licked her lips. Hilde Clayton was as insane as the son she'd killed on the lawn, even if Sam couldn't see it reflected in the black eyes. With sudden realization, Sam knew Hilde would kill everyone in the room if she had to, just like her son, Tarz Broderick.

Across the room, Star hugged her grandmother's knee. At the other point of the triangle, Addison had his eyes closed, but Mandy made like to get to her feet, her eyes burning with anger. Sam stilled her with a quick shake of her head. All the people she cared most about, threatened by her mother-in-law.

Hilde's eyes cut back and forth around the chamber, keeping everyone under observation. She pulled the hood forward to cover her face, and that gave Sam an idea. There was no way Hilde could know Addison was the detective from Steerman—his face was turned away from her, and he'd lost consciousness again. Sam raised her hands and slowly rose to her feet.

"If it's me you want, then take me." Then she indicated the others with a move of her head. "They can't hurt you."

Doubt flickered across Hilde's face, visible only to Sam in the emergency light. Before the woman could rethink the situation, Sam took one sideways step toward the open doorway. Rain splashed in, soaking the floor, and bringing with it the fresh scent of ozone. Lightning flashed again, but the following thunder was four or five seconds delayed. Perhaps the worst of the storm had passed. The worst was only beginning for Sam.

She took another cautious step closer to the door, turning Hilde away from the others. If she could get outside, maybe she could make a break after a lightning flash. They'd both be blinded momentarily, but Sam knew the steps and the grounds. A steel pipe railing led down the stairs. She could hurdle it and sprint off to the left around the lighthouse base. Or, if they walked a ways on the lawn, she could break away near the hedge.

One more step. Sam lifted her foot but froze as clarity and fury captured her foe's face. The pistol came up. Hilde intended to shoot her right here.

Before Sam could react, a brilliant flash lit the doorway and high windows, casting macabre shadows in every direction. The explosive thunder was immediate and deafening, rattling everything in the room as well as the very foundation of the tower.

Sam dropped and rolled toward Hilde's legs. She could feel the concrete vibrating as she rolled over and over. The pistol fired once somewhere above her, but then she bowled into Hilde and the woman fell heavily on Sam, a bony knee plunging deep into her stomach. Sam fought for breath, but it was gone. No matter how she tried, her diaphragm refused to pull air into her lungs. She gasped like a beached fish, clutching her stomach and trying to slide from under Hilde.

The weight disappeared and Sam rolled onto her side, opened mouth, willing air to enter her starving body.

Hilde stood above her, the weapon shaking as it came to center on Sam's forehead. Fury contorted her mother-in-law's face into a hideous mask. Her lips pulled back and her eyes contracted. Sam saw Hilde's right hand tighten on the pistol.

This was it. She would die here on cold, wet concrete. But that's not what concerned her most. What would happen to Mandy, Addison, Millie, and Star? Could they get free? Addison's head was turned toward her now, eyes half-open, registering the scene but unable to act. Surely Hilde would kill at least him. Tears welled as she thought of all they would miss together. At least friendship. Perhaps love.

And Star. She'd already lost a mom and dad, and her grandmother had only a short time to live. The girl would be completely alone. Sam would never know if she was cut out to be a mother to the girl—never have a chance to try.

Hilde's index finger turned white on the trigger. When the shot came, would Sam feel anything? Would it be instant?

And what about afterward? Was God real? Would she meet him in heaven where all was peaceful? She longed for that peace, weary of the running, the attempts on her life, the hiding.

But those were the events of the past. This was reality. A single shot to the head.

Hilde's lips opened in a snarling gash. "Die, you—"

Between Hilde's legs, Sam saw another figure.

Something swinging, descending. Star. No!

The gun blast peppered Sam's face with burning powder, but the bullet missed, pinging off the floor and ricocheting off the rock walls like an old-time western movie. All at the same time, Sam saw the two-by-four knock the pistol from Hilde's hand and heard it clatter away.

Star wound up for another hit, but Hilde reacted faster. She backhanded the girl across the face and knocked her to the floor. The two-by-four clattered to the cement like a dropped baseball bat after tagging a fly ball.

Sam clutched Hilde's ankle and yanked. Her mother-in-law went down on all fours, but kicked a glancing blow to Sam's wounded side. She doubled up in agony and lost her grip. Hilde crawled away, searching for the gun.

Star leaped on Hilde's back, circling her neck with desperate arms. Hilde rolled right and landed on top of the girl, breaking free and coming up with the two-by-four. She raised it to strike Star.

A gunshot rang through the room. Hilde dropped the board and stared in amazement at the blood running down her right arm. Then she stumbled back against the curved wall and slid to the floor in a sitting position.

Across the room, Mandy held the pistol in a two-handed police stance, arms straight, feet slightly apart. A wisp of smoke curled from the gun's barrel.

From Sam's vantage point on the floor, the girl looked impossibly tall. Soot smudged across her cheeks and forehead added to the dangerous glint in her eyes. An Amazon warrior princess, absolutely deadly. No fear or doubt marred her countenance. Though her left wrist was bent at an odd angle, the gun barrel didn't waver, and it was pointed squarely at Hilde who remained where she was. Her hood had fallen open, fully revealing her pinched face.

"You so much as twitch, lady, and I will shoot you dead. No warnings, no hesitation. You understand?"

Hilde sagged, looking like a wet, frail bird, caught in a storm too powerful to fight.

How had Sam once been so terrified of this pitiful woman? Gone were privilege and official power, leaving a hollow shell in their place.

Defeated, Hilde gripped her wounded arm and whispered a question. "Who *are* you people?"

Star got to her feet and swiped a hand across her bleeding mouth. The other hand held the two-by-four. She positioned herself between her grandmother and Hilde, mouth set in grim determination.

"We're a family."

Sirens sounded in the distance, drawing closer. Unlike before, when Sam's house exploded and Donna died, this time the sirens promised help and hope.

EPILOGUE

"You'd be proud of the daffodils this spring, Millie. They're two-feet tall and the brightest yellow you've ever seen. And the mustard plant covering the fields by Simpson Creek is as high as a man's head with all the rain we've had. I brought some for you—daffodils, I mean, not the mustard."

Sam arranged the cheery flowers in the vase, filled it with water from her sports bottle, then set the container in the recessed receptacle. The matching one on the other side held delicate white lilies—from Alejandro, no doubt. Through Millie's ordeal, he'd become a good friend, but nothing more.

Sam stood and brushed at her eyes with the back of her hand. "I miss you, Millie."

The new, brilliant white marble marker of Millie's choosing stood tall in the verdant surroundings. The inscription never failed to bring a smile to Sam's lips.

Sorry I missed you. I'm at His place and won't be back. Eighty-one years old and I loved every minute of it. Go have a fantastic life! - Millie Trafford.

She had died in January, and there wasn't a day Sam's eyes stayed fully dry. But now, as she and Star remembered the old woman's humor and quirky ways, not all the tears were of sorrow.

Sam settled her Cardinals baseball cap in place. Her hair still wasn't long enough to put in a ponytail. She arched her back, skin around the bullet wound in her side pulling tight. Agonizing physical therapy under the watch of Carl the Cruel—as Star dubbed him—had assured minimal scar tissue. One day she might be able to thank him.

She gathered her things, whispered goodbye to Millie, and set off down the sloping cemetery grounds at a brisk pace.

On her way through town she swung by Maxine's and picked up two large containers of clam chowder, then poked her head into Last Drop to say hi to Connie. By the time she hiked up the road to the house, sweat had broken out on her brow. She placed the soup on the kitchen counter and picked up a note, penned in Star's careful hand.

Went for a hike. Back soon. Love, Star.

She peeled off her sweater. Winter had been one for the record books, a hundred year storm they said, and county officials were still repairing flood damage. But today, the sun shone brightly and the temperature had climbed into the mid-70s. She poured a glass of iced tea and stepped out onto the front porch of Millie's house—hers and Star's now—letting the brisk ocean breeze cool her skin.

She relaxed into the chase lounge and sipped from the sweating glass while gazing over the harbor to the sparkling sea beyond. Millie had given them all one last surprise when her lawyer read the will, bequeathing the home to Samantha Riley and Starfire Trafford.

The changes in the past few months were still shocking. Sam had lost her husband and discovered his betrayal, run for her life, been shot twice, broken her foot, been burned, nearly drown, and lost two homes to fire. Her two best friends, Donna and Millie, were dead. Her mother-in-law was in jail awaiting trial for attempted murder, conspiracy for murder, and several other charges. Hilde's political career had evaporated. Sharon Tanner of the Steerman Police Department had given birth in the county jail hospital to Jack's baby.

What a sick and twisted family. And it had all been about money for Jack's failing business and Hilde's campaign.

Tarz Broderick—confirmed as Hilde's son by a bizarre teenage marriage to Frank Crane, the name Sam found in Wena's genealogy record—had disappeared the night of the storm. Police had found a stolen car on the road by Millie's with fingerprints matching his. Sam hoped she'd never see him again.

But the nights were hard. She couldn't look at a dark window without expecting his face to pop up. Motion sensor lights covered every corner of the house and yard. A shiver ran through her. It wasn't the day's cool air.

Sam went to the shooting range every week with her nine millimeter, a gift from Addison. Mandy laughingly said Sam would soon be a better shot than she was. But the girl's aim had been perfect that night in the lighthouse.

Sam stood and rubbed her arms while scanning the bluff. Brilliant with blue lupine, orange California poppies, and dozens of other wildflowers, the April coast shook off the wet winter like a new puppy. Even the burned hulk of Sam's stone cottage was surrounded by color. Ben and Addison had lined up a crew to rebuild it this summer.

But for all the pain and loss, these past months had brought even more new and good things. She had a townfull of new friends, anxious to help when they found out the details of that stormy night. Her career as a marine tour guide had expanded into talks at local schools and field trips to the tide pools. Her notorious ocean rescue of the boy from the boat hadn't hurt, either, and she now gave talks on boating safety at the local harbors and lakes. She suspected people came to the sessions as much to meet Blew—Captain Tom had insisted the dog accompany her anytime she spoke—as to hear what she had to say.

As Millie had approached the end of her life, her church had rallied around the three of them. At Millie's request, most of her art pieces had been sold at a show sponsored by one of the local galleries. To Sam's surprise, art lovers and dealers from all over the western states came, and the proceeds had covered all Millie's medical expenses and set up a college fund for Star.

Sam had been attending church with Star, at first because she knew the girl needed the people in her life. But lately Sam admitted the teaching and her own Bible reading were beginning to make sense. The love the people had for Sam and Star echoed what Donna had said about her church in Steerman.

The legal adoption was in process and she'd soon be Starfire's official mom, though Star called her that all the time now. Sam hoped she could live up to the girl's high expectations. Mandy had reversed the tables and announced she officially adopted Sam into *their* family, and used her computer to produce a legal-looking adoption certificate, which included Star as her sister.

Sam wasn't quite sure what that meant for her relationship with Addison and Mandy. It was made even more confusing when Addison resigned from the Steerman police force before Christmas and moved them to a rental at Storm Lake, not far from Ben's house. Addison hadn't decided on a job yet, but he'd had offers from two security consulting firms in Mission Peaks.

She smiled at the memory of their half a dozen dates—innocent things like movies, lunch at Blue Rock Harbor, a day trip up Highway 1 to Big Sur—and the Christmas gift from he and Mandy: a brand new Kit-Cat clock.

As if on cue, Sam heard voices and turned again toward the harbor. Across the driveway and field, Addison, Mandy and Star crested the hill from the cliff path, stopped and turned toward the bay. Boats bobbed lazily in the harbor, while beyond the breakwater, sailboats sporting bright canvases sliced through swells. Addison pointed to something and the girls shielded their eyes exactly like him. Star broke away and twirled, arms outstretched, head back, soaking up the warming sun. Mandy knelt to pick wildflowers and Star ran to join in.

Sam observed Addison's strong profile as he continued to stare at the distant water. Then, as if his radar clicked on, he turned, caught her with his eyes and grinned.

She dipped her head, embarrassed to be caught watching, then met his gaze. She let out a breath and moved down to the top step of the porch, hesitating, hand on the painted banister.

Addison didn't move, only reached out his hand to her in silent invitation. The corners of her mouth raised into a smile. Sam stepped down onto the shell path that led to the three people she loved.

Donna had been right those months ago. Tomorrow was a better day.

~ The End ~

ABOUT THE AUTHOR

Rich Bullock writes stories of ordinary people put in perilous situations, where lives are changed forever. Perilous Cove is his first published novel—it was a semi-finalist in the Zondervan First Novel Contest, 2009. His second novel, Storm Song, won the ACFW (American Christian Fiction Writers) 2010 Genesis Contest in suspense.

He is a member of American Christian Fiction Writers, and the Quills of Faith writing group in Redding, California.

His first writing experience was at ten years old on a well-used typewriter, where several keys added extra spaces after striking, and clearing the tangled print arms was a continual chore. The old machine lasted through high school all-nighters.

Fortunate to grow up in small-town San Luis Obispo, California, he developed an eye for settings that remind people of home. He now lives and writes in Redding, California where, on most days, he sees Mount Lassen, Mount Shasta, and the inside of Starbucks.

Connect with Rich Bullock
www.PerilousFiction.com
www.facebook.com/PerilousFiction

16622258R00152

Made in the USA
Charleston, SC
02 January 2013